KU-376-173

PENDRAGON

THE REALITY BUG

WITHDRAWN
FROM STOCK

D. J. MACHALE

SIMON AND SCHUSTER

Laois County Library
Leabharlann Chontae Laoise

Acc. No. ...09/20939...........

Class No. ..J.F..................

Inv. No. .....11006...............

SIMON AND SCHUSTER

First published in Great Britain in 2004 by Simon & Schuster UK Ltd.
1st Floor, 222 Gray's Inn Road, London WC1X 8HB
A CBS COMPANY

This edition published in 2009

Originally published in the USA in 2003 by Aladdin Paperbacks,
an imprint of Simon & Schuster Children's Division, New York.

Copyright © D. J. MacHale, 2003

This book is copyright under the Berne Convention.
No reproduction without permission.
All rights reserved.

The right of D. J. MacHale to be identified as author of this work
has been asserted in accordance with sections 77 and 78
of the Copyright, Designs and Patents Act, 1988.

A CIP catalogue record for this book is
available from the British Library

ISBN 978-1-84738-447-8

This book is a work of fiction. Names, characters, places
and incidents are either a product of the author's imagination
or are used fictitiously. Any resemblance to actual people
living or dead, events or locales is entirely coincidental.

10 9 8 7 6 5 4 3 2 1

Printed by CPI Cox and Wyman, Reading, Berkshire RG1 8EX

This is for my sister, Patrica,
the true artist of the family

Dear Readers,

Time to hit the flumes again.

Since the *Pendragon* books have been published, I've heard from lots of readers, and one question keeps coming up more than any other: Will Bobby ever see his family and Uncle Press again?

Good question. *Very* good question. But I'm not telling.

You see, as much as each *Pendragon* book contains its own unique adventure, there's also a much larger story being told here. It has to do with the Travellers and Saint Dane and the battle of good vs. evil for control of Halla. The origin of the Travellers and why they have the responsibility of protecting Halla will unfold over the course of all the books. So I can't go giving away future secrets now, can *I*? That would be like opening up presents long before your birthday and ruining the surprise. Okay, maybe that's a bad example because everybody likes to open presents no matter when they get them, but you know what I mean. Right?

I will tell you this much: Bobby may be growing and learning some incredible truths about himself and about the nature of existence, but his family and his uncle Press are always in his thoughts and his heart. I think you'll see what I mean as you read *The Reality Bug*. There are lots of surprises in store for Bobby and the Travellers, and for you readers. But *I* can't give them away until it's time.

Because that's the way it was meant to be.

Hobey ho,
D. J. MacHale

☻ SECOND EARTH ☻

Bobby Pendragon slipped the heavy ring on to his finger, where it belonged. But no sooner was it back in place when surprisingly, it began to twitch.

"What's the matter?" Mark Dimond asked.

"It . . . it's activating," Bobby said with surprise.

"Really? You mean there's a gate around here?" Courtney Chetwynde asked.

The grey stone in the centre of the ring began to glow, then sparkle. A second later a sharp beam of light shot from its centre. With a flash, the light blossomed into an image that hovered in front of the group.

Mark and Courtney took a surprised step backwards. Gunny Van Dyke stepped protectively in front of them. But Bobby held his ground. Of the four of them standing on the empty lot at 2 Linden Place, Second Earth, Bobby was the only one who had seen this particular phenomenon before.

Floating before them was the image of a girl. Actually, it was a girl's head. Just a head. It was bigger than life, but definitely a girl. She had blonde hair pulled back in a ponytail and wore small, yellow-tinted glasses.

"Whoa," said Courtney in awe.

"Yeah, whoa," added Mark.

"Aja Killian," whispered Bobby.

"Who?" Gunny asked.

"The Traveller from Veelox."

"Where have you been?" the floating head demanded angrily. "I've been trying to contact you for ages!"

"Long story," Bobby answered.

"I don't want to hear it, Pendragon," Aja's head shot back. "You'd better get back to Veelox."

"Why?" Bobby asked.

Aja-head hesitated. She looked nervous. Or at least as nervous as a 3-D floating head could look. "I'm not saying I made a mistake," she explained with a touch of embarrassment. "This may be a total false alarm, but –"

"Just say it!" Bobby shouted.

"All right!" Aja snapped. "Saint Dane may have slipped through my security system. He is here on Veelox."

Bobby smiled and asked teasingly, "You're telling me your perfect security system isn't all that perfect?"

"Are you coming or not?" Aja demanded. She didn't like being challenged.

"On my way," Bobby answered.

"Don't take your time," Aja said snottily. Then the image vanished. The beam of light shot back into the ring and all was normal.

"Well," said Courtney with a sigh. "That was . . . strange."

"I guess I'm going to Veelox," Bobby said. Then looked to Gunny and asked, "Want to come?"

"Wouldn't miss it," Gunny answered with a smile.

Bobby turned to face Mark and Courtney. "This has been

the best week of my life," he said sincerely.

The three friends had just spent an excellent week together, forgetting for a short while that Bobby Pendragon was a Traveller who shot across the universe, protecting Halla from an evil demon. Mark was nearly in tears. Courtney wasn't far behind. She walked up to Bobby and before he realised what was happening, she grabbed him and planted a serious kiss on his lips. Bobby didn't fight it. Once the shock was over, he wrapped his arms around Courtney and held her close.

Mark and Gunny turned away.

"So?" Gunny asked Mark. "How 'bout them Yankees?"

When Courtney and Bobby finally unlocked lips, Bobby's eyes were a little watery. But Courtney's gaze was razor sharp.

"Let's not wait another year before the next one, okay?" she said.

"Uh . . . sure. Sounds good," Bobby replied, trying to keep his knees from buckling.

Mark looked at Bobby, his best friend, and said, "Remember what we talked about, okay?"

"I promise," Bobby answered sincerely.

Bobby and Gunny walked towards the street and the limousine that was waiting to take them to the Bronx, and the flume.

"How are you feeling, shorty?" Gunny asked. "I mean . . . where is your head you know, with things?"

"I feel like Saint Dane got the better of me on First Earth," he answered thoughtfully. He then locked eyes with Gunny and said with total confidence, "And I'm not gonna let it happen again."

Gunny chuckled.

"What's so funny?" Bobby asked.

"Shorty, you're starting to sound just like your uncle Press."

Bobby smiled. He liked that. The two got into the back of the big car, the driver gunned the engine, and they were on their way.

Mark and Courtney watched as the black limo picked up speed with Bobby's hand still out the window, waving goodbye.

"What was it you guys talked about?" Courtney asked Mark.

"All sorts of things," he said with a sly smile. "But I'll tell you one thing: I'll bet we're going to see Bobby Pendragon again, a lot sooner than you think."

They took a last look at the departing limousine and saw Bobby pull his arm back inside. The car turned on to the main road and disappeared.

☻ SECOND EARTH ☻

Mark Dimond was ready for an adventure.

He had spent the first fifteen years of his life on the sidelines, watching everybody else have all the fun. It was getting old. He was tired of being wallpaper, tired of being the brunt of geek jokes, and *really* tired of wishing he was somebody else. Anybody else. But even Mark had to admit that it was going to be tough pulling himself out of the deep hole of dorkdom he had been digging since birth.

When he was a baby, his parents barely let him out of the house because he was allergic to everything but air. In three years of Little League he got on base only once, because he was hit by a pitch that broke his glasses. Girls scared him, but that wasn't much of a problem because most girls never looked at him twice anyway. They weren't interested in a guy who constantly gnawed on carrots (to improve his vision), sat in the first row of class (because he had every correct answer, always), and had a stringy mop of hair that always looked like it should have been washed yesterday.

No, Mark hadn't exactly been living large. But now that he

was fifteen, he was determined to make a change. He was ready to seize the day and kick start a new life filled with adventure and excitement. Why?

Because he had a best buddy named Bobby Pendragon.

They had been friends since kindergarten, though most people thought they were as different as east and west. Bobby was athletic and funny and people loved to be around him. Mark was quiet and tripped a lot. But that was just surface stuff.

Mark and Bobby liked the same things, and not always the normal things that other kids thought were cool. They loved old Abbott and Costello movies, eighties music, Thai food, and James Bond novels (not the movies, the original novels). They laughed at the same jokes. They started a band, but Bobby could barely play the guitar and Mark only had an ancient set of bongos. Neither could sing. They were terrible. They had a blast.

They liked to fish in the small river that wound its way through their little town of Stony Brook, Connecticut. It didn't matter that they hardly ever caught anything. It was all about getting away for hours to just hang. Like most guys, they talked about girls and sports, and about what teachers they wanted vaporised. But they also talked about ideas, about travelling and seeing different places, and about the future.

Each always seemed to know when the other needed encouragement, or a kick in the butt. For Bobby, Mark was the only guy he knew who thought outside the box. For Mark, Bobby was his lifeline to the rest of the world. Both knew that no matter what twists their lives took, they would always be best friends.

What they *hadn't* known was that during the winter of their fifteenth year, Bobby and his entire family would mysteriously disappear. A huge investigation by the local police turned up nothing. Literally. It was like the Pendragons had been magically erased from existence.

But Mark knew the truth.

He wasn't sure what had happened to the rest of the Pendragon family, but he knew where Bobby had gone. He had left with his uncle, Press, to become a Traveller. Bobby Pendragon and his uncle had flown through a portal called a flume that took them to strange, distant territories where they joined with other Travellers to do battle against a demon named Saint Dane. In the year and a half since Bobby had left home, he had helped prevent a medieval territory called Denduron from blowing itself up, halted the spread of a poison that would have wiped out the entire population of a water territory called Cloral, and travelled back in time to stop Nazi Germany from developing the world's first atomic bomb.

What was Mark doing while Bobby was defending humanity? Watching a lot of *SpongeBob SquarePants*. Yes, Mark was desperately ready for an adventure. He needed an adventure.

He was about to get one.

"Courtney!" Mark shouted.

Courtney Chetwynde had just stepped off the school bus that brought her to the first day of classes at Davis Gregory High School. Courtney hated the bus, but school was too far from home to bike, and her parents wouldn't let her ride in cars with the older kids yet. Courtney was the only other person who knew the truth about Bobby Pendragon. But unlike Mark, Bobby and Courtney had started out as rivals – athletic rivals. Courtney had done her best to beat Bobby's butt at everything. It had been her way of covering up that she had an incredible crush on him.

Now not a day went by where she didn't think back to the night a year and a half ago when she finally admitted to Bobby that she liked him. That moment got better when Bobby told her that he liked her, too. It got *seriously* better when the two of them kissed. But it all went south when Bobby's uncle Press showed up to break the magic and whisk him away on the back of a motorcycle to begin his life as a Traveller. If Courtney had one wish, it would be that she could wind back the clock to that night and stop Bobby from riding off with his uncle.

As she stepped off the hated school bus, Courtney saw Mark scurry up to meet her.

"Anything?" she asked hopefully.

"Nope," Mark answered.

He knew she was asking if another journal had arrived from Bobby. It hadn't.

These two made an odd couple. Courtney was beautiful, popular, confident, and athletic. Mark . . . wasn't. If it weren't for their connection with Bobby, they never would have been on each other's radar screens.

"First day of high school," Mark said. "Nervous?"

"No," she answered truthfully. Courtney didn't get nervous.

They were starting the tenth grade, which was the first year of Davis Gregory High. Last year they were on the top of the pyramid at Stony Brook Junior High. Now they would have to start over again at the bottom of the school food chain.

As the two walked towards school, Mark had to hurry to keep up with Courtney's long strides. "Courtney, there's s-something I want to talk to you about."

"Whoa, you're stuttering," Courtney said seriously. "What's the matter?"

"N-Nothing," Mark assured her. "I just need to talk to you is all."

"About, you know, journals and stuff?" she asked while glancing around to make sure nobody heard her.

"Sort of. Can we talk after school?"

"I've got soccer practice."

"I'll come watch. We'll talk after."

"You sure everything's okay?"

"Yeah. Good luck today!"

The two then separated and began the first day of their high school careers.

Courtney pretty much hung with her regular friends, though she made sure to check out any new kids. In English class she found herself staring at a cute guy named Frank. It felt a little weird, like she was cheating on Bobby. But Bobby had written in his journals about how fantastic the Traveller girl named Loor was. Courtney thought that if Bobby could like a girl from a far-off territory called Zadaa, then why couldn't she like a guy from two desks over in a class called English?

Mark stepped into high school with expectations of starting a new life. Three junior highs emptied into Davis Gregory, which meant at least two-thirds of these kids didn't know the dorky truth about him. The Etch-A-Sketch of his life had been turned over and given a healthy shake.

Unfortunately, by the end of the last period, Mark had got lost six times, showed up late for every class, made a girl in chemistry gag because his trainers smelled like an experiment gone sour, and got laughed out of the cafeteria when he made the mistake of sitting down to eat lunch next to an all-county wrestling jock. As punishment for invading his space, the guy made Mark stand up on the table and sing "Wally the Green-nosed Tuna" to the tune of "Rudolph the Red-nosed Reindeer".

It was junior high hell all over again, only with bigger kids.

While Mark was discovering the horrible truth that his life of humiliation was going to continue, Courtney was learning that things for her were going to be very different. Courtney was tall and pretty with long, light brown hair, deep grey eyes and a nice smile. She had lots of friends, too. Except when it came to sports. In sports, Courtney had no friends. She hated to lose and had the goods to back it up. It didn't matter what sport, either.

Baseball, athletics, basketball, even judo. She had absolute confidence in herself. In fact, she had got so used to winning that she was looking forward to high school because she desperately wanted more competition.

She got it.

"Chetwynde! Get your shoes on the right feet!" the soccer coach yelled at her.

Courtney's autumn sport was soccer. She had played centre forward on the junior high team and led the town in scoring. She fully expected to step on to the high school varsity field and dominate like always.

She didn't. Courtney realised she was in trouble during the very first drill. It was a dribbling drill. Courtney brought the ball forward with a confident smile, ready to give these high school girls a taste of Hurricane Courtney. She ducked right, moved left . . . and the defender stole the ball.

Whoa.

When it was her turn to play defence, the girls put moves on her and dribbled past like she wasn't even there. One girl made such a hot move that Courtney got her feet crossed and fell on her butt – prompting the comment about her shoes being on the wrong feet.

All afternoon Courtney was one step behind. These high school girls were good. Really good. They shot no-look passes, stole the ball from her, and basically made her look like she was a little kid playing with grown-ups. One girl stole the ball, flipped it up with her foot, bounced it off her knee, and slammed a header downfield. She then looked to Courtney and said, "Welcome to the big time, superstar." When it came time for sprints, Courtney was nearly last every run. That was unheard of. Nobody beat Courtney Chetwynde. Ever! What had happened?

The truth was, nothing had happened. Courtney was always

big for her age. It was one of the reasons she had been so good at sports. But between the ninth and tenth grades, the other girls caught up. Girls who had been too small to compete with Courtney were suddenly eye to eye with her. It wasn't that Courtney had suddenly got bad, it was that everybody else had grown up and got better. Much better. For Courtney it was an absolute, total nightmare. But she wouldn't let it show. No way.

On the sidelines Mark sat under a tree, watching practice. He couldn't believe what he was seeing. Everybody had bad days, but seeing Courtney struggle like this was disturbing. There were some things in life that were absolute. He knew that pi times the radius squared gave you the area of a circle; he knew that water was made up of two parts hydrogen and one part oxygen; and he knew that if you challenged Courtney Chetwynde, you would lose.

The last one of Mark's all-time truisms was now being proved wrong. It was the perfect way to end a totally crappy day.

"Looks like she ain't so tough after all," came a familiar voice from behind Mark.

Mark looked up quickly to see that the horror of this day wasn't yet complete. Standing over him was Andy Mitchell. The guy snorted back a lougie and spit, barely missing Mark's hand. Mark spun out of the way, but Mitchell flicked his cigarette butt in the other direction and Mark nearly rolled into it. Mark had to pop to his feet or risk getting gobbed on.

"What'sa matter, Dimond?" Mitchell laughed. "Twitchy?"

"What do you want?" Mark grumbled.

"Hey, don't get all testy with me," Mitchell shot back. "I'm just out here having a smoke. Seeing Chetwynde getting whupped up on was a bonus." Mitchell wheezed out a laugh through yellowed, smoke-stained teeth.

"Go away," was all Mark managed to squeak out. He turned and walked off, but Mitchell followed.

"I didn't forget, Dimond," Mitchell snarled. "About them journals. Pendragon is out there somewhere. You know it and I know it and I know you know I know it."

Truth be told, there was a third person who knew about what happened to Bobby Pendragon. It was Andy Mitchell. Mitchell had seen one of Bobby's journals and blackmailed Mark into showing him the rest.

Mark turned to Mitchell, standing toe to toe with him. "All I know is, you're an idiot. And I'm not afraid of you any more!"

Mark and Andy held each other's gazes. Mark had had enough of this bully and would almost welcome a fight. Almost. Mark wasn't a fighter. If Mitchell called his bluff and took a swing, things would get real ugly, real fast. For Mark.

"Hey, Mitchell," Courtney said.

She stood behind Mitchell with her gear bag in one hand and her trainers in the other. She looked tired and dirty and not in the mood to be messed with. "What are you doing in high school? I thought you'd be out stealing cars by now."

Andy ducked away from her. He didn't mess with Courtney, no matter how bad she looked playing soccer.

"Real funny, Chetwynde," Mitchell sneered. "You two think you're being all smart, but I know."

"What do you know?" Courtney asked.

Mark said, "He knows we know he knows . . . or something like that. You know?"

Mark and Courtney chuckled. They knew Mitchell wasn't a threat to them any more. He wasn't smart enough for that.

"Yeah, you laugh," he sneered. "But I read those journals. You gonna laugh when that Saint Dane dude comes here looking for them?"

With that, Mitchell snorted back another good one, then turned and hurried away.

Mark and Courtney weren't chuckling any more. They silently watched Mitchell jog off. Then Courtney said, "Well, today pretty much . . . sucked."

The two walked to catch the late bus home. Normally Courtney would sit in the back of the bus with the cool kids and Mark would sit up front with the not-cool kids. Not today. There were a couple of girls in the back who had just taken Courtney apart on the soccer field. They were sitting with some guys from the football team, laughing and flirting. Courtney wasn't welcome. She had to sit in the front of the bus with Mark. It was the final indignity.

"You want to tell me about your day?" Courtney asked.

"No," answered Mark. "You?"

"No."

They rode in silence, both wondering if the rest of high school was going to be as painful as the first few hours. Finally Courtney asked, "What did you want to talk to me about?"

Mark glanced around to make sure nobody was listening. He kept his voice low, just in case. "I've been thinking," he began. "Remember what I said before? In spite of what Mitchell just said, I think we dodged a bullet. When the Travellers stopped Saint Dane on First Earth, I think they saved all three Earth territories. Remember?"

"Yeah, I remember," Courtney said, then added with growing annoyance, "and I remember you saying how disappointed you were because you wanted Saint Dane to come here so you could help Bobby fight him. And I remember saying that you were totally crazy. Do *you* remember that part, Markie boy?"

Mark nodded.

"Good," Courtney said. "Then stop thinking so much."

"But still," Mark added. "I want to be able to help Bobby."

"We *are* helping him," Courtney corrected. "We're holding his journals."

"But that's like almost nothing," Mark countered. "I want to *really* help him."

"We *can't,* Mark."

Mark gave her a sly smile. "Don't be so sure."

Courtney gave Mark a long, probing look. "*Now* what are you thinking?"

"I want to become an acolyte. I want us *both* to become acolytes."

"Aco-whats?"

"You know, acolytes. Bobby wrote about them. The people from the territories who help the Travellers. They put supplies by the flumes for the Travellers. They're the ones who kept Press's motorcycle, and had his car ready when he got back. It's totally safe, but really important."

"Safe?" Courtney shot back. "You think going to that abandoned subway in the Bronx and getting past those quig-dogs is safe?"

"Maybe there's another flume here on Second Earth," Mark added hopefully. "They have more than one flume on other territories, why not here?"

"And what if it's in Alaska?" Courtney lobbed back. "You want to move to Alaska?"

"After the day I had, absolutely."

"You don't mean that."

The two rode in silence for a few more stops. A couple of the soccer girls got off and made a point of ignoring Courtney. Courtney didn't care. Her mind was back on the journals, and Bobby.

"I know you care, Mark," Courtney said softly. "I do too. But even if I thought this acolyte thing was a good idea, how would we do it?"

Mark sat up straight, encouraged that Courtney was at least considering it.

"I don't know, but when Bobby was home I talked to him about it –"

"You already asked Bobby?" Courtney interrupted. "Without talking to me first?"

"All I did was ask him to look into it," Mark said. "He didn't know any more about acolytes than he wrote, but he promised to try and find out. What do you think?"

"I think I gotta think about it. And I think this is my stop." Courtney stood.

"Promise me that?" Mark asked. "You'll think about it?"

"Yeah," Courtney answered. "But I gotta know more."

"Absolutely," Mark said.

Courtney swung down the bus stairs and out of the door. Mark felt better than he had all day. He felt sure that if Bobby got them information about the acolytes, Courtney would join up with him. It was a great feeling to know he might actually have a shot at helping Bobby in a real way.

As Mark lay in bed that night he couldn't stop his mind from imagining the possibilities. If they became acolytes, could they actually fly through the flumes? That would be awesome! He imagined himself on Cloral, speeding underwater with Bobby. He could see himself racing a sledge down the snowy slopes of Denduron, dodging the charging quig-bears. He even saw himself on Zadaa, battling through the capture the flag game alongside Loor.

Mark had to force himself to think of something else for fear he'd never get to sleep. He turned his mind to maths problems. He thought of lying on the beach at the Point. He imagined looking up at puffy clouds on a warm summer's day. He pretended his ring was twitching and another journal from Bobby was about to show up.

Mark sat bolt upright in bed. That wasn't his imagination. Mark's ring *was* twitching. He looked at his hand. The stone in the heavy silver ring was dissolving from dark grey into crystal clear. That meant only one thing . . .

Mark wouldn't be getting to sleep any time soon.

He threw his feet over the side of his bed, yanked off the ring, and placed it on the rug. The small circle became larger, revealing a dark hole where the floor should have been. Mark knew this was the conduit to another territory. He heard the jumble of sweet musical notes that sounded far away at first, but quickly grew louder. Sparkling light then blasted out of the hole, lighting up his room like a thousand fireflies. Mark had to shield his eyes from the brilliant show.

Then, as always, the event abruptly stopped. The lights went out and the music was gone. Mark peeked through his fingers to see that the ring had returned to normal. As always, the mysterious ring had made a delivery.

Lying on the rug was Bobby's latest journal.

But this was unlike anything Bobby had sent before. In fact, it didn't even look like a journal. It was a small, shiny silver device that was roughly the size and shape of a credit card. Mark curiously picked it up and saw three square buttons on it. One was deep green, another was bright orange, the third was black. The thing didn't weigh much more than a credit card either. There was a piece of paper stuck to the device. It was a short note, written in Bobby's handwriting.

It read: GREEN – PLAY. BLACK – STOP. ORANGE – REWIND.

It seemed to Mark like CD player instructions, but this tiny little card didn't look like any media player he had ever seen. But if Bobby sent it, who was he to argue? So he touched the green button.

Instantly a narrow beam of light shot from one end of the card. Mark dropped the device in surprise. The silver card hit the floor and the beam swept across the room. Mark jumped over his bed and crouched down on the far side for protection. Was it a laser? Was he going to get sliced? A second later the beam grew until it projected a holographic image in the middle of the bedroom. Mark had to blink, then rub his eyes, then look again, because standing in front of him was Bobby Pendragon. The image looked as real as if his friend were standing there in the flesh. The only thing that reminded him it was a hologram was the beam of light that came from the device on the floor.

"Hiya, Mark. Hey, Courtney," Bobby's image said as clear as can be.

Mark fell back on his butt, stunned.

"Greetings from the territory of Veelox. What you're seeing and hearing right now, is my journal number thirteen. Pretty cool, aye?"

VEELOX

Hiya, Mark. Hey, Courtney. Greetings from the territory of Veelox. What you're seeing and hearing right now is my journal number thirteen. Pretty cool, aye? I'll bet it beats having to read my lousy handwriting. Heck, it beats having to write everything down, too. I'm loving this. But this projector thing is a toy compared to the science fiction stuff they've got going on here. It's totally incredible.

Just to tease you a little, imagine the most amazing video game you ever played. You know, great graphics, realistic sound, 3-D environments, excellent challenges, the whole deal. Now, imagine that game being about twelve billion times better. That's what they've got on Veelox. I'm not exaggerating. There's no way I could give you a quick description beyond that. You'll have to learn about it the way I did, a little at a time. Be patient. It's worth it.

But before we dive into the wonders of Veelox, I want to tell you what happened after I left you guys on Second Earth. Borrowing one of Spader's phrases, I found myself in the middle of a tum-tigger.

Again.

Gunny and I were given a limo ride to the Bronx by the old gangster, Peter Nelson. We were headed for the abandoned subway station and the flume to the territories. Our ultimate destination was Veelox. Where Saint Dane goes, we go.

Unfortunately.

As we rode towards the Bronx, my head was in a strange place. It was because of what happened on First Earth. Simply put, I failed. On First Earth Saint Dane tried to prove I wasn't worthy of being a Traveller, and that's exactly what happened. It all came down to the moment when the airship *Hindenburg* was about to be destroyed. As horrible as that was, the *Hindenburg* was *supposed* to be destroyed. If history was changed, it would have been Armageddon for Earth. As I stood over the rocket that was about to shoot into the air and blow it up, I knew I had the future of all three Earth territories in my hands.

And I choked. In that horrible moment, I couldn't bear to let the innocent people in that zeppelin die. So I made a move to kick over the rocket, save the *Hindenburg,* save those people, and send the Earth territories spiralling towards doomsday.

But Gunny held me back. He stopped me from making the worst mistake possible. The rocket took off and the *Hindenburg* exploded. Gunny saved the Earth territories. That was the way it was meant to be.

Though the Travellers had beaten Saint Dane, Saint Dane had beaten *me*. Call it what you want: a moment of truth, a test, whatever. But I blew it. From that moment on I questioned whether or not I was up to this job. Heck, I've questioned it from day one, but my screw-up on First Earth totally rocked me. I think Saint Dane expected me to shrivel up and crawl into a hole, never to bother him again in his quest to rule Halla. Believe me, I thought about it.

But that wasn't going to happen.

My screw-up on First Earth had the opposite effect. It got me mad. I wanted to prove to that monster I'm not the loser he thinks I am. Or maybe what I really wanted to do, was prove it to myself. Whatever. Bottom line was, for the first time since I left home to become a Traveller, I felt like I wanted the job. Seriously. I wanted to live up to the trust Uncle Press had in me. Saint Dane's plan had backfired. Rather than making me go away, he fired me up. If he thinks I'm too weak for the job, that's cool. That means he won't see me coming.

And I am definitely coming.

After the limo dropped us off at the abandoned subway station, Gunny and I stood on the pavement, enjoying our last few moments of Second Earth sunlight. Gunny's a great guy and I'm proud to call him my friend. There's a lot of great things I can say about him, but probably the most important is that he was strong enough to take the heat for me on First Earth.

But at that moment, standing on a Bronx pavement, he didn't seem to be in any hurry to go Saint Dane hunting. He was a tall, African-American guy, about 6'4", who looked pretty happy being there with his eyes closed and the sun on his face.

"What're you thinking?" I asked the Traveller from First Earth.

Gunny opened his eyes and glanced around at the busy city intersection. It must have looked strange to him. After all, he was from 1937.

"Tell me, shorty," he said. "Do you think the day will ever come when we can all go home and get back to normal?"

I had been asking myself that same question from the minute I first left home with Uncle Press.

"Don't know," I answered truthfully. "But then again,

I'm not so sure I know what normal is any more."

I led him down the rubbish-strewn stairs of the closed station. It was a familiar route. The entrance was boarded over with wooden planks that were plastered with flyers and advertisements. But I knew the way in. Two of the boards were loose and a quick tug revealed our entrance.

The empty station looked the exact same as it had the first night Uncle Press brought me here. It was a long forgotten piece of New York history – forgotten by everyone but us, that is. A subway train rumbled through, kicking up pieces of crusty paper full of yesterday's news. Once it passed we quickly jumped down on to the track and made our way along the oil-stained wall towards the wooden door with the star symbol. A few seconds later we entered the rocky cavern that would be our last stop on Second Earth. The first leg of our trip had been easy. Now things would get interesting. The two of us stood there for a moment, silently gazing into the long, dark roadway to the territories . . . the flume.

"Tell me about this Veelox place," Gunny said.

"Not much to tell," I answered. "I was only there for a few minutes and never left the flume."

"That floating-head girl?" he asked. "You sure she's a Traveller?"

"So she says," I answered.

Gunny shook his head in wonder. "Heads floating in space," he said philosophically. "What next?"

"I think we're about to find out," I answered.

He gave me a small smile, then stepped into the mouth of the flume. *"Veelox!"* he shouted and the flume came to life. The rock walls cracked and groaned as if they were stretching out the kinks after a long sleep. Deep in the tunnel a faint light appeared that would soon come to sweep Gunny away. Along with it came the faint jumble of sweet musical notes that always accompanied the spectacular light show.

Gunny turned to me. I saw a hint of tension in his eyes. "Did I ever tell you I'm not a big fan of this fluming business?"

I laughed. "Gunny, there's plenty of stuff out there to be scared about. The flume isn't one of 'em."

As the light grew closer, the dark rock of the tunnel began its transformation into clear crystal.

"I'll hold you to that," Gunny said. The light flashed nuclear, music echoed throughout the space, and Gunny was gone. I dropped my hand in time to see the light disappear into the depths of the tunnel. The flume had returned to normal, waiting for its next passenger. Me.

"Veelox!" I shouted, and the process began again.

As the light and music came for me, I closed my eyes, waiting for the first tug that would signal the beginning of my trip.

Here we go again.

The flume ride to Veelox wasn't different to any other. I crossed my arms, kicked back, and enjoyed the sensation of shooting through the crystal tunnel. I gazed out through the clear walls at the star field beyond, trying to pick out a constellation, but none looked familiar. I still didn't know exactly what happened when a Traveller went through a flume. I was beginning to understand that it wasn't like moving through the regular old three dimensions of space that we're used to. You know: up, down, forwards, back. I believe a flume trip sent you through a fourth dimension, which was time. That's why the Travellers are able to show up where they need to be, *when* they need to be there.

Uncle Press explained to me about Halla. It was everything . . . all times, all places, all people, and all things that ever were. And they all still existed. If that were true, then maybe there was a fifth and even a sixth dimension, and the flumes were interdimensional highways between them. Something like that would make sense, or the universe would be getting pretty crowded.

Did I say that made sense? Who am I kidding? Does *any* of this make sense? There was only one thing I knew for sure: All this thinking about multiple dimensions was ruining my cool flume ride. I had to lighten up.

Too late. The jumble of notes grew more furious, which signalled I was nearing Veelox. A few seconds later gravity kicked in and I was gently set down. The first thing I saw was Gunny's back. He stood at the mouth of the flume a few feet in front of me. The second thing I saw was . . .

Saint Dane.

Whoa.

"Hello, Pendragon," the demon said with an oily smile. "Welcome to Veelox."

VEELOX

Saint Dane stood facing us in the dark room.

His sharp blue eyes cut through the gloom like cold fire. He was in his normal form, standing seven feet tall with long grey hair that fell over his shoulders. To say I was shocked to see him doesn't cover it.

"I'm surprised, Pendragon," Saint Dane continued. "After your embarrassment on First Earth, I thought you would have given up your foolish pursuit."

I couldn't talk. I was in total brainlock.

"No matter," he continued. "My work here is complete. Veelox is on the verge of crumbling. I must say, I didn't expect Veelox to be the first territory to fall, but in the end it won't matter, since all of Halla will ultimately meet the same fate."

"Veelox is about to crumble?" Gunny asked, stunned.

"I don't believe you," I said, finally kick-starting my brain.

Saint Dane smiled from one corner of his mouth and said, "You say that as if I should care. Now, please, step aside. I have business elsewhere."

"You're not leaving," I announced defiantly.

Gunny gave me a quick, nervous look. That was a pretty bold threat, especially since I had no idea of how to back it up.

"What are you going to do?" Saint Dane chuckled. "Hold me here?"

"If we have to," I said, trying not to let my voice crack. I meant it too. If Saint Dane ran for the flume, I was ready to tackle him. We had to know what had happened on Veelox.

"Isn't that a little unimaginative?" Saint Dane said. But the words didn't come from his mouth. They came from our right. Huh? Gunny and I both turned quickly to see . . .

Another Saint Dane was standing there. There were two of them! "Certainly you can be more creative than that," the second Saint Dane said.

"Or maybe you've reached your limit for resourcefulness," came another voice.

Uh-oh. Gunny and I spun to our left to see a *third* Saint Dane.

"Press would be so disappointed in you."

We turned to see yet another Saint Dane behind us, standing in the mouth of the flume. "They're not real, Gunny. They're holograms," I said. "Like movies."

"Correct!" Saint Dane announced. The *fifth* Saint Dane. We were now standing in a circle of Saint Danes. There were twenty of them, all the exact duplicates of one another. They started to move together, circling us.

"The question is," they all said in unison, "which one of us is real?" They let out a chilling laugh. "What to do? What to do?" they sang together.

Gunny and I stood back to back, trying to spot any sign that would tell us which was the original. It was impossible.

They were perfect clones. Then, in one unified voice, they all shouted, *"Eelong!"*

Uh-oh. The flume came to life. If we were going to do something, it would have to be fast. Gunny made the first move. He jumped forward and wrapped his arms around the closest Saint Dane. But all he got for his trouble was an armload of air.

The Saint Danes laughed. This was fun for him. Or them, or whatever.

Light from the flume lit up the room and the musical notes were nearly on us. Gunny lunged at another Saint Dane, but his arms swept through the hologram like it wasn't even there. Because it wasn't. In seconds Saint Dane would escape to another territory and we'd be left to pick up the pieces. As scared as I was, I lunged at one of the Saint Danes . . .

And wrapped my arms around the demon Traveller. The real one. I had guessed right. First try. Lucky me.

It's hard to describe the feeling. Yes, I was petrified, but I guess that's obvious. What I remember most is that Saint Dane felt cold. It was like hugging a block of ice. With my chin stuck in his chest, I looked up into his eyes. For an instant I was afraid the blood in my veins would freeze solid. Maybe it did, because I couldn't move. When he opened his mouth to speak, his breath smelled like something had crawled in there and died.

"Does this mean you're coming with me?" he asked with a wicked sneer.

That threw me. I felt as if holding on to him wasn't going to stop him, but instead make me his prisoner. The thought was so gruesome, I automatically let go. Bad move, because Saint Dane instantly bolted for the flume. Gunny lunged at him, but the demon was too fast. He leaped into the flume at the exact instant the light came to take him. All that was left was the echoing sound of his laughter as he flumed away.

Saint Dane was gone.

So were the holograms. Gunny and I were left alone in the big empty room, staring at a dark flume.

"I'm going after him," Gunny announced.

"No!" I shouted. "We've got to figure out what he did here on Veelox."

"He's going to start in on a new territory, Pendragon," Gunny declared. "What's done here is done."

"We don't know that for sure," I countered. "Just because he said it, doesn't mean it's true. He's not exactly an honest guy."

We were at a crossroads. What was the best thing to do? Stay here and do damage control, or stop Saint Dane from digging into a new territory called Eelong?

"You've been here before," Gunny said. "You know the Traveller. What's her name?"

"Aja Killian."

"Right. The floating head. I think you should find her. She'll know what Saint Dane has been up to."

"What about you?"

"I'll follow him to Eelong and see what we're up against there. Then I'll be back."

"I don't like splitting up," I said. "Remember what happened on First Earth when Spader took off on his own? That was nearly a disaster."

"I know," Gunny reassured me. "But this is different. Spader had his own ideas. You and I are working *together*."

I didn't want him to go, but if we had the chance of heading off Saint Dane before he could get started on Eelong, we had to take it.

"Promise me you'll bolt if something wacky happens," I demanded.

Gunny laughed. "Shorty, seems to me like everything is pretty wacky."

"You know what I mean."

"Course I do. Don't you go worrying; I'll be fine," Gunny said.

The two of us hugged, then Gunny pushed me back and asked, "What was the name of that territory again?"

"It sounded like 'Eelong'," I answered.

Gunny stepped into the mouth of the flume, stood up straight, and faced the tunnel. *"Eelong!"*

On cue, the flume sprang to life. The moment before he was taken away in the shower of light and music, he smiled at me and said, "What is it that Spader always says?"

"Hobey-ho, Gunny."

"Hobey-ho, Pendragon. See you soon."

I hoped so. An instant later he was gone and I was alone. I stood there, trying to collect my thoughts. The idea of Gunny being lost to me was horrible. I was a fraction of a second away from jumping in the flume and going after him, when I heard a familiar voice.

"What took you so long?"

I spun quickly to see a giant face. It was Aja Killian. The hologram-head was back. I looked up at the bizarre image and said, "You called. I'm here. Now what?"

The head vanished. A second later I heard a faint sound from across the room. I looked to see a door opening, by itself. Light spilled in from whatever lay beyond.

It was time to meet Aja Killian and get my first look at the territory of Veelox.

VEELOX

I found myself in a long, narrow tunnel that stretched far off in two directions. Light came from overhead bulbs, but it was pretty dim because every other bulb was burned out or smashed.

Slam!

The gate shut behind me. It was a plain, metal door that practically disappeared because it was the same grey colour as the cement walls around it. The only thing that told me it was there was the star symbol that marked it as a gate. I hoped I wouldn't have to find it again in a hurry.

I saw that I was standing on tracks. Uh-oh. Another subway. My adrenalin spiked. Was I going to have to run from a speeding train? A closer look showed me there was no danger. Big chunks of the track were missing and a thin coat of brown rust covered the silver steel. There hadn't been a train through here in a very long time.

"Walk to your right," Aja's voice boomed from nowhere. "You'll find a ladder."

"Where are you?" I shouted. I was getting tired of all this mystery. "Why don't you just show yourself?"

"Find the ladder, Pendragon," Aja's voice commanded.

Fine. Whether I liked it or not, the mystery was going to continue. As I walked through the tunnel, I wondered if the people on Veelox were giants. If Aja's projection was life-size, then I was in for a whole *Gulliver's Travels* adventure. That wouldn't be fun.

I came to a metal ladder that disappeared up into a dark opening in the ceiling. I was about to climb up, when a thought hit me. I was still wearing the flannel shirt and jeans you loaned me on Second Earth, Mark. We weren't supposed to mix things from other territories, including clothes. But there hadn't been any Veelox clothes at the flume. What was I supposed to do? I actually had a quick thought that since I had only seen Aja's head, maybe the people on Veelox didn't wear clothes at all. How's *that* for an image? Big, floating, naked giants. Sheesh. No way I was taking my clothes off.

The ladder led up through a round shaft that wasn't much wider than my shoulders. A few more steps up the ladder and I hit the ceiling. I tested it with a push. It moved. This was it, my portal into Veelox. With a quick breath to calm myself, I pushed the heavy hatch up and climbed through to get my first look at this new territory.

I'm not sure what I expected to see, but this wasn't it.

First off, I was relieved. Since Saint Dane had said he had already done his dirty work here, I was nervous about finding a territory that was on fire, or laid waste, or had people running around screaming in panic. But there was none of that. What I did see was totally strange, if only because it wasn't strange at all.

Veelox looked like Second Earth. I found myself standing on a city street that could have been a neighbourhood from home. The hatch I had just climbed through was a manhole in the street. The buildings were city-style town houses. There were pavements and trees and even streetlights. If I didn't know any better I'd say I had pulled a U-turn in the flume and landed back on Second Earth.

Still, as familiar as this place was, something felt off. I looked around, trying to figure out why I was getting such a strange vibe. It took me all of three seconds to understand.

The place was deserted.

Not just empty, I'm talking desolate. No people, no cars, no music, no nothing. The only sound was the whisper of wind as it blew through the buildings and rustled the trees. It was totally eerie. The place was . . . dead. That was the word. Dead. Veelox was a ghost territory.

Great. Giant, naked, floating *ghosts*. Could this get any stranger?

"Over here!"

I spun to see a welcome sight. Standing on a street corner not far away was Aja Killian. The real deal. I was relieved to see she had a body to go with the head. Better still, she was normal size. Still better, she was wearing clothes. Phew.

I jogged over to her. Aja was shorter than I was, and I'm guessing a little bit older. She wore a dark blue jumpsuit that fitted her pretty well. She was kinda cute, with big blue eyes behind those yellow-tinted glasses. The only thing non-Second Earth about her was a gizmo she had strapped to her right forearm. It was a wide, silver bracelet with lots of buttons that looked like a high-tech calculator.

And she was cute, too. Did I say that?

"Hi," I said, being all sorts of charming.

I held out my hand to shake. She didn't take it. Aja snapped angrily, "What took you so long to get here?"

Whoa. Where did *that* come from? I had been here for a

grand total of ten seconds and she was already giving me grief. Not a good start.

"What are you talking about?" I asked.

"I've been trying to contact you about Saint Dane, but you haven't been responding," she scolded. "I was ready to give up on you when —"

"Whoa. Hang on," I interrupted. "I didn't get your message because my ring was stolen. The second I got it back, your message came through and here I am."

She couldn't argue with the logic but still wanted to fight. So she changed her tack.

"How could you let your ring get stolen?" she demanded to know. "Do you know how important these rings are? If you're not —"

"*Stop!*" I yelled. "I got here as soon as I could. Let it go at that, all right?"

"Fine," Aja said, sounding snotty. "But everything's fine now, so you can flume off with that Gunny person and worry about some other territory. Goodbye." She turned and walked away.

My head was spinning. What just happened here? Was she blowing me off?

"Time out," I said while running after her. "Did you hear what Saint Dane said?"

"Of course. I have the flume monitored, remember? I know everything that happens down there."

"Good, then you know he said Veelox was ready to crumble."

"He was wrong," Aja said without looking at me.

"Explain, please."

Aja came to an abrupt stop and I nearly ran into her. "Technically he's right," she explained. "Veelox *is* ready to crumble. But it hasn't yet, and it won't. I made sure of that."

"So what was he up to?" I asked. "Is there some kind of battle going to happen? Are there armies going to march on one another? Who's fighting here?"

Aja shook her head like she pitied me for being totally pathetic. "No, Pendragon. There is no big war. There are no guns or bombs. Nothing is going to explode, which I'm sure is disappointing to you."

I let that comment slide. "So then what's the conflict? What's the turning point on Veelox?"

Aja stepped up to me and touched my forehead. "The turning point is in the head of every single person on Veelox. There are no good guys or bad guys here. This is a war that is being fought in people's minds, not on any battlefield."

"I have no idea what you're talking about," I admitted.

Aja smiled. I think she liked feeling superior.

"It doesn't matter. Everything is under control. I contacted you because that's what I was supposed to do, but you aren't needed here, Pendragon. Veelox is safe. Go away."

She turned and walked off again. I wanted to believe her. One less territory to worry about was, well, one less territory to worry about. But I couldn't just take her word for it. So I ran after her again.

"What do you mean, you were *supposed* to contact me?" I asked.

"Because you're the lead Traveller," she said, throwing me a look of disdain. "Hard to believe."

Yikes. New twist. Lead Traveller? Nobody told me that. "Uh . . . who said I was the lead Traveller?"

"Everyone," she answered.

"Everyone who?"

"The Traveller from Denduron, for one. Alder was his

name. Did you really blow up an entire castle?"

"Yes. Alder told you I was the lead Traveller?"

"I first heard it from Press Tilton. Now *that* guy I could see being the lead Traveller. Do you know him?"

"Yeah," I answered. "Press was my uncle. He's dead."

Aja stopped walking. It was kind of harsh to give her that news so abruptly, but at least I had got her to stop being annoying for a few seconds. "I . . . I'm sorry, Pendragon," she said with sincere sympathy. "I didn't know."

I didn't want to have to battle this crazy Traveller girl. So at the risk of getting insulted again, I decided to put it all on the table. "I'll be honest with you, Aja," I began. "Up until you just said it, I had no idea I was a lead Traveller. I don't even know what that means. But whether it's true or not, I'm not your enemy. So cut me a little slack, all right?"

I looked her in the eye, trying to will her into trusting me. I wasn't sure if Traveller mind persuasion worked on other Travellers, but I was willing to give it a try.

"Come with me," she finally said, and walked off.

Phew. That was a start. The two of us walked along the centre line of the empty street. The place reminded me of those big movie sets I saw on the tour of Universal Studios. Everything looked normal, but totally without life.

"Where is everybody?" I asked tentatively.

"Almost everyone is in Lifelight," she answered.

"Lie flight?"

"No, Lifelight."

"Sorry," I said. "I don't know what that means."

Aja stopped walking and touched her silver bracelet to my head. I felt a short, warm buzz, then she pulled it away.

"What was that?" I asked nervously.

Aja then pointed her hand, hit a few buttons, and said, "Look."

I looked to where she was pointing and saw something that made me want to laugh and cry at the same time. It was Marley, my golden retriever. She stood facing me, wagging her tail so hard her whole backside wiggled. She had a goofy grin on her face and wore the green collar I got her for Christmas two years before. This wasn't just any golden, this was *my* golden.

"Marley?" I called out tentatively.

Marley wagged her tail harder and ran to me. She was all set to jump and I was ready to catch her, but the second her front paws left the ground, she disappeared. Poof. Gone. All I caught was air. After a frozen moment, I looked to Aja and squeaked out a stunned, "How did you do that?"

"Lifelight," she answered. "It pulled that from your memory."

"Huh?" was all I could get out.

Aja smiled. She was back in charge again. "Veelox is the perfect territory, Pendragon, because we can live any existence we choose."

I was sinking deeper into the land of confusion. "Now I'm totally lost," I said.

"Imagine the perfect place," she continued. "It could be anywhere you want and populated with the people you choose. Like that dog. That's Lifelight. People here can live a life tailored specifically for them."

"So Lifelight sends people all over the territory and sets them up in whatever perfect life they want?" I asked.

"No," she answered. "I said people live any life they choose. They don't go anywhere."

"Still not getting it," I complained.

Aja motioned for me to follow her. She took a few more steps, rounded a corner and pointed to a sight that actually took my breath away. No kidding. For a second I couldn't breathe. That's how awesome it was.

Sitting in the centre of the city, maybe a mile away from us, was a huge, four-sided pyramid. It dwarfed the buildings around it, looking as if a massive, alien spacecraft had set down in the centre of town. The shiny black walls reflected the sun towards us, making the immense structure seem more like a shadow than a building.

"You're telling me everybody from this city is in that pyramid?"

"Not everybody. Most."

"Why?"

Aja shook her head like I was a lousy student, then walked to the side of the road. Parked near a lamp-post was a strange, two-seater pedal car. The seats were side by side and it had three wheels, like a tricycle. Aja climbed on to the left seat and said, "I could tell you, or I could show you. Which would be easier?"

Man, this girl really thought I was a dimwit. But I didn't want to argue anymore, so I took the right seat. Aja kicked off and the two of us pedalled towards the monster pyramid.

"Is Lifelight some kind of virtual reality game?" I asked.

"It's no game," Aja scoffed.

"But it's all just holograms, right? Like my dog, and your big floating head."

"Don't pass judgement until you know what you're talking about."

Fair enough. I decided to see what Lifelight was about

before asking any more questions. The two of us rode in silence and I took the chance to check out more of this forlorn, deserted city. We passed grocery stores and clothing shops and office fronts. All very normal, but empty. Looking closer, I saw that the buildings were run down. Signs were turning yellow, rubbish was collecting in corners, windows were thick with grit. It was like the people had just . . . walked away.

I saw lots of signs for something called "gloid". There was NEW GLOID and TASTE SENSATION GLOID and even GLOID PLUS. It was one of the few words that my Traveller brain didn't translate into English, so I assumed it was something unique to Veelox. Another unique word I kept seeing was "Rubic". Street signs pointed to RUBIC CENTRAL. Stores used the word too, as in RUBIC LAUNDRY. I even saw a sign that said: BEST GLOID IN RUBIC. That one put me over the edge. I had to ask.

"What is Rubic?"

"That's the name of the city," she said. "Rubic City."

"And what's gloid?"

"That one I'll have to show you," she answered.

As much as this place looked like Second Earth, these subtle differences reminded me that I was nowhere near Second Earth. That's when I remembered something else.

"My clothes!" I blurted out. "I need Veelox clothes."

Aja looked me over. "Nobody will notice," she said calmly.

If she wasn't worrying, then maybe I shouldn't either. Besides, there were more important things to worry about. Looming up before us was the Lifelight pyramid. Man, it was massive! I'm guessing that it had to be fifty storeys high. The shiny black surface made it seem even more imposing because it was such a contrast to the lighter-coloured buildings that surrounded it.

"I'm off duty, so I can give you a tour," she said.

"You work here?"

"Yes, I'm a phader."

"Huh?"

"Don't think too hard. I'll show you what that means."

I was beyond caring about Aja's intellectual digs. I was way more interested in this strange pyramid. We headed towards a revolving door that looked tiny at the base of this massive building. As we rode closer I finally saw some of the other people of Veelox. They were walking around the pyramid, wearing coveralls like Aja's. Some were blue, others were red. That was it. Blue and red. Not a whole lot of fashion going on here.

"The people in red are vedders," she explained. "No way I'd want their job."

"What do they do?" I asked.

"You'll see."

Aja guided our bike right up to the revolving door and hopped off. "Open your mind, Pendragon. Don't judge until you've experienced it."

"Experienced what?"

"Lifelight, of course. I'm going to take you on the most amazing trip you could possibly imagine." With that, she turned and entered the pyramid.

I had been on plenty of amazing trips lately. She would have to go a long way to top any of them. To be honest, I wasn't so sure I wanted her to try. But there was one thing I was dead sure of: If I wanted to figure out what Saint Dane had been up to on Veelox, the answer would be inside this pyramid.

So with one last quick glance around at the world outside, I stepped into the dark pyramid and a world called "Lifelight".

VEELOX

Forget everything I said about Veelox being like Second Earth.

Stepping into that pyramid was like entering a different world. Inside the revolving door we walked through a narrow tunnel that was lit by long tubes of purple neon light. As soon as we stepped inside, the hair stood up on my arms. It was like the room was charged with electricity.

"Sterilisation," Aja explained.

Sterilisation? That sounded like something the vet did to your dog when you didn't want it to have puppies. Gulp.

"It's totally safe," she assured me. "The process kills any foreign microbes that might foul the grid."

"Sure, wouldn't want to foul the grid." Whatever *that* meant.

At the end of the corridor, we walked our newly sterilised selves through another revolving door that led to a quiet, dimly lit room. There was a long counter, behind which were four people wearing red coveralls. "Vedders" is what Aja called them. She led me up to a guy I guessed to be about my age. He had coal black hair parted in the middle that went right down to his shoulders. There was definitely a Goth vibe going on, but I doubted they called it that on Veelox.

"Hello," the vedder said to Aja flatly.

"This is my friend's first time; I wanted to walk him through."

The vedder snapped a look at me like I had two heads. "You've never jumped before?"

"Uh . . . not that I can remember," I said, then held out my hand to shake. "My name's Pendragon."

The Goth vedder stared at me blankly. He didn't care what my name was. He didn't shake my hand, either. Creep.

"Yes, well, welcome to Lifelight," he said, sounding totally bored. He reminded me of somebody who had worked at McDonald's selling burgers for too long. He finally reached out to take my hand, but rather than shaking it, he flipped it over and jabbed a tiny needle into my pinkie.

"Ow!" I quickly pulled back and sucked on my stinging finger. "What was that for?"

"You need a bio workup," Aja explained.

I had already been sterilised, dissed, and stabbed. So far there wasn't much to like about Lifelight. The vedder put the needle into a computer-looking thing that I assumed was doing the bio-whatever analysis on the blood he had just stolen from me. While we waited for him to finish, I glanced around the room. It reminded me of the ticket counter at an airport. It was all very modern. There were no signs, but on the wall behind the counter was a big oil portrait of a kid. He looked to be about ten years old, with short, blond hair and a blue jumpsuit like Aja's. He was a serious-looking little dude, too. He seemed to be staring right at me.

"Who's that?" I asked.

The vedder shot me a look as if I had suddenly sprouted a third head to go with my other two.

"You're funny," Aja said, covering for me. She then looked at the vedder and said, "He's always making dumb jokes."

The vedder wasn't laughing. "Give me your hand, please."

"Not if you're gonna poke me again," I protested.

Goth boy gave Aja an impatient look.

"Hold up your hand, Pendragon," she commanded.

Reluctantly I held up my hand again, prepared for more pain. But the vedder quickly snapped a silver bracelet around my wrist. It looked more like a high-tech device than jewellery. It was smaller than Aja's, about two inches wide, with three square buttons that were flush to the surface.

"Enjoy your jump," the vedder said, though I was betting he didn't care one way or the other.

I smiled at the guy anyway, then followed Aja towards a door at the far end of the room. "Who was the kid in the picture?" I whispered.

"Dr Zetlin, the person who invented Lifelight."

"A kid invented all of this?" I asked, unbelieving.

"A very smart kid," was her answer.

"Yeah, no kidding."

Aja then pushed open a door, and we continued into a long corridor that can be best described as mission control . . . times about a thousand. The walls were made of glass. Through them I saw a series of high-tech workstations that looked like they each had enough electronic muscle to launch about a million space shuttles. Each station was its own separate, enclosed cubicle. I guessed that there were around fifty of these workstations on either side of the corridor. Then there was a whole nother row of workstations above them. So a rough guess was that there were around two hundred of these high-tech rigs.

There was one phader in each, wearing the signature blue jumpsuit and sitting in the coolest looking chair I had ever seen. It was black, with a high back, and wings near the head that spread out to either side. The arms of the chair were wide, with a silver control panel on each side where the phader could touch the myriad of buttons that worked . . . whatever.

In front of each phader was a wall of computer screens. A quick count told me that each phader was looking at around thirty screens. Here's the strange part (as if everything up until now *wasn't* strange): Each of the computer monitors was showing a different movie. Multiply the thirty movies playing in each cubicle by two hundred cubicles and that's like six thousand movies, all playing at the same time. I figured this might be some kind of satellite TV operation that beamed shows all over Veelox.

I couldn't have been more wrong.

"This is where I work," Aja explained. "It's called the 'core'. The phaders troubleshoot the hardware, upgrade when necessary, and monitor the jumps to make sure everyone is okay."

"And what do the vedders do?"

"They take care of the jumpers physically. That's why they took your blood. They make sure the jumpers are safe and healthy."

"What are the movies they're watching?" I asked.

"Those are the *jumps*," Aja answered, trying not to sound too impatient.

I looked through the glass at one of the banks of monitors and saw that the action on the screens wasn't continuous. Every few seconds each screen changed to another bit of action, like turning the channels on a TV. I focused on one screen to see a hot sailing boat gliding through tropical waters. The image then changed to the point of view of a skier flying down a snowy mountain, expertly dodging through trees. On the screen next to that I saw what looked like a stadium full of people watching a game that was like soccer, but played with a big orange ball the size of a monster pumpkin. That screen then changed to the quiet scene of a cozy fireplace and an older woman drinking tea.

"People come here to watch movies?" I asked.

Aja chuckled. "Something like that. Come on."

She led me down the long corridor of cubicles. I glanced into the different workstations that made up the core to get an idea of what kind of movie I'd choose when it came my turn. I figured I'd want to watch a movie about basketball. I hadn't played in a long time and missed it. I hoped they knew what basketball was on Veelox.

When we reached the end of the corridor, Aja said, "Are you ready for this?"

"Uh, yeah. I guess." I had no idea if I was ready or not because I didn't know what to expect.

Aja shook her head again, amused by my innocence . . . or stupidity. We pushed through the next revolving door, and what I saw beyond proved only one thing . . .

I wasn't ready for it.

We stepped into the central chamber of the pyramid. Everything up to this point had been pre-game. This was the main event. I took a step inside, looked up, and my knees buckled from seeing the sheer size of the place. The pyramid was pretty much hollow so I could see all the way up to the point. In the centre of the structure was a tube that ran from the floor right up to the uppermost tip. Off this central tube were hundreds of walkways that spread out like spokes of a wheel in different directions and levels. They attached to the inside walls of the pyramid, which had hundreds of levels, with walkways ringing all the way around.

Aja didn't say anything at first. I guess she wanted me to get my mind around it all. She shouldn't have bothered. There was no way I could get my mind around any of this.

"You asked me before where everybody was," she finally said. She then pointed up to the walls of the pyramid.

"You're telling me everybody from Veelox is up there, right now?"

"No," she said. "But almost everybody from Rubic City is. There are at least eight hundred more of these Lifelight pyramids all over Veelox."

The idea was staggering. "So, everybody's in here watching movies?" I asked.

Aja lifted her arm to look at her wide, silver bracelet. She touched a few buttons while staring intently at the high-tech device.

"What are you doing?" I asked.

"Looking for a vacant station," she answered, and started walking. Like an obedient puppy, I followed. She led me to the centre of the pyramid, which was not a short walk. Along the way we passed several phaders and vedders who were ferrying equipment or supplies of some sort. Nobody said much to anyone else. To me, they all seemed a little depressed. Maybe not as bad as the miners of Denduron, but these guys weren't exactly whistling while they worked, either. We got into a lift and quickly rose up the central tube.

When Aja stopped and opened the door, my palms instantly went wet. We were seriously high up in the air. Worse, the guardrails on the walkways were only about knee-high. Aja stepped out. I didn't.

"It's safe, Pendragon," she said. "Look straight ahead

and follow me." She walked out on one of the bridges that led to the far wall of the pyramid. "Don't look down."

Yeah, right. That's the first thing I did. Yikes. We were about halfway up the pyramid, but that was plenty high. It felt like I was standing on a rickety Lego structure. I could only hope these walkways were sturdier than they looked. I didn't want to be on that bridge any longer than I had to, so a few seconds later I caught right up with Aja and blew past her. I made it to the far end and the balcony that ran the length of one side of the pyramid.

Aja gave me a disapproving look. "Are you sure you're the lead Traveller?" she asked.

"No. Where are we going?"

Aja checked her high-tech bracelet once more, then walked along the balcony. I followed, hugging the wall to stay as far away from the edge as possible. There were doors every few feet. If you figured this was only one side of one level of the pyramid, there must have been hundreds of thousands of doors just like it. Each door had a small round, white light next to it. Most were lit. Aja stopped at a door marked 124-70. The light over the door was out so I guessed that meant nobody was home. Aja touched the door and it instantly slid back into the wall like we were about to step on to the bridge of the starship *Enterprise*.

The room inside was pretty bland. It reminded me of a doctor's examination room because it looked simple and sterile. There was no furniture or anything, just a round, silver disc on the back wall about three feet wide. Next to it on the wall was a square silver panel that looked like a bigger version of the control bracelet Aja wore. On the panel were several rows of flat, silver buttons, none of which were marked. Above the rows of buttons was a narrow black section that I guessed was some kind of computer screen that gave read-outs of . . . whatever. Aja went right to this silver panel and began hitting buttons. The narrow computer screen flashed with green numbers.

"This pyramid is operating at about eighty-seven percent capacity," she explained.

She touched one button and, with a slight hum, the round silver disc slid sideways into the wall to reveal a circular tube that stretched back into the wall space for about seven feet. Another touch of a button and a white table slowly emerged from the tube.

"Lie down," Aja ordered.

Yeah, right. If she thought I was going to lie on that table and get sucked back into this sci-fi-looking tube without an explanation, she was dreaming.

"Tell me what's going to happen first."

"Don't you trust me?" she asked with a sly smile.

"It's not that I don't trust you," I said quickly. "It's just that this is all . . . I mean, I've never seen . . . I don't understand . . . uh, no, I don't trust you."

"Even though I'm a Traveller?"

"Look," I said. "I don't know why you have an ick against me, but if you want me to trust you, you gotta start acting a little more human."

It bugged me that Aja had such disdain for me. I had no idea why. Yeah, she was a Traveller, but I didn't see her out there fighting quigs or getting shot at or jumping out of aeroplanes or doing any of the scary things I'd had to do. What made her so special?

"Sorry," she said. "Lifelight is such a normal part of life that it's hard for me to understand how someone doesn't know all about it."

"Fine. Start explaining or I'm not lying down on that thing."

"It's totally safe," Aja began. "Nothing happens to you physically. It's all about expanding your mind into areas of your own choosing. You lie on the table, the table slides back into the tube and I close the round disc. To be honest, some people get a little nervous because it's dark and the space is closed. But the sensation doesn't last long. I promise."

"Then what do I do? Lie there and watch a movie?"

"You focus your thoughts. Think about a place you'd like to be. Or a person you'd want to see. That's all it takes."

"And it reads my mind? Like when my dog appeared?"

"Exactly."

It seemed impossible, but Marley sure as heck looked real. It may have been a holographic illusion, but it was a good one.

"What if something goes wrong? Like if I get claustrophobia or something?"

"You won't," she assured me. "But if it makes you feel better, the vedders and phaders monitor all the jumps from the core. If something goes wrong, they'll stop the event. Believe me, they know what they're doing."

I lifted my arm and touched the silver bracelet on my wrist with the three buttons. "What's this for?"

"It's your ultimate control over the jump. If you want to talk to your phader, push the left button. If you want to end the jump, push the right button."

"And the middle button?"

"That's for advanced jumpers. Don't push it."

Oh man, that was like saying: "Don't look down." Now all I wanted to do was push that middle button. "How long will I be in there?" I asked.

"I'm going to time your jump to last only a few minutes.

The point is to show you what Lifelight is all about. After that, I'll be able to explain why Saint Dane doesn't pose a threat to Veelox."

We had come full circle. That's exactly why I was here. This was all about figuring out what the turning point of Veelox was, and how Saint Dane had tipped the territory towards chaos. I was beginning to understand why Aja wanted me to see this for myself. Hopefully after I completed my jump, or whatever they called it, I would be up to speed and could focus on the main problem. Saint Dane.

"Now lie down," Aja instructed. "Feet first."

With a shrug, I laid down on the table. It was soft and moulded to my body. Very comfy. I guess it would have to be if people were lying down for long periods of time.

"Try to relax," Aja said in a surprisingly soothing voice. "Fold your arms over your chest. I'm going to retract the table and slide you inside. Be sure to breathe. If it helps, close your eyes. Then I'm going to close the front panel and the tube will go completely dark. It's okay. That's supposed to happen. Your job is to focus your thoughts."

My heart rate started to climb. Should I trust this girl? Or was she sending me into some high-tech atom smasher that would pulverise me into pocket lint? But she was a Traveller. I had to believe she knew what she was doing.

"Ready?" she asked.

"Yes," I lied.

With a slight shift and a soft hum, the table began retracting into the tube, bringing me along with it. Gulp. I wanted to yell: "Time out!" but that would only prolong the torture. I had to suck it up. A few seconds later I looked up and saw the top of the tube pass by my face as I slid inside. I didn't close my eyes. Maybe I should have, but I wanted to see what was happening. I lay there in this tight, round tunnel, staring up at the top, which was only a few inches above my nose. I never had a problem with claustrophobia, but if there ever was a time to get it, it was now.

"You okay?" Aja asked.

"Fine," I lied again. I had one question. It wasn't sophisticated. It wasn't smart and maybe it proved I was a weenie. But I had to ask it. "Aja?" I asked, trying not to let my voice quiver. "Is this going to hurt?"

Aja leaned down until she was just behind my head. When she spoke, it was the first time I sensed that there was actually a human being with feelings behind those yellow-tinted glasses.

"Pendragon," she said, "it's going to be the most fun you've ever had."

With that, the round panel hummed and began to close behind me. Seconds later the last of the light from the chamber room was cut off and I was in total darkness.

⚙ SECOND EARTH ⚙

It was an act that required a huge amount of willpower.

Mark reached down to the floor and touched the black button on the small silver projector. Instantly Bobby's hologram disappeared. It killed Mark to stop it, especially at such a crucial moment. Bobby's image was about to reveal the mystery of Lifelight. But that's exactly why he had to stop it.

Courtney wasn't there.

Mark felt like he had already cheated on their pact by watching so much of the journal without her. But the hologram thing was so incredible, Mark couldn't wait. In fact, he had been so captivated by the 3-D image that it took a while before he even realised what he was doing. Rule #1 was that they would always read Bobby's journals together. He had just broken it. Sort of. He would have to explain to Courtney how he was so surprised by Bobby's image that it took him a while to get his head back together. He didn't deliberately choose to watch the journal without her. It just happened. She would understand.

No, she won't. She's going to be totally ticked off, Mark thought.

He started getting sweaty. He had betrayed Courtney's trust once before by not telling her that Andy Mitchell found out about the journals. Now he had done it again. Courtney was going to be mad and Mark knew she had every right to be.

He took the small, silver projection device and put it in his bedside drawer. He then crawled back into bed and tried to relax. He had had trouble getting to sleep before the journal arrived. Now it was impossible. He was dying to know what happened to Bobby in Lifelight. The answers were in the drawer only inches from his head. Talk about torture!

In his mind he replayed all that Bobby had recorded. It was an incredible device. Not only did it look as if Bobby were standing in the room talking right to him, Bobby was able to act out the events he was describing. He played the different parts, changing his voice to mimic the different characters and using hand gestures for emphasis. Bobby knew how to tell a story, too. His written journals were great, but seeing him tell the story aloud was awesome. Mark couldn't wait to hear more.

He ended up staring at the ceiling for the rest of the night.

When morning finally came, Mark tucked the silver device safely into a small zipped pocket of his backpack and took it to school. His hope was that as soon as Courtney saw it, her curiosity would overpower her anger. Neither of them shared any classes, so Mark didn't see her all day. The best thing he could do was meet her after soccer practice again. He hoped she would have a better practice than the day before. He didn't want her in an ugly mood.

Mark's second day of high school wasn't as painful as the first. That was because he mostly kept to himself. It wasn't hard. His body may have been at Davis Gregory High, but his mind was on Veelox. The day went by without any major incident, until the end of the last period. He barely listened to his chemistry teacher because he was spending so much time staring at the clock, willing the hands to move faster. The instant the final bell rang, he quickly packed up and was the first one out of the door.

"Excuse me? Mark Dimond?"

Mark spun around and saw a teacher calling to him from down the hall. His name was Mr Pike, the physics teacher. Everybody knew who he was because he was one of the younger, cool teachers. His hair was kind of long and he wore jeans and a cotton sweater. To Mark he looked more like an artist than a science teacher.

"Yeah?" Mark answered tentatively.

"I've been looking forward to meeting you," the teacher said, holding out his hand to shake. "My name's David Pike. I teach physics."

"Y-Yeah, I know who y-you are." Mark wasn't used to grown-ups introducing themselves by their first names. Especially not teachers.

"How do you like Davis Gregory so far?" Mr Pike asked.

"Uh . . . fine, I guess." Mark didn't understand where this was going. "You were looking forward to meeting *me*? Mark Dimond?"

"Absolutely." Mr Pike laughed. "I saw your battling robot at the county science fair. I was impressed, but when it took the state prize, I knew I had a star coming to school."

Mark had built a battling robot as a science project that literally destroyed the competition. It had a hook that trapped its prey, a shovel that flipped its victim over, and then a buzzsaw that went in for the kill. Mark never lost. He had thoughts about going on one of those TV shows to test his baby against the big boys, but after the state prize he decided it was better to go out on top, and intact. So he retired his killer robot and forgot all about it. Until now.

"Your design was light-years ahead of the other students," Pike continued. "I was thrilled when I heard you were coming to Davis Gregory."

Mark wasn't used to getting compliments. "It wasn't all that hard," he said with his eyes down.

"You're being modest," Pike said. "Have you thought about joining Sci-Clops?"

Mark couldn't believe it. Sci-Clops was a science club that was made up of the brainiest students at school. It was legendary. At least with the science-geek crowd. Having Sci-Clops on your record was an incredible plus if you wanted to go to a top engineering school after high school. There were even a few former Sci-Clops students who got into MIT.

"Are y-you serious?" Mark asked. "You mean, *the* Sci-Clops?"

Pike laughed. "Sure, how many are there?"

Mark's face turned red with embarrassment. Pike put a reassuring hand on his shoulder. "Think about it," he said. "We'd love to have you."

Mr Pike left Mark standing there speechless. It took a while for him to put his brain back into gear and say, "Y-Yeah. Sure I'll join!"

But it was too late. Pike was already gone.

Mark was stunned. It wasn't just because he had been given the chance to join a club that he had never considered himself good enough for, it was more that somebody had actually recognised him for having done something well. As he stood in that hallway, he sensed an alien feeling growing inside. It was pride. He still wasn't sure if he was good enough to join Sci-Clops. Confidence was still something he had to work on. But it made him feel great that at least one person, besides his mother, thought he had something special going on. Mark's second day of high school was definitely turning out better than the first.

Except he still had to face Courtney. The thought made his stomach turn, so instead of going directly to the practice field, he ran after Mr Pike.

Courtney, on the other hand, was *not* having a great day. She had tried to shake off the horrible practice of the day before and arrived at school ready to regain her rightful place as the girl who set the standards by which everyone else was judged.

She failed.

Word had spread how Courtney the Unbeatable had suddenly become Courtney the Diminished. Friends gave her sympathy and wanted to know what went wrong. Girls and guys she had intimidated for years wanted to know if it was true. Had Courtney lost it? Some kids were devastated at the thought that their hero could have feet of clay. Others simply wouldn't believe it. Many quietly enjoyed seeing someone so mighty get knocked down a few pegs.

Courtney did her best not to show how upset she was. People always envied her. Now that envy had turned to pity. That was the worst. As the day wore on, she kept smiling and telling people she was fine and simply had an off day. But inside, the fire was burning. She couldn't wait for the end of school so she could blast on to that soccer field and put some serious hurt on the nonbelievers.

A crowd had gathered around the field. More kids showed up for this practice than Courtney had heard showed up to watch the games. She was used to having an audience when she performed, but not like this. They were there to bear witness. They wanted proof that all was right with the world, or that it was the end of an era.

From the moment she stepped on to the field, Courtney played angry. It was the worst thing she could have done. It meant she tried too hard and allowed the other girls to hang her out to dry. They dribbled around her; they wouldn't pass to her; they stole the ball from her. During sprints, they left her in the dust.

Courtney looked really bad. The harder she tried, the worse it got. Her confidence was shattered. As she ran down the sidelines she'd see the faces of kids she had dominated in years past. Some looked disappointed. Others stunned. Still others had smug smiles that said: "Payback is sweet." She tried not to look into anyone's eyes, friend or foe. They all hurt the same.

The crowd didn't hang around long. They saw all they needed early on. The rest was like staring at a car wreck long after the dust settled. But the worst indignity was yet to come. When practice was mercifully over, Courtney ran towards the school locker room.

"Courtney! Hang on!" It was the coach, Ms Horkey. She jogged up to Courtney and the two walked towards the school together. "Tough day," Ms Horkey said with sympathy.

Courtney could only shrug.

"Look," Horkey said. "I know this is hard for you. I've watched you play since you were barely old enough to kick a ball. I know how good you are. Don't get discouraged."

"I won't," Courtney said, feeling totally discouraged.

Then Horkey dropped the bomb. "I think it would do you a world of good to start playing with the junior varsity team."

Courtney stopped short. "You're cutting me?" she said, barely able to say the words.

"No," Horkey assured her. "But you need to work on fundamentals. It's not a horrible thing. It's rare for a sophomore to be on varsity anyway."

"There are two other sophomores on varsity," Courtney pointed out. "Look, Ms Horkey. I just had a slow start."

"I know. But look at the big picture. You're not up to the level of the varsity players. If you stayed here, you'd be working to keep up, rather than getting better. On the JV level you'll be more competitive. Then next year you can —"

"Next year! I'd have to wait a whole year to get back on the team?"

"You're still on the team, Courtney. You're just playing at a level that's better for you."

"On the loser level, you mean," Courtney snapped at her.

"No," the coach corrected. "On the level that is going to help you improve. You're not a quitter, Courtney. You're going to get better, but you're going to have to work at it. Maybe you're not used to that."

Courtney wanted to scream. But the truth was, the coach was right. Courtney had never had to work all that hard to be good. Maybe she didn't know how to.

"It's really for the best," Horkey concluded.

"Yeah, sure," Courtney said under her breath. Horkey then jogged ahead towards the school.

Courtney wanted to run home. She didn't want to go into that locker room and get changed with all those girls who looked at her like a loser. She wasn't a loser. But at that moment, she sure felt like one.

"Courtney!" Mark yelled as he ran up to her. "The most amazing thing happened! I got asked to join Sci-Clops!"

"Cyclops? Like the monster with one eye?"

"No," Mark laughed. "Sci-Clops with an s-c-i like in science. It's only the most respected science club in the state. Is that incredible or what?"

"Yeah, that's great, Mark," Courtney said, not sounding as if she meant it. She continued walking towards the school.

"Uh-oh. Bad practice again?"

"I just got cut."

"What!"

"Not really. I've been demoted to JV."

Mark didn't know what to say. This was alien territory. He wasn't used to boosting Courtney's confidence.

"You know you're better than that," Mark said sincerely.

"Am I?" she said softly.

Courtney had never admitted defeat before. Mark glanced around quickly to make sure he was the only one who heard it. "Don't say that," he chastised. "You just had a slow start." Then a thought hit him and he added, "Besides, I've got more good news."

He waited for her to react. A few moments went by, then Courtney looked at him and actually smiled.

"Are you serious?" she asked cautiously.

"It showed up last night," Mark answered with a big smile. "I've got a confession to make, though. I think you'll understand why it happened when you see the journal, but I already saw the beginning part."

Courtney stopped walking and stared at Mark. Mark didn't let the moment hang. He had to explain himself, fast.

"I didn't mean to, but it's not a regular journal. It's a hologram."

"Say what?"

"Bobby recorded the journal like a 3-D movie. I was so surprised that I didn't turn it off right away. But I only heard the beginning. I stopped it before he got to anything really important. I didn't want to hear it without you."

That was the truth, mostly. Mark could only hope that Courtney would understand. A long moment went by. Mark wasn't sure if Courtney was going to forgive him or kick him in the head.

After an eternity, Courtney said, "It's cool. I get it. Can you come over tonight?"

"Right after dinner," he said, totally relieved.

Courtney then continued on, jogging into the school. Mark

nearly leaped into the air. This was an incredible day. Sci-Clops, then Courtney's forgiveness. As he jogged around the school building to catch the late bus, Mark was elated. Things were turning out perfectly.

But still, he felt a little strange. He wasn't used to taking the upper hand when it came to Courtney. He thought she would have at least made him feel a little guilty for what he had done. But she forgave him and let it go at that. It was like they had reached a new level in their friendship.

Mark wasn't entirely sure he liked it.

A few hours later Mark and Courtney sat together on the big, dusty old couch in Courtney's basement. They usually read Bobby's journals there because it was a workshop full of rusty tools that Courtney's father never used. She called it the "Tool Museum". It was a perfectly private place for them to read and discuss the journals. Being private was even more important this time, because they weren't going to be reading, they would be listening and watching.

"How does it work?" Courtney asked. She was all showered and feeling a little bit better. Time and a good dinner will do that. A new journal from Bobby didn't hurt either.

Mark was in the same clothes he wore at school. He hadn't eaten dinner. He was too excited. He reached into his pack and took out the small, silver device that contained Bobby's journal.

"It's like a CD player," Mark explained. "I'll rewind to the beginning." He touched the orange button. There was no sound or feeling of movement.

"How much did you see?" Courtney asked.

"Just a little," Mark fibbed. He figured since they would both see it from the beginning, he could get away with stretching the truth.

"Is he okay?" Courtney asked.

"Seems so," Mark answered. "But you can see for yourself." Mark put the silver device down on the table in front of the couch and pressed the green button. Instantly the beam of light shot out and projected Bobby's life-size image in space.

"Hiya, Mark. Hey, Courtney," Bobby's image began.

"Wow!" shouted Courtney. "It's like the hologram with the floating head."

Mark let out a relieved breath. Up until that moment he wasn't sure if the device had actually rewound all the way. Now he was totally off the hook with Courtney. He didn't mind that he was going to have to rehear Bobby's story from the beginning. All that mattered was that they were under way.

Together this time.

And they were about to learn about Lifelight.

VEELOX

"**B**obby! It's getting-up time!" came a familiar, singsong voice.

I was still asleep. It was one of those perfect moments when no matter what position you roll into, it's more comfortable than the last. No, I didn't care what time it was, I was staying in bed.

"Big day today!" came the pleasant voice again.

I was too comfortable to care. I rolled over, determined to continue the bliss. But then I felt a huge weight land on me. I knew what was coming next. Any chance of staying in bed would soon dissolve because . . .

A slippery, sandy tongue started burrowing into my ear. I don't know what was so tasty about my ear, but it was the spot that Marley would lick when she wanted me to get up.

"All right, all right!" I laughed and pushed my golden retriever away. I think she liked the whole ear-licking-while-I-was-trying-to-sleep thing because it was one of the few times she had complete control over me. That, and of course when I walked her and had to pick up her poop. She pretty much called the shots then, too.

A second later another weight landed on the bed. I knew

what this was too. It was my little sister, Shannon.

"Breakfast is ready," she informed me. "You have to eat or you won't be strong enough to play."

Shannon thought she pretty much knew everything about everything, and for an eight-year-old she wasn't far from wrong. She was cute, too, with long dark brown hair that she always tied into two ponytails. She had these big brown eyes and a broad smile that lit up the room. People always told Mum that Shannon should be a model, but Mum wasn't hot on the idea. I think she was afraid Shannon was already growing up too fast.

"Eat soon so you can digest," she continued. "I don't want to see you barfing on the court." With that last little nugget of wisdom, she jumped off the bed and ran out of my bedroom. Marley bounded off the bed and scampered after her.

The smell of bacon found my nose. That was the last bit of convincing I needed. I loved bacon and we didn't get it that often because Mum thought it was too fatty or something. But every so often when there was a special occasion, she would give in. I guess today's basketball game counted as a big occasion. Fine with me. I threw my legs over the bed and stood up, now fully awake. I was wearing boxers, but pulled on a pair of tracksuit bottoms because sitting at the breakfast table in my underwear wasn't cool. I then picked a T-shirt off the floor, sniffed it to make sure it wasn't rank, and pulled it over my head. It was going to be a good day. Big breakfast, basketball game, maybe Courtney would come to watch and . . .

What the hell?

Reality struck. My knees went weak and I actually fell back down on to the bed. What was happening? I looked around my bedroom and it looked as familiar as always. My desk, my computer, my trophies, my stack of CDs, my New York Jets posters, even my clothes strewn on the floor. This was my bedroom. At home. In Stony Brook.

On . . . Second . . . Freakin' . . . Earth!

Nothing was out of the ordinary but *everything* was out of the ordinary. How could this be happening? I started to hyperventilate. Nothing made sense, even though it made perfect sense. Could everything that had happened since the night I left home with Uncle Press have been a dream? Denduron, Cloral, the *Hindenburg,* Saint Dane . . . everything. Had it all been a nightmare? I glanced at my window, half expecting Professor Marvel from *The Wizard of Oz* to poke his head in to see if I was okay.

"C'mon, Bobby, breakfast is getting cold!" came a voice from outside my room. It was my father. What was happening? I had faced a lot of scary situations since I became a Traveller, but on the strange scale, this was at the top. It took every ounce of courage I had to get my legs moving. I had to find out what was going on.

I cautiously left my room. The upstairs hallway had all the same pictures, the same rug, the same doors, the same everything. I half walked, half floated down the stairs, through the living room, past the dining room and straight into the kitchen. When I poked my head in, I saw a scene that was totally normal and totally impossible at the same time.

The table was set for breakfast. Mum was scooping scrambled eggs from a pan; Dad was sitting in his normal spot, pouring orange juice for everyone; Shannon sat at her place, politely waiting for everyone to sit so she could begin; and Marley sat on the floor at Shannon's side, waiting with equal patience for somebody to drop food on the floor.

I stood in the doorway, staring. Part of me wanted to dive into that kitchen, throw my arms around everybody and cry like a baby. Another part of me wanted to turn and run.

Finally Mum saw me and said, "Eat. You can't be late."

I didn't know what else to do, so I drifted over to the table and sat down at my place. It was the place by the window where I had eaten since I was old enough to sit up. It was the place I never thought I'd take again, since my house and family and everything I had ever known had disappeared.

But now they were back.

I must have looked as stunned as I felt, because my father said, "You all right, Bobby?"

I wasn't sure how to answer him, because I wasn't. "To be honest, Dad, I'm a little confused."

"About what, sweetheart?" Mum asked innocently.

I chose my words carefully, knowing just how ridiculous they would sound. "Has anything . . . odd happened?"

Dad asked, "Like what?"

Shannon chimed in. "We're having bacon for breakfast. That's odd."

"What are you talking about?" Mum asked while taking her place at the table. I sat looking at my family. The three of them looked back at me over their plates of bacon and eggs, waiting for me to say something. Marley poked her brown rubbery nose up from below the table and looked at me too, though I think she was more interested in sniffing out the bacon. I didn't say anything. Instead, I picked up a piece of bacon and took a bite. It was as delicious as any bacon I'd ever had. Done just the way I liked it too. Not too crispy. I didn't know why that surprised me, but it did.

Finally I dropped the bacon on my plate and stood up. "I . . . I'm not hungry. I better get dressed." I left the table, heading for the door to the dining room.

"But you have to eat something before the game!" Mum called after me.

"I'll get something later," I yelled back.

I was going mental. If my parents had said: "Well, Bobby, you were in a coma for the last year and a half," I would have understood. That would have meant that everything about the territories had been a dream. But they didn't. They acted as if nothing out of the ordinary had happened at all.

There was only one possible explanation. It must have been a dream. A really long, detailed, incredible dream that happened all in one night. Isn't that how it worked with Scrooge from *A Christmas Carol*? I read somewhere that dreams may seem long, but they really only last a few seconds. I figured that must have been what happened to me. As I walked back towards the stairs, I began to accept that possibility. A few moments crept by where I actually started to relax. I was home. The nightmare was over. Everything was going to be normal.

That warm, fuzzy feeling didn't last long.

I walked by a mirror and saw my reflection. What I saw wasn't the image of the guy who had kissed Courtney, then got on the back of Uncle Press's motorcycle bound for the flume. No way. This guy was older. About a year and a half older, to be exact. Everything in this house was the exact same as I remembered it . . . except for me. In that instant, my dream theory came crashing down. There was no way I could have slept for one night and dreamed up the whole adventure, because I wasn't the same guy anymore. No, the answer wasn't as simple as that.

It was then that a single word came to my mind. I didn't know what it meant at first, but it definitely felt like it was the key to unlocking this mystery.

The word was . . . Lifelight.

No sooner did I remember that word, than I felt something on my wrist. I looked down and saw I was wearing a wide, silver bracelet with three buttons. It surprised me at first because it wasn't there a second ago. But still, it seemed familiar. What was I told? If I needed to talk with someone, push the left button. Well, I couldn't imagine a bigger need to speak with someone than right now, so I pressed the button on the far left. The button glowed white for a moment and gave off a soft, quick hum.

"Not bad, Pendragon," came a voice from the top of the stairs. "You put it together faster than most."

I spun around and looked up the stairs to see someone sitting on the top step. It was the one thing that was out of place in this house. Besides me, that is. She was a pretty girl with a blonde ponytail, blue eyes, and yellow-tinted glasses. I stared at her for a few seconds, confused. It was like having an answer on the tip of your tongue, but you couldn't quite get it out.

"Breathe, Pendragon," she said. "It'll come back."

"Aja . . ." I said.

Aja smiled and clapped. "Very good. There's always a little disorientation at first, especially if you've never jumped before."

I looked around the house. My house. It seemed so real, but it wasn't. It was an illusion. An incredible, wonderful, heart-wrenching illusion. It was all coming back. I wasn't home. I was lying in a dark tube in a giant pyramid on the territory of Veelox, and this was all happening in my head.

"I know what you're thinking," Aja said. "You've seen a little of what Lifelight can do and you're pretty impressed." She walked down the stairs and came right up to me. "But you've just had a taste. The only limits to Lifelight are the limits you put on it yourself." She touched her finger to my forehead. "It's all up there, waiting to come out."

"There's more?" I asked.

Aja laughed. "Pendragon, you're just getting started."

VEELOX

I walked around my living room in a daze. Or should I say, I walked around the *illusion* of my living room. The dazed part was real, though. No illusion there. I ran my hand along the back of my couch and felt the soft, cotton fabric. I turned the switch on a table lamp, and the light came on. I picked up a frame that held a picture of me holding a newborn Shannon the day she came home from the hospital. Everything looked and felt totally normal, and *real*.

"You shouldn't be surprised," Aja said. "Everything is going to be right because it's coming out of your head."

"But I can *feel* things," I said. "And I tasted bacon. How is that possible?"

"You know how it should taste, so that's what it tasted like. Simple as that."

Simple as that? Who was she kidding? This was the furthest thing from simple I could imagine. I had about ten miles of questions. "What if I hurt myself?" I asked, my mind racing with possibilities. "Do I really get injured?"

"No. You'll feel the pain if you get injured, and you'll stay that way until the jump is complete, but you're not really here.

You're in the Lifelight pyramid. Nothing physical happens to you; it's all in your head."

"So I can't, like, die or anything?"

"If you die, the jump is over."

I looked at the silver wrist bracelet that had magically appeared when I began to remember Lifelight.

"Why didn't I see this at first?" I asked, holding my arm up.

"The goal of jumping is to completely immerse yourself in the experience," she answered. "Having that control band on your wrist would be a constant reminder that none of this is real. You'll only see it when you need to."

"Really? It's like my mind tells the band when to appear?"

"Exactly. Your mind controls everything."

"So I could, like, wish for a pizza to appear? Or for a swimming pool to be in the garage? Or for a spaceship to land on the front lawn and take me to Mars?"

Aja laughed. That was a surprise. For a change she didn't sound annoyed. I think she liked showing off what Lifelight could do. "Sure, but only if those kinds of things would normally happen. Lifelight was designed to create a perfect experience. A *realistic* experience. You can't suddenly sprout wings and fly away. Your mind wouldn't let you because you know that can't really happen. You're governed by the rules of reality. But the thing is, it's a *perfect* reality."

She reached over to me and lightly touched the middle button on my wrist controller. *Dingdong.* The front doorbell rang. Mum hurried out of the kitchen to get it.

"You expecting somebody?" she asked me on her way to the door.

I shrugged. I was expecting nothing . . . and anything. When she opened the door, I saw that standing outside was a pizza delivery guy from Domino's Pizza.

"Large pepperoni, extra cheese," the guy announced.

Mum gave me a look. "No wonder you didn't want breakfast." She paid the guy and took the pizza. "Do you have any idea how disgusting it is to eat this so early in the morning?"

"Uh, yeah," I answered, dumbfounded.

Mum then smiled and said, "Fine, you can have this because it's game day, but do not give any to Shannon or Marley, or your father. And eat it in the kitchen."

She disappeared back into the kitchen along with the pizza. She hadn't even said anything about Aja.

"Lifelight read my mind," I said to nobody in particular.

"That's what I've been telling you," Aja said.

"Why did you press the button? What did it do?"

"This starts getting a little advanced," she explained. "When you started the jump, I told you to think about a place you'd like to be. Lifelight read those thoughts and created this house and your family. That's the basic jump. That middle button is only used if you want to vary it. Let's say your family wanted to go on a picnic, but it was raining. All you'd have to do is touch the button and the storm would clear. Or let's say you wanted an old friend to be part of the jump. Think about the person, touch the button, and they'll show up."

"So it's like controlling the experience?"

"That's exactly what it is. But it's also a safety feature. When you first enter a jump, Lifelight creates the environment you're thinking of. Once you're in, Lifelight only reacts to what is actually happening. The trouble is, you can't control every idea that pops into your head. You might suddenly get a thought about being on a boat. But Lifelight won't do anything with that unless you push the button. If not for that button, there would be too much input coming from your brain and the jump would be a mess."

"So I could think about climbing a mountain right now —"

"And nothing would happen unless you pushed that button. Then a friend of yours might show up to tell you he's going on a trip to the mountains and ask you to join him."

"That is so cool!" I said.

"That's one way of putting it," Aja replied.

"So then, where are you?" I asked. "I mean, Lifelight isn't reading your thoughts, is it?"

"I'm your phader for the jump. Remember the core we passed through on our way into the pyramid? I'm sitting in one of those control cubicles, watching your jump."

"Those video monitors!" I exclaimed. "They're showing you what the jumpers are experiencing."

"Exactly. The phaders monitor the jumps to make sure everything goes well. To be honest, it's a boring job. Things rarely go wrong. But every so often a jumper needs some help or his wrist controller needs replacing or some minor problem arises and we get sent into their jump. But the thing is, we can't become part of a jump unless the jumper presses the left button. That's why I was able to show up when I did. If you hadn't pressed that button, I wouldn't be able to join you."

"So can you control the jump now too?" I asked.

"No, I'm only a visitor."

"Bobby? Are you going to eat this pizza before it congeals?" asked Mum. She stood in the doorway of the living room.

"Uh, yeah. As soon as I finish talking to my friend here." I had no idea how to explain Aja.

Mum gave me a strange look. "You want to run that by me again?" she asked.

"She can't see me," Aja said with a chuckle. "I'm not part of this jump."

How weird was that? Aja was like a ghost. There were a lot of rules to this bizarro experience.

"Never mind," I called to Mum. "I'll be right there."

Mum did a double-take, then left again.

"So what do I do now?" I asked.

"Anything you want. I think you have some kind of game to go to?"

"Yes! The basketball game! I can play ball?"

"If you want."

"Oh, man, this is great! How long does this go on?"

"Don't worry about it. Have fun. When you get back, we'll talk about the big picture."

"C'mon Bobby!" shouted Shannon impatiently. She stood at the door to the living room with her hands on her hips, looking irritated with me for holding up the show.

I looked to her and said, "Coming!" I then looked back to Aja, but she was gone. Just like that. My silver control bracelet was gone too. At least I couldn't see it any more. I had a moment where I wasn't sure what to do, but then decided if I was going to learn all about Lifelight, I had to go along with the programme. And heck, if it meant playing a little round-ball, that wouldn't be so bad. So I decided to give myself over to the experience and ran into the kitchen and tucked into the most delicious pizza I had ever eaten. But better than that was being together with my family. Shannon told me all about a play she was in at school, Dad talked about a newspaper article he was having trouble finding the inspiration to write, and Mum announced she was up for a promotion at the library. It was all so . . . excellent. I was home. The only sour note was that I couldn't tell them anything about me. My guess was that would have thrown a monkey wrench into the whole illusion, so I kept quiet. Then again, nobody asked me anything either.

After breakfast we all piled into the SUV and headed for my basketball game. I had played some pick-up hoops with Spader on First Earth – when we went there together in pursuit of Saint Dane – but that wasn't the same as putting on a uniform and playing five-on-five in a gym. The last time I played organised ball was for Stony Brook Junior High. If I hadn't left home I would be going to Davis Gregory High right now. Question was, where would my mind take us? Junior high, or high school?

Dad drove us to Davis Gregory High. I had been there before and even played a city final in their gym, so I knew the place. I left my family and went right to the locker room, not entirely sure of what I'd find. For a moment it felt like one of those dreams where you've got to take a test, but suddenly realise you never went to any of the classes. But I didn't panic. After all, Lifelight was supposed to deliver a perfect experience, right?

It did. When I stepped into the room, I was thrilled to see all my teammates from junior high. But they weren't getting dressed in the yellow jerseys of the Stony Brook Wildcats. They were putting on the crimson jerseys of the Davis Gregory Cardinals. I had always dreamed about playing for the Cardinals. My dream was about to come true. Sort of.

The guys all greeted me, but didn't act like anything was out of the ordinary. I wanted to grab them all and hug them and tell them how psyched I was to be back, but I played it cool. For some reason I knew which locker was mine. Hanging up inside was a Cardinal jersey with my number: 15. Any doubt I had about being in the right place went away when I picked up that jersey, turned it around, and saw the stitched lettering over my number. It read: PENDRAGON.

As I look back and analyse what happened, I can figure

out why Lifelight did what it did. But at the time, I was totally taken up with the illusion. Even though I knew what was going on, it didn't matter. I'm not sure if it was Lifelight doing it to me, or it was my own brain guiding things, but it was like I had forgotten that I was lying in a vast pyramid with my mind tripping through a computer. As far as I knew, I was really there.

And the game was awesome. The stands were full, and rocking like it was a championship. The band pounded out a war rhythm. The cheerleaders fired up the home side. Our opponents were the crosstown rival Black Knights of Easthill High. Our starting five were the same as back in junior high: me, Jimmy Jag, Crutch, Petey Boy, and Joe Zip. Man, I missed those guys. Coach Darula was on the bench looking confident, the same as always. As we came out of the locker room and headed for the court, I got that old familiar feeling in my stomach. The butterflies. They always started dancing right before tip-off. It meant I was ready to play.

And man, did I play.

From the opening tip-off, I was on fire. Being a point guard, I was used to shooting and scoring, but what happened in that game was nothing short of phenomenal. Everything clicked. We played together like a dream team. Almost every shot I took found nothing but the bottom of the net. I didn't gun the ball, though. Oh no. I dished it around. I shot no-look passes to Joe Zip, who laid it in. I alley-ooped a few to Crutch, who could leap high enough to jam it home. I stole the ball a bunch of times and generally ran the offence like a pro. It was a dream game. Yeah, that's *exactly* what it was.

We didn't win by a hundred points either. The game was close, which made it that much more exciting. With only a few seconds left to go, we were actually down by two points.

Jimmy Jag passed me a give-and-go, I drove the lane, and as I went in for the lay-up, I got hammered by their centre. Yeah, you guessed it. Two points down, seconds on the clock, and I was on the foul line. It doesn't get any sweeter than that. I stood at the line with my hands on my hips, totally exhausted and sweating. It was awesome.

I looked around at the crowd. Everyone was on their feet, cheering for me. The ref bounced me the ball. I dribbled once, bent my knees, lined up my shot and . . . swish. All net. The crowd went nuts. I took another second to soak it all in before my next shot. I gazed around at all the excited faces. Some I recognised, others were people I had never seen before. But they were all cheering for me.

Then I saw something that made a great moment even greater. Sitting on the bleachers behind our bench was my family. Mum, Dad, and Shannon. But that's not all. Sitting behind them was you, Mark. Next to you was Courtney. You were all waving and cheering. It was the best moment I could imagine.

The ref bounced me the ball; the crowd grew silent; I put up the shot and . . . oh yeah, it was good. The buzzer sounded. We were going to overtime. I jogged over to our bench while looking up at you guys. You were going nuts. I couldn't have imagined a better scenario. Come to think of it, from what I learned about Lifelight, it was the *exact* scenario I imagined.

The team manager threw me a towel and I sat down on the bench to catch my breath. I wiped the sweat from my face and did my best not to smile too broadly. That's when I heard a voice I didn't want to hear.

"Having fun?" asked the intruder.

I looked up and saw Aja sitting next to me on the bench. It actually took me a second, again, to remember who she was.

But I did, and I didn't like it. I didn't want her there, no way. Not then. She was going to ruin it.

Aja looked around at the screaming crowd and added, "Wow, you really like to get the old adrenalin pumping, don't you?"

"Yeah, so?" I shot back. "It's my fantasy. I can do what I want, right?"

"Absolutely," Aja continued. "Only one problem. Your jump's over."

"What?" I shouted. "It can't be over, we're going into OT!"

"Sorry," Aja shrugged. "I told you, the jump was timed."

"Give me twenty more minutes," I begged.

"Sorry. Besides, it's good to end like this," Aja said. "It's the perfect demonstration."

"There's nothing perfect about ending this now," I complained. I then noticed that the silver band had returned to my wrist. The button on the right was blinking red. I didn't like the look of that.

Aja picked up another towel and threw it at me. "Wipe your face. You're all sweaty," she ordered.

I caught the towel and wiped my face. But when I dropped it, I realised with horror that I had gone blind. At least that's what it seemed like because the gym had gone black. Worse, I had gone deaf, too. A moment before, the place was rocking with the sound of hundreds of frenzied fans. Now it was like somebody had pulled the plug on the TV. Everything had gone dark and silent. I was totally disoriented, until I heard a voice. It was a calm, familiar voice that brought me back to reality.

"Relax, Pendragon," Aja said. "Nothing is wrong. You're coming out of the jump."

I then realised the truth. I wasn't deaf or blind. I was lying in a dark, silent tube.

"Just lie still for a few minutes," Aja said. "I'll be right there to bring you out."

I was filled with all sorts of emotions. First off, I was angry. Lifelight had just given me the most incredible gift I could imagine, only to snatch it right back. But I was also still high from the excitement of the game. I wasn't physically tired because I hadn't actually done anything. But the emotions were still there. I could remember the thrill of sinking those foul shots. But most of all, I felt sad. I had been given a small taste of being back with my family. It all seemed so real, and it made me miss them even more.

I heard a slight hum as light entered the tube. The silver disc behind my head was sliding into the wall. It was now official. I hadn't moved an inch since I was first sealed in. I had "jumped" into a computer simulation. I felt a slight movement and the table slid out of the tube. The first thing I saw was Aja. She stood at the control panel looking down at me.

"How do you feel?" she asked.

"Like I need another twenty minutes in there, thank you very much."

"I'm glad it ended that way, because it only helps illustrate the point I need to make."

"What point?"

Before she could answer, an alarm sounded. At least I thought it was an alarm. It was a loud, persistent horn that sliced through the quiet pyramid. Aja quickly glanced at her wrist band.

"What is it?" I asked.

"Medical call," she said, suddenly sounding all official. "It's in this sector."

Without another word of explanation, she bolted for the door. I was still a little dazed after coming out of my jump, but

I wanted to know what was going on, so I threw my legs over the side of the table and stood up. I was a little wobbly at first, but a second later I was running after Aja.

I blasted out through the door and almost lost my balance again when I was hit with the sight of the interior of this vast pyramid. Man, talk about a rude awakening. I had to shake off my disorientation, fast. I looked both ways and saw Aja sprinting along the balcony. I sucked it up and ran after her.

Up ahead, a red light was blinking outside one of the cubicle doors. It didn't take a genius to know that was where the alarm was coming from. Just before Aja got to the door, I saw a red-suited vedder running up from the other direction.

"Where is this jumper's phader?" Aja demanded.

"I don't know," the vedder answered.

They both entered the cubicle with the flashing red light. I ran up and peered into the open door to see what was happening. Aja was at the control panel, quickly pushing buttons. A second later, the alarm stopped blaring.

"It came out of nowhere," the vedder said nervously. "There weren't any signs."

"Did the jumper try to abort?" Aja asked.

"No! His vitals just suddenly spiked."

A second later the silver disc in the wall slid open and the table emerged with the jumper lying there. The vedder immediately attended to the person. The jumper was a man maybe around my father's age. He didn't seem to be in any kind of trouble. It looked like he was sleeping peacefully. The vedder had a device that resembled a Game Boy. He put it to the jumper's chest, then checked the readings. A second later he took it away and shook his head.

"Too late," he said sadly.

"Too late?" I asked, entering the room. "What do you mean, 'too late'?"

"What do you think he means, Pendragon?" Aja said quietly. "He's dead."

Whoa. Left field. I hadn't expected that. "I thought this was supposed to be safe!" I said, feeling numb.

"It is," Aja shot back. "But sometimes . . . things happen."

The vedder started for the door.

"Where are you going?" Aja asked. "You've got to fill out a report!"

"Not me," the vedder said haughtily. "My shift's over. I'm jumping. The next shift can handle it."

The guy left. What a tool. Someone just died on his watch, and all he cared about was jumping into his own fantasy.

"Aja, what happened?" I asked.

Aja looked shaken. She tried to collect her thoughts. "I don't know. We'll have to look at the records of his jump. There are thousands of people in the pyramid. Sometimes they die of natural causes. But . . ."

"But what?"

"But it's starting to happen more often," was her sober answer.

I didn't like the sound of that.

"You've seen Lifelight at its best, Pendragon," she continued. "It's a wonderful tool that has brought joy to the people of Veelox. But it's got a downside, too. That's what you've got to see next."

I'm going to end this journal here, guys. While Aja did a postmortem on the dead jumper, she put me in a room by myself with this incredible recording device. I wanted to be part of their investigation, but Aja didn't know how to explain who I was. Still, I'm curious to know what they come up with. Once they're finished, Aja is going to take me to her home. Then tomorrow she's going to show me more of Rubic City.

But the truth is, I'm not here to sightsee. I'm not here to learn about the wonders of Lifelight or tour the city or take a trip into my own fantasies. I'm here to find out what evil Saint Dane has brought to this territory. After seeing what happened with the jumper, I have the sick feeling that I just got my first taste of it.

So I'll sign off now. This is the end of my Journal #13. By the time I record #14, I should have more answers. Goodbye, guys. I miss you.

END OF JOURNAL #13

☻ SECOND EARTH ☻

After a quick goodbye wave, Bobby's image disappeared in a flicker, leaving Mark and Courtney staring into the empty space of her father's workshop. Neither could say anything. They had been watching Bobby's story unfold before them, spoken by Bobby himself. It was like he had been standing in front of them, in the flesh.

"Well," Courtney said after several silent seconds. "That was . . . *different*."

"I can't imagine something like Lifelight being real," Mark said thoughtfully. He reached forward and picked up the silver, credit card-size projector. He turned it over in his hand, inspecting it. "Then again, I can't imagine something like this, either, so what the heck do I know?"

"Do you think Saint Dane sabotaged Lifelight?" Courtney asked.

"That's my guess," Mark answered. "But I'll bet it's not as simple as that. Man, what I wouldn't give to try it out."

"What would you do?"

"A million things," Mark answered quickly. "I'd ride a horse.

I've always wanted to do that. I'd fly an aeroplane, and play in a rock band, and run the New York marathon."

"But you can do all that for real," said Courtney.

Mark shrugged. It didn't feel to him as if any of those things were within his reach. "What would *you* do?" he asked Courtney.

Without hesitation Courtney said, "I'd put some major whup-ass on that soccer team."

Mark said, "Same thing, you can do that for real."

Like Mark, Courtney shrugged. Her confidence was so low, the idea of putting major whup-ass on anybody seemed like a fantasy. Mark then looked back at the silver hologram projector. A thought came to him, and he frowned.

"What?" Courtney asked.

"This is wrong," Mark answered. "Bobby shouldn't have sent this to us."

"Why not? It beats having to read the journals."

"But he's not supposed to mix things from other territories," Mark answered while fingering the device nervously. "It's totally against the rules."

"We'll put it in the safe-deposit box at the bank," Courtney offered. "Nobody will ever see it."

"Good idea. I'll go first thing after school tomorrow," Mark said. "Man, why didn't Bobby think of this?"

"Maybe they don't use paper on Veelox. It might have been the only way he could send a journal."

"Still," Mark said. "It might cause —"

Mark's ring started to twitch. He stopped talking and held his hand up.

"You're kidding?" Courtney said with surprise. "That was fast!"

Mark stared at the ring quizzically. "It feels different" was all he could say.

He quickly took off the ring and put it on the table. Courtney stood next to him and the two gazed at it. Normally when one of Bobby's journals was arriving, the grey stone in the centre of the ring would turn crystal clear. The band would then grow and the journal would arrive in a flash of light and music. But that wasn't happening this time. The large grey stone didn't change. But something else did.

Engraved in the silver band and circling the stone was a series of odd characters. Each symbol was unique, with no apparent pattern. When Mark first got the ring he did a search on the Internet, thinking he could decipher them. But he came up empty. After tons of research there was only one thing he knew for sure: The symbols had no relation to any language or culture on Earth.

Now one of those symbols was starting to glow. It was as if there were a light inside the ring, shining out through the engraving. The glowing symbol was nothing more than a squiggle with a straight line passing through it. Mark and Courtney watched, dumbfounded, as the ring finally began to grow.

"Something's coming in," Mark gasped. "I think."

The ring didn't grow as large as usual. But they heard the familiar jumble of sweet notes that accompanied every trip. The light from the symbol then flashed across the room, momentarily blinding Mark and Courtney. A second later they looked back at the ring. As always, the event was over quickly. The ring had returned to normal. No more light, no more sound, nothing unusual . . .

Except for what the ring had deposited. It wasn't a journal. It was an envelope. A regular old white, Second Earth-style envelope.

"What is it?" Courtney asked.

"It's an envelope," answered Mark.

Courtney rolled her eyes. "Duh. Why did Bobby send us an envelope?"

Mark cautiously leaned over and picked up the piece of mail. He turned it over, examining it. There was nothing weird about it. It was sealed, with no writing on the outside. Courtney gave Mark a nod of encouragement and he carefully opened it, trying not to rip it more than he had to. Inside was a piece of plain white paper.

"I don't think this is from Bobby," Mark announced.

Courtney looked at the page. There was handwriting on it, and it was definitely not Bobby's. Bobby wrote in a kind of classic script. This note was written with block letters. It was actually jittery looking, as if the person who wrote it didn't have a sure hand. The note was simple. It was an address.

"'Four twenty-nine Amsterdam Place. Apartment Five-A. New York City'," Mark read aloud. "You know anybody who lives there?"

"No," Courtney answered. "Why would Bobby send us an address? With no explanation?"

Mark suddenly looked up, as if he were hit with an idea.

"What?" asked Courtney.

"Could it be?" he asked, half to himself, half to Courtney.

"Could it be what?" Courtney asked, growing impatient.

Mark looked at the address again, then back at the ring. "Could this be about the acolytes?"

Courtney deflated. This wasn't the answer she wanted to hear. "Are you still on that kick?" She plopped back down on to the couch.

Mark was gaining energy. "I asked Bobby to find out about the acolytes. Maybe this is his way of pointing us in the right direction!"

"I don't want to hear about it," Courtney said sharply.

"You promised you'd think about it," Mark shot back at her.

"I did. I decided I don't want to hear about it."

"But this could be our chance to help Bobby, for real!"

"Mark, I've got enough stuff to worry about."

Mark didn't back down. "Like what?" he asked sarcastically. "*Soccer*?"

It was like Mark had flashed a red cape in front of an angry bull. Courtney jumped to her feet. "Yes, soccer!"

In the past Mark would have backed off when faced with Courtney's rage. But not this time. He stood his ground. "How can you care about stupid sports when there's so much more important stuff going on?"

"It's important to me!" Courtney defended herself.

"But it's just a game!" Mark countered.

"It's not! Can't you see that? I've never failed, Mark. Never. You just can't relate!"

Mark stiffened. "Why? Because I'm used to failure?"

Courtney forced herself to calm down and speak with more control. "I'm sorry, I didn't mean that." She sat back down on the soft couch and took a deep breath. "It's not just about soccer," she continued. "Everybody's got a role. You know? An identity. I liked mine. I liked how people looked up to me. But after what's been going on the past few days, I'm beginning to think I might not be the person I thought I was."

"Courtney," Mark said with sympathy. "It's just a *game*."

"Yeah, maybe," Courtney said. "But who knows what might turn up tomorrow? It's the first time I've doubted myself. Ever."

Mark thought for a moment, then picked up the silver hologram projector and the envelope with the address, and put them in his backpack.

"I'm sorry, Courtney," Mark said. "I hear what you're saying about roles and stuff. I always thought mine was to be the lamewad who everybody made fun of. But I'm beginning to think I'm better than that. You might not be the person you thought you were either, and maybe that's not such a bad thing. Maybe it means you've got more important things to do."

Courtney gave Mark a quick look; then Mark headed for the stairs. "Tomorrow's Friday," he said. "I'll put this stuff in the safe-deposit box at the bank. On Saturday I'm going to the address on this paper. I hope you come with me, but I'll understand if you don't."

Mark left her alone in the basement.

The next day in school Mark and Courtney had no contact. Mark met with Mr Pike about Sci-Clops and was given a schedule of meetings for the rest of the semester. He tried to be enthused about it, but it was hard to focus. All he could think about was being on the verge of a much bigger adventure.

When school was over, Mark went to the National Bank of Stony Brook on the Ave. The pruny Ms Jane Jansen brought him into the vault where he deposited the projector that held Bobby's Journal #13 in the same safe box where he was keeping Journals #1–12. He didn't put the mysterious slip of paper with the New York address in the box though. He needed that.

As for Courtney, she'd made the tough decision and took the demotion to play for the junior varsity. Her plan was to prove herself so superior that Coach Horkey would have no choice but to bring her right back up to the varsity.

Things didn't work out that way. It was clear from Friday's practice that she was one of the better girls on the team, but definitely not the best. She didn't let it get to her though. She wouldn't go so far as to accept her fate, but forced herself to try and make the best of it. At least for the time being.

The next day, Saturday, Mark got up early and told his parents he was going to take the train into New York City to go to a science museum. He was old enough to do that on his own now. Taking the train into the city was easy. The station was at the bottom of Stony Brook Avenue, a short distance from Mark's house. He checked the schedule and planned on catching the 8:05 local that would get him into Grand Central Station around 9 A.M. He figured that would leave him plenty of time to go to the address on the note and be back home before dinner.

He was hoping to get a call from Courtney, but that call didn't come, and he wasn't going to beg. So he found himself early Saturday morning standing on the train platform, alone, ready to begin the next chapter in the adventure that had begun so long ago when Bobby first left home.

The train pulled into the station and the doors opened quietly. During the week this train would be packed with commuters heading in to work. But on Saturday not many people took the train, so Mark pretty much had the car to himself. He picked a seat directly in the middle because he knew it was the smoothest ride. He threw his backpack in the overhead rack, then plunked down into the seat.

"What's the matter?" came a voice from the seat behind him. "Don't want to sit with me?"

Mark spun in surprise to see . . .

Courtney.

"I called your house," she said. "Just missed you. Your mum told me you were catching this train. I got on one stop back."

"You sure about this?" he asked cautiously.

"No, but who else is going to watch your back?" she answered with a smile.

Mark broke out in a huge grin and moved into the seat next to her. For the time being, they were a team again. As the train took them into the city, they talked about everything except the mysterious note. It wasn't that they were avoiding the subject, it was more that they had no idea what to expect on Amsterdam Place.

They arrived in Grand Central Station and went right to the subway. Courtney knew that Amsterdam Place was on the upper East Side of Manhattan, so a quick scan of the subway map showed them the trains they had to take. The ride took twenty minutes, with only one change. Soon enough they found themselves emerging from the underground station on Amsterdam Place. Mark double-checked the building number, 429, and they walked two more streets north.

Finally they found themselves standing in front of an old, brick apartment building. It looked like a pretty nice neighbourhood, with a view of the East River. There was a park across from the address with little kids running around and a bunch of guys playing touch football. Since it was September, the leaves were just beginning to show autumn colours. But the air was warm and the sky was the kind of deep blue that only showed up in the autumn. The whole scene was about as normal and safe as could be.

Except that Mark and Courtney now had to find out what was waiting for them in apartment 5A. With a quick look at each other, they climbed the cement stairs that led to the entrance. The double door looked like it had about five hundred coats of black paint on it. Mark grabbed the brass handle and pulled it open, letting Courtney go in first. Inside was another set of doors, but these were locked. The only way to get in was to be buzzed in by a tenant. On the right wall was a grey metal panel that listed all of the occupants of the building. Mark and Courtney eagerly checked for 5A.

"'Dorney,'" Mark said, reading the typed name. "Nothing weird about that."

"What did you think it was going to say?" asked Courtney. "Acolyte Headquarters?"

In spite of his nervousness, Mark laughed. The two stood staring at the name. Next to it was a black button. Neither was quick to push it.

"What are we going to say?" Mark asked.

"How about: 'Hi! We're here to interview for the acolyte position.'"

Mark gave Courtney a smirk. Before he could change his mind, he pushed the button. They waited. Nothing happened.

"Maybe they're out doing acolyte stuff," Courtney offered.

Mark hit the button again. Still nothing. Mark then said, "I guess we should come back –"

"*What*?" came a man's gruff voice from a speaker near the names.

Mark and Courtney shot each other a look. Courtney got her head together first and said, "Uh, Mr Dorney?"

"Who is it?" the gruff voice demanded.

"Uh, my name's Courtney. I'm here with my friend Mark. We were wondering if –"

"Go away!" the man barked, and the speaker went dead.

"Now what?" Courtney asked.

Mark hit the button again.

"Whatever you're selling, I don't want any!" the voice growled at them.

"We're not selling anything," Mark said politely. "We're here to talk to you about . . . uh . . . Bobby Pendragon."

No response. Mark and Courtney exchanged looks again. Mark reached forward to hit the button one more time, but was jolted by the harsh sound of a buzzer.

"What's that?" Mark said nervously.

Courtney glanced at the door, then pushed it open.

"He just buzzed us in," she answered. Courtney stood in the doorway, holding the door open. "Last chance," she said.

"Don't say that," Mark threw back. "I might change my mind."

He took a quick breath, then turned and walked quickly past Courtney, through the door. Courtney followed, letting the door close behind them.

Next stop, apartment 5A.

☻ SECOND EARTH ☻
(CONTINUED)

The creaky lift took them up to the fifth floor. Mark and Courtney anxiously watched the numbers above the door light up as they ascended.

"What if it's Saint Dane?" Courtney blurted out nervously. "He could be, like, luring us in."

"I thought about that," Mark responded, almost as nervously. "But why would he bother with us? We're just a couple of kids."

"Yeah," said Courtney. "Two kids he could use to get even with Bobby."

Mark shot Courtney a look. He hadn't thought of that. The lift clunked to a stop and the doors slid open. Should they keep going?

"If he wanted to get us," Mark said, trying to sound confident, "he wouldn't have to go through so much trouble."

Courtney nodded and stepped out of the lift. Mark was right behind her. The hallway was carpeted and pleasant looking. There were windows on either end that glowed with warm, autumn light. Under each was a table with a pretty flower arrangement. They were probably fake, but still made the place look homey. It wasn't a fancy place, but it wasn't run down either. There looked to be around a dozen apartment doors spaced evenly on either side of the corridor. All were painted glossy black like the front door. Each had a brass knocker with the apartment number engraved on a metal plate. Mark walked right and Courtney looked left in search of 5A. The "A" apartment was right next to the lift.

"Go? No go?" Courtney asked.

Mark's answer was to reach for the brass knocker. He rapped twice. Not too hard as to sound insistent, but strong enough not to appear wussie. They heard the sound of footsteps inside shuffling towards the door. The person stopped, probably to peer out at Mark and Courtney through the peephole. Both of them sensed this, so they stood up straight, trying to look sincere. A moment later the door was unlatched and pulled open a crack. Just a crack. Mark and Courtney looked at each other as if to say: Now what? Courtney stepped forward and cautiously pushed the door open.

The first thing they saw was the back of a man shuffling away from them – an old guy, wearing a checked shirt and khaki trousers. His hair was grey and clipped short.

"Close the door," he called without turning around.

Mark and Courtney stepped inside the apartment and closed the door. But not all the way. With a silent look, Courtney showed Mark that she was leaving the door open a hair, just in case they needed to make a quick getaway.

"Come on!" the man shouted at them impatiently. "You got this far, don't be shy now."

Mark and Courtney walked cautiously after the man, staying close to each other for support, ready to bolt at the first hint of danger.

The apartment was normal enough. It looked exactly like the

kind of apartment one would expect an old man to live in. The furniture was old, but in good shape. There were oil paintings of landscapes on the walls and framed photos of smiling people on polished mahogany tables. There wasn't a single modern touch to the whole place.

Two things stood out though. First was the books. There were thousands of them. In bookcases, on tables, in stacks that reached the ceiling. Whoever this guy was, he liked to read. The other thing was the plants. The apartment was like a greenhouse. There were dozens of potted plants, as well as viney tendrils, that travelled along the walls and across the bookcases every which way, with no beginning or end.

The apartment in general looked very clean, even with all the plants. This wasn't some slobby old guy who couldn't take care of himself. So far, Mark and Courtney learned that the guy was neat, he read a lot, and had green fingers. None of that helped to solve the bigger mystery of who he was though.

"Sit down," the old guy said while pointing to an overstuffed couch. He then shuffled over to an easy chair and slowly settled into it. Courtney and Mark didn't take their eyes off him. As he sat, he had to hold on to the arm for support, as if his legs weren't strong enough to do it on their own. The guy wasn't frail, but he wasn't going to run a marathon either. Mark and Courtney did as they were told and sat next to each other on the couch. Both thought it had the vague smell of mothballs. Neither mentioned it.

Now that they were facing each other, they saw that the old man wore small, wire-rim glasses. His short grey hair was almost military in style. He sat with incredibly great posture, which made both Mark and Courtney sit up straight as well. He stared at them with a steady gaze, as if sizing them up. The guy may have been old, but he looked sharp.

Mark got the ball rolling. "I'm M-Mark Dimond."

"And I'm Courtney Chetwynde."

A long moment went by. The man kept staring at them. Finally he asked, "Why do you care?"

Mark and Courtney exchanged confused looks.

"About what?" Courtney asked.

"You're here, aren't you?" the man said. "Why do you care?"

Mark said, "W-We got your address —"

"I know that," snapped the old man. "You wouldn't be here if you hadn't. What I want to know is, why?"

There was no nonsense about this guy. He didn't care about being polite or pleasant or anything else that would have put a visitor at ease.

"We're here because we want to help our friend, Bobby Pendragon," Mark said.

"Good," said the man quickly. "Why?"

"He's our friend," Courtney chimed in. "Isn't that enough?"

"Depends," answered the man.

"On what?" Courtney shot back.

"On whether or not you're willing to die for him."

Whoa. The tension in the room had just jumped a few dozen notches. The old man didn't even blink. Mark and Courtney didn't know how to respond.

And then Mark's ring began to twitch.

He quickly looked at his hand. Courtney saw it too. The grey stone was beginning to change colour. Mark shot his other hand over the ring to hide it.

Too late.

"Take it off!" ordered the old man.

Mark looked at him, his panic rising.

"I said take it off! Put it on the table."

Mark didn't have a choice because the ring had already

begun to grow. He pulled it off his finger and placed it on the coffee table in front of them. Bright light blasted from the stone, dazzling the apartment. The ring quickly grew until it was the size of a frisbee, revealing the dark hole inside. Then came the musical notes. After a final blast of light and music, the ring returned to normal.

Mark and Courtney looked to the table to see what the ring had delivered. Sitting there was another small, silver hologram projector. Bobby had just sent his next journal. It was a totally awkward moment. Mark grabbed his ring, swiped up the journal, and stood up.

"This was a mistake," he said nervously. "We're outta here."

Mark turned for the door. Courtney didn't know what else to do, so she followed him.

"Stop right there!" the old man demanded as he struggled to his feet.

Mark turned and faced him head-on. "L-Look, mister," Mark said with passion. "We came here for answers, and all we're getting are questions. Well, you know what? I don't trust you. Why should I? If you think we're going to sit here and get grilled and threatened, then you'd better give us a good reason why, or we're gone."

Courtney gave Mark a quick look, as if surprised he had that in him. She looked back to the old man and added, "Yeah!"

The old man held their gaze, then slowly nodded. He turned away from them and walked over to a cabinet that was built into the wall.

"My name is Tom Dorney," he said firmly. "I've lived in this apartment for nearly fifty years. I'm not married. Never was. I have two sisters and three nephews." Dorney took a key ring out of his pocket and unlocked the cabinet door. He swung it wide to reveal several metal boxes, each about two-foot square.

"I served in the military for twenty years," he continued. "Saw action in World War Two. South Pacific." He pulled one of the boxes out of the cabinet and carried it over to the coffee table. It looked heavy, but neither Mark nor Courtney made a move to help. He didn't look like he wanted or needed any.

"These boxes are fireproof," he explained. "This whole place could burn to the ground and nothing would happen to what's inside." Dorney took another key from the ring and unlocked the box. He gave one more look to Mark and Courtney, as if debating whether or not to open it.

He then said, "And I'm an acolyte. You want proof of that?"

Mark and Courtney nodded dumbly.

Dorney lifted the lid on the box to reveal it was full of papers. Some were in folders, others were rolled up scrolls that were tied with twine. Mark and Courtney stared down at them in wonder.

Mark said, "Are those . . . ?"

"They're the journals of a Traveller," Dorney answered.

"Which Traveller?" Courtney asked.

"They were written by my best friend, Press Tilton."

Dorney then raised his hand to show he wore a ring just like Mark's. "I brought you two here because I'm getting old, and need help. Now, my question still stands. Why do you care? If I don't get the right answer, you can walk right back out that door. I don't care what that Pendragon kid thinks about you.

VEELOX

Hey, guys. Getting used to watching me like this yet?

It's weird, after Lifelight, the idea of recording myself as a hologram seems pretty low tech. Lifelight is an incredible invention . . . that's also incredibly dangerous. The thing is, I'm afraid Saint Dane knows that, and we may not be able to stop him from taking advantage of it. I'm serious. We may already be too late to save Veelox. But I'm not ready to give up yet. Aja and I have come up with a plan. To pull it off I'm going to have to jump back into Lifelight. To be honest, it scares the hell out of me because this time it won't be the wonderful, fantasy visit back home like before.

This jump is going to be hairy.

I know, I'll bet you're thinking: How hairy can it be if it's all taking place in my mind? Well, the mind is pretty powerful. So is imagination. Trust me. I've just seen what can happen when things go bad. It isn't pretty. I don't want to risk jumping again, but I don't see any way around it. I've got to go back in. I know what has to be done.

I think.

Let me tell you what brought me to the point of having

to make this insane trip back into Lifelight . . .

After my first jump I was thinking Lifelight was pretty cool. Going home and spending time with my family and kicking some serious butt against Easthill High was excellent, even if it was just an illusion. I'm sure this is hard to understand, but while I was in Lifelight, I sort of forgot that it was fake. The experience was so real, my brain wanted to believe it actually was. Or at least my heart did. Does that make sense? It would if you had been there.

But then I left the jump and witnessed the death of a fellow jumper. That made it pretty clear that Lifelight wasn't without risks. When Aja found me after her debriefing, I began to learn what those risks were.

"I'll take you to my home," she declared as she hurried into the office where I was recording my journal. "We'll have something to eat and I'll continue your education."

Education. Wow-wee. Aja really liked showing me what a brain she was. Lucky me.

"What happened to that jumper?" I asked. "Why did he die?"

"It happens," she said quickly. "There are a lot of people in the pyramid."

"But you said it's happening more often."

"It was an accident, all right!" she snapped. "I told you, things are under control here."

Yikes. She was a raw nerve. Things didn't seem like they were under control at all. But it wouldn't help to argue. Without another word, Aja left the office. I guessed she expected me to follow, so I did.

We left the Lifelight pyramid and went back to the three-wheeled vehicle that had brought us here. We climbed aboard and started pedalling along the quiet street. There were a million questions I wanted to ask about Lifelight and how it worked and why she was so sure Saint Dane's plan was doomed to failure and, for that matter, what the heck Saint Dane's plan *was*. But I didn't think it was a good time to grill her. She looked pretty upset. As she pedalled the odd bicycle, she stared ahead with a vacant look that told me her mind was miles away.

I was faced with a real dilemma. From all I've described to you, it must be clear that Aja wasn't the easiest person to get along with. She had a quick temper that flashed nasty the instant someone challenged her. She was a proud person, and totally brainy. And she took every chance she could to prove it. That was the exact opposite of somebody like, say, Uncle Press. Uncle Press knew pretty much everything about everything, but never rubbed it in your face. I think that came from confidence. With Aja, I got the feeling that beneath it all, she wasn't totally sure of herself, which is why she was always trying to demonstrate her brilliance.

But she was the Traveller from Veelox and we had to get along. If she was right and Saint Dane's plan was already derailed, then everything was cool. We didn't have to be friends and I could be on my way. But after hearing from Saint Dane about how he had already won on Veelox, and learning how Lifelight might have some problems, I had some serious doubts. I was pretty sure Aja and I were going to have to learn how to work together, and it was up to me to make that happen.

"Did you grow up here?" I asked, trying to make small talk.

"Yes."

"In Rubic City?"

"Yes."

"When did you find out you were a Traveller?"

"Two years ago."

She wasn't exactly being talkative. But I kept trying.

"How old are you?"

"Eighteen."

"Wow, are all the phaders so young?"

"You want my life story, Pendragon?" she snapped suddenly. "Here it is. From the time I was a baby I was raised in a group home. I never knew my parents. To this day I don't know if I was taken from them or given up for training."

Whoa. Lots of baggage in that one little sentence. I wasn't sure which topic to go after first.

"Training?" I finally asked. I figured it was less emotional than the whole "raised in a group home" thing.

"The directors find gifted babies and train them to become phaders and vedders. From the time I was old enough to sit up, I was at a key panel learning how to write code. I was a full-time phader by the time I was twelve. Now I'm a senior group leader."

This was good. She was opening up. "Who are the directors?" I asked.

"They make all the decisions when it comes to Lifelight. But to answer your question, yes. All the phaders are young. The vedders, too. The directors want the sharpest minds possible at the controls. But it's more than that. As people grow older, they want to spend their time jumping, not monitoring. By the time a phader gets to be twenty-five, they pretty much take themselves offline."

"And do what?"

Aja didn't answer. Instead, she looked around. I took the cue and looked around too. What I saw was . . . a deserted city. Like I described before, it pretty much looked like any city on Second Earth, except there were no people. Rubbish kicked around in the wind and collected in alleyways. Glass windows were so grimy there was no way to see through them. Vehicles were parked along the kerb, but many sat tilted on flat tyres. I had the feeling that at one time this was a busy place.

I was starting to understand the problem.

"They're all in Lifelight, aren't they?" I asked softly.

"Why would they live anywhere else when they can create the life of their dreams?" was Aja's sharp reply.

"Is it like this everywhere?" I asked. "I mean, other than Rubic City?"

"It's the whole territory, Pendragon," she said. "Reality on Veelox only exists to support the fantasy." She then looked right at me. "That's why Saint Dane thinks he's won. This territory is about to fall apart, and we have nobody to blame but ourselves."

It made all sorts of sense. If nobody wanted to live in reality, then of course the territory would crumble. It made me think of a guy we used to go to school with. Remember Eddie Ingalls? He got caught up in playing one of those online fantasy games. He'd stay in his room on the computer for hours. I don't think he even slept very much, especially at the weekends. He ended up spending so much brain time playing that game, he lost most of his friends because he never wanted to come out and do anything. Then he started messing up in school. I'm not sure what happened to him, but I think his parents had to send him away to some kind of special school to help him catch up with real life. Well, what happened to Eddie Ingalls is what was happening on Veelox . . . times about eight billion.

The idea staggered me. My pulse started to race. We had lost Veelox before we had the chance to save it!

"Then Saint Dane was right," I declared. "We're too late. He *has* won!"

"Relax," Aja said sternly. "I told you, I've got things under control."

"Control? I'm seeing a lot of things here. *Control* isn't one of them! This city is falling apart. How long until Lifelight itself crashes? That's what'll happen, you know. Is that why jumpers are dying? Is that the future of Veelox? Are all the jumpers going to die in the middle of their fantasies because nobody bothers to take care of reality? We've got to get them out of there! Maybe we can pull the plug and force them to wake up! It's the only way they can —"

"Stop!" Aja shouted, and slammed on the brakes. I rocked forward, nearly launching out the front. Aja stared at me with such anger that I thought my brain would melt.

"I am trying to teach you about what's happening here," she said sternly. "We can't just 'pull the plug' and tell everybody to go back to their normal lives, though I'm sure you wish it were that easy. Salvation here can be found in only one place: the imagination. If you can't understand that, you might as well flume out right now."

I had to calm down. Though common sense told me otherwise, I had to believe Aja knew what she was talking about. The technology on Veelox was totally alien to me. If she said things were under control, I had to give her the benefit of the doubt. At least for a while, anyway.

"I'm sorry," I said, forcing myself to chill. "I'd like to stay and learn more about Veelox."

Aja stared at me. I wasn't sure if she was going to throw me out or take my head off again. Or both. Luckily she did neither. She started to pedal again. We didn't say another word until we arrived at her home.

Aja lived in a beautiful building on a quiet, tree-lined street. Did I say "quiet"? Hah, everything here was quiet. Her building was three storeys high and made of brick. It looked like a millionaire's home. Completing the picture, the street was lined with huge, leafy trees that gave the neighbourhood an inviting, parklike feel.

"Do all the phaders live in places this nice?" I asked as we walked up the marble steps to the entrance.

"They live pretty much anywhere they want," was her reply. "Most of the homes are abandoned. This place belongs to one of the directors. The prime director, actually, Dr Kree Sever."

"Nice of him to let you live here," I said.

"It's not a him, it's a her," Aja corrected me. "And Dr Sever couldn't care less. She's been on a Lifelight jump for over a year."

A year. Unbelievable.

She opened the heavy door and we entered the mansion.

"I'll be right back," she said, and ran up the stairs to the first floor.

The mansion was beautiful inside, too. There was a large entryway with thick, ornate carpets. A stairway led up to the first floor with a fancy wooden banister that was polished and gleaming. A hallway led deeper into the house with rooms off to either side. A quick glance showed me that the rooms were big, with high ceilings. It stunned me to think that somebody who lived in such a beautiful place would abandon it to live in a fantasy world. But then again, maybe the mansion Dr Sever had in her fantasy was twice as nice. Or maybe she had twelve mansions. If it was a fantasy, she could have whatever she wanted.

As I looked around, something felt a little bit off. It was because the place was totally clean. I mean, immaculate eat-off-the-floor clean. The wood was polished, the crystal cases of knick-knacks sparkled, and there wasn't a speck of dust anywhere. Rubic City was a falling-down mess because nobody cared, but this place was spotless. I couldn't imagine Aja taking the time to be so neat. Who was taking care of the place?

My answer came right away.

"You must be Bobby Pendragon!" came a warm voice from deeper in the house.

I looked to see an older woman hurrying towards me. She was the perfect image of a way-cool grandmother. Her grey hair was long and tied back in a ponytail, much like Aja's. She wore a deep blue sweater, dark trousers, and black boots . . . no granny-style dresses for this lady. She hurried up to me and held out her hand. I took it, not sure of how hard to shake. But her grip was solid. This lady may have been old, but she still had it going on.

"Oh, this is silly, give me a hug," she said.

Before I could react, she pulled me in and gave me a strong hug. I figured it would be quick, but she surprised me by squeezing tight and holding on. It was totally awkward. I wasn't sure if I should hug back or not. We hadn't even been introduced.

"I was so sorry to hear about Press," she said. "He was a wonderful man."

Okay, now I got it. She was being sympathetic about my uncle. I still felt awkward, but a little less so. She then held me at arm's length and said, "You are exactly as he described you."

The woman had kind eyes, with a hint of sadness.

"Thanks," I said. "Uncle Press was a great guy."

"We're all going to miss him." She then smiled and said, "Come. You're just in time for dinner."

Dinner. Excellent. I hadn't eaten since I had breakfast with you guys back on Second Earth. The fantasy pizza in Lifelight didn't count. The woman held my hand and led me towards the back of the house.

"You didn't tell me your name," I said.

The woman laughed warmly. "I am so rude. It's Evangeline. I'm Aja's aunt."

Whoa. That didn't compute.

"Aunt? I thought Aja didn't know her family."

"Well, I'm not her real aunt. Not by blood, anyway. I worked in the group home where Aja was raised. Still do. I love all the children, but there was something special about Aja. When it was time for her to leave, it was like losing a child of my own. So we decided to move in together and, here we are."

"Your house is beautiful," I said, figuring it was the kind of thing an older lady would like to hear.

"Thank you, but it's not really ours," she said in a whisper, as if it were a secret. "I don't think Dr Sever is coming back any time soon, but I make sure to keep the place tidy just in case. Are you hungry?"

"Starved."

"Perfect! Then you're in for a treat."

I was beginning to like Evangeline. First off, she was nice. She had a pleasant personality. She had a sense of humour. And she seemed to like me, too. In other words, she was nothing like Aja. We entered the big kitchen which had a table set for two. Evangeline busied herself setting a third spot for me. I was getting hungrier by the second.

"What's for dinner?" Aja said as she entered the room behind me. She had taken off her blue phader jumpsuit and now wore grey tracksuit bottoms and dark, trainer-like shoes. If I didn't know any better I'd think she was a normal kid, instead of an obnoxious, brainy, Traveller geek.

"Your favourite," Evangeline answered. "Tricolour gloid."

Gloid. I remembered the signs in the shop windows advertising gloid. I hoped it was as good as the pizza from Lifelight.

It wasn't. Evangeline placed a small cup at each of the

place settings. Each was filled with something that looked, well, it looked tricolour. It was a thick liquid, like soup, divided into half-inch-wide stripes of bright green, orangy rust, and royal blue. It looked like finger paint.

Evangeline and Aja both sat down and grabbed spoons.

"Sit, Bobby," Evangeline said. "Enjoy!"

I reluctantly sat and looked down at my bowl. My appetite was suddenly gone. But Aja and Evangeline dug in like it was the tastiest treat in the territory. And for all I knew, it was. I watched as they dipped their spoons into the goo. It had the consistency of bird doo. Evangeline was delicate. She tasted one colour at a time. Aja was less discriminating. She dug up all three at once.

"We don't often have tricolour gloid," Evangeline explained. "It's getting harder to come by."

I smiled like I was impressed. I wasn't.

"I don't mean to be rude," I said. "But I've never had gloid."

Aja and Evangeline exchanged glances. Oops. It was the wrong thing to say. Aja knew I wasn't from this territory so she would understand. But if gloid was such a big deal, how would I explain why I'd never had it? It was like admitting I didn't know who Dr Zetlin, the inventor of Lifelight, was. My mind searched for excuses, but I didn't know enough about Veelox to come up with any.

"It's pretty much all we eat," Aja said. "It was developed for Lifelight by the vedders to feed the jumpers when they're in the pyramid for long periods. It gets absorbed through their skin."

I had wondered how people could survive in Lifelight for so long without eating. I was bracing myself for Evangeline to ask me why I didn't know about gloid when Aja said to her aunt, "I don't think they have gloid on Second Earth."

Whoa. Did Evangeline know about the territories and the

Travellers? I mean, she knew Uncle Press, but Uncle Press knew a lot of people from the territories. He never told them about being a Traveller, though. He always made up some story about being from another part of the territory. At least, that's what I thought.

Evangeline then said to me, "Press once told me about something you had called . . . 'Gatorade'? Is that anything like gloid?"

"Uh, not really," I said dumbly. "Gatorade is a drink for when you're exercising hard and . . . I'm sorry. I'm confused. You know about Second Earth?"

I figured I had nothing to lose at this point. After all, she was the one who brought it up.

"Of course, silly," she answered with a smile. "Why wouldn't I?"

Okay. I figured I might as well cut right to the chase. "Evangeline, are you a Traveller?" I asked.

Both Aja and Evangeline laughed.

"No, silly," Evangeline giggled. "Of course not."

Now I was totally confused. If she wasn't a Traveller, why did she know about Second Earth?

Evangeline reached to her neck and pulled out a silver necklace. Dangling on the end of the chain was something very familiar. It was a silver ring with a heavy, grey stone at its centre.

"I'm not a Traveller," Evangeline said. "I'm an acolyte. Now please, eat your gloid."

VEELOX

Acolyte.

There was that name again. Uncle Press had told me they were people from the territories who helped the Travellers. But the only evidence I ever saw of them was when I'd flume into a territory and there would be clothes and stuff to change into. I had never met an acolyte . . . until now. I was pretty psyched because it felt like another piece of the Traveller puzzle was about to fall into place.

"Eat your gloid, Bobby," Evangeline said sweetly.

Man, I didn't even like the name. Gloid. It sounded like a body part, as in: "I'm afraid we have to operate and remove your gloid." Ick. But I couldn't be rude, so I picked up my spoon and cautiously took a scoop of the orange stripe. It was gooey, like pudding. I don't mind pudding, but the bright colour was throwing me off. Still, Aja and Evangeline seemed to like it, so how bad could it be? I wanted to hold my nose to kill the taste, but that wouldn't have been cool. So I took a quick breath and put the spoon in my mouth.

It wasn't bad. It was sort of bitter, like nuts. I then tried the green colour and discovered it was pretty good too, though totally different from the orange. The green was more like berries, sweet at first but with a tart aftertaste. With more confidence I dipped into the blue . . . and nearly puked. Blue was bad. I had to force myself not to spit it out. It was like a brussel sprout had gone south and got mixed in with kitty litter.

At that exact moment I looked up and saw Evangeline put a big spoonful of blue into her mouth. My stomach twisted. But I felt like I had to finish my cup o'gloid, so I used the Aja technique and mixed all three colours together. It was a good move. The orange and green mellowed out the foul blue and I was able to choke it all down.

When I finished, I was surprised to find I wasn't hungry any more. It wasn't because the weird taste had shut off my appetite, either. I really felt satisfied, like I had just polished off a big meal. I had all sorts of energy, too. Whatever the stuff was, it definitely did the job. I still wished it had been a big old pepperoni pizza, but I wasn't complaining.

"That was . . . delicious," I lied. "You make great gloid."

"Thank you," Evangeline said with a chuckle. "Not everybody knows how to scoop gloid from a container like I do." She winked at me. Ah, it was a joke. The gloid probably came ready-made, like ice cream. Oh well, so much for being a brownnoser.

"Gloid is pretty much the only thing we eat any more," Aja said. "There's hardly anybody left to grow real food."

"It's a shame," Evangeline said. She cleared the plates and Aja went to the sink to wash them.

"What can I do to help?" I asked.

"Nothing. We'll be done in a second," Evangeline said.

I was looking for an opening to ask Evangeline about the acolyte thing, but wasn't sure how to bring it up without sounding stupid.

"You have no idea what an acolyte is, do you?" Aja asked with a snotty edge.

Gee, thanks, Aja. Never missed an opportunity to point out something I didn't know. Just as well, it broke the ice.

"Uncle Press told me about them, but didn't go into a whole lot of detail," I answered. "I'd like to know more."

Evangeline wiped her hands on a towel and sat back down at her place at the table. Aja kept her back to us, washing the dinner dishes.

"Everyone needs a purpose," Evangeline said while looking me right in the eyes. "What better role could someone play than to support those who have a higher calling?"

"Higher calling?" I said.

"What else would you call it?" Evangeline said quickly. "The Travellers are concerned with the well-being of the territories. You can't get a much higher calling than that. I, for one, am comforted by the fact that you Travellers are out there. It makes me sleep easier at night."

Yikes. Evangeline was sleeping easier because I was keeping the territories safe? How wrong was *that*? I wondered if she knew about Saint Dane. I'll bet she wouldn't be getting so much sleep if she knew the wicked stuff he was up to.

"I have to admit, Evangeline, I'm a little shaky on the whole Traveller thing," I said. "Uncle Press wanted me to learn as I went along, but I don't think I've learned all that much."

Evangeline gave me a little smile. She then reached out and held my hand.

"What about Denduron?" she asked. "I heard you saved that territory from a horrible civil war."

Whoa. She knew about Denduron?

"It wasn't just me," I said quickly.

"And Cloral would have been ravaged by a plague if you

and the others hadn't intervened," she said.

"The people of Faar saved Cloral," I corrected her.

"And First Earth? Saint Dane was trying to change the destiny of three territories by saving that zeppelin and altering history."

I guess she knew about Saint Dane after all.

"You're making it sound more dramatic than it was," I cautioned.

"Am I?" she said quickly. "You've got quite a reputation, Bobby. I think you've learned a lot about being a Traveller."

"How do you know so much about what I've been doing?" I asked.

Evangeline glanced to Aja, who turned away. She looked annoyed again. What was her problem?

"The acolytes share information," she answered, holding up the ring on her chain. "Many of us keep the journals that the Travellers write. Aja asked me to keep hers. It was a great honour, but I wanted to do more. That's why I became an acolyte."

"Now that you mention it," I said, "I have some friends who want to become acolytes too. They're the ones I send my journals to."

"Can you trust them?" Aja asked.

I was getting sick of Aja always challenging me. I decided to zing her back. "If I didn't, I wouldn't be sending them my journals, would I?"

"I'm not talking about holding on to a bunch of papers for safekeeping, Pendragon," Aja countered. "I'm talking about being there, any time of the day or night, no matter what the situation, whenever they get the call."

"They're my friends. I trust them," I said firmly. I didn't

like the way she was questioning you guys, or me.

"I'll take care of it, Bobby," Evangeline stepped in, trying to be the peacemaker. "Your friend will get the chance."

"Two friends," I corrected her. "Mark Dimond and Courtney Chetwynde."

"Can we deal with the real issue here?" Aja asked impatiently.

"And what is that, dear?" Evangeline asked.

"I'm trying to convince Pendragon that Veelox isn't in danger from Saint Dane and he's wasting my time by being here."

That was it. Aja had pushed me over the edge. I looked to Evangeline and said, "Sorry for this."

Evangeline nodded as if she knew exactly where my head was and said, "I understand."

I then turned to Aja and said angrily, "Let's cut through it, all right? You've been treating me like an idiot since I met you. I took it because I didn't know how your territory worked, but now I do, and I gotta tell you, I think Saint Dane was right. He's already won. Veelox is falling apart. You say you've got it under control? I don't see it. You better start giving me some real answers or I'm going to flume out of here and come back with a whole bunch of my friends who have the same higher calling as me and —"

"And what?" Aja shouted back. "Blow up the pyramids? Destroy Lifelight? Convince everybody how they're better off living in reality than in their fantasies? Is that what you'd come back and do?"

I was really ticked off, but the truth was, I had no idea what I would do. Still, I couldn't let her think I was winging this. No way. I forced myself to calm down, but not lose my edge.

"You have no idea of what Saint Dane is capable of," I said through clenched teeth. "Have you even gone to another territory?"

Aja faltered. "Well, no, I'm too busy here and —"

"Well, I have, and even after all the horrible things I've seen, I'm not sure I know the true depths of Saint Dane's evil. That's the difference between you and me. I worry about the things I *don't* know. If I were you, I'd start worrying a little more."

This seemed to tweak Aja. She turned away from me, reached into a pocket, and pulled something out.

"I don't care what happened on the other territories, Pendragon. You can't beat Saint Dane here with a fight. There are no bad guys to battle or zeppelins to destroy. But it's every bit as dangerous as anything you've faced before. That's because the real enemy here is *perfection*."

"I get that," I said. "The people have to be shown what's happening to the real world."

"They already know!" Aja shot back. "They don't care! They think they've created the perfect system that runs itself. But the truth is the phaders and vedders would rather jump than do their jobs. You saw that vedder today. Someone died and all he cared about was starting his own jump. You only got a taste of Lifelight, Pendragon. And you know what? You didn't want to come out, did you? What was it you wanted? Twenty more minutes? They *all* want twenty more minutes, twenty more hours, twenty more days, weeks, months! Most of them don't even realise it's a fantasy any more. If I hadn't timed your jump, you'd still be in there."

I had to admit it. She was right.

"Okay, you convinced me," I said. "Lifelight is, like,

addicting. But my question stands. What makes you think you've got it under control?"

Aja threw the thing she had taken out of her pocket on to the table. It was a small, silver disc about the size of a quarter in a clear, plastic case. It looked like a tiny CD.

"I've been working on that for nearly a year," she said with pride.

Evangeline picked it up and handed it to me reverently. "It's all she thinks about," she said.

"Saint Dane was right in some ways," Aja said. "He's done here. If things continue the way they are, it would only be a matter of time before Veelox falls apart for good. Lifelight itself wouldn't be far behind. But I know how to save the territory."

"With this?" I asked, holding up the disc.

"With that," she answered with confidence.

"What is it?"

"I call it the Reality Bug," she said. "And tomorrow you're going to jump back into Lifelight and get a first-hand look at exactly how it works."

VEELOX

I wasn't so sure I wanted to jump back into Lifelight, not after seeing that jumper die. On top of that, I was starting to get nervous about Gunny. He had followed Saint Dane to the territory of Eelong and was supposed to take a quick look around and come right back to Veelox. Since Aja had the gate monitored, I asked her to let me know the instant Gunny arrived. I couldn't help but wonder what he'd found on Eelong. My guess was it wasn't good, but then again I always assume the worst.

Trouble is, I'm usually right.

I decided the best thing I could do was stay focused on Veelox and trust that Gunny could take care of himself. I spent the night in a guest room of the mansion. It was really comfortable and I would have had a great sleep if it weren't for the fact that I couldn't turn my brain off. It was all jammed up with worries about Gunny and jumping back into Lifelight. I ended up tossing around most of the night, nervous about what the next day would bring.

In the morning, Evangeline made us a yummy breakfast of, what else, gloid. We weren't treated to the tricolour stuff this time. This batch was all orange. That was okay by me, as long as it wasn't blue. I was surprised again by how filling the little cup of goo was. I would have preferred a stack of pancakes with maple syrup, but the gloid did me just fine.

Aja had on her blue jumpsuit, ready for business. She gave me a jumpsuit of my own, only mine was dark green. She said jumpers wore green when they spent long periods of time inside Lifelight. I didn't want to hang out inside Lifelight any longer than necessary, but figured I should be wearing Veelox clothes anyway. So I traded in my jeans and flannel shirt for this new suit. Aja also gave me some lightweight, black boots. I kept my boxer shorts, though. Rules or no rules, I always keep the boxers.

When we were ready to leave, Evangeline gave me a big hug. This time I hugged back. I liked her. Besides, she had to be pretty special to put up with Aja.

"Be safe, Bobby," she said to me.

"Don't forget, Evangeline," I said. "I told my friends I'd find out about the acolytes for them."

"I promise," Evangeline assured me.

I gave her one last squeeze of thanks and followed Aja outside. Evangeline watched as we went down the marble steps to the street and the vehicle that would take us back to the Lifelight pyramid.

"Bye, Vange," Aja called to her aunt. "I'll be home when I get home."

The two of us boarded the three-wheeled vehicle and began pedalling back towards Lifelight.

"Tell me about the Reality Bug," I said.

"I'm going to give you a demonstration," she said back.

"I know. Humour me."

"It'll be easier to show you," she argued.

"I'm sure," I countered, letting a touch of impatience creep into my voice. "But it would help if I knew a little bit about what to expect."

Aja sighed. I got the feeling that she thought of me as an inferior intellect who couldn't put two thoughts together without drooling.

"It's a computer program," she reluctantly explained. "Lifelight is designed to take the jumper's thoughts and give them the perfect experience. The Reality Bug alters the program . . . slightly."

"How?"

"It attaches to the data stream, changes it, and makes the experience less than perfect."

"Really? How?"

"That's what I'm going to demonstrate," she snapped. "You'll have a lot less questions after I show you."

I didn't want to argue. This was her show. I figured I was going to get the answers I needed soon enough anyway. Doing it on her terms was going to be less painful. So I shut up and we rode the rest of the way to the pyramid in silence.

When we arrived, we followed the same route as before. We went through the long hallway of freaky purple sterilisation, then to the airline-like ticket counter where I was fitted with another silver bracelet with three buttons. They didn't take any blood this time, I'm glad to say. I was already in the system.

As I waited for my control bracelet, I looked at the portrait of the kid Aja called Dr Zetlin. After having been in Lifelight, I had even more trouble understanding how a kid could have invented such an incredible device. But then again, didn't Beethoven write symphonies when he was, like, four? I guess you've either got it or you haven't.

We left the bracelet counter and continued on through the core. This time Aja stopped at one of the control stations. A glass door opened and we stepped into the high-tech room. Sitting in the coolio chair was a skinny little phader who looked like he was around twelve. He was gazing up at the wall of monitors, scanning each, looking for signs of trouble on the jumps while slurping down some blue gloid. Ick.

"Hey, Alex, we're doing a dual. I need you to phade for us," Aja said.

The kid, Alex, didn't take his eyes away from the screens. I noticed that he had a wicked case of acne. I wondered which colour gloid caused that.

"I'm off soon," he said with a high voice that sounded as if he were talking through his nose.

"But you're the best, Alex," Aja implored, sounding a little flirty. "I hate jumping with anybody else."

Alex gave a little smile. Aja had him. She knew how to manipulate the guy.

"You need a vedder?" he asked.

"Nah, this is gonna be short and sweet," Aja answered.

I liked that.

Alex then tore himself away from the screens and looked at us. He checked me out, then looked to Aja and gave a sly smile. "Careful what you do in there. I'll be watching."

"Do you have any idea how creepy that sounds?" Aja said to him coldly.

Alex instantly lost the smile and went back to watching the screens, embarrassed.

"Don't be long," he said while shovelling more blue gloid into his mouth. "When my shift's up, I'm jumping."

"Don't worry," was Aja's reply as she turned and left the control room. I followed right after her.

"He's a jerk," Aja explained. "But he's the best phader there is. Next to me, of course."

"So then why aren't you going to be the phader for my jump?" I asked.

"Because we're jumping together. Didn't you hear what I said?"

"Yeah, but I didn't know that was possible," I said with total surprise.

Aja didn't explain. Instead she entered another control room. This one was empty. Nobody sat in the control chair and all the screens were dark. She gave a quick glance back to the corridor to see if anyone was watching, then sat in the control chair and expertly hit a few buttons on the control pad that was built into the arm. Instantly a small section of the console in front of us sprang to life with indicator lights. Aja reached into the pocket of her jumpsuit and took out the tiny, silver computer disk she called the Reality Bug. After another quick glance outside, she stood up, went to the console, and inserted the disk into a slot in the board. She quickly sat back in the chair, hit a few more buttons, then ejected the disk and popped it back into her jumpsuit. Another few keystrokes and the console went dark. The whole event took a grand total of twenty seconds.

"It's loaded," she announced, and left the control room.

She either knew exactly what she was doing, or knew how to put on a good show.

"What did you just do?" I asked.

Aja shot me a quick look that had "Shut up, idiot" written all over it.

We entered the centre of the pyramid and I was once again stunned by the enormous size of the place. We took the lift up, made the scary walk across the bridge to the far side, and found an empty cubicle. This one was different to the others I had seen. It was bigger, with two silver discs on the wall rather than just one. Aja went right to the control panel and started to program our jump.

"How does this work?" I asked. "I mean, how can we jump together?"

"It's your jump," she explained while programming the panel. "Lifelight will take all of its cues from you. I'm just along for the ride."

"Can you control anything that happens?"

"No, I told you. It's your jump. We'll experience everything the same way, though. We'll be in this together."

With a few more keystrokes, the two silver discs on the wall slid open, and the two tables slowly ejected.

"There's something I don't get —"

"There's a *lot* you don't get," she interrupted.

I ignored the insult. "If people spend months and years in here, how do they eat? And go to the bathroom?"

Aja pointed inside the tube. "See those two pads?"

There were two black squares that were flush with the top of the white tube. "If there's going to be an extended jump, those pads drop down and the vedders attach them to the stomach of the jumper."

She showed me that there were two zippers on the front of our jumpsuits. They were about four inches long, the exact same length as the black pads.

"Attach? That sounds gruesome."

"It doesn't hurt," Aja assured. "They rest on the skin. One pad excretes a form of gloid that gets absorbed into the jumper's system. The other pad removes waste."

"So you eat and, well, do your, uh, *business* through those pads?" I said, totally disgusted.

"Business?"

"You know what I mean."

"The system bypasses the body's normal metabolic processes. It's all about breaking everything down into its base chemical structure so it can pass through the skin. I'm not exactly sure how that happens. It's not my field. But I do know this much: perfecting the feeding system was the last piece in the trouble puzzle. Once people could stay alive inside the tubes for long periods of time, they had no reason to come out."

The idea of lying in a dark tube, being fed through my skin by a pad that took away waste was kind of gross. I was glad our jump was going to be quick.

"Let's go," Aja said, and climbed on to one of the tables.

"What do I do?" I asked while climbing on to the other one.

"Same as last time. Think of a place you want to be, and that's where we'll go."

"But the Reality Bug is going to make it different?"

Aja chuckled. "Oh yeah."

I didn't like that. I wanted to know exactly how much different it was going to be, but I didn't get the chance to ask. A second later Aja hit a few buttons on her wrist controller and our tables slid into the tube.

"You know what you're doing, right?" was all I could get out before my head went inside.

Aja answered with a laugh. I hoped that meant yes. A second later I was all the way into the tube, and the door closed behind me.

I was in the dark again. In more ways than one. Where was Lifelight going to send me this time?

VEELOX

My body started to feel heavy, like I was being pushed into the table. I felt a little sleepy too. This was pretty much what happened the last time I was in here, so I wasn't worried. But my heart was starting to beat faster with anticipation.

I felt something dry and scratchy brush against my face. It didn't scare me or anything because even though I didn't know what it was, it somehow felt . . . right. I reached up to find out what it was, and discovered there was something covering my face. It felt like a towel. How did a towel end up on my face? I grabbed hold of it and pulled it away as . . .

The roar of the gymnasium crowd came flooding back like someone had just swung open a soundproof door. I pulled the towel away to find myself sitting on the bench between Petey Boy and Jimmy Jag. I was back at the basketball game at the exact same moment where I'd left it. Yes! It looked like I was going to get my extra twenty minutes after all.

It took a few seconds for me to get my head back into the situation. I glanced up at the scoreboard. It was all tied up at fifty-eight and we were heading for overtime. I had just sunk two free throws and the crowd was going ape. Coach

Darula came over and knelt down in front of us.

"We've been here before!" he shouted over the noise of the crowd. "Five minutes of OT. We've got the experience, we've got the conditioning, and now we've got them scared. All we have to do is keep our poise and the game is ours. Bring it in."

We all brought our hands together and Coach shouted, "One, two, three . . ."

We all answered with "*Win!*" then dropped our hands and jumped up to take the court. I was back up to speed, warmed up, and ready to go. Oddly, I even felt a little tired and sweaty, as if I had just played a full regulation game of basketball . . . which I had, in my fantasy. As we trotted out on to the court I heard a lone voice calling from the stands. Though it wasn't very loud, it cut right through the noisy crowd.

"Good luck."

I turned back and saw Aja sitting in the stands behind the bench, dressed like a high school kid with jeans and a sweat-shirt. She was holding a red pennant that said "Cardinals" and waved it with absolutely no enthusiasm. She really stood out against the rest of the crowd that was going totally nuts.

There was something about the way she said "good luck" that gave me an uneasy feeling. There was more. I looked up into the stands where I remembered you guys, Mark and Courtney, were sitting. But you weren't there. Odd. Everything was the same as when I left the fantasy before, except that the two of you were gone. Another look told me my family wasn't there either. I figured this was the kind of thing Aja was talking about when she said the Reality Bug made the jumper's experience less than perfect.

As soon as I got to the centre of the court for the tip-off, I noticed something else had changed. The players from Easthill High seemed bigger than before. It wasn't like they were suddenly giants or anything, but they definitely had more muscle and a few inches of height. They didn't look all that tired, either. I wasn't sure of what was going on, but there was one thing I felt certain about.

This was going to be a long overtime period.

The ref threw the ball up, it got tipped away from us, and the fun began. It was horrible. This was an entirely different game. I'm not sure if it was because these guys were suddenly better, or we had got a lot worse. Didn't matter. The result would have been the same.

They ate us for lunch.

Skill-wise, they dribbled around us, passed behind their backs, and alley-ooped for a bunch of slam dunks. Physically, they pushed us around like we were little kids. I'd dribble to the top of the key with my back to the basket, and the guy guarding me would put a hand on my back so I couldn't move. If I tried to pass, he'd swat the ball away and steal it for a fast break, followed by an easy layup on the other side of the court.

Three minutes into the overtime period and they had outscored us twelve to one. It was worse than embarrassing. The only reason we got a point was because I took a jump-shot and the centre hammered the ball back into my face so hard that it bounced off my head and landed two rows deep in the stands.

To be honest, the rejection was clean. No foul. But the ref took pity and called it. Unlike the last time I stepped up to the foul line, the crowd had grown deathly silent. I didn't think it was possible to have so many people in one place make so little noise.

I sank the first free throw, which was our one point. But I missed the second. It was a costly miss in more ways than one.

The ball bounced off the rim and rebounded back towards me. I jumped for it. So did their big centre. He grabbed the ball and came down hard . . . elbow first.

Yeow! He nailed me right in the nose. Man, I saw stars! I landed on my butt with the gym swirling around me. This might have been a fantasy, but that shot to the nose felt totally real. They had to stop the game and Coach Darula ran over to help me up. Blood was spurting from my nose like a lawn sprinkler. My head was spinning. I wasn't sure if I could make it back to the bench. Crutch and Joe Zip had to help me get there.

The crowd gave me a decent ovation. At least that proved they were still alive. Then, just before I sat down, I caught a glimpse of Aja. She had a big smile on her face like she was all sorts of happy that I had got nailed. All I could do was give her a dirty look. She shrugged. I sat down on the bench with my nose bleeding and my head swirling. I was done for the day.

But the day wasn't done with me.

Even though we were getting our butts kicked, Coach Darula was still coaching like crazy. He was running up and down the court, shouting encouragement, calling plays, crying foul when the other team got too rough (which was pretty much all the time). I had never seen him so excited. His face was all sorts of red. It worried me that he was overdoing it. As it turned out, I was right.

There were thirty seconds left in OT. We were down by fifteen with no hope of making a comeback. At this point our guys were only trying to survive. I had a moment of guilt, thinking that it was my fault they were getting beat up like this. I had to keep reminding myself that it was all a fantasy. But at that moment, it didn't feel like one. I know my aching nose felt all too real. Easthill had just scored, again, and Coach Darula wanted a time-out. He jumped up from the bench, shouting at the ref, making the T symbol with his hands . . . and that's when it happened. Coach Darula clutched his left arm, his face went blank, and he fell to his knees. I'm no doctor, but I was pretty sure of what was happening.

He was having a heart attack. The game was stopped. The referee ran over and laid him on his back. He then motioned for the timekeeper to get the paramedics. Seconds later two guys in uniform hurried over to the coach to take care of him. I didn't think it was possible, but the crowd was even more quiet than before. Within minutes Coach Darula was on a stretcher, being wheeled out as the crowd applauded nervously.

Nobody wanted to play after that. There was no point. Everybody just kind of wandered away in shock. Even the Easthill guys didn't celebrate their victory. It was all so very strange. I looked around for Aja, but she was gone too. Not knowing what else to do, I followed my team into the locker room and took a shower. My nose had finally stopped bleeding and the warm water felt good. I stood alone in the shower with my sore nose, washing the dried blood from my face and watching it swirl down the drain.

"Any questions?" came a familiar voice.

Aja stood in the entrance to the shower with her arms folded, looking smug. I quickly grabbed my towel and covered up. Sheesh, could this get any worse?

"I've got a ton of questions," I said while turning off the shower. "But first I want to know why my nose hurts so bad if this is all happening in my head?"

Aja chuckled. "You're not hurt, Pendragon. Not really. When we leave the jump, your nose will be fine."

"Good. Would you mind turning around so I can get dressed?"

Aja rolled her eyes and looked away. I went quickly back to my locker and changed into the clothes I had put there in my earlier fantasy. The locker room was empty now. The other guys were long gone. As I tied up my hiking books, Aja came over and sat down next to me on the bench.

"Lifelight took your thoughts and created a perfect fantasy," she explained. "The Reality Bug took those same thoughts and also found the flaws and fears. Rather than only pulling out the good, it also found the bad. Just like reality. Getting beaten like that was something you feared might happen. You probably even worried that one day your coach would overdo it and get sick. The Reality Bug found those fears and made them real."

"But what's the point?"

Aja stood up and paced. "Haven't you learned anything? The people of Veelox will never leave Lifelight on their own. The territory is crumbling because nobody wants to take care of real life. Reality is too much trouble. People have to work and repair their homes and grow food and have babies and deal with other people who might not agree with them, and basically do all the things that it takes to run a world. But in Lifelight they don't have to worry about any of that. That's why Saint Dane is winning. He's got fantasy on his side. But my Reality Bug is the ideal solution. It makes Lifelight less than perfect so people aren't staying in as long as they used to. It's forcing them to return to real life."

"So . . . you've already tried it with other jumpers?"

"A few. Every time they ended their jumps earlier than planned. It works, Pendragon. Once I've fully installed the bug, it will affect every jump in every pyramid on Veelox."

Aja sat down beside me. It was the first time she seemed happy.

"Don't you see?" she said. "The bug will make Lifelight more like reality, so it won't be as attractive any more. And nobody will know why. I've buried the bug so deep that no one will ever find it."

I hated to admit it, but Aja's plan made a whole bunch of sense. Still, there was something that bothered me.

"I think it's great, Aja, I really do," I said, still trying to form my thoughts. "If everything works out the way you say it will, then you did it. You beat Saint Dane."

"Thank you!" she said with a big, dramatic breath, as if this were the one thing she had been waiting for me to say all along.

"But —"

"There's no buts," she jumped in.

"Maybe not, but you said the battle on Veelox was going to happen inside people's imaginations. I understand that now. But aren't imaginations hard to control? I mean, look at me. I got hammered. You said this came from my own fears. What if somebody fears something really big? I mean, the jumps could get dangerous."

"So what?" Aja shot back. "It's a fantasy. Nobody gets hurt. They're all lying safely inside the pyramid."

"So when we come out," I asked, "my nose won't hurt any more?"

"Exactly!"

I wanted to believe her, but something else was bugging me, so to speak. The Reality Bug was nothing more than a really advanced computer virus. And computer viruses were scary. You never knew where they'd turn up or what damage they'd do. I once got a virus on my computer at home that trashed my hard drive. If a virus could wreck my little PC, I'd hate to think what it might do to a system as complex as Lifelight.

"Tell you what," Aja said. "I'll prove it to you. Let's do the final test. Right here, right now."

"Test?" I asked nervously.

"Your control bracelet," she said. "Remember the middle button?"

I lifted my arm to see that the silver band with the three buttons had reappeared. "The middle button alters the jump, right?"

"Exactly. Press the button. Let's see what happens."

"Are you crazy?" I shouted, jumping to my feet. "What if things go wacky?"

"I hope they do," Aja countered. "It'll be the only way I can prove to you that no matter how wrong a jump goes, all we have to do is end it and everything will be fine."

I shook my head and paced. This was getting scary.

"This is the final test, Pendragon. Pressing that button is the first thing the jumpers will do when their jumps go bad. They're all going to try and change their fantasy. Let's see what will happen when they do."

"What do *you* think will happen?" I asked.

"I don't know. It all depends on you."

Truth be told, I was scared to death of what might happen. What if a fire broke out? Or an earthquake hit? I didn't want to have to go through that kind of mayhem, even if it was just a fantasy. My nose hurt bad enough.

"C'mon, Pendragon," she cajoled. "You're the big brave Traveller who beat Saint Dane all those times. Be the hero again. Push the button. Let's prove the Reality Bug works once and for all."

"You promise we can end the jump right away? I mean, all I have to do is say 'Stop!' and you can make all of this go away?"

"You can end it yourself, remember?" she said, pointing to my control bracelet. "Just press the right button. That ends the jump. Everything should work exactly as normal, except the Reality Bug will alter the fantasy."

Aja seemed to have found the solution to the turning point on Veelox. If her Reality Bug worked, it would force people to live in the real world again. The Travellers would have beaten Saint Dane and set the territory back on the right path. If all that was left to do was test the middle button, we had to do it.

"You sure you know what you're doing?" I asked.

"You already asked me that," she answered impatiently. "Haven't I impressed you yet?"

Okay, she had. I took a deep breath, raised my arm, and put my finger over the middle button on the silver control bracelet.

"Ready?" I asked her.

"Always," she answered.

I pushed the button. It glowed red for a moment and then . . .

Nothing happened. The ground didn't shake, the roof didn't collapse. We stood there like a couple of dopes.

"Nothing changed," I said. "Maybe it didn't —"

Then it all hit the fan.

Aja lifted her arm with the large, silver control bracelet. "My controller," she said with surprise. "It's activating."

"What does that mean?"

A second later a beam of light shot out of the wrist controller and projected a holographic image. If the idea of the Reality Bug was to dig into my subconscious and pull out all my fears, it did a very good job. Because standing in front of us in that locker room was the one thing I feared most.

Saint Dane.

"Checkmate!" the demon laughed.

"Is this my fantasy?" I asked Aja, stunned.

"No!" Aja answered with a shaky voice. "Your jump isn't tied into my controller. This is real. It's a recording."

"Aja, you sweet thing," the image of Saint Dane said. "Did you really think I'd let you sabotage Lifelight? I worked too hard for too many years helping those programmers create Lifelight to allow you to destroy it with a simple computer virus."

Aja shot me a look. This wasn't my horror fantasy.

It was hers.

"Sweet, little Aja," Saint Dane's image said. "I've watched you from the day you were born. I made sure the directors picked you for the phader program; I saw you grow into an arrogant little Traveller; and I even helped you program your nasty little bug. I'm sure Pendragon has told you I'm always around. I'll bet you didn't believe him."

She didn't. But she was beginning to.

"You see, dear girl," Saint Dane continued, "you're my back-up plan. If Veelox didn't crumble from neglect, then I wanted to make sure your Reality Bug worked far better than you could imagine. And it will!"

Saint Dane laughed. It was chilling.

"Either way, I win," he continued. "Thank you so much for all your help, Aja. You've made destroying Veelox such a pleasure! Give my regards to young Pendragon."

The recorded image disappeared and Saint Dane was gone. Aja looked like she was about to faint. None of this made sense to her. Unfortunately it made a whole bunch of sense to me. Saint Dane knew exactly what was going on from the beginning. He was in total control. Just like always.

"He's lying," Aja said. "The Reality Bug won't fail."

"I think that's the problem," I said. "He's saying it's going to work better than you planned."

"How could he know that?"

"I've been telling you from the start, Aja!" I shouted. "That's what he does. He works people, pushing them towards answers they think they want, but it leads them to disaster. You don't see him coming until it's too late. You're smart, Aja. But you made a huge mistake. You thought you were smarter than Saint Dane."

Aja shot me a look full of hurt and anger. But it was the truth. Just when you think you've got the better of Saint Dane, he comes back to bite you in the butt. And right now, our butts were stinging.

"Aja? You in there?" came a voice from outside the locker room.

"Who is that?" I asked.

"It's Alex," Aja answered with surprise.

She ran for the locker room door. I was right after her. The door led to a short corridor that led to the gym. We stopped, still inside the locker room, when we saw that standing outside in the empty gym was Alex, our phader. We stood on either end of the short corridor, Aja and I in the locker room, Alex in the gym. He was nervously punching buttons on his wrist controller.

"Aja, what's going on?" he called to us.

"What do you mean?" Aja shot back.

"I'm losing control of the jumps," he whined. "A surge of data shot through the grid in my quadrant, and I traced the source to you!"

"What does that mean?" I asked.

"I'm not sure," Aja answered, trying to stay in control. "It could mean the Reality Bug has activated."

"I thought it was already activated?" I asked, rubbing my stinging nose.

"Not fully. I had it isolated to our jump," Aja answered. "But it's programmed to spread through the entire grid once I give the command."

"I think that command was just given," I said soberly. "Saint Dane took care of that."

"Reality Bug?" Alex called to us. "What is that?"

"End the jump," she ordered me. "We've got to get back to the core."

I quickly hit the jump-ending button on my control bracelet.

Nothing happened.

"Why are we still here?" I asked.

"I'll override you and end it myself," Aja said. She hit a few buttons on her wrist controller, and frowned.

"What's the matter?" I asked.

"It's not responding."

"Not responding?" I yelled. I hit the right button on my controller a dozen more times. It still didn't work. Aja's fingers sped over the silver buttons on her wrist controller, trying to find the right combination that would put her back in control. She didn't find it.

"Alex!" Aja yelled out to the phader, who was still standing on the opposite end of the corridor, working his wrist controller. "Get back to the core and jam a shutdown. Get us out of here!"

"Are you sure?" Alex called back. "What if —"

Grrrrrr.

The sound came from out in the gym, where Alex was.

"What was that?" Aja asked. She started to walk curiously towards the corridor that led to the gym, but I grabbed her arm to stop her.

"I don't know," I answered. But the truth was, it sounded familiar.

"Alex," I shouted, "is something out there?"

The phader looked around the gym and shrugged. "I don't see anything."

GRRRRRRRR . . .

There was something out there all right, and it was getting closer.

"We gotta get outta here, Aja," I insisted.

"I'm trying!" she said while pounding out buttons on her useless controller.

I then heard what sounded like a scraping sound, as if something sharp were being dragged over a hard surface. I *knew* that sound. It felt so familiar, yet I couldn't place it. What was it?

A second later it hit me. But it was impossible. Not here. Not on Veelox. Or on a fantasy version of Second Earth for that matter. Or wherever we were. There was only one other place where I had heard a sound like that. It was on a territory far from here. The sound brought back horrible memories from a place I would never forget.

Denduron.

"Hey!" shouted Alex with surprise.

Aja and I both looked up. We saw the phader framed in the doorway to the gym. He was now looking off to his right . . . and he looked scared.

"Who thought *this* thing up?" he asked with a shaky voice.

"What is it, Alex?" Aja asked.

Alex took two steps back, the fear showing in his eyes. "I'm gonna get back to the —"

He never finished his sentence, because a set of strong jaws closed around his throat. Aja screamed. I took a step back in surprise. The beast had appeared from nowhere. It leaped at Alex, knocking him down.

"How could that happen? I thought the phaders aren't really here?" I yelled, trying to keep my head together.

"They aren't!" Aja screamed. "This is our jump. He's not part of this."

"Yeah?" I cried. "Tell that to Alex . . . and the quig that just killed him."

At that moment the beast looked up from its victim and stared down the corridor at us. The sight of blood dripping from its teeth was all too familiar. It was a quig from Denduron. It was in my high school gym, in my fantasy . . .

And it had just set its sights on us.

VEELOX

A nightmare from my past had just sprung out of my brain and was standing in front of us. In the flesh.

Somehow Aja's Reality Bug had found it in my memory and brought it to life. It was impossible, yet here it was. The quig looked exactly as it had on Denduron. It was like a prehistoric bear with an oversize head that was mostly jaws. It had big sharp teeth on both top and bottom that jutted out like a wild boar's. Its body was covered with dirty-grey fur. Yellow spikes of bone ran down its spine. Its paws were huge and strong, with knife-sharp claws. But the thing I remember most about these quigs, like all the quigs from all the territories, were its eyes. They were yellow and angry and focused . . .

On us.

This one was smaller than the ones I remembered, about the size of a grizzly bear. But that was bad news because it was small enough to move through doors. We were only a doorway and a short corridor away from being eaten. The quig stepped over Alex's lifeless body, stalking towards the locker room . . . and us. There was only one thing I could think of doing.

I closed the door on our end of the corridor.

Just in time too. A second later I heard the quig smash against the door with a sickening thud. I knew the beast wasn't smart enough to open a door latch, so I didn't worry about locking it. The only thing I could hope was that the door would hold if it tried to bash it down.

Aja was frozen in shock. Her eyes were wide and frightened.

"Where did that come from?" I demanded.

"F-From your mind," she stammered out. "I told you, it'll find things in your memory that you fear."

"But you said Lifelight can only use reality," I shot back.

"Isn't that thing real enough for you?"

As if in answer, the quig smashed against the door again.

"But those monsters don't exist on Second Earth. It's from a different territory. From Denduron."

"That's impossible!" Aja shouted. "Lifelight can't do that!"

The quig slammed into the door again, letting out a bellow of pain and anger.

"Well, it can now!"

The door began to splinter. A couple more hits like that and it would be on us.

"C'mon!" I grabbed Aja's hand and ran. I didn't know where to go, but we couldn't stay there. We found a door on the far side of the locker room and blasted through. The door led outside, but once we were out, we both froze in horror.

We were near the large, football practice field. But there were no players scrimmaging today. Instead, we were faced with more quigs! The grass was swarming with them. They were all sizes, too. Some were as big as the beasts that had fought in the Bedoowan stadium on Denduron, others were smaller than the one from the gym. A few quigs were battling each other, trying to tear into each other's necks. I knew where that would lead. These quigs were cannibals. If one went down, the others would pounce and chow.

"The door!" I shouted.

It was closing behind us. If it locked, we were history. Aja reacted quickly and threw her foot out, wedging her shoe into the doorway just before it closed. If she had missed, we would have been quig lunch and I guarantee we were tastier than blue gloid.

I glanced back at the herd of quigs to see a few of them were lifting up their heads. They had caught our scent. In a few seconds they'd zero in on us and the dinner bell would ring.

"Back inside!" I shouted, and pulled the door open. After we ducked back in, I made sure to pull the door all the way shut. It was a good thing too, because a handful of quigs had spotted us and they were beginning to charge.

"Is there another way out of here?" Aja asked in desperation.

"I—I think so."

We ran back through the locker room, past the door to the gym, just as . . . *crash*! The gym door smashed open and the quig stood there looking totally ticked off that he had to go through so much trouble to get lunch. Aja and I kept running through the locker room, heading for the door that connected it with the girls' locker room. The quig chased us, awkwardly smashing into lockers that gave off a hollow, metallic thunder each time the monster slammed into one.

The door to the girls' locker room didn't have a latch, but it opened towards us. That was a huge break. There was no way the quig could pull a door open. We shot through and into a mirror-image locker room on the other side. We were safe, but for how long?

"Get us outta this!" I screamed at Aja.

"This isn't as bad as it seems, Pendragon," she answered.

"You're kidding, right?"

"No, this is a fantasy. Even if we got attacked and killed by one of those beasts, we'd just wake up inside the Lifelight pyramid."

"No," I said. "This isn't how it's supposed to work! You said it's impossible for those quigs to be here, but they are. And our control bracelets should work, but they don't. And Alex shouldn't be lying dead out there in the gym because he wasn't part of this jump, but he looks pretty dead to me. There are too many impossible things happening for me to risk letting one of those monsters eat us back to reality!"

"But —"

"You heard Saint Dane. He *knew* what you were trying to do with the Reality Bug. He messed with your program. Who knows what it's capable of now? We've got to get out of here alive and figure out what happened."

Aja nodded. I was making sense to her, for a change.

"I have no idea how to get us out," I added. "It's up to you."

I could tell the wheels were spinning in Aja's head, trying to figure a way to escape from the jump. Finally she said, "Our controllers were somehow taken offline. Whatever Saint Dane did, it happened when you pushed the reset button."

"Right, no more pushing the reset button," I agreed.

"But Alex's controller is tied into the general grid. It's on a different string."

"Can you use it to end our jump?" I asked.

"Absolutely," she answered with authority. "If it still works."

I knew what had to be done. We had to go back into the gym, get to Alex's body, and get his wrist controller. No problem, right? Yeah, sure. We quickly found the door that led from this locker room back into the gym. Aja and I cautiously opened it a crack and peered out.

The big gym was eerily empty. Not long ago it had been full of screaming basketball fans. Now the only person left in the gym was Alex, and he wasn't doing any screaming. Not any more. Question was, where was the quig?

"You sure this is the only way out of the jump?" I asked Aja in a whisper.

"No, but it's the only way I can think of."

"Then we've gotta take the chance," I said. "Wait here."

I started into the gym, but Aja grabbed my arm.

"Where are you going?"

"To get the controller, where do you think?"

"You don't know how to get it off his arm."

Good point. We had to go together. Aja and I then shared eye contact in a way that hadn't happened up until this point. Though we were both Travellers, our relationship had been a battle from the get-go. But now we were about to step into danger. The look between us said it all. We were in this together, like it or not. I gave her a quick nod, and the two of us stepped into the gym.

The distance to Alex was only about twenty yards, but it might as well have been a mile. If the quig caught us in the middle of the gym, there was nowhere for us to run. We started out by walking slowly, but I think we both realised the faster we did this the better, because with each step we picked up the pace.

Alex's body was lying right in front of the open doorway to the boys' locker room. The quig was probably still in there. I had my eyes fixed on the door, waiting for it to spring out. Neither of us said anything for fear of alerting the monster.

As we got closer to the body, I realised I didn't want to see what horror the quig had done to the poor guy. Fantasy or not, this was all too real. But there was no chickening out. Not now. We were only a few feet from the body and I felt as if we were going to pull this off.

I was wrong.

The quig sprang from the doorway, exactly as I feared. Without thinking, I grabbed Aja and pulled her underneath the bleachers. It was the only place to go. Because of the basketball game, the bleachers were extended out into the gym. The move saved our lives, for the moment.

The quig swiped at me with its massive paw just as I ducked under a metal rail. The monster's hand smashed the rail, but one claw caught the back of my arm, slicing open the fabric of my jumpsuit. The stinging pain told me it had sliced through a part of my arm, too. But no matter how bad it hurt, I wasn't about to stop now.

"Keep moving!" I shouted at Aja.

A complex steel framework held up the bleachers. The two of us crawled through the labyrinth, moving up and over and around and under, desperate to get away from the quig. I glanced back to see the quig was still coming. It was having a lot more trouble getting through the tangle of steel than we were. But that didn't stop it. This thing was tearing the bleachers apart to get at us.

That's when I got a brilliant idea.

"Get to the far side, hurry!" I shouted at Aja.

If my idea was going to work, we had to get out from under here as soon as possible. I kept pushing Aja from behind, forcing her to snake through the metal rails. Finally we made it to the far side and out from under.

"Which way?" she shouted.

"Stay right there!" I commanded.

Aja looked at me like I was crazy. But I didn't have time to explain. Aja may have known computers, but I was a gym rat. Before I became a Traveller, I had spent every moment I could in gyms. I knew how they worked. I ran to a small silver box on the wall, flipped up the safety cover, and pressed the red control button inside.

Instantly the bleachers began to retract, with the quig trapped underneath.

"Brilliant!" Aja exclaimed.

It was the first nice thing she said to me. The two of us stood there, both hoping the quig would get crunched in the tangle of steel that was closing around it. All we needed was a minute to get the controller.

We didn't get it.

With a horrifying roar, the quig crashed out from under the retracting bleachers, pulling pieces of steel frame along with it. Turned out my brilliant idea, wasn't so brilliant. There was nothing we could do but run for our lives. We sprinted across the gym, maddeningly close to Alex's controller. But there wasn't time to get it. We ran out of the gym and down the corridor that led to the rest of the school.

I always felt like there was something spooky about an empty school building. I'm not sure why. Maybe it's because I was used to schools being busy and loud. A quiet school seemed wrong. Well, this school was definitely wrong. The fact that it was empty was the least of the reasons. Aja and I ran down the long, glass-walled corridor from the athletic wing into the student centre that was the main hub of the school. It was a huge, aeroplane hangar-size room from which all the rest of the school wings could be accessed. Aja and I ran to the centre of the big room so we would be able to get a complete 360 view around. If anything was going to enter the place looking for us, we'd see it in plenty of time to run the other way.

"There's gotta be another way to end the jump," I said, gulping for air.

Aja once again hit a series of buttons on her wrist controller, then grunted in frustration. "This can't be happening!" she shouted. "I have no control!"

There was no way around it. We had to figure a way to get past that quig, or at least distract it long enough to get Alex's controller.

"You know this place," Aja said. "Are there any weapons?"

"In a school? Yeah, right."

"Think, Pendragon! Is there anything we can *use* as a weapon?"

My first reaction was to say no, but that wasn't helpful. I had to give it some thought and be creative. Was there anything in this school we could use as a weapon to beat a quig? Uncle Press had killed some quigs with spears, but there was nothing like that here at Davis Gregory High. We had also blown up a quig using the explosive tak, but there was none of that stuff around. What else could we use?

That's when an idea started to form.

"These quigs," I asked. "Lifelight created them, but are they real? I mean, are they just like real quigs?"

"They're as real as you remember them," Aja explained. "Lifelight took them from your mind. It doesn't matter what real quigs are like, only what you remember about them. If you believe they can sing a song, they'll be able to sing."

"Then we need a dog whistle," I announced.

"A what?"

"Quigs are incredibly sensitive to high-pitched sound.

They go nuts when they hear it. If we can find some kind of whistle, we can keep that quig back long enough to get to Alex's controller.

"Perfect!" Aja exclaimed. "Where can we find a whistle?"

"I don't know," I admitted.

"Ugh!" Aja exclaimed in frustration. "Think! Is there anything we can use to make that kind of sound?"

We heard something that sounded like the rumble of thunder. I took a quick look around and saw movement outside the windows. I wanted to scream. The quigs outside had found us! They were peering in through the windows, staring at us, probably deciding the best way to attack. Suddenly I wished that I could find a *hundred* whistles.

A hundred whistles.

An idea was sneaking around the edges of my brain.

"Pendragon," Aja whispered. "We don't have much longer."

I had it. A hundred whistles. Plan B was starting to take shape.

"This way!" I shouted, grabbed Aja's hand and ran off. I led her through the student centre to the wing housing the school offices. It's where the principal hung out and where the secretaries worked. If I was right, we'd find something there that would help us stop the quigs.

The office was dark and deserted. I made my way towards the long reception desk when suddenly . . . *crash!* A window blew out. Aja and I jumped in surprise and looked to see that a quig had smashed it and was now crawling in. *Crash! Crash!* Two more windows blew, followed by more squirming quigs. They knew exactly where we were. Either my idea was going to work, or Plan B was going to put us on the quig menu.

"What are we doing in here?" Aja asked. I could hear the growing terror in her voice.

"A hundred whistles," I answered while continuing on towards the reception desk. "We may not have a single whistle, but I might be able to come up with a hundred."

I was looking for the public address system. Every school had one for announcements and whatnot. I really hoped that Davis Gregory High was one of them. It was our last, best hope.

Crash! Crash! Two more windows shattered and glass rained down. The quigs were coming from all over. It was now or never. I found the PA system under the long reception desk. Now the trick was to figure out how to use it.

There was a power switch that I immediately threw. The lights on the machine blinked to life. There was a long row of buttons that I guessed operated the speakers throughout the school. I was about to turn every one on, when I saw a toggle switch marked "All speakers". Duh. I flipped it on.

The first quig had got inside and was now standing up. It would charge in seconds.

I cranked the volume knob to fifteen. If it had gone to twenty, I would have cranked it to twenty. I then grabbed the microphone. It was on a stand, with a trigger to turn it on. With a quick look at Aja, I hit the button and turned the microphone toward the amplifier.

They call it feedback. We've all heard it before, a thousand times. I'm not exactly sure what causes it, but it always seems to happen when the volume is turned up too high on something that is amplified. I think it has to do with an overload that the system can't handle and . . . to tell you the truth, I didn't care how it happened. I only cared that it happened now.

It did. The piercing sound screeched out from the speakers. It was horrible . . . and beautiful. The quigs began to bellow, just as they had on Denduron when I blew the dog whistle. It was perfect. They couldn't function. I quickly took some Scotch tape and wrapped it around the microphone to keep the button depressed, then leaned it against the amplifier. Unless it blew a fuse, we had our hundred whistles.

Aja grimaced in pain from the horrible sound, but still managed to smile.

"Can we go now?" she shouted.

The two of us ran out of the office, heading back towards the gym. The horrifying sound was piercing the entire school. As we ran, I looked outside and saw quigs fleeing in terror. Compared to a little old dog whistle, this feedback was monstrous.

Aja and I ran through the student centre and down the long corridor back to the athletic wing. I had no doubt that the quig in the gym was in just as much agony as the rest of them. Now all we had to worry about was whether poor Alex's wrist controller would work.

We made it back to the gym and peered inside. Sure enough, our friend the quig was on its back, writhing in pain. With a quick look of relief at each other, Aja and I started into the gym.

And the screeching stopped.

Just like that. Maybe the amplifier blew. Maybe the power went out. Maybe, maybe, maybe. All that mattered was that our hundred whistles had fallen silent.

And the quig was back on its feet, ready to roll.

VEELOX

Aja and I froze. The quig didn't. It was back in control and madder than ever. It saw us and started to charge. All we could do was run.

That's when I saw it. I didn't know why I hadn't thought of this before, and didn't care. I saw it now, and we had nothing to lose by giving it a shot. So before we ran from the gym, I reached out next to the door and pulled the fire alarm.

Instantly the grating horn sound filled the gym, louder than the feedback from the PA system. Question was, would it be enough to bother the quig? Aja and I both turned to see . . .

The quig had fallen back down, clutching its head. We were back in business. Without stopping to think, Aja took off towards Alex. I was right after her. We dodged the squirming quig and made it to the body of the poor phader. I couldn't bring myself to look too closely at him. His body was still. Blood pooled on the gym floor. That's all I needed to know.

Aja quickly reached for his arm and pulled it towards her so she could have access to his elaborate wrist controller.

"Does it work?" I asked.

"We'll know in a second."

She expertly hit a few keys, and the strangest thing happened. I felt dizzy. It was like the whole gym started to spin. I wondered if all the sound of the feedback and the blaring fire alarm had finally got to my inner ear.

The next thing I knew it was pitch black. Was I back in the Lifelight pyramid? The odd thing was, I still heard the fire alarm blaring. But that didn't make sense. Either I was back or I wasn't. A second later I was bathed in light. The next thing I saw was my black boots. I was lying inside the Lifelight tube. I was back!

But why was I still hearing the alarm? The table slid out of the tube and I looked quickly to my left to see Aja was already jumping off her table.

"What's going on?" I asked.

"Come on!" she shouted.

We ran outside the cubicle into the centre of the pyramid. One look around told me the problem. There were hundreds of lights flashing red outside the cubicles. Phaders and vedders were running around like crazy. The alarm sounding here had nothing to do with the fire alarm I had pulled in my fantasy. This was a full-out emergency . . . for real.

"We gotta get to the core!" Aja exclaimed, and ran for the lift tube. We sprinted over a bridge, jumped in the tube, and flew down.

In the glass corridor of the core, things were frantic. There were alarms blaring and red warning lights flashing everywhere.

A phader grabbed Aja and yelled, "We've got hundreds of jumps going bad!"

"Contact the directors!" Aja shouted at the phader, and ran past him down the corridor. I kept up with her. As we ran by the control stations I saw that several of the screens showing jumps were flashing off and on. Phaders were in their control chairs, desperately hitting buttons on their arm controllers, but it didn't seem to be doing any good. A few seconds later I saw where Aja was heading. She threw open the door to Alex's control station.

"Alex! What happened?" she yelled.

Alex couldn't answer. He was sitting in his chair with blank eyes still staring at the screens.

Alex was dead. On his neck were bite marks. There was no mistake. The quig in my fantasy jump had somehow killed Alex out here in reality. Whatever the Reality Bug had done, it had turned Lifelight inside out. Right now, in cubicles all over the pyramid, all over Veelox, people were in mortal danger as they faced their worst nightmares in their own fantasies . . . for real.

"Shut it down," I said.

Aja continued to stare at Alex, unbelieving. She couldn't move.

"Aja, shut it down!" I shouted. "You gotta save those people!"

"This can't be happening," she said, stunned. "They're just *fantasies*!"

I grabbed Aja and forced her to look at me. "Not any more they're not!" I shouted.

"But it's illusion!" Aja argued. "It's not real!"

"Is that real enough for you?" I asked, pointing at poor, dead Alex.

"There must be some other explanation," she argued.

"Yeah?" I shot back. "Then how do you explain this?" I let her go and turned my back to her, shoving out my arm. What I wanted her to see was proof positive that what was happening inside Lifelight was no fantasy. I showed her my arm. It was the arm that got sliced by the claw of the quig when we escaped under the bleachers. My jumpsuit was cut, with dried blood around the edges.

"That blood is real," I said. "It hurts, and so does my nose. My injuries didn't go away when we got back."

Aja stared at my arm as if her brain wouldn't let her accept what her eyes were seeing.

"Aja," I said softly. "It's not a fantasy any more."

She looked at me with confusion. Her orderly world had just been blown apart. Then the door to the cubicle flew open and a phader ran in.

"Aja!" he shouted with terror. "It's happening all over Veelox. Lifelight has been totally corrupted."

Aja forced herself to think. She blinked once, then her eyes focused. "Did you contact the directors?" she asked.

"They're all jumping!" the phader answered. "Every one. We can't get to them!"

Aja looked to Alex's control board.

"Shut it down, Aja," I said again.

"I can't," she finally answered. "There's no such thing. People would die."

"But we have to do something!" I demanded.

Aja was thinking fast. I saw a spark in her eye. An idea. She turned back to the phader and said, "We've got to suspend the grid."

"What?" the phader shouted. "We can't!"

"Do you have a better idea?"

The phader didn't.

"Get your key!" Aja commanded him. She reached around her neck and pulled out a black-cord necklace from under her jumpsuit. Attached to it was a large, green card.

The phader hadn't budged.

"Move!" Aja commanded.

The phader was shocked back to reality. He hurried to the control panel while pulling out his own cord necklace. He had a green card on it, just like Aja's. The two stood at opposite ends of the complex array of controls.

"I hope you know what you're doing," the phader said softly.

Aja shot the guy a look. "Insert!"

They both took their green cards and inserted them into slots on either side of the control array. Aja then flipped about a dozen switches, the last of which was behind a clear, plastic cover. She lifted the cover to reveal a red toggle switch. The phader was working a duplicate set of switches, with the final being a similar red toggle switch.

Aja took a breath and said, "On my mark. Three, two, one . . . *suspend*."

They both flipped the red switches.

Instantly all the monitors went blank. The thousands upon thousands of images that were being displayed had been replaced by the same single, flat colour of green. The alarms all stopped as well, leaving everything eerily quiet.

I looked to the phader. He was crying.

"What happened?" I asked.

Aja stared ahead blankly. Her voice was calm and even. "We just suspended the grid."

"You mean, you shut it down?" I asked.

"No, the jumpers are still in Lifelight, but the jumps are frozen. Nothing will happen to them. All over Veelox. Millions of people are lying in the grid, waiting."

"For what?"

Aja then looked at me. Her eyes were red and frightened. "They're waiting for me to figure out what went wrong."

VEELOX

"How could you do that?"

"What happened?"

"This is impossible!"

Aja was in the centre of a storm of phaders and vedders, all screaming at her, wanting to know why she had suspended the grid. Whatever *that* meant. No sooner had the two switches been thrown, than the blue- and red-suited technicians came flooding into the control room, demanding answers. Most of the computer screens now showed live images of phaders and vedders from all over Veelox who were demanding to know what had happened. It wasn't until those faces started showing up on all those screens that I realised the full deal.

Aja hadn't only suspended Lifelight here in Rubic City, she had suspended the *entire territory*. At that moment millions upon millions of people all over Veelox were lying in suspended animation.

"Everybody, listen to me!" shouted Aja. Nobody did. They were too scared. I can't blame them. Their world was on the verge of crashing. Heck, if they weren't scared, they should be.

"Please, let me speak!" Aja begged. But the questions kept coming.

"My whole family is on a jump!"

"We've got to get back online and get them out!"

It was borderline chaos. All I could do was stay out of the way and hope that Aja could handle this. Finally she went to the control panel and with a look of pure determination, pressed a large green button. A screeching horn sounded that forced everyone, including me, to cover their ears. I saw that the technicians on the monitors were cringing as well.

After a few seconds Aja took her finger off the button and the horn fell silent. The phaders and vedders went silent too. They must have been afraid Aja would blast them again. Aja hit another switch and spoke into a microphone on the console. Her voice was amplified throughout the pyramid and heard by the technicians on the monitors.

"My name is Aja Killian," she said calmly. "I'm the senior phader on duty here in Rubic City. I'm the one who authorised the suspension of the grid."

Everyone started shouting again.

Aja jammed on the horn. Again, everybody quietened down. She released the button, but kept her finger close, ready to blast it again if anybody got out of hand.

"We had an emergency," she explained. "Jumpers were in trouble throughout Veelox."

I looked at the wall of monitors and saw several of the technicians nodding. For the first time I noticed how young they all looked. I scanned the monitors, searching for at least one grey-haired, wise scientist who would save the day. There weren't any.

"As best as I can tell," Aja continued, "the processing code has been corrupted."

People gasped. Whatever that meant, it must have been bad.

"How can that be?" a phader shouted, risking another blast from the horn. "That's never happened before!"

I looked to Aja. This had to be one of the toughest moments of her life. She knew *exactly* how it could be. Things had gone whacko because she had introduced a bug into the system. A Reality Bug. Worse, it was a bug that Saint Dane had somehow made even more powerful than it was supposed to be.

"But it *has* happened," Aja said firmly. "The jumpers are in danger. Suspending the grid was the only way to buy us time to solve the problem."

Everybody seemed to agree. Score one for Aja.

"With the grid suspended, the jumpers are totally safe," she continued. "I've been monitoring the situation and I believe I can ferret out the problem."

"We can't leave them inside like that," a vedder called out.

"We don't have any choice," Aja shot back. "If we go back online without solving the problem, we'll be back where we started and the jumpers will still be in danger."

I saw a lot of nervous heads nodding in agreement.

Aja then said, "Who is the senior vedder on duty?"

A guy stepped forward who looked like he wanted to be anywhere but here. "I just came on duty when the alarms started going off," the guy said softly.

I'll bet he wished he had overslept.

"How long are the jumpers safe with the grid suspended?" Aja asked.

"Theoretically, forever," the senior vedder answered. "But it's never been tried before, so who knows?"

"That's okay," Aja said confidently. "It won't take forever

to fix the problem. I'm going into the Alpha Core to start unravelling this."

"What do we do in the meantime?" the senior vedder asked.

"Nothing," Aja answered. "Just don't go far from the pyramid. When I crack this, everyone should be ready to go back online."

She then looked up at the faces on the monitors. "The same goes for all of you," Aja said to them through the microphone. "Let me work on the processing code. I'll keep you updated on my progress."

It was a great performance. Aja had shown total authority, and from the looks on everybody's faces, they believed she was going to solve the problem. The question was, did *Aja* believe she could solve the problem? I wanted to think so, but when she flipped the switch to turn off the microphone, I saw that her hand was shaking. Oh man. She was barely keeping it together.

She then glanced at me and we made eye contact. There was no mistake. She was scared. I hoped nobody else saw it. She then looked to the senior vedder and said softly, "You'll take care of Alex, right?"

The vedder nodded sadly.

Aja gave me a quick look and said, "Let's go."

She then walked away from the console, through the crowd of technicians, and out of the control room. I'm sure she felt the heat of everyone's eyes on her, searching for some sign of assurance that she would solve the problem.

I followed her to the far end of the glass corridor and up to a solid door marked ALPHA CORE — AUTHORISED PERSONNEL ONLY. She took the same green card from around her neck and inserted it into a slot near the door handle. A metallic *click* signalled that the door was unlocked. Aja entered and I followed right behind her.

Inside was another control room that was a little different from the others. This one felt more important. Maybe it was because it was behind solid walls instead of glass. There was only one large monitor on the wall, and one control chair facing it. Beneath the monitor was a vast array of switches and knobs and lights, just like in the other control rooms. One arm of the control chair was extra long and held a silver keypad that looked way more complicated than the ones in the other control stations. I had no doubt that this was where we would have to undo the damage and save the territory.

Aja fell into the chair and started to cry.

Uh-oh. Not a good start. It must have taken every ounce of willpower she had to hold it together in front of the phaders and vedders, but now that we were alone, she lost it. I felt bad for her, but I was feeling worse for all those people who were stuck in the vacuum of Lifelight. Their only hope of getting out safely rested with Aja, and she wasn't looking all that capable of saving anybody. Finally she took off her glasses and rubbed her eyes.

"I didn't want you here on Veelox, Pendragon," she said. "Do you know why?"

"Uh . . . no," was my dumb but truthful answer.

"Because you're you," she said.

"What's *that* supposed to mean?"

"Give me a break," she said with tears forming again. "You're the lead Traveller. You swoop into a territory and take on Saint Dane like some kind of fearless saviour. Denduron, Cloral, First Earth . . . every one a victory for the good guys. It's all so simple for you."

I wanted to laugh. I really did. Fearless? Saviour? Me? Yeah, right. I didn't know what stories she had heard, but her information was definitely twisted.

"I'm not like you," she went on. "I'm not some big adventurer. What I am is smart. Smarter than you. That's not a boast; it's fact. My whole life I was trained to maximise my intellect. I lived with teachers and scientists. Evangeline was my only friend. It was a cold way to grow up. I hated it. Then one day your uncle showed up to tell me I was a Traveller. Suddenly it all made sense. I knew what I was meant to do. All the training and studying and loneliness I had to endure meant that I had the tools to protect Veelox. It was like I had suddenly come alive, because my life had purpose. I was all set to take on Saint Dane with the weapon I knew how to use best . . . my brain."

Aja stopped talking. I think she was trying to hold back tears. She swallowed and said, "The reason I didn't want you here, Pendragon, was I didn't want you to take that chance away from me."

I was slowly starting to get the picture. Finally. Aja had been cold towards me because she feared I would take away the one thing that gave her life meaning.

"But as it turns out," Aja continued, barely keeping her emotions down, "I not only failed to save Veelox, I made things worse. I didn't stop Saint Dane, I *helped* him!"

"We don't know that yet —"

"No?" she shouted, spinning the chair towards me. "I created the Reality Bug. It's my fault that millions of people are in danger. And that Alex is . . . I thought I was being so smart, and all along I was doing the worst possible thing."

"Aja, you have to understand," I said carefully. "Saint Dane may have had a bigger part in this than you know."

"No! I programmed it. I installed it. It was all me."

"I know that, but like I told you, Saint Dane is more devious than you can imagine. I'm not saying he was by your side helping you program the thing, but he probably put ideas in your head. It could have started years ago. He might have been a teacher who first planted the idea about how Lifelight would be better if it weren't so perfect. He could have been a phader who suggested it might be possible to alter the program, or a vedder who said it was impossible to be hurt while jumping. That's what he does, Aja. He plants ideas. He gets you thinking in directions that seem right, but are totally wrong."

Aja didn't turn her gaze from me. It was the first time she actually listened to what I had to say.

"And it probably wasn't just you," I added. "I'll bet he was doing the same thing with other phaders, and getting them to monkey with Lifelight so that when you installed the bug, it would blow up the way it did."

Aja let this information work its way through her brain. I wished she had done that when I first met her, but hey, no sense in looking back.

"There's something else," I said. "I don't know where you've been hearing these stories about me, but things didn't exactly happen the way you think they did. Yeah, we've been able to slam Saint Dane a couple of times, but it wasn't because I was a brave guy who charged in to kick butt and take names. Most of the time I was so scared I couldn't think straight."

"So how were you able to beat him?" she asked with a touch of confusion.

"Luck, as much as anything," I said. "To be honest, I blew it on First Earth. If I had been alone, there would have been a disaster worse than what we're looking at here. I'm still trying to figure out how to live with that."

"But it all worked out," Aja said.

"That's because I wasn't alone. Gunny bailed me out. I don't think any one of us can stand up to Saint Dane alone, Aja. Working together is our only chance."

I hoped I was getting through to her. The future of Veelox depended on it, not to mention the rest of Halla.

I then added, "But what we've got here is a little bit different."

"How?" she asked, confused.

I walked over to the vast console and looked at the sea of buttons and switches.

"The Reality Bug was a brilliant idea. If Saint Dane hadn't stuck his nose in, it might have worked. But he did. We can't change that. We can only look forward. Our job is to save Veelox. But first we have to stop the Reality Bug. I have no idea how to do that. But you do. I can be here to bounce ideas off of, but only you can stop the bug. So when it comes right down to it, you *are* going to get the chance to save Veelox."

Up until that moment Aja looked like she was ready to crawl into a corner and shrivel up. But now the sparkle returned to her eyes. She sat up straight and put her yellow glasses back on. She stood up and faced me with the same confidence that I saw when she spoke with the technicians outside.

"Not a problem," she said. "All I have to do is tap into the grid and purge the bug from the processing code."

Whatever *that* meant.

"That won't solve the larger problem though," she added. "Once I'm done, Lifelight will go back to normal and Veelox will still be in trouble."

"One step at a time," I said.

Aja walked over to me and turned me around. I wasn't sure

why until I realised she was examining the cut on the back of my arm.

"Go see a vedder and get that taken care of," she said. She even sounded like she cared. A little.

"You sure you don't need me?" I asked.

Then . . . a miracle. She smiled. Was it possible? I'd like to take credit for getting her to lighten up, but the truth was that nearly causing the deaths of millions of people was probably earth-shattering enough to get anybody to see things differently . . . even an ego case like Aja. All I could do was smile back.

"It'll take me less time to purge the Reality Bug than it will for you to get your arm fixed," she said, then spun away from me and sat back down in the control chair. She pulled the control arm in front of her, ready to work. A few keystrokes later, the large monitor flashed to life. She had slipped into computer world, so I left her alone and went looking for some Bactine and Band-Aids.

The glass corridor of the core was empty and quiet. The technicians were gone and all the monitors at the control stations were showing the same blank green colour. It was creepy seeing the place so dead, so I hurried to the end of the corridor to get out as fast as possible.

I stepped into the room with the long counter where I had been fitted with my silver bracelet for the jumps. It was empty too. I walked up to the counter and gazed at the portrait of young Dr Zetlin, the inventor of Lifelight. He didn't look like a genius. He just looked like a regular kid.

"Hiya, Doc," I said. "This what you had in mind when you invented Lifelight?"

A voice then came from behind the counter. "Who are you talking to?"

For a second I thought it was the portrait, and it made me jump. But it turned out to be the Goth-looking vedder who had pricked my finger the day before.

"Uh, nobody," I answered, embarrassed. "Hey, you think you could take a look at my arm?"

The vedder rolled his eyes. "If I have to," he said, as if it were the last thing he wanted to do. I wasn't sure why he minded so much. It wasn't like he had anything else to do. I unzipped my jumpsuit to my waist and pulled my arm out.

"Where did everybody go?" I asked as he examined my cut.

"They're all up in the pyramid," he answered. "They're going to jump as soon as Aja gets Lifelight back online."

Unbelievable. Even during a crisis, all these guys could think about was jumping out of there.

"What about you?" I asked. "Don't you want to jump?"

"Not any more, I don't," he said. "I'm beginning to think real life is safer than make-believe."

That was good to hear. Maybe there was hope for the territory after all.

"It's not a bad cut," he said. "Your jumpsuit got it worse than you did."

The vedder put an ointment on it and the stinging immediately went away. He then put a yellow pad over the cut and I was good to go.

"Thanks," I said.

"Don't worry," the guy said sincerely. "Aja is the best. If there's anybody I trust around here, it's her."

I nodded. I really hoped he was right.

There was nothing else to do, so I wandered back to the Alpha Core to see how Aja was doing. The door was unlocked, and I slipped in quietly, trying not to disturb her.

Aja was totally focused on her work. I glanced at the large

monitor to see that it was filled with several lines of computer code, each in a different colour and each more complex than the last. Aja was furiously entering figures, and the data kept scrolling up with each new entry. She was good. My confidence rose.

"We've got a problem," Aja said flatly.

So much for my confidence.

"I thought you said it would be easy to purge the bug from Lifelight?"

"It would be, if I could get to it," she answered. As she talked, she kept inputting data. "The problem isn't the Reality Bug, it's the origin code."

"You lost me," I said.

"The system is programmed with security codes that make it difficult to get in," Aja explained while she worked. "It's to keep unauthorised people from monkeying with the grid. I know most of the codes because I'm a senior phader, but . . . but . . ." She slammed her fist down in frustration.

"But what?"

"When the Reality Bug infected the grid, it went so deep that the only way to reach it is to get past the final code, the origin code. And I don't know it!"

"Well, somebody's gotta know it, right?" I asked, trying to be helpful.

Aja jumped out of the chair and paced. "Only one person knows that code."

"So let's go and get them!"

"That's not so easy. He hasn't been seen in three years."

"Three years? Who is it?"

"Dr Zetlin," answered Aja.

"That kid in the painting? How come he's the only one with the code?"

"Oh, I don't know," Aja answered sarcastically, sounding like her old self. "Maybe because he *invented* Lifelight!"

Good answer.

"Besides," Aja continued, "he's not a kid any more. He's got to be in his seventies by now."

"Fine. Let's find him, make him some warm milk, tell him the problem and get the freakin' code!"

"It's not that easy," Aja said.

"Why not?"

"Because Dr Zetlin is in Lifelight, Pendragon."

Oh.

That was definitely a problem. A really big problem.

Aja looked up at the screen and said, "Without that code I can't purge the Reality Bug. And if I can't purge the bug then we can't put Lifelight back online."

"And if we can't do that, almost everybody on Veelox is as good as dead," I concluded. I was getting the sick feeling that Saint Dane was right. The battle for Veelox was over and he had won.

"I don't suppose you've got a Plan B?" I asked.

I fully expected Aja to shout something like, "No, Pendragon! There is no Plan B, idiot!" Instead she looked down. The wheels were spinning in her head. That was good. She had a good head with good wheels.

"What are you thinking?" I asked.

"There is one possibility," she said reluctantly. "But it's too much to ask."

"Ask!" I shouted.

Aja sighed and said, "It's possible to jump into Lifelight and find Zetlin."

"But I thought the grid was in suspense?"

"Suspended," she corrected.

"Whatever."

"It is, but there's another way," Aja said.

She walked to the far side of the Alpha Core, where there was another door. She took out her green card and inserted it in a slot. Instantly the door slid open. I peered into the room beyond and was surprised to see a room similar to the jump cubicles in the pyramid. Only this one had three large silver discs on the wall.

"This is the original unit," she explained. "The alpha grid. It operates independently from the main grid. I could bring it back online by itself."

I gazed into the cubicle as the reality of what she was telling me slowly sank in. "Are you saying —"

"Yes. Dr Zetlin is in there."

Whoa. The father of Lifelight was lying only a few feet away. It felt like I was peering into a tomb. But it was no time to pay respects.

"So fire up the alpha grid and pull the old guy out of there!" I said.

"I can't," Aja said. "He doesn't want to come out."

"So what!"

"It's the same problem," Aja said, trying to be patient. "He programmed the jump so nobody could end it. He doesn't even have a phader or vedder assigned to him. Without the origin code, I can't end his jump." She glanced into the cubicle and added, "But I can put somebody else in."

"You're telling me we could enter his jump, the way you were in my jump?"

"Well . . . sort of."

"Tell me everything, Aja. C'mon!" I suddenly understood the term "like pulling teeth". Sheesh.

"Yes, it's possible to enter his jump. The trick then is to

find Zetlin and convince him to give up the code."

"Then let's do it!"

"We can't! I mean, I can't. I mean . . . I can't go with you."

"Why not?"

"Because somebody has to stay out here and phade the jump or you might not get back out again. You'd have to go alone, Pendragon. That's why I said it's too much to ask."

Gulp. A few minutes ago I thought Aja was going to sit down at that control console and make everything okey-dokey. Now I was faced with the possibility of going back into that crazy fantasy world.

"Let me ask you something," I said. "If Zetlin's jump is on a different circuit —"

"Grid."

"Yeah, grid, whatever, stop correcting me. Since it's different, did the Reality Bug infect it?"

"I can't be absolutely sure," she said slowly. "But I would have to say . . . yes. The overall operating software is the same, and that's what I designed the bug to attack."

"So let me understand," I said. "The only way we can get rid of the Reality Bug is for me to jump into Dr Zetlin's fantasy and get this code from him. But it might be a horror show if the bug is doing its thing?"

"Yes, that's about it."

Oh, man, no way I wanted to go. After what happened in my own fantasy with the quigs, the idea of jumping into somebody else's fantasy was truly horrible. Worse, I was going to have to do it alone.

"I don't want you to go, Pendragon," Aja said quietly. "It's too dangerous."

"Yeah, me neither. But what choice do I have?"

Aja shook her head. "What you said before makes sense.

We're stronger together. It's way too risky for you to jump in by yourself. I don't know what to do."

The reality of the situation was beginning to sink in. I was going to have to jump by myself.

That's when an idea hit me.

"There might be another way," I said. "What if I got somebody else to jump with me?"

"Who?" Aja asked quickly. "You can't ask one of those technicians out there. If they find out what's really going on, there'll be a riot."

"I'm not talking about one of them," I said. "I'm talking about another Traveller. Somebody who knows the bigger picture and how important this is. If anybody is going to jump with me, it has to be another Traveller."

Aja let the idea sink in, then nodded. "Sure. I could send you both in. Do you have somebody in mind?"

"Absolutely," I answered. "And I can't think of anybody I'd trust more to get us out of a gnarly situation . . . alive."

VEELOX

"If I thought there were a better way of doing this, I swear I wouldn't be here asking you to come along," I said.

This was tough. I was asking a friend and fellow Traveller to go on a dangerous mission. In some ways it was more dangerous than anything we had faced so far, because we were dealing with the unknown. When we were in my own jump, the Reality Bug searched my brain for things I was afraid of and came up with those vicious quigs. As scary as that was, at least I knew all about the quigs and could figure out a way to beat them. But once we were in Dr Zetlin's jump, the dangers would be from *his* memory, and we wouldn't have a clue as to how to battle the nastiness that might come flying out of his genius brain.

"I could go myself," I said. "I will if I have to, but I think we have a better chance of pulling this off together."

I could have asked any of the Travellers to help me, except for Gunny because I still wasn't sure what happened to him on Eelong. But of all the Travellers, there was one I felt had a superior chance of helping me battle whatever boogeymen we found on the jump into Dr Zetlin's fantasy world.

That was Loor.

"You have explained this Lifelight very well, Pendragon," she said. "Yet, it is hard for me to believe it is possible."

"Weren't you the one who told me that after all we've seen, we shouldn't think *anything* is impossible?"

Loor looked right into my eyes and gave a little smile. That didn't happen often. Loor wasn't the smiley type. But when she did, it made my heart melt. It wasn't until I saw her again, here on her home territory of Zadaa, that I realised how much I had missed her.

Aja had taken me back to the gate, where I flumed to Zadaa. I have to admit, part of me wanted to flume to Eelong to find Gunny, but I needed to find Loor. I could only hope that Gunny was okay.

I had been to Zadaa once before, with Spader, so I knew the way to Loor's home. I arrived at the gate on Zadaa and quickly changed into the white robe that was waiting for me. (Boxers stayed on, as usual.) I then made my way quickly through the labyrinth of underground tunnels that brought me out to the wide, subterranean river flowing under the city of Xhaxhu. Behind the waterfall that fed the river was a portal that I knew would lead me to the ramp up to the city. Everything was pretty much the same as I remembered it, except for a few disturbing changes.

Through the portal behind the waterfall was the giant gizmatron that controlled the flow of the underground rivers of Zadaa. It was a coolio-looking device with dozens of different-size pipes that ran floor to ceiling. In front of the pipes was a control platform with a series of levers and dials and switches they used to control the river water. Spader and I had watched a guy work this bad boy when we were there before. Well, when I entered the chamber this time, there was a guy working the controls again, but with one big difference.

"Stop right there!" a gruff voice shouted at me. "Where are you going?"

It was a big, beefy guard with a long, nasty-looking club that would do some serious damage if it made contact with any part of my body. In fact, three of these bad boys stood there, guarding the water controller. The people who lived underground were called Rokador. Loor told me that there was some tension between the Rokador tribe and the people who lived on the surface, the Batu. Whatever the tension was between these tribes, it must have got worse since I had been here. Before, the Rokador didn't need guards.

"I'm, uh, I'm going up to the city to, uh, get some supplies," I said, trying to sound like I wasn't making this up as I went along. Which I was. The Rokador were light skinned, like me, so they assumed I was one of them. Good thing. I didn't want to be a piñata.

"Do you want an escort?" the guard asked. That wasn't a bad idea. If I was safe down here with the Rokador, then it followed I might be in danger up with the Batu. But I had no idea how I would explain that I was going to visit Loor, who was a Batu.

"Thanks, but no," I said.

"Be careful," the guard grumbled. "Return before sunset."

Now I was getting nervous. If things had gone south here on Zadaa, then it was going to be tricky finding Loor without getting hammered by some Batu guy who had an ick against the Rokador. The only thing I could do was try to be invisible. I hurried up the winding ramp that brought me into a building on the surface, and for the second time I saw the beautiful city of Xhaxhu.

If you remember, guys, I told you that it looked like ancient Egypt, with tall sandstone buildings. The streets were paved with stone and lined with palm trees. There were statues of all sizes, some towering as high as the buildings. It was a beautiful oasis in the middle of a vast, dry desert. Its water source was the river that ran below ground. Without that water, Xhaxhu would dry up and blow away like a forgotten sand castle. Knowing that, I saw something that made me nervous.

Running beside many of the streets were troughs that carried water throughout the city. At nearly every intersection was a fancy fountain that sprayed arcs of water in complex patterns. At least that's what I saw last time I was here. This time the troughs were nearly dry. Only a small trickle of water ran through them. The fountains weren't spraying water either. This was a really bad sign. If there was a problem with the water, the city was in trouble.

But that was something to worry about another day. Right now, I had to find Loor. It was a scary trip. The streets were alive with people, most of them Batu. As I described before, the Batu were dark-skinned warriors. They wore light, leather clothing that showed off their lean, muscular bodies. With my light skin and white robe, I stood out like a flashlight in the forest. I was getting some seriously bad vibes from these people. If looks could kill, I wouldn't have lasted two minutes. Seriously. I could feel pure hatred coming from them as soon as they laid eyes on me. It wasn't just the tough-looking dudes, either. The women were giving me the evil eye too. So were their kids. Heck, if a Batu dog walked by he probably would have peed on me. I put my head down and kept moving, hoping to make it to Loor's home in one piece.

Loor lived in a large, one-storey building that was reserved for the military. She was a warrior in training, and was given a small apartment. I found it pretty easily, and was within a few yards of her place when my luck ran out.

Without warning, somebody grabbed the back of my robe and lifted me up like a doll. The guy spun me around and I came face-to-face with a giant Batu warrior. No, make that four giant Batu warriors. They all stared at me and none of them looked happy to see me.

"You have lost your way, little Rokador sheep," the guy snarled. "Are you looking to take back more of your precious water?"

"Uh, no, actually," I said, trying to be friendly, "I'm looking for —"

"Water!" he shouted. "Water is all you know, water is what you will have!"

The other Batu warriors cheered, egging him on.

"But my friend lives right —"

"Here is your precious water!" he shouted.

The Batu warrior dragged me over to a wall near the front of the building. I tried to break away, but the guy was too strong. It wouldn't have mattered anyway. If I broke loose, there were three other goons there to grab me. Behind the wall was the community bathroom. On one side of the enclosure was a trough of fresh running water for drinking and washing. On the other were holes in the ground with water running underneath for, yeah, you guessed it, going to the bathroom. It was basically an outhouse. Unfortunately we didn't stop at the fresh-water trough.

The warrior stopped at one of the open sewer holes, then stuck his nose in my face. "You love water so much," he seethed, "then have it."

The guy lifted me up and turned me upside down. The other warriors laughed and cheered.

"Hey, stop!" I yelled. "You're making a mistake."

I know, pretty lame, but I didn't know what else to say. The guy lowered me towards the open latrine hole. I was going into the sewer headfirst! I was in such a panic, I didn't even think to try and use my powers of Traveller persuasion on him. All I could think about was landing in smelly sludge. My head got closer to the hole. I did a quick calculation and unfortunately figured that it was plenty big enough for me to fit through. This was going to be gruesome. My head was only a few inches away from crossing the portal into the land of stench and disgust, when someone shouted out, "Put him down!"

I really, *really* hoped they were talking about me. Sure enough, the warrior flipped me over. I landed on my feet and looked up to see . . .

Loor.

I could have kissed her, but that would have been a major-bad move.

"I know this one," Loor said. "He gives me information on the Rokador. He must not be harmed."

The warriors grumbled in disappointment and shuffled off. Loor had spoiled their fun. Gee, too bad. Bullies. I hate bullies.

"Come with me, Rokador!" she barked at me. She then walked away quickly. I was all too happy to follow. Seconds later we were in her apartment.

"Nice friends you have," I said.

"They do not like the Rokador," Loor said with no emotion.

"Yeah, I got that. Thanks for saving me."

"No need to thank me. If they had finished what they started, I would have had to smell your stench in my home."

The two of us looked at each other, then I burst out laughing. Loor relaxed too.

"Man, I'm glad to see you, Loor," I said. I went over and hugged her. She didn't hug back. It wasn't that she didn't like me, it's just that Loor never showed affection. So as I hugged her, she only gave me a couple of friendly pats on the back. What can I say? That's Loor.

She started a fire and we settled into her woven chairs. I first told her all that had happened on First Earth and the *Hindenburg* disaster story. I left out the part about my chickening out at the last second. I didn't want Loor to know that.

Loor told me how tension between the Batu and the Rokador was worse than ever. She feared there would be a war. The Batu had strength, but the Rokador controlled the water. In her heart she knew this would be the turning point of Zadaa, but had no idea what to do about it.

I then told her about Veelox and Lifelight and the Reality Bug. Being a warrior from a territory that had no technology, it was hard for Loor to imagine the concept of a wristwatch, let alone something as amazing as Lifelight. Still, she listened and did her best to understand.

As I sat in that room with the dirt floor and the fire crackling in the fireplace, I couldn't take my eyes off her. The fire gave her dark skin a warm glow that looked as if she had stepped out of a painting. An amazing painting. And she's cut like an athlete. The leather outfit she wore showed off the long, strong muscles of her shoulders and arms. I've seen her battle guys nearly twice her size and kick butt. But more important than the physical stuff was that she had an incredibly clear way of seeing things. She didn't overthink things the way I sometimes do. Okay, the way I *always* do. With Loor there are only two ways: the right way and the wrong way. She wouldn't think twice about cutting down an enemy, or risking herself to save a friend.

That's why I was here. I needed Loor to cut down some enemies and risk herself for a friend. Me.

"I want to help, Pendragon," she said. "But I worry about what will happen here on Zadaa. I do not want to be somewhere else when trouble finally arrives."

"I get that," I said. "And when the time comes, I want to be here to help you. But the flumes will always put us where we need to be, *when* we need to be there. I don't understand it, but it's true. When the time comes that you're needed on Zadaa, you'll be here."

"And what if this Lifelight is as dangerous as you say, and we do not survive?"

Ooh. Good question.

"I don't know," was my only answer. "But I do know that millions of people are in trouble right now. If they die, Veelox will die along with them and Saint Dane will have his first victory. I can't let that happen."

Loor stoked the embers of the fire. In this light she looked like her mother, Osa, the woman who died saving my life. Loor was a little older than when we had our adventure on Denduron. So was I. Hard to believe this was possible, but she was even more beautiful. I was suddenly hit with the realisation that I didn't want anything to happen to her. Not here, not on Veelox, and certainly not in the fantasy world of some wacky old scientist.

I was about to get up and walk out when she turned to me and said, "I want to return as soon as possible."

"No," I said quickly, and I stood up. "This was a bad idea. You don't need to be watching my back. Your place is here. I'm sorry. It was wrong of me to ask. I'm gonna go back and —"

"Pendragon!" she said firmly. "I am a Traveller. It is what we are meant to do."

She stood up and grabbed a nasty-looking sword that was leaning against the fireplace. She twirled it expertly, the sharp blade flashing with light from the fire. "What weapons will I use on Veelox?"

"We won't know until we jump into Lifelight."

Loor gave the sword one last swing, then put it back down. I knew she wanted to take it with her, but that was against the rules.

"What is it that Spader says?" she asked.

"Hobey-ho?" I answered with a smile.

"Yes. Hobey-ho, Pendragon. We belong on Veelox."

We were a team again.

We made it through the streets of Xhaxhu with no problem. Nobody was going to mess with me since I was with a Batu warrior. But we then had to go into the underground. Rokador territory.

"We have to get by some Rokador thugs," I warned. "They're guarding this machine that controls the water."

"Stay behind me," was all that Loor said. She wasn't worried.

We hurried down the ramp into the bowels of the underground. I thought that if we moved fast enough, nobody would notice us.

I was wrong.

Before I could stop her, Loor walked boldly into the room with the guards. It was a good move because she took them by surprise. I think the last thing they expected to see was a Batu warrior babe strolling into their secret subterranean chamber.

Before they had a chance to recover, Loor pounced. She took care of the first guy with a kick to the chest; the second guy fell to a leg sweep followed by a roundhouse kick that caught him on the side of the head; the final guard got the worst of it. He charged Loor from behind and grabbed her in a bear hug. Loor pumped her legs and drove the guy backwards, through the room and out of the portal. She finished him off by flipping him over her back into the waterfall, sending him plummeting into the fast-moving river.

I looked up at the Rokador guy who was operating the water controls. He didn't stop working, but gave me a nervous glance.

"You should see her when she's *mad*!" I said to the scared guy.

I thought the poor dude was going to faint. I hurried out of the room, jumping over the bodies of the groaning guards, and joined Loor on the ledge behind the waterfall.

"Finished playing?" I asked.

She gave me a sly wink and we were off. A few minutes later we made it to the gate and hit the flume.

When we arrived on Veelox, I was glad to see that there were two sets of green coveralls waiting for us. Evangeline had been here. I made a mental note to ask her how the acolytes knew when to bring stuff to the flumes. We changed quickly and made our way along the derelict subway tracks and up the ladder to the manhole that brought us out on to the quiet street in Rubic City.

I was happy to see that Aja was waiting for us. She was at the wheel of a new vehicle. This one still used pedal power, but it had four seats rather than two.

"I didn't think it would take so long," was the first thing Aja said.

"Good to see you too, Aja," I shot back. "This is Loor. Loor, Aja."

Aja gave Loor an up and down once-over. She then said, "Is Loor a man's name or a woman's name?"

Ouch.

Loor answered, "It is the name of a legendary hero on Zadaa. A woman."

"Really?" Aja said. "What did she do that was so heroic?"

"She killed her enemies and ate them."

Aja's eyes opened in shock. She turned forward and clutched the wheel of the vehicle nervously. Loor looked at me and winked. She was kidding. Great. That's all I needed.

"Let's get to the pyramid," I said, and hopped in next to Aja. Loor climbed in the back and we pedalled our way back to Lifelight.

On the way I filled Loor in on everything about Lifelight that I hadn't explained before. I wanted her as prepared as possible, because there were bound to be plenty of surprises along the way. I kept expecting Aja to correct my descriptions, but I think she was too scared to speak. Just as well.

After a few minutes of my lecture, Loor put her hand up to stop me.

"Am I going too fast?" I asked.

"You must understand, Pendragon," Loor said. "The things you describe are beyond my imagination. You talk of computers and codes like they are as normal as air and water."

Aja scoffed and rolled her eyes. I wanted to smack her.

"If Aja is as smart as you say she is, then I trust she will take care of us and get us to where we should be. I do not need to know all the details. My trust is with Aja."

I looked to Aja for her reaction. Aja looked to me and I saw the surprise on her face. She even let out a little smile.

"Thank you, Loor," Aja said. I think she meant it too.

"For what?" Loor asked.

"For trusting me . . . and for coming. We really need you."

We had reached an understanding. And we were under way.

This is where I'm going to end the journal, guys. While Aja prepped Lifelight for our dual jump into Zetlin's fantasy, I took the time to finish this. I'll send it to you with a reminder that you might be contacted by somebody named Evangeline. If you're serious about wanting to be acolytes, you're going to get the chance.

I have no idea what to expect when Loor and I make this trip back into Lifelight. Finding Dr Zetlin will probably be the easy part. Finding his deepest fears is what I'm worried about. But having Loor with me gives me all sorts of confidence. It's great that we're together again.

Be safe and think about me every once in a while. I'll catch you on the other side.

END OF JOURNAL #14

☉ SECOND EARTH ☉

Bobby's image vanished.

Courtney and Mark kept staring at the empty space where the hologram used to be. Neither were sure of what to say or do next.

Then Dorney started to laugh. It started out as a chuckle, grew into a belly laugh, and finally changed into a wheezing, uncontrolled, coughing fit. Courtney jumped up and got a glass of water. Dorney took it gratefully and gulped it down.

"You all right?" Courtney asked as she sat back down next to Mark.

Dorney cleared his throat, took a deep breath. He was fine.

"What's so funny?" Mark asked.

"Just like his uncle, that one," Dorney said with a smile. "Always jumping out of one frying pan into another one that's even hotter."

Mark glanced at the metal boxes that held Press's journals. "Can we read some?" he asked.

The smile fell from Dorney's face. He glanced over at the journals, then back to Mark and Courtney. "Depends."

"On what?" asked Courtney.

"On whether or not I like what you have to tell me."

"We're here for Bobby," Mark exclaimed. "You heard what Bobby said to Evangeline."

"Evangeline?" he scoffed. "If the devil himself told that lady he was misunderstood, she'd invite him in for tea."

"You know her?" Courtney asked in shock.

"How do you think I knew to send you my address?"

"But she's from –"

"Veelox, yeah. So what?"

"But, you said you weren't a Traveller," Mark said.

"I'm not! Are you thick or something?"

Courtney and Mark were dumbfounded.

"I'm s-sorry if we're being dense," Mark said. "But I thought only Travellers could fly through the flumes. If you're not a Traveller, how could you know somebody from another territory?"

Dorney stared at them for a moment, as if debating about whether or not to answer. Finally he held up his hand – the hand with his Traveller ring.

"It's the rings," he said. "It's all about the rings."

Mark and Courtney sat there patiently, waiting for Dorney to explain. But he didn't. Instead he pushed himself out of the easy chair with a grunt and began moving the metal boxes with Press's journals in them back into the cabinet.

"I was a practical guy," Dorney finally said, sounding serious. "I always thought that everything had its place. B always came after A. Two always followed one. But then Press Tilton came into my life. He opened my eyes, so to speak, and I began to realise there was something else going on. Something bigger than me and my safe little life. I don't mind telling you, it scared me. All this business about fluming and territories that exist in different times – it's enough to make a fella want to lock his door and never poke his nose out again."

Mark and Courtney nodded. They knew how he felt.

"But what scares me even more," Dorney continued, "is that somebody out there is causing problems. Knowing Saint Dane is trying to make it all fall down has kept me from getting a good night's sleep in nearly ten years. Only thing that gives me a little piece of mind is knowing the Travellers are trying to stop him. That's why I'm an acolyte. I do what I can to help the good guys."

Dorney put the last of the metal boxes into the cabinet, then closed and locked it.

"Trouble is, I'm getting too old for this. Now that Press is gone, I'm not so sure I've got the energy. That brings me to you two. Pendragon seems to trust you. Question is, should I?"

"We told you!" Courtney shouted defensively. "Bobby is our friend and —"

Mark put a hand on her arm to quiet her down.

"You're right," Mark said calmly. "You don't know us. All we can say is that we're just as freaked out about Saint Dane as you are. Besides that, you've gotta trust that Bobby knows what he's talking about."

Dorney looked between the two of them. Finally he shrugged and said, "Don't matter anyway. It ain't my choice."

"What does that mean?" asked Courtney. "Whose choice is it?"

Dorney shuffled towards the front door. "Go home," he said.

Both Mark and Courtney jumped up in surprise.

"Mr D-Dorney," Mark stuttered, "we came here because we wanted to learn about being acolytes. You can't throw us out."

Dorney opened the door and stood to the side. "I can do whatever I please," he said. "Truth is, you two ain't ready."

"But w-we are!" Mark protested.

"Not from what I'm hearing," Dorney countered. "When the

time is right, come on back. I'll help you then, not before."

Mark and Courtney looked at each other. They knew it was no use to argue. So Mark grabbed the silver hologram projector from the table and jammed it into his pack.

"How are we going to know when the time is right?" Courtney asked.

"Believe me." Dorney chuckled. "You'll know." He opened the door further, expecting them to leave.

"We'll be back," Mark said as they backed out the door. "Count on it."

"I hope so," Dorney said seriously. "I truly do."

He shut the door, leaving Mark and Courtney in an empty corridor.

"Well, that sucked," Courtney said. "We came all the way here and all he can say is we're not ready?"

Mark walked towards the lift. Courtney hurried after him.

"We're not giving up so easily," she asked. "Are we?"

"We're not giving up at all," Mark said. "I think Dorney believes we can be acolytes, but the time isn't right."

"I think he's a crazy old coot who likes pulling our chain," Courtney said.

"Yeah, that too," Mark said. "But I'll bet you anything we'll be back here."

The two rode the lift down and left the building. All the way back to Stony Brook, Mark and Courtney tried to analyse what Bobby had told them about Lifelight and the Reality Bug. Mark was fascinated with the idea of a computer that could read your thoughts and make them real. Courtney was too, but was more interested in talking about Loor. She thought Bobby made a bad choice. She thought he should have got Spader. Mark pointed out that Bobby wasn't a hundred percent sure he could rely on Spader. Courtney didn't care. She felt Spader would have been the better choice.

Mark had a pretty good idea of what Courtney was *really* thinking. She was jealous. From what Bobby said in his last journal, it was obvious he had feelings for Loor. But Mark decided not to point that out. He didn't want to risk a punch in the head.

When the train brought them home, the two stood on the empty station platform at the bottom of Stony Brook Avenue.

"Now what?" Courtney asked.

"I don't know," Mark answered. Then added, "Does this mean you officially want to be an acolyte with me?"

Courtney had to think about that for a second. "It means I still want to find out what it means," she said. "I can't promise any more than that."

"Good enough," Mark said. "Maybe Bobby's next journal will tell us more."

Courtney nodded. "You'll tell me when —"

"Soon as it comes in," Mark assured her.

With a quick smile Courtney turned and headed for home. Mark stood there for a moment, twisting the ring on his finger. When Bobby was in the middle of an adventure the journals came pretty close together. Mark expected the next delivery to come through his ring at any moment.

It didn't.

Mark had to get his mind off Bobby and back into his own life. He busied himself at school and went to his first meeting of Sci-Clops. It was better than he could have imagined. Mr Pike, or David as he insisted on being called, introduced him to the other members, all of whom were older than Mark. They were all working on different projects, like mixing unique metals to create a new lightweight alloy, and making a computer processor that responded to eye movement. It was heady stuff for Mark and he feared he was out of his league. But he quickly discovered they all spoke the same language. He had found a home.

Courtney focused on classes and soccer. She continued to practice with the JV team and did pretty well, but she always had one eye on the varsity squad that practised on the other side of the field. More than anything she wanted to prove herself worthy of being back there.

Several days passed with no word from Bobby. Mark started to fear that something horrible had happened when he and Loor jumped back into Lifelight. But he forced himself not to worry. He had to keep reminding himself that time between the territories wasn't relative. Still, as days passed, Mark found himself thinking more and more about the trouble on Veelox.

Then, towards the end of the week, something finally happened.

There was no Sci-Clops meeting that afternoon, so Mark caught the early bus home after school. The bus stopped a few blocks from Mark's house and he always walked the direct route home. But today he took another route. He wasn't sure why; he just felt like walking. So he took the long way home.

Mark was pretty familiar with every other house in the neighbourhood. Though a few were modern, most dated back a long time, some over a hundred years. All the yards were big, with huge leafy trees that shaded the grass. Autumn was coming on fast now and many of the trees had already traded their green leaves for brilliant colours of orange and yellow. It was Mark's favourite time of year. Chilly but not yet wintry. The wind was brisk, the sky was blue, and he even loved the smell of burning leaves. It was the perfect afternoon to walk a roundabout route home and try not to think about territories and Travellers.

His holiday didn't last very long.

As he walked along the cracked pavement, kicking leaves,

Mark's ring began to twitch. He stopped short. Naturally his first thought was: "Bobby's next journal!" But when he looked at his ring, he saw that the large grey stone in the centre wasn't making the change. It was the odd symbol that glowed brightly – the same symbol that foreshadowed the arrival of the note from Dorney. Maybe it was a message from the old man to say the time was right to learn about being an acolyte!

Mark ducked into the bushes near a tall cement wall. He didn't want anybody to see what was about to happen. He dropped his pack on the ground, then took the ring off and put it down next to the pack, waiting for it to start growing.

It didn't. The light continued to glow from the symbol, but the ring didn't change size. What was going on? Mark picked up the ring and put it back on his finger. The symbol glowed, but that was it. No change, no note, no nothing. Weird. With a shrug, Mark continued walking home. When he got to the next corner, he noticed that the glowing symbol had gone dark.

False alarm, he thought, and continued walking.

When he got halfway across the street, he realised he'd left his pack next to the cement wall. *Duh!* He did a quick about-face and jogged back to get it. But no sooner did he arrive at the pack than the ring twitched and the symbol began to glow again. Mark waited a few minutes to see if the ring would do anything more dramatic, but it didn't. He grabbed his pack, slung it over his shoulder, and hurried towards home. But when he reached the street, the symbol stopped glowing. Mark felt sure something was going on, but had no idea what it could be.

Then an idea struck him. He turned and slowly walked back towards the cement wall. Sure enough, as soon as he got close, the symbol grew bright again. Uh-oh. This was no false alarm. Something was happening, and it had to do with where he was.

Mark looked up at the cement wall to see where he was, and his heart sank.

"Oh great," he muttered.

He was standing in front of the Sherwood house. Everybody knew it. It was the biggest property in the neighbourhood. The house was built in the early 1900s by some rich guy who'd made his fortune raising chickens and selling eggs, of all things. At one time there was a poultry farm on the property, but that was long gone. The house was still there, though. It was surrounded by the high cement wall that Mark was standing in front of now. It was actually more of a mansion than a house. The place was huge.

The thing was, nobody had lived there for years. Mark's mum told him that once old man Sherwood died, none of his kids wanted to run a chicken farm. But they couldn't agree on what to do with the property. So there it sat, a giant piece of land with a big old mansion on it, going to waste, falling apart.

Of course, all the kids in the neighbourhood made up ghost stories about seeing shadows walking past windows and hearing strange sounds on Hallowe'en. Bobby once made up a story about how the ghosts were actually chicken spirits looking for revenge. That was Mark's favourite. But he didn't believe in ghosts and didn't think for a minute that the place was really haunted. Still, he never went near the place by himself.

Until today.

The glowing symbol on his ring was telling him something, and he had the sick feeling that whatever it was, it was inside the Sherwood house. *Gulp.* Mark had a quick thought of putting this off until he could come back with Courtney, but his curiosity was stronger than his fear.

Halfway down the street was a big old set of black iron gates, but a heavy steel chain and padlock told him this wouldn't be the way in. He only had one choice. He had to go over the wall. So he walked alongside the high wall until he found a tree that was close enough to climb up and get over the top. As he stood looking up, he wasn't worried about ghosts or banshees or dead chickens running around with their heads chopped off. That was kid stuff. He was more worried about getting caught trespassing. The idea of calling his parents from gaol was not a good one. Still, the insistent glowing of the symbol on his ring told him he had to keep going.

He pushed his hair out of his eyes and dug his trainers into the tree. Moments later he was up and over the wall, landing in tall grass. So far so good. He looked at his ring to see the small symbol was glowing brighter. He was definitely on the right track.

He looked up at the house and could see why kids thought it was haunted. The place was ancient. The wind kicked up and the autumn trees swayed back and forth, slashing against its walls. The yard was a mess too. A caretaker could be seen every month or so, cleaning up dead branches and making simple repairs, but that wasn't enough to make the place look lived in. No, this was a big, empty, lonely old haunted-looking house.

And Mark was on his way in.

The ground floor was surrounded by a wide porch. He imagined people sitting there in rocking chairs on a hot summer night, drinking iced tea and swapping chicken stories. But they were long gone. The only thing on the porch now was dead leaves. Mark walked up the five stone steps that led to the porch.

He thought he saw something move past a window inside the house. It was fast, and he wasn't completely sure he really saw it, but the hair went up on his arms just the same. He stopped at the top of the stairs, looking into the dark windows for any sign of movement. There was none.

He started walking towards the front door . . . and saw something again. It was a quick shadow moving past the window. For a second he actually thought it was a ghost. But there were no such things as ghosts. Then again, he never thought there were such things as Travellers, either. He looked around and decided the ghost was nothing more than the reflection of a tree branch waving in the wind. At least, that's what he told himself.

Mark walked cautiously up to the front door and tried the knob. It was locked.

"Great," he said to himself. "Now what?"

That's when he heard something inside the house. It was fleeting, but it sounded like something had run past, just inside the door.

"Heeeere, chickie, chickie, chickie!" Mark croaked nervously, though the idea of there still being chickens around was absurd. He looked at his ring. The symbol was glowing with a fierce intensity. He needed to know why.

He moved over to the big window next to the door and put his nose right against the glass to try and block as much of the outside light as possible. That helped a little, and he got a better view of the inside of the Sherwood house.

The place was empty. The only illumination inside came from windows farther back in the house, and they didn't do much to light the place up. Very creepy. There was no furniture, or pictures, or any sign of life –"

GRRRRRR!

A hideous, black animal face leaped out of the shadows inside. It stared Mark square in the eyes. Drool dripped from its white fangs as it snarled viciously, trying to bite through the glass and get a chunk of Mark-meat.

Mark yelped in surprise and fell backwards, landing on his butt. He stared up at the window to see two more animals join the first. They were awful-looking black creatures that could have been dogs, but no dog Mark had ever seen looked as evil as these beasts. They were focused on him, with only a thin pane of glass holding them back.

Mark pushed himself along the floor of the porch to get away. The beasts barked and snarled. Mark's mind was reeling. What were dogs doing in there? Were they watchdogs? They definitely weren't ordinary dogs. They were vicious, uncontrollable demons, and they were out for blood. They were . . .

It suddenly hit him. It was something from Bobby's very first journal. What gave it away were the horrible, yellow eyes. There was no mistake.

"Quigs," Mark whispered to himself.

⚬ SECOND EARTH ⚬
(CONTINUED)

Smash!

The beasts threw themselves against the glass, desperate to attack Mark.

Mark knew the glass would be no match for these demons. He had to get out of there, fast. He jumped up and ran. He suddenly realised he had left his backpack on the porch, but the pounding on the window meant he wasn't going back for it. No way. Mark sprinted across the overgrown yard, heading for the wall and safety.

He now saw that he was in deep trouble. When he first arrived, he had been so worried about getting caught trespassing that he hadn't taken the time to figure out a way to climb back over the wall. Now he had another worry. He was worried about being trapped and eaten.

Crash!

The window shattered. The quigs were coming. Mark could hear them yelp and snarl as they tumbled over one another to get through the broken window.

He was still twenty yards from the nine-foot wall. He desperately scanned left and right, looking for a way to scale it. Without some kind of help, Mark didn't think he could make it over. He dared not look back, because he knew what he'd see. Every second counted. If the quigs got to him before he got to the wall, there wouldn't be enough of him left for anyone to find.

Mark saw nothing to help him climb.

The snarling quigs drew closer. In seconds they'd be on him. But Mark was focused. He had no plan, but had to think of one fast or in seconds he'd be dog food. He was almost at the wall, but didn't slow down. He thought to himself, "I'm gonna run right up the side!"

He hit the wall running and dug his trainer into the crumbling cement. His toe caught. He launched off it and grabbed the top of the wall. Normally Mark couldn't even vault over the pommel horse in gym. But normally Mark wasn't jet powered by surging adrenalin. He heaved himself up by his arms, threw both his legs to one side, and flung his body up and over.

No sooner did he clear the top than all three quigs hit the other side of the wall, yelping and crying for having missed their prey. Mark sailed down and hit the ground, rolling away from the wall, lucky not to have broken an ankle. He jumped up and did a quick check to make sure all body parts were intact. They were. He stood there for a second, trying to catch his breath. He listened as the quigs snarled from the other side in frustration.

Mark smiled. He had made it. It was probably the most exciting moment of his life. He even dared to think that this adventure rivalled some of the stories that Bobby had told. He had met a pack of hungry quigs and lived to tell the story.

But his joy didn't last long. The glowing ring on his finger took it away. The truth was, the adventure wasn't over. Whatever was in that house, whatever was making his ring glow, he was going to have to come back and find it. Running away wasn't going to cut it. He was going to have to get past those quigs.

But next time, he was bringing Courtney.

Courtney knew this was her golden opportunity.

There was going to be a practise scrimmage between the varsity and the JV soccer teams. She had been practising hard with the JV, swallowing her pride and improving her skills, waiting for the chance to prove herself worthy of being back on the varsity. This was her chance. She was going toe-to-toe with the very girls who had tarnished the golden reputation of the unbeatable Courtney Chetwynde. Revenge was not too strong a word to describe what was on Courtney's mind when she stepped on to that field. Her game face was on; her emotions were in check; she was ready.

So was the varsity. It seemed as if its entire game plan was about stopping Courtney. She was double-teamed all day and pretty much taken out of the action. Making things worse, with only a few minutes left to play, the JV team was losing 5-3. But truth be told, Courtney didn't care if they won or lost. All she wanted was to prove that she could compete. That wasn't happening.

Finally, with only seconds on the clock, she got her chance. She was playing forward and the ball was passed to her. She was being double-teamed and one of the defenders fell. Courtney used the player's body as interference and got past the second defender. It was now one-on-one between Courtney and the goalie. This was her moment . . . her chance to put a solid exclamation point on the game. She wanted this goal badly. She *needed* this goal. She dribbled the ball in quickly, deeked a kick that made the goalie move right, then drew back to fire the ball into the opposite corner of the net. It was perfect.

Almost.

Just as she was about to deliver the killer kick, the defender sprinted up from behind and took her out. It was a totally illegal move. The defender slid into Courtney's feet like a baseball runner sliding into second base. Instead of putting her foot into the ball, Courtney landed on her back. Hard. Whistles blew, a penalty was coming, but it didn't matter to Courtney. Her moment was lost.

She jumped to her feet, screaming, "What was *that*?"

Before the defender knew what was happening, Courtney gave her a wicked shove that sent her sprawling back on to the grass. She put her knee on the player's back so she couldn't get up. All her frustration finally came pouring out.

"I beat you and you know it!" she shouted.

A second later the other players descended and pulled the two girls apart. It was tough pulling Courtney away because she was so enraged. The defender got back to her feet and was ready to take Courtney on.

"Come on!" she taunted Courtney.

Courtney tried to lunge at the girl, but the other players held her back. Finally Coach Horkey ran in between the two girls and restored order.

"Enough!" she shouted. "Laura," she said to the defender. "Inside. All of you, locker room."

The fight was over. So was the scrimmage. The girls walked off, grumbling.

"Courtney," Coach Horkey said firmly. "Stay here."

As Laura, the defender, walked off, she looked over her shoulder and snarled, "Loser."

"Enough!" shouted Coach Horkey. Laura put her head down and kept walking. Courtney didn't budge. She was breathing hard, still fired up from the fight.

"She deserved it, Coach," Courtney pointed out. "It was a total cheap shot."

"It wasn't," Horkey countered. "She had a point to give and made the aggressive play."

"But don't you see? All they care about is shutting me down! It's been that way since day one!"

"I'll tell you what I see," Horkey said. "I see a girl who is faced with a challenge for the first time in her life. A *true* challenge. And she is losing. Courtney, you are a talented athlete. But it takes more than skill to be a winner. You know how to handle success, but not failure. Until you can do that, you won't help this team, or any other."

Courtney didn't say anything. As much as she hated to admit it, Horkey's words rang true.

"I'm suspending you for two weeks," Horkey added.

"What!"

"Players on my team don't fight. Especially with each other. Think about that and come back in two weeks." Horkey jogged off the field.

Courtney was left stunned. Not only was she demoted from varsity to JV, now she was kicked off JV! She stood in the middle of the field, covered with dirt, unable to accept this impossible turn of events. How could this have happened? How could she have fallen so far? In her heart she still believed she was as much of a competitor as ever, but reality was telling her otherwise.

Courtney walked off the field, but didn't go into the locker room. She didn't want to face the other girls. She knew the *old* Courtney would have walked right into that locker room and taken the heat. But then again, she'd never had to take any heat before. Not like this. Courtney began to wonder if there was ever such a thing as the old Courtney. Maybe this is who she always was . . . a gutless coward.

She walked past the locker room and made the commitment

to walk all the way home. It was going to be a long walk. But she wasn't about to take the late bus, either. All she wanted to do was crawl into bed. Since it was Friday, she wouldn't have to worry about facing anybody for a couple of days.

"Courtney!" a familiar voice shouted.

Courtney had rounded the school and was heading for the street when Mark came riding up on his bike. He was out of breath and excited.

"You're not going to believe it!" he exclaimed. "I was – " Mark focused on the fact that Courtney was still in her soccer uniform, totally dirty, still wearing her football boots, and walking away from school. "What's going on?"

"Don't ask," was all Courtney could get out. Mark got off his bike and walked alongside her.

"You're walking home?" he asked, confused.

"I'm really hurting, Mark," she said. "Can we talk about it some other time?"

"Yeah, sure." They walked in silence. Mark was dying to tell Courtney what had happened at the Sherwood house, but wasn't sure if she was in the mood to talk about anything. Still, she had to know.

"Can we talk about something else?" he asked tentatively.

"Whatever."

"Something happened today," Mark said. "I . . . I'm not sure exactly what it means, but I'm guessing it has something to do with the acolyte thing."

Courtney stopped short. A second before, she looked like the walking dead. Now a spark had returned to her eyes. Mark thought that whatever had happened at soccer, it had beaten her up pretty badly. But the fire still burned inside her. He knew Courtney too well to think otherwise.

"Another journal?" she asked.

"No," Mark answered. "Let's go for a ride."

Mark tried to ride Courtney on the handlebars of his bike. It didn't work. Courtney was too tall and Mark was too . . . Mark. So they switched places and Courtney gave Mark the ride. Along the way Mark told her everything that had happened at the Sherwood house. Courtney didn't ask any questions. She just listened. By the time Mark had finished the story, they found themselves parked right back where the mystery began. They were in front of the locked iron gates of the spooky old house.

Mark held up his ring. The symbol was glowing again.

"What do you think?" Mark asked.

"I think we've got to find out what's inside that house," Courtney answered.

"Easier said than done," Mark replied. "You didn't see those dogs."

Courtney looked up at the sky and said, "It's gonna be dark soon. I say we come back tomorrow, with some help."

Courtney's idea of help was an obvious one. They waited until the next morning, then Mark came over to Courtney's house and they put a call in to their friend on the Stony Brook police force, Captain Hirsch.

They had met Captain Hirsch when Bobby and his family first disappeared. Since then Hirsch had been working on the missing persons case. Of course, Mark and Courtney knew the truth about what had happened to Bobby, but decided not to tell, for fear of interfering with Bobby's mission as a Traveller. Still, they kept in touch with Hirsch. He was a good guy. Now, they hoped, he was going to help them get one step closer to unravelling the mystery of the acolytes.

Mark told Captain Hirsch about there being strange dogs running around the Sherwood property. He really built it up, saying how the dogs were vicious and wild. There was no way these dogs were somebody's pets. Of course, Mark left out the part about having been trespassing on the property. He also didn't mention that the dogs might be evil quig beasts who were guarding a secret inside the house. That wouldn't have been cool.

Half an hour later Mark and Courtney met two uniformed police officers outside the front gate to the Sherwood house.

"Hi, guys," one of them said. "Remember me? Officer Wilson?"

"Sure we do!" Courtney said.

Officer Wilson had once given the two kids a ride to the police station. He was a good guy, too.

"This is Officer Matt." Everybody shook hands. "Tell us what you saw."

Mark again explained how there were three dogs inside. Big, vicious, slobbering dogs with sharp fangs. Mark wasn't exaggerating. He wanted to make sure the cops knew exactly what they were getting themselves into.

Officer Wilson had a key to the lock on the front gate. They explained to Mark and Courtney that the Sherwood family had given it to the police in case of an emergency. This definitely qualified. While Wilson unlocked the gate, Officer Matt opened the trunk of their squad car and pulled out two pieces of equipment. One was a long metal rod with a loop of cable on the end. It was a snare that animal control officers use to capture dogs. The other thing Officer Matt pulled out was a tranquilliser rifle. Mark knew that if one of these dogs got the chance, it would tear a person apart. He wasn't so sure that a tranquilliser dart would do anything to stop it either. Still, it was better than nothing.

"Don't bother with the snare," Mark advised. "You aren't going to want to catch one of these monsters."

Officer Matt chuckled, but kept the snare.

"We'd like to come with you," Courtney said.

The two cops shared looks. They didn't like the idea of putting the kids in danger.

"C'mon!" Courtney cajoled. "We'll stay behind you. And you've got guns and snares and stuff, right?"

Wilson shrugged. "Okay. Just stay close."

They followed the two cops on to the property. Wilson held the snare, Matt kept the tranquilliser gun pointed at the ground, but ready.

Mark made sure to close the iron gates behind them. He also took off his ring and put it in his pocket. He didn't want the cops to ask him why he had a ring that was shooting off light.

Officer Wilson whistled. "Here, boy! C'mon!" He whistled again.

Nothing happened.

The four walked up to the porch. Mark kept glancing behind them, making sure that one of the black dogs wasn't sneaking up quietly.

"Uh-oh, what's this?" Officer Matt said. He reached down and picked up the shredded remains of Mark's backpack. Oops. Mark had totally forgotten.

"That's mine," he said. "I dropped it outside. They must have dragged it in here." It was a small lie, but Mark didn't want to admit he had been trespassing. "Look," he added to change the subject. "That's where they broke through the window."

Wilson pointed out the shards of glass on the porch. "It was broken from inside," he deduced. "They must have cut themselves up pretty good."

"How did you know they broke through the window?" Officer Matt asked Mark. "You can't see it from the gate."

Oops. Mark had to think fast. "I heard the glass break and then saw them running around."

Were the police going to buy this story? Of course they were.

Mark wasn't the type to trespass on private property . . . or so they thought. Mark held up the remains of his backpack. The quigs had really chewed it up. He'd lost two textbooks, a library book, a chocolate bar, and all his carrots. Mark knew that chocolate wasn't good for dogs and hoped they'd choked on it.

"Let's check inside," Officer Wilson suggested.

Wilson had a key for the front door as well. When they all stepped inside, both Mark and Courtney had the same thought: *haunted house.* The place was huge, with high ceilings and a curved staircase that led to the first floor.

"Here, boy!" Wilson called out again, and whistled.

Again, no response. Mark looked to Courtney and shrugged. He really wanted to look at his ring, but didn't risk taking it out of his pocket. The policemen then led the kids on a tour of the house, checking each and every room. They first checked the ground floor, walking through the grand entryway, through the living room, the huge dining room and into the big kitchen. Besides the broken window, there was no sign of any dog.

They went down to the basement. It was a vast space with a cement floor. There were a few wooden doors that were closed. The officers opened them all. One room had nothing but empty, wooden racks. The wine cellar. Another room had a long wooden table that was scarred and stained. The workshop. Another room was nothing more than a large, cool space with wispy remnants that looked like dead weeds hanging from the ceiling. Mark had heard of places like this. Root cellar is what his grandmother used to call it. It was a cool, dry place for storing onions and potatoes and the like. It looked to be dug out of the earth, with one wall being nothing more than a vast chunk of the rock that the house had been built on top of.

It was all very interesting, but there were no dogs.

The caravan then went up to the first floor. There was one long corridor with empty bedrooms off either side. Each of the rooms was connected by an inner door, so that you could choose to travel from one end of the house to the other through the corridor, or by going from room to room. Again, no dogs.

The next stop was the second floor. This was a smaller floor than the others. There were two bedrooms on one side, and a large attic on the other with a high, pointed ceiling where you could see the rafters of the house. It was empty. No dogs and no sign that dogs had ever been there. Once they stepped into the attic, the last room of the house, the police officers relaxed.

"Whatever you saw, Mark," Wilson said, "they're gone now."

"Are you sure? I mean, maybe we should check the yard."

Wilson shrugged. "Sure, why not?"

They all went downstairs and out on to the porch. The four of them moved cautiously around the whole property. Mark had no idea it was so big. They saw some old wooden buildings that probably had something to do with the chicken farm. There were a lot of trees and an empty swimming pool and even a small golf green. At one time this was a busy place. Now it was forgotten and sad. The policemen even inspected every inch of the wall along the ground to see if an animal might have tunnelled its way in or out. But there was no sign of anything like that.

"Any other ideas?" Officer Wilson asked. The cop respected Mark. If any other kid had given them this story, they probably wouldn't have believed a word.

"No," Mark answered. "Sorry."

Courtney glanced at Mark with a "You *sure* you saw dogs?" look. Mark could only shrug.

"Don't be sorry," Wilson said. "You did the right thing. Whatever was in here got away somehow, that's all."

They walked out through the front gate and Officer Matt locked it up. Officer Wilson returned the tranquilliser gun and the snare to the boot of the police cruiser.

"If you see anything else, be sure to call, okay?" Wilson said.

"Okay," Mark answered.

The two cops got back into their cruiser and sped off, leaving Mark and Courtney alone in front of the house.

"I'm not lying, Courtney," Mark said.

"I didn't think you were."

"So then what happened to the quigs?" he said as he reached into his pocket and pulled out his ring. The strange symbol was glowing brightly.

"I don't know," answered Courtney. "But we saw pretty much every inch of that place and there was nothing strange that would make that ring glow."

"Then we missed it," Mark announced.

The two looked at each other. Each knew what the other was thinking.

"We gotta go back in," Mark said with finality.

"Yeah, I know. Where's the tree we gotta climb over?" Courtney asked.

◉ SECOND EARTH ◉
(CONTINUED)

Mark led Courtney around to the side of the property and the tree that was their ladder. Courtney gave Mark a leg up, then Mark reached down and gave Courtney a helping hand. Seconds later the two of them jumped off the wall and landed back inside the property.

"Wait," Mark said. He looked back at the wall, scanning both left and right.

"What are you looking for?" Courtney asked.

"There!" Mark pointed to an old, wooden tool shed. "If we gotta get back over fast, head for that shed. We can climb up the side."

He wasn't going to make the same mistake twice. This time he wanted to be ready. Courtney nodded and headed for the house. Neither was nervous, since they had just done a thorough inspection and knew the quigs were gone.

"I say we start inside the house," Courtney said. "There are a lot of rooms we may have missed."

They climbed up on to the porch and stopped at the broken window.

"That's our door," Mark announced. He made a move to go in, but Courtney stopped him.

"Mark, I'm in," she said.

"What do you mean?"

"I mean I want to be an acolyte."

Mark couldn't help but smile. "You sure?"

"Yeah, it just took some time to get my head around it," Courtney said sincerely. "I think it's an important thing to do. And I don't want to let you down. Or Bobby."

Mark smiled. "I never thought you would," he said as he lifted one leg through the broken window.

Mark's confidence in her made Courtney feel better than she had in weeks. Maybe Mark was right. Maybe she had a more important role to play than sports superstar. She knew one thing for certain: She wanted the chance to find out. But there was no time to feel warm and fuzzy. They had work to do. So Courtney followed Mark inside.

The two of them stood in the grand entryway, once again taking it all in.

"Where to first?" Courtney asked.

Mark lifted his ring and saw that the symbol was still glowing brightly.

"Let's start in the attic and work our way –" Mark stopped talking. He had heard something. Courtney heard it too.

"What was that?" Courtney asked.

"Sounded like something scratching across wood."

"There it is again!" Courtney exclaimed. "It's outside, on the porch."

They both turned to the broken window they had just come through.

"It could be squirrels," Mark said hopefully.

More scratching. Whatever it was, it was moving quickly back and forth on the porch.

"Or birds," Courtney offered.

"Or . . . quigs."

Courtney laughed nervously. "Don't even joke –"

Smash! Smash! Smash!

Three windows shattered as black quig dogs came crashing into the house.

"C'mon!" Courtney grabbed Mark's hand and they ran up the stairs. The quigs were slightly dazed by the hammering their heads had just taken, and it gave Mark and Courtney enough time to make it to the top. But a second later the quigs had their wits back, sniffed the air, and charged up the stairs after them.

Mark and Courtney sprinted along the hallway, not sure where to go.

"The window at the end!" Mark shouted.

"We'll never make it," Courtney yelled, and pulled Mark into one of the empty bedrooms. They quickly closed the door. There were two other doors in the room. They were the doors that led to the adjoining bedrooms.

"Close those doors!" Courtney ordered.

They each ran to one of the doors and closed it.

"We're dead," Mark said.

Courtney ran for the window. She tried to lift it up, but it had been closed for years and wouldn't budge.

Mark then noticed something. "Look," he said, holding his hand up. His ring had stopped glowing.

"Not now, Mark. Wait here," she said, and ran to the other door that led to an adjoining room.

"Where are you going?"

Slam!

The quigs had found them. They were trying to batter down the door Mark had just closed. Mark leaned against it to keep them out. He could hear their angry growling.

"Get ready to open that door," Courtney ordered, and ran out of the room.

"What?" Mark screamed in shock. There was no way he was opening the door.

Courtney moved quickly and quietly through the next bedroom and poked her head out into the hallway. It was empty. She could hear the sound of the quigs slamming themselves against the door that Mark was holding shut.

"Hey!" she shouted. "Devil dogs! Suppertime! Come and get it!"

The banging stopped. Suddenly all three quigs came charging out of the far bedroom and into the hallway, heading for her.

"Psyche," she shouted, and ducked back into the bedroom. She then sprinted through the room and back into the bedroom where Mark was. She didn't close the door behind her either.

Mark yelled, "Close the door!"

"No!" Courtney shouted. "Open yours!"

Mark hesitated. He didn't know the quigs had left. But it was clear that Courtney wasn't stopping. If he didn't open the door, she'd run right into it. So he swallowed hard and pulled it open. It wasn't a second too soon, because Courtney blasted through at full throttle.

"Close it behind you!" she shouted.

Mark didn't know what she was doing, until he looked back and saw the three quigs flying towards him, through the bedroom. They had come through the door Courtney left open. Mark jumped out through the door and pulled it closed as . . . *slam slam slam!* All three quigs hit the door. Now Mark and the quigs were on opposite sides from where they had been a few moments before. He still had no idea what Courtney was doing.

Courtney never stopped running. She turned into the hallway and sprinted along the same route the quigs had just taken after her. She knew that either her plan was going to work, or she was about to serve herself up for lunch. She ran into the third bedroom and ran towards the connecting door that led back to the second bedroom. Her plan was to lock them inside.

The quigs had figured it out. They stopped trying to beat down the door, and turned back for the door they had just entered through. But Courtney was too fast. She reached inside the room, grabbed the doorknob, said, "G'night kids!" and slammed the door closed, trapping the quigs in the bedroom. Again the quigs slammed at the door in a blood rage.

Mark poked his head into the room. "Can we go now?" he asked.

The two of them ran back along the hallway and hurried down the stairs. They were just about to exit through the broken window when Mark stopped.

"Look!" he exclaimed and held up his hand. His ring was glowing again. "Whatever it is, it's down here. Or down *there*," he said as he pointed at the door to the basement.

"Forget it! Those dogs are —"

Mark wasn't listening. He ran to the basement door and opened it. Sure enough, the symbol on his ring glowed even brighter.

"It's down there!"

"If the quigs get out, we'll be trapped," Courtney warned. Too late. Mark was already heading down the stairs. Courtney ran right after him. She made sure to close the door behind her this time, just in case.

The large basement didn't look any different from a few

minutes before, except for one thing: Mark's ring was blasting out light as if it were alive.

"This is it!" Mark declared.

"There's nothing here," Courtney exclaimed. "We looked behind every door!"

A horrifying sound came from above. It was the sound of the quigs running down the stairs from the first floor. They had got out of the bedroom. Mark and Courtney looked up in fear. Mark was about to say something, but Courtney held her hand over his mouth. She put her fingers to her lips for him to "Shhhh". They didn't move. They didn't make a sound. They thought that with any luck, the quigs wouldn't find them.

Slam!

No such luck. The quigs found them and were trying to batter down the door.

"We gotta find a way out," Courtney said with a shaky voice.

"No," Mark yelled back. "We gotta find out what's down here." Mark looked around. He went to the door that led to the wine cellar and threw it open.

Slam! Slam!

The quigs threw themselves at the basement door with a horrifying fury. They seemed even more out of control than before.

"They know we're close," Mark said. "They don't want us to find it."

Courtney saw something they hadn't noticed before. A raggy curtain was hanging on the wall, covering it from ceiling to floor. Courtney pushed it aside to find another door. She quickly pulled it open and shouted for joy. Daylight flooded into the basement.

"Yes! It's the way out! Mark, c'mon!"

Mark ignored her. He threw open the door to the workshop, but nothing was out of the ordinary.

"Mark, c'mon!" Courtney yelled.

Crunch!

The basement door was starting to splinter. A few more shots and it would come down . . . and so would the quigs.

"Mark!" Courtney cried.

Mark wasn't going to run. Not now. Not when they were so close. He was about to open the next door, the one that led to the root cellar, when he felt something strange. He looked down at his hand, then grimaced in pain.

"Ahhhh!"

Courtney ran to him. "What's the matter?"

CRASH!

The wooden basement door gave way and clattered down the stairs. The quigs were on their way.

"It's burning hot!" Mark yelled, and pulled off his ring.

Courtney turned to see the quigs had begun their final, fatal charge. "This is gonna hurt," was all she could say.

Mark threw the burning ring on to the floor. Instantly a high-pitched sound came from it. It wasn't a painful sound; it was more like a jumble of high musical notes that were all being played at the same time.

Courtney grabbed Mark. Mark grabbed Courtney. The two turned to face the charging quigs to see . . .

They had stopped. The three beastly dogs, their yellow eyes still intensely focused, had stopped. They twisted their heads as if the strange sound were irritating them. A second later the three dogs turned and ran back up the stairs, tails between their legs, whining in fear.

Mark and Courtney looked back down to the ring to see that it was moving. It wasn't growing though. It began to spin. It was slow at first, but picked up momentum until the ring was up on end, spinning so fast that it was nothing more than a blur. The high-pitched notes grew louder.

"Look!" Mark said, pointing at the door to the root cellar.

Courtney looked to see the door was starting to rattle on its hinges.

"Something's in there," Courtney said in shock.

"Maybe," Mark said. "Or m-maybe something's coming."

The rattling continued, then an intense light began to leak from around the edges of the door. Whatever was behind there, it was giving off a light so bright that Mark and Courtney had to squint, even though it was only coming from the crack around the edges. The strange sound from the ring grew even more intense. Now it was so loud it started to hurt. Mark and Courtney both had to cover their ears. The light from behind the door grew even brighter. The door shook furiously. Mark was ready for it to blow off its hinges.

It was then that the most incredible event of all occurred. As the ring continued to spin, a laser light shot from it, aimed at the wooden door. Mark and Courtney watched in awe as the intense white light hit the door at head level. Smoke rose from where the light hit the wood. The door was burning.

And then, like somebody had pulled the plug on a lamp, everything stopped. Everything – the beam of light from the ring; the bright light from behind the door; the strange, piercing sound. And finally the ring itself stopped spinning. It rolled one last time, then came to a stop with a slight, metallic *ping*. It was over. All was back to normal.

All but one small thing.

"Oh, man," Courtney said in awe.

Mark saw that she was looking at the door to the root cellar. At first, Mark wasn't sure why she was so stunned, and then he saw it. It was on the door, right where the beam from the ring had hit it. There was no mistake. They had seen this once before and read about it many times over.

It was a star. The sign of a gate.

Mark reached down and picked up the ring. It was no longer glowing and was now cool enough to touch. It had done its job. Courtney walked over to the door and touched the blackened symbol.

"It's still hot," she said. She looked at Mark and asked, "Could it be?"

"Open the d-door," Mark said. "My hand's shaking."

Courtney reached down and grabbed the door handle. "My hand's shaking too," she said.

Mark put his hand over Courtney's and the two of them pulled the door open.

The room looked pretty much the same as it had when they searched it before. It was a large, empty space with a dirt floor and bits of dried weeds hanging from the beams of the ceiling. It was cool inside, just the way a subterranean root cellar should be. It was the exact same room that they had been in before, except for one small change. The rock that made up one whole wall of the cellar was gone.

Mark and Courtney stood together, staring, not breathing. Instead of a rock wall, they now looked into a craggy opening. It was unmistakable.

It was a flume.

Neither could speak. They both stood there, staring into the infinite tunnel. It was Mark who first broke the silence.

"D-Do you think m-maybe this means the time is right for us to be acolytes?"

Courtney stared into the tunnel a moment more, then started to laugh. "Yeah," she said through the laughter. "I'd say this is a pretty good sign."

Mark laughed too. The two laughed and hugged. Neither knew what the future held, but one thing was for certain: They were no longer just bystanders whose job it was to read Bobby's mail. They were in the game now. For real.

Mark's ring twitched.

"Uh-oh," he said, and held his hand up.

"Now what?" Courtney exclaimed. "I don't know if I can take any more fireworks."

But this event was safe and familiar. The centre stone of the ring started to glow. Mark took it off and placed it down on the dirt floor. This time the ring grew, opening up the portal to the territories. The familiar musical notes grew louder, bringing with them a special delivery. The sparkling light filled the underground room. For Mark and Courtney, it was like being held in a warm embrace. The lights flashed one final time, the notes fell silent, and the ring was once again back to its normal size.

Lying next to it was the silver projector that held Bobby's next journal.

"Hobey-ho," whispered Mark.

VEELOX

We were good to go.

Loor and I stood facing the three silver discs in the wall of the alpha jump cubicle, wearing our dark green one-piece suits. Loor had been through the prep routine. Her blood had been scanned and she was fitted with a silver control bracelet. I got my own control bracelet too, but after what had happened during my last jump, I wasn't going to put a whole lot of faith in that thing.

Our safety was in the hands of Aja Killian. She had put the alpha grid that controlled Zetlin's jump back online. She would now monitor our jump into Zetlin's fantasy and yank us out if anything went wrong. At least, that was the plan. Once we were in Dr Zetlin's jump, the Reality Bug might have plans of its own.

"Any questions?" Aja asked us. She stood at the door of the jump cubicle.

"No," Loor answered calmly.

What could Loor ask? This was a girl from a territory of primitive, tribal warriors. The idea of jumping into somebody else's fantasy was about as alien to her as, well, I seriously doubt if there's anything that comes close to being that alien.

Aja stepped back into the Alpha Core and sat in the big chair. She hit a few buttons on the silver control panel on the arm. Two of the three silver discs in the wall retracted, and the tables slowly slid out. These tubes were on either side of the centre jump tube where Dr Zetlin was lying. It was creepy to think there was a guy in there, and we were about to leap into his mind.

I hoped there was room for all of us.

"Lie down on the table," I instructed Loor. "Get comfortable."

She did. Loor trusted me. Man, I hoped she wasn't making a mistake. I walked out of the jump cubicle and went to Aja.

"Do you have any idea where we might find him?" I asked.

Aja frowned. "I'm sorry, Pendragon," she said. "It all depends on the fantasy he created."

She showed me a picture. It was the old-man version of the little kid in the oil painting outside. There was nothing unique about him. He just looked like a smart old man. He was bald and wore round little glasses. I memorised the face.

"So all I have to do is ask him for the origin code, right?" I asked.

"Yes. Tell him the main grid has been suspended because the processing code has been corrupted. Tell him we have to clean the string."

"Origin code, corrupted processing code, clean the string – got it."

"I doubt he'll give it up easily," Aja added. She leaned over my shoulder and glanced at Loor, who was now lying quietly on the table. "You may have to force him to end his jump."

"Let's find him first," I said.

"Right," she said.

There was something bothering me, and I had to say it. "Aja, if the Reality Bug is doing its thing, you might be in danger too. I mean, look what happened to Alex."

Aja shrugged and gave a cocky reply. "I'm not Alex."

Gotta love this girl. She wasn't short on confidence.

"Just be careful," I said, then turned and walked towards my jump tube.

"Pendragon," Aja called to me. I stopped at the door to the cubicle and looked back at her.

"I'm glad you're here," she said.

It was the nicest thing Aja Killian had ever said to me.

"We're gonna fix this, Aja," I said, trying to sound as confident as she was.

"We don't have a choice," she replied.

She was right. If we were to have any hope of rescuing Veelox from itself, and from Saint Dane, we had to purge the Reality Bug. I walked back to the jump tubes and looked down at Loor.

"What do I do, Pendragon?" she asked.

"Nothing," I answered. "Just relax. You'll slide inside, it'll be dark for a few seconds and then we'll be together in the jump." I called out to Aja, "Right?"

"Exactly," Aja called back. "I'll be watching it all on the monitor."

I hopped up on to my table and settled in. My heart started to beat faster. It was game time.

"Hobey-ho, let's go!" I called out.

Loor called out, "Aja? What should I be ready for?" I could sense the slight tension in her voice. Loor was the single most fearless person I had ever met. But this was scary, even for her.

Aja answered with one, simple word. "Everything."

Funny. That was exactly what I was *afraid* of.

Everything.

I was hit with a blinding flash of light and threw my hand up to cover my eyes. My first thought was that something had gone haywire and I was floating in limbo. But a second later I realised what had happened.

I was staring up at the sun.

I quickly looked down to see I was standing on hard-packed dirt. I didn't think there was a sun or dirt in limbo, so everything was cool. A few seconds later my eyes adjusted, and I got the first look at my surroundings. I was standing in the centre of a rocky canyon. The walls rose steeply on either side of me. In the distance, the canyon made a few gentle turns, and emptied out into a green meadow. Beyond that in the far distance were snow-capped mountains. Not bad. Dr Zetlin's fantasy took place on a warm, sunny day in the great outdoors.

"Where are we, Pendragon?" Loor asked.

Oh, right. Loor. I almost forgot. I spun around to see her standing behind me. I smiled and said, "Howdy there, buckaroo."

Loor gave me a strange look that said, "What the heck are you talking about?"

I didn't blame her, but I couldn't resist, because Loor was now dressed like a cowboy. Or cowgirl. Or cow-Traveller. Whatever. She had on blue jeans, a deep red shirt, and black cowboy boots. Her long black hair was tied back in a tight ponytail that reached down to the small of her back. Tied around her forehead was a rolled black bandana. She looked great.

I was pretty much dressed the same way: blue jeans, a deep green shirt, and the same kind of black boots. I even had a bandana around my neck. Dr Zetlin's fantasy was something right out of the Old West, which raised a weird question. Was there an Old West on Veelox? I guess there had to be, because we were in it.

Loor knelt down and picked up a handful of dirt, then let it spill through her fingers.

"It is real," she said. "How can that be?"

"It's real because our minds are telling us it is," I answered. "Or Zetlin's mind is telling us it is."

Loor stood up and gazed around at the canyon. "This is what the man Zetlin is thinking?"

"Yeah," I said. "He must have wanted to be a cowboy when he grew up."

"What is a cowboy?" Loor asked.

Before I could answer, I heard a sound. It was a rumble, like far-off thunder.

"You hear that?" I asked.

The curious look on her face told me she did. We both stood there, listening, as the rumbling grew louder.

"It is coming from that direction," Loor said and pointed deeper into the canyon.

Behind us the canyon walls made a sharp turn. There was no way to know what lay beyond. But Loor was right. Whatever was making that sound was around the bend, and getting louder. That meant it was coming closer. I took a quick look in the other direction. The mouth of the canyon had to be at least a half mile away.

"Look," Loor said.

I looked back the other way to see a huge, brown cloud of dirt drifting out from around the bend in the canyon. What was coming? A storm? A rock slide? Godzilla? The thunder grew louder. The sound bounced off the walls of the canyon. Whatever was making that sound, it didn't seem happy. I took another quick look around to see if there was a place we could hide. But the rock walls to either side of us were steep and unforgiving. No way we could climb up. If we were in trouble, the only safe place would be out of this canyon . . . half a mile away.

I kept my eyes on the bend in the canyon, but started to back towards the mouth.

"I think we'd better get outta here," I said.

"If this is happening in Zetlin's head, are we in danger?" Loor asked.

"That depends," I answered.

"On what?"

"On what's coming around that corner."

A second later we had our answer. Charging around the bend of the canyon, running full throttle, was a herd of cattle. There must have been a thousand of them, heading right for us.

"Stampede!" I shouted. "Run!"

Loor and I turned and sprinted away from the charging mass of animals. I took a quick look back and saw that the swarm of beasts was packed nearly wall-to-wall in the canyon, all snorting and grunting with wild eyes. I'll bet the animals in front of the herd were just as scared as we were. If one of them went down, they'd be trampled by the others charging up from behind. No way they were going to stop. They were running for their lives. Just like us.

"What are they?" asked Loor breathlessly. "Do they eat meat?"

"No, but if they catch us there won't be anything left to eat anyway!"

There was no place to go for protection. We had to get out of that canyon. But it was too far away. No way could we outrun this charging herd. I looked back again and saw that they were catching up, fast. It was like racing against an avalanche and we were losing. I started to feel the prickle of grit on my neck from the cloud of dirt they were stirring up. In seconds we'd be roadkill. Or canyonkill.

"There!" shouted Loor.

She pointed to the canyon wall ahead of us, where I saw a single, brown vine that snaked down from somewhere above.

"Follow me!" Loor ordered, and ran for it.

There was only one vine. Even if it was strong enough, which I wasn't sure about, there was barely time for one of us to climb. The herd would be on us in seconds.

"Jump on my back!" Loor commanded.

What? Was she crazy?

"Now!" she demanded, and grabbed the vine.

I wasn't about to argue. I could feel the ground rumble with the thumping of oncoming hooves. Loor grabbed the vine and I grabbed Loor, wrapping my arms around her neck. She climbed, hand over hand, with her boots on the wall, walking up. I dangled from her neck, hoping she had the strength to do this and hoping the vine was strong enough to hold us both.

The cattle were on us. But we were high enough to be out of harm's way. They charged past as if we weren't even there. The mass of animals thundered by only inches below us. I could feel the heat coming up from their bodies. Or maybe it was my own sweat.

"You okay?" I asked Loor.

Loor gave a quick nod. No problem. I could feel the strength in her shoulders and arms. I shouldn't have doubted her. This was easy for her. Now all we had to worry about was whether the vine would hold until the herd was past.

The cattle kept coming. I couldn't believe how many there were. Finally, after what felt like a lifetime, the herd started to thin, so they weren't close to the canyon wall any more.

And the vine snapped. Loor and I tumbled to the dirt. Luckily I broke Loor's fall. Lucky for her, that is. It wasn't so hot for me. She landed on me full force and knocked the wind out of my lungs. Ooof! It took me about a minute to catch my breath, but I didn't care. We had survived. I glanced up and saw a few straggling cattle trotting after the herd. The rumbling sound of hooves grew faint. I glanced to the end of the canyon and saw the herd spreading out over the green meadow.

"How do you feel?" Loor asked. She was sitting in the dirt, barely winded from the ordeal.

"I feel like a genius," I said.

"A genius?"

"We've only been here two minutes and you've already saved my butt. I knew it was the right move to bring you along. Thanks, Loor."

Loor stood up and helped me to my feet. We started to brush the dust off our clothes when we heard: "What in blazes are you two doing here?"

We looked up to see two cowboys on horseback trotting up to us. These guys were definitely out of the Old West, complete with cowboy hats, leather chaps, and coils of rope around the horns of their saddles.

Neither looked like Dr Zetlin.

One cowboy asked, "Are you all right?"

"Yeah, we're fine," I answered.

"We checked the whole canyon before we drove the herd through," the other cowboy said. "Where did you two come from?"

"We must have wandered in right after you checked," I said. It was sort of the truth.

"You coulda got killed! What're you doing all the way up here?"

"We're looking for somebody," I answered.

"Up here? In the pass?" the first cowboy asked, totally confused.

"Yeah, well, we got lost," I said. "His name is Zetlin. Do you know him?"

The first cowboy looked at the other and asked, "That the name of the fella staying down in Old Glenville?"

"Could be," the second cowboy said with a shrug.

The first guy then looked at me and Loor and said, "There's a man living down in town who might be the one you're looking for. You been through there?"

"No," I said with growing excitement. "Could you point the way?"

"Sure," he answered. "Where are your horses?"

Loor and I looked at each other and shrugged.

"We lost 'em," I said. Wow, could I have given a more lame excuse?

"Lost your horses?" the second cowboy exclaimed. "How did you go and do that?"

"Long story," I said. "We can walk."

"It's too far," the first cowboy said. "We'll lend you horses."

"Really? That's great!"

"Climb on," the second guy said.

Loor and I each climbed on to the back of one of the

horses, behind the cowboys. A second later we were trotting out of the canyon. It wasn't exactly comfortable, but way better than walking.

When we reached the mouth of the canyon, I got a full view of the beautiful mountain pass. It was awesome. The dry, rocky canyon gave way to green, rolling meadows that stretched out as far as I could see. The mountains in the distance were immense. I had never seen the Rockies, but this was what I imagined they looked like. It was another example of Veelox looking like Second Earth. Or at least an example of Dr Zetlin's fantasy looking like Second Earth. Whatever. It was great.

The two cowboys rode us over to a wagon where they had two more horses hitched. While they saddled up the fresh horses, they explained that they were bringing in the herd for the winter, and often stayed up in the mountains for weeks at a time. That's why they had four horses. If one got hurt, they didn't want to have to go back into town to get a replacement. They said that they were nearly done for the season, so they wouldn't mind lending us these two. They told us to leave them with the blacksmith in town. They'd be down in a few days to pick them up.

Man, these guys were pretty trusting. But then again, this was Dr Zetlin's fantasy. Maybe he only put trustworthy people into his jumps.

I had ridden horses a couple of times, at summer camp. So I was comfortable enough to mount up and trot along. But I wasn't sure about Loor. Did she know how to ride? The answer came when Loor jumped up on her horse like a pro, tugged the reins, and got her horse to spin in a circle one way, then the other. Show-off. I should have known.

"Follow the worn trail down out of the pass," the first cowboy explained. "It's pretty well travelled; you won't miss it. You should reach town before sunset."

"Thank you," Loor said.

"Yeah," I added. "You really saved us."

"Aw, heck," the second cowboy said. "It's the least we could do for nearly getting you killed back there."

After a few more thank-yous, Loor and I were on our way to town. It was an awesome ride. The slope was gentle, the air was warm, and the countryside was spectacular.

Loor didn't look half bad, either. Ever since I first met Loor, I had been trying to prove myself to her. She was an athlete and a warrior. I'd seen her battle guys twice her size and make them look bad. Next to her, I was a total weenie. But she wasn't all about muscle. Loor had a strong sense of right and wrong. She totally believed in the Travellers and our mission. Her mother died battling Saint Dane's evil, and I think that made her even more dedicated. But after all we'd been through, I didn't know how Loor felt about me. Yeah, she was on my side because we were both Travellers, and I know she respected me for some of the things I had done, but I think that's as far as it went. I thought of Loor as a good friend. I think she only thought of me as a teammate.

We had a long ride into Old Glenville, and there was a lot I wanted to talk to her about. I figured this was as good a time as any.

"When I was on First Earth," I said to her, "things didn't go too well."

"Saint Dane failed," she said. "That is all that matters."

"Did he?" I said. "We saved the territory, but no thanks to me."

"And how did that make you feel?" she asked.

"Like I never want to let him get the better of me again," I said. "And I won't."

Loor looked at me and said, "I know you, Pendragon. Your heart is in the right place, but you have been unsure of yourself, and of our mission."

I wanted to argue, but she was right.

"It sounds to me as if Saint Dane tried to take away your confidence, but instead made you more determined. If that is the case, he made a very bad mistake, for all he managed to do was bring you fully into the conflict. He will regret that."

In that single moment, things became incredibly clear. I had been struggling with my failure. But now, Loor made me believe that my weakness at that critical moment on First Earth might actually have been the best thing that could have happened. Any doubt I had up to that point about wanting to battle Saint Dane was taken away. Uncle Press always said that this conflict was about more than a single battle. Heck, even Saint Dane said that. By facing my own weakness, maybe I was now ready for the long haul.

"I missed you, Loor," I said. I wanted her to tell me she missed me, too.

She didn't. "I will always be there when you need me," she said. "As I know you will be for me. That is our destiny."

Okay, maybe not exactly a statement of undying friendship, but it was better than nothing. I guess.

We rode for a long time, mostly in silence. I was beginning to think those cowboys had pointed us in the wrong direction, when . . .

"Look!" Loor exclaimed, pointing ahead.

I looked to see the tops of buildings peeking up over some trees. This had to be Old Glenville.

"Last one there buys the sniggers," I exclaimed.

"The what?" Loor said.

Too late. I kicked my horse into action and galloped towards town. Loor probably could have beaten me, but I had got such a head start that there was no way she could catch up. A few minutes later, I rode straight down the centre street of Old Glenville.

It was a ghost town. I pulled up my horse and Loor stopped right beside me. The two of us sat there in the middle of the dirt street, looking around at the empty town.

Old Glenville was something right out of an old-time Western movie. There were two-storey wooden buildings down either side of the main street, with wooden sidewalks and hitching posts in front. I saw painted signs on the stores that identified them as: GENERAL STORE AND DRY GOODS; BARBER AND DENTIST; SHERIFF; TELEGRAPH OFFICE; and even one that said: CORONER. At the end of the street was a church with a tall steeple that dwarfed the rest of the buildings. It was the perfect little frontier town. The only thing missing was people.

"Here we go again," I said. "Just like Rubic City."

I kicked my horse into gear and we walked slowly down the centre of the street. I listened for any sign of life, but there was none.

"I'm surprised there's no tumbleweed blowing through," I said.

"What is tumbleweed?" Loor asked.

As if on cue, a big piece of brown tumbleweed rolled past us. This was getting strange, in more ways than one. I guess I could believe that another territory was just like Earth, but this meant the territory of Veelox also had the same kind of history as Earth. This town of Old Glenville was exactly like a typical town from the Old West in America. Very strange.

"There," Loor said. She pointed to a barnlike building that was off the main road.

There was a hand-painted sign leaning against a fence that said: BLACKSMITH. This was where we were supposed to leave the horses. We rode over to the barn, but didn't find a soul. Even stranger, all the tools of the trade were lying around. There were hammers and nails and coal and all the stuff you'd think a blacksmith used. The barn even had a few horses in stalls, but they were the only sign of life. This town looked like it had been recently abandoned.

We tied the horses to a hitching post near the barn. I was about to suggest that we start on one end of town and work our way down the street, searching each and every building, when we heard something strange.

"Music," Loor said.

It was old-fashioned, honky-tonk piano music, which is the exact kind of music you'd expect to hear in a Western town.

"I'll bet you a dollar there's a saloon around here," I said.

"What is a saloon?" Loor asked.

"I'll show you."

Not that I had ever been in a saloon, but I had seen enough Western movies to know that's usually where the music was played. And since everything about this town smelled of the Old West, I had no doubt we'd find a saloon. So we took off walking back to the main street. The closer we got, the louder the music became. Sure enough, across the street I spotted a sign over a balcony that said in fancy gold letters: OLD GLENVILLE SALOON.

We walked across the dusty street like a couple of gun-slingers heading towards the O.K. Corral. The music was definitely coming from the saloon. As we got closer I saw a set of swinging doors in front. Classic Western. We got as far as the wooden sidewalk and were about to step up, when the piano suddenly stopped.

Loor and I did too.

We then heard the sound of a chair scraping across the floor inside, as if someone were standing up. It was followed by the sound of footsteps walking across the floor, heading for the swinging doors, and us.

Loor and I didn't move. Whoever was inside, we were about to meet them. I really hoped it was Dr Zetlin.

It wasn't.

When the swinging doors flew open, I saw something that made me question whether this was Dr Zetlin's fantasy nightmare . . . or mine. Because standing in the door before us was Saint Dane.

He wore black from head to toe, like a gunfighter. On his hips were twin six-shooters. His grey mane of hair fell down to his shoulders, topped off with a black cowboy hat. The demon acted as if he were expecting us. He smiled a yellow-toothed grin, stared at us with those cold blue eyes, and said, "Looks like it's time to liven up this dead little town!"

VEELOX

"Howdy, Pendragon!" Saint Dane exclaimed jovially while leaning against the hitching post. "I see you brought along your violent little girlfriend. What a nice surprise!"

This didn't compute. How could Saint Dane be in Dr Zetlin's fantasy? This wasn't like before where he was a pre-recorded hologram. This was him. For real. Or should I say, in fantasy. My brain locked.

"You seem surprised!" he laughed. "This can't be possible, yet here I am. It seems as though Aja's Reality Bug has completely scrambled Lifelight."

Loor looked at me and said softly, "This is real, isn't it?"

"Real enough!" Saint Dane answered for me.

He pulled out one of his six-shooters, aimed it at the sky and pulled the trigger. The sharp crack sounded pretty real to me. A moment later four more cowboys with six-shooters appeared from the saloon. They moved quickly behind us, cutting off any chance we had of escape. These guys didn't look like the friendly cowpokes from the mountains either. The word that came to mind was, desperados.

"Since this is a fantasy," Saint Dane continued, "let's have some fun."

He stepped off the wooden walkway and strolled over to us with his thumb in his gun belt. He was enjoying this. We weren't.

"The man you're worried about?" he said. "I know where he is, and I'm going to give you the chance to rescue him."

I shot a look at Loor. This had just got interesting.

"Rescue?" I asked.

"About a mile south of town is a dam. It's an immense structure. Holds back an extremely large lake. Without that dam, this town would be underwater. On top of the dam is a small, stone hut. That's where you'll find him."

"That's it?" I asked. "Simple as that?"

Saint Dane laughed. "Pendragon, please, is it ever as simple as that?"

He pulled out a golden pocket watch and checked the time.

"Dynamite has been placed all over that dam, thanks to my associates here. In just about, oh, ten minutes, it's all going to explode and things around here are going to get very wet."

My adrenalin spiked.

"So you're giving us ten minutes to get to the hut and get him out? Is that what you're saying?"

"With one small complication. I'll give you a two minute head start. After that I'm sending my associates here, to stop you. Won't that be exciting?"

Saint Dane leaned down and looked me square in the eye, saying, "You didn't have the strength to succeed on First Earth. How will you handle this little challenge?"

Without thinking, I reached forward and quickly grabbed one of Saint Dane's guns from its holster.

"Nicely done, Quick Draw," he said, barely showing surprise. "Now what?"

I grabbed Loor's hand and started to run.

"Yahoo!" Saint Dane called after us.

If we had any chance of getting to that dam in ten minutes, we needed the horses.

"What is dynamite?" Loor asked as we ran.

"It's like tak," I answered. "It'll destroy the dam."

We made it to the blacksmith's barn in a few seconds. I jammed the six-shooter into my belt and we started to untie the horses.

"Does it matter if this town is destroyed?" Loor asked. "It is not real."

"It's not the town," I answered quickly. "It's Zetlin. If something happens to him we'll never get the origin code and Lifelight will —"

Crack! Ping!

A bullet zinged off a metal bucket that was hanging near the barn door. It barely missed us.

"That wasn't two minutes!" I shouted.

Either the desperados didn't care, or they couldn't tell the time, because I was answered with a series of gunshots.

"Inside!" Loor commanded.

We grabbed the bridles of the horses and ran them inside the barn. Loor quickly closed the big doors. We were safe, but trapped, and the clock was ticking.

"What do those noisemakers do?" Loor said while pointing to the gun I had jammed in my belt.

"It shoots out small pieces of metal. They're deadly. But it only fires six times and they have a lot more guns than we do. And to be honest, I've never even shot one before."

More shots were fired from outside, shattering a window, making the horses whinny in fear.

"We gotta get outta here," I said and ran to a door in the back of the barn. I opened it and was met with a gunshot that splintered wood just over my head. To use a cliché Western phrase, they had us surrounded. I ran back to Loor and shouted, "You're the soldier-in-training! What are we supposed to do?"

Loor wasn't panicking, I'm not surprised to say. She coolly looked around the barn, seeing what we had to use.

She then said calmly, "The animals. What did you call it before? Stampede?"

I could have kissed her. It was brilliant and insane. There were about a dozen horses in stalls, plus ours. If we could get them moving together out of the barn, we might be able to use them as shields. I was more than ready to give it a try.

"Get them together!" Loor commanded.

We ran to opposite sides of the barn, throwing open the stalls and yelling at the horses to get out. It was kind of scary. The horses were already nervous because of the gunshots. Having two crazy people running around waving their arms made them even more excited. This was dangerous. One quick horse kick to the head and it would all be over.

After a few frantic seconds, we had all the horses gathered together in the centre of the barn. They were bumping into each other, kicking at the ground, and whinnying. They weren't happy about this at all.

"Go to the doors!" Loor yelled.

I ran to the big barn doors and grabbed the handles. Loor took our two horses with saddles and led them to the back of the pack.

"Are you ready?" she called out.

I was. So were the horses. They were starting to rear up and I was nearly stomped a couple of times.

"Let's go!" I shouted.

"Open the doors!"

I threw open both doors. Loor gave off a sharp whistle, and the herd of horses charged out of the barn.

I barely had enough time to jump to the side before getting trampled. Loor ran forward with our two horses. Without a second to think about how crazy this was, I jumped on mine and we charged out after the fleeing herd.

Outside, it was a chaos of wild horses and dust. The horses blasted into the open and ran together towards the main street. Loor and I pushed our horses forward to stay as close to the wild herd as possible. We both crouched low in the saddle, trying to offer smaller targets. I kept expecting to hear gunshots, but they didn't come. I guess there was enough confusion going on that the desperados didn't want to waste their ammunition. Good for the horses, good for us.

We were out, and we had our horses. Now it was a race. We had to get to that dam and find Zetlin before the whole thing blew up, or the desperados stopped us.

"Which way?" Loor yelled.

I figured we came into town from one direction, so the dam must be in the other. I gave my horse a quick kick in the butt, and we were off. We charged down the main street of Old Glenville, flew past the church, and blasted along the dirt road leading south. Side by side we galloped along the road like a couple of bandits on the run.

I soon realised there was something else to worry about. As much as I'd like to pretend otherwise, I'm not a very good rider. This was freaking scary! The horses were fast, which was good, but I barely knew what I was doing. If I fell off at the speed we were going, something would get broken. Probably my head. I grabbed the reins with one hand, and had a death grip on the saddle horn with the other. I didn't even look at Loor. She knew way more about riding than I did. I had no idea how much time had gone by, but every second counted. Slowing down was not an option.

"There it is!" Loor called to me.

Sure enough, looming up in the distance, tucked into a ravine, was a huge stone dam. Saint Dane said it was a mile out of town, but it was so big it looked much closer. I could even see the small, stone building on top, right in the middle.

Bang!

We weren't alone. I didn't turn around to look because I was afraid I'd lose my balance. But Loor did.

"They are coming," she announced.

"How many?" I asked.

"All of them. Saint Dane, too."

Swell.

More shots were fired. I kept expecting to feel the sting of a bullet, but they must have been too far back to be accurate. We had to keep it that way.

The road forked. It was clear that the right fork would take us to a trail that led up the side of the ravine, and to the top of the dam. Without a word we both steered our flying horses on to the right path. The trail quickly grew narrow as it rose up along the side of the steep ravine. But we still pushed the horses on. We couldn't risk being caught. Soon, we had risen up so high that there was a steep drop off to the left. I was in the lead. If my horse took one wrong step, adios.

The trail then entered a forest. Branches slapped at us from both sides, trying to knock us off. It was getting painful.

"We gotta slow down!" I said.

Loor and I both pulled on the reins and slowed to a trot. I could see through the trees up ahead that we were nearly at the top of the dam. There were only about a hundred yards to go.

"Give me the noisemaker," Loor ordered.

I looked back and was shocked to see that Loor was getting off her horse.

"What are you doing? We're almost there!" I shouted.

"Keep going," she said. "Find Zetlin and get him out. I will stop the others from following."

There was no way I was going to leave Loor here alone. "Loor, I won't —"

"You are wasting time, Pendragon!" she shouted at me. "We must save Zetlin! That is all that matters. Give me the noisemaker!"

It killed me, but I pulled the six-shooter out of my belt and tossed it to her. She looked at it curiously. My confidence wasn't high.

"Hold the handle, point the long end at the bad guys and pull the trigger," was the quickest instruction I could think of. "Hold it tight, it'll probably kick."

"Go!" she ordered.

I snapped the reins, kicked my horse, and galloped for the dam. I took one last look over my shoulder to see that Loor had pulled her horse into the trees. She was setting a trap. Man, what a brave girl. But then again, if the dam blew up, she wouldn't be on it. I would. I didn't know which was worse, facing the desperados, or standing on an exploding dam. Suddenly I wasn't feeling so bad for her any more.

It was all about time now. I had no idea how soon the dam was going to blow. A few seconds later, I broke out of the trees on top of the ridge to see the huge lake that Saint Dane told us about. A quick look to my left showed me that I had made it to the top of the dam. The stone hut was about halfway across, which I'm guessing was about fifty yards away. Fifty very long yards. I figured I could cover the distance faster on horseback.

That's when I heard gunfire. The quick, sharp pops told

me that the desperados had caught up with Loor. I could only hope that she'd be safe, and keep them back long enough for me to get to Dr Zetlin.

"Yah!" I slapped the horse's flank, and we charged out on to the dam. It was only about ten feet wide, with water on one side and a very long drop on the other. I hugged the water side.

Crack! Crack!

More gunshots, followed by splinters of stone kicking up around me. The desperados weren't gunning for Loor, they were shooting at me through the trees. I ducked down on the horse and begged it to run faster.

Ping! Crack!

A piece of flying stone stung my arm. They were getting better, but there was no way I would be stopped. Not when I was so close. We had played Saint Dane's evil game and nearly won. I made it to the stone hut and jumped off my horse. I tied it on the far side of the hut, making sure to use the building for protection against the shooting desperados.

A million thoughts flew through my head. What was my next move? I would get Dr Zetlin out, get us both on the horse, and then go . . . where? If we went back the way we came, we'd land right in the laps of the desperados. But I couldn't abandon Loor! The only choice was to keep going to the far side of the dam. But then once the dam blew up, Loor would be trapped with the desperados.

It was a familiar, horrible feeling. I was faced with a choice. Which was more important? The future of Veelox, or the safety of my friend? It was the *Hindenburg* all over again. Was this what Saint Dane wanted to do all along? Did he want to put me in the same, horrible position just to see me fail again?

These thoughts took all of three seconds to flash through my head. I truly didn't know what to do. All I knew for sure was that I had to keep going. But when I threw the door of the hut open, I was rocked by a sight so incredible that it made all my other concerns seem trivial.

"Dr Zetlin!" I shouted as I opened the door. "We've got to get off the dam or —"

When I saw the man inside the hut, I froze. It wasn't Dr Zetlin. This wasn't playing out the way it was supposed to. But to be honest, Saint Dane hadn't lied, either. He told us that the man I was worried about was in this hut. And he was.

It was Gunny.

"Shorty!" he yelled when he saw me. "What in heck is going on?"

Gunny was tied to a chair with a long length of rope. Seeing him was such a shock, I couldn't function.

"Wha — how did you get here?" I stammered.

"Saint Dane sandbagged me! Get these ropes off!"

My brain clicked back into gear. I ran to Gunny and started working on the knots. I wasn't sure if I was happy to see him or totally freaked out.

"You're not gonna believe what's been going on," I said. "This isn't real. None of this is." I then stopped working and looked at him. "Wait, I don't get how you can be here. Did Saint Dane bring you into a Lifelight pyramid?"

Gunny was about to answer, when I felt a sharp rumbling. It felt like a short, quick earthquake. But it wasn't. Our ten minutes were up. More rumbling followed. The dynamite was exploding. There was no way we could get off in time. The dam was about to collapse, with Gunny and me still on it.

VEELOX

"What's happening?" Gunny asked. His eyes were wide with fear.

"The dam is exploding," I said. "Saint Dane loaded it with dynamite."

I caught a glimpse of my horse charging away. He had pulled free and was galloping off in terror. Smart horse. He knew what was about to happen.

"Get yourself outta here," Gunny ordered.

I wanted to argue. I wanted to be all sorts of brave and say: "We're getting out, together!" or something equally heroic. But the truth was, there wasn't time. The exploding dynamite was tearing the dam apart. The floor shook, the stone ceiling started to fall down around us. In a few seconds there would be no more dam and no more us.

"Run, Pendragon," Gunny implored.

It was too late. I knew there was only one possible way to get off this crumbling dam. I lifted my arm and pulled up my sleeve to reveal my silver control bracelet with the three square buttons. The button on the far right was supposed to end the jump. The last time it failed, but I couldn't think of anything else to do, so I pushed it, and prayed.

The stone hut shuddered. We were going down.

"Goodbye, shorty," Gunny said.

Everything went black.

I sat up fast and slammed my head.

"Ow!"

I was totally disorientated. My head hurt too. What had happened? A second later, the answer came. With a slight hum, the silver disc that enclosed the jump tube slid back and filled my little tunnel with light. I was back in the Lifelight pyramid! The table slid out, depositing me back in the jump cubicle off the Alpha Core. My bracelet had worked. I had ended the jump. I looked quickly to my left to see a welcome sight. Loor was sliding out of the other tube, safe.

"Pendragon! What happened?" she asked. "I was shooting the noisemaker at Saint Dane and suddenly the world went black."

She was breathing hard and her eyes were wild. I can honestly say it was the first time I saw Loor rattled. But who could blame her?

"I ended the jump," I said. "We're back. Are you all right?"

"I am confused, but not injured," she answered. "Did you find Zetlin?"

I looked at the tube between us to see it was still closed. Zetlin was still inside.

"No," I answered. "Something is whacked." I jumped off the table and ran out of the cubicle. "Aja?" I called. "What went wrong?"

But Aja wasn't there. Her control chair was empty. The large monitor was still showing images of our jump though. On screen, I saw a horrific sight. It was a view of the collapsing dam. The explosions had weakened the stone structure and tons of water from the lake came crashing through. The dam crumbled like wet sand. I saw the small stone hut on top fall into the chaos of crashing stone and water.

"Gunny," I said to myself.

The screen went blank. The jump was over.

"What went wrong?" Loor asked. She was standing behind me, watching the disaster. "Where is Aja?"

"I don't know," I answered.

I led Loor out of the Alpha Core in search of Aja. Where was she? Why had she left the controls in the middle of the jump? Of course, my mind rushed to all the worst possible answers. I feared she had somehow gone into the jump and got hurt. Stranger still, how had Gunny ended up in Zetlin's jump? Worse, if he was in the jump, did he go down with the crumbling dam? There were a ton of questions that needed answering. But first we had to find Aja.

We ran quickly through the core to see all was exactly as we had left it. The monitors were still showing green and there were no phaders or vedders around. There was no Aja, either. We left the glass corridor and hurried back to the counter where we had been fitted with our control bracelets. The Goth vedder was still there, looking as bored as ever.

"Have you seen Aja?" I demanded.

"She left a while ago," he answered. "She was in a big hurry, too. She said to tell you she had to get home."

"Home?" I shouted. "But the grid is still suspended!"

"Hey, don't ask me," the guy said. "I'm just a vedder."

This made no sense. What was so important at home that she would leave us alone in the jump? I looked at Loor, hoping she might have an answer, and saw she was staring at the oil portrait of the young Dr Zetlin.

"We must find him," she said.

"Yeah, I know. But we can't do it without Aja. C'mon."

We started to leave when the vedder called to us. "Hey!"

We looked back at him and he pointed to his wrist. Right. We still had our jump bracelets on. Loor and I quickly unclasped the bracelets and put them on the counter.

"Thank you," the vedder said. "This is the way it was meant to be."

I shot the guy a surprised look. "Why did you say that?"

The Goth guy shrugged. "Just something to say," he answered, and smiled.

That was weird.

"Let's go," I said to Loor, and headed out.

I was confused and angry and frightened all at once. How could Aja abandon us? Loor and I jumped on to one of the three-wheel pedal vehicles and quickly made our way back towards the mansion that Aja made home.

"I am having trouble understanding what is happening, Pendragon," Loor said.

"Yeah, me too," I answered truthfully. "Nothing is making sense, but I guarantee that if Aja went home, it was for a good reason. Let's not sweat about it until we find her."

We pedalled the rest of the way in silence. The empty streets of Rubic City seemed even more chillingly quiet than before. This was a ghost town in the middle of a ghost territory, and we weren't doing much to change it.

We arrived at the mansion and ran up the marble stairs. I wanted to burst through the door, screaming for Aja, but that would have been rude. This was still Evangeline's house too. So I grabbed the door knocker and pounded it a few times. A few agonising seconds later, the door opened and Evangeline was there. When she saw me, her face lit up with a bright smile.

"Pendragon! What a surprise!" she exclaimed. "And who is this?"

"This is my friend Loor," I answered. "She's a Traveller. Where is Aja?"

"Another Traveller?" Evangeline said. "How wonderful! You two are just in time for dinner."

She stepped back to let Loor and me inside.

"We need to find Aja, Evangeline," I said urgently.

"But surely you have time for some gloid," she said sweetly. "We're having your favourite. Blue. You like blue the best, don't you?"

Yeah, right.

"Where is Aja?" Loor demanded. She didn't care if she sounded rude.

"She's not here," Evangeline answered. "Please, come into the kitchen and eat."

She turned and walked down the hallway, heading for the kitchen.

"If she is not here," Loor said, "where else could she be?"

"I don't know," I answered.

We followed Evangeline through the house, towards the kitchen. No way I was going to get near any of that blue gloid, but we had to find Aja. I stepped up to the kitchen door, swung it open, and saw something that froze both Loor and me in our places. It was impossible, yet as real as can be.

Evangeline was scooping big ladles of blue gloid into white bowls. But that wasn't what shocked us.

"Sit down, you two," she said with warm hospitality. "Plenty of room."

Loor and I didn't move. That was because there were already two dinner guests seated at the table. As impossible as it was, sitting there, chowing down on huge spoonfuls of blue gloid, were the two cowpokes from the mountain ravine in Zetlin's fantasy.

"Howdy there, you two!" one of them said. "You come by to return our horses?"

"That's right nice of you to go out of your way!" the other one said. He then looked at Evangeline and said, "Ma'am, this chow sure is tasty."

"That's kind of you to say," Evangeline said, blushing.

What was going on?

Loor asked me, "Do you smell that?"

At first I thought she meant the gloid, but I took a whiff and realised it was something else. Something was burning.

"Evangeline, are you cooking something?" I asked.

Before she could answer, a door opened on the far side of the kitchen and another guest arrived.

"Gunny!" I shouted.

Yup. In walked Gunny Van Dyke, dressed in his bell captain uniform from the Manhattan Tower Hotel.

"Hey there, shorty!" he said. "I see you made it off that dam. You going to introduce me to your friend?"

I was numb. My brain wasn't computing any of this.

"This is . . . this is . . . Loor," I said numbly.

"Osa's daughter?" Gunny exclaimed. "I am very pleased to meet you."

Gunny reached across the table, holding out his hand to shake Loor's. Loor reached out, looking as dazed as I was.

And there was a gunshot.

The smile froze on Gunny's face. He pitched forward and fell face first on to the table. Gunny had been shot. Both cowpokes dived away from the table and hit the floor. Evangeline screamed and huddled behind a counter. I looked across the room to where the shot had come from.

Standing in the doorway was Saint Dane. He was still dressed in his black cowboy outfit and had a smoking six-shooter in his hand.

"You cheated, Pendragon," Saint Dane exclaimed. "There's no fun in a challenge if you cheat. Now you two will just have to pay the price."

From behind him, the desperados entered with guns drawn.

I was absolutely, totally frozen in shock. Things were happening so fast and seemed so impossible, I couldn't even begin to figure out what to do.

Luckily, Loor could.

She quickly grabbed the end of the kitchen table and flipped it up on end. Cutlery and gloid flew everywhere as the desperados opened fire. Bullets slammed into the table, shredding it. But Loor's quick thinking had protected us. At least for the time being.

"Outta here!" I shouted, and we ran for the door to the hallway.

More gunshots were fired as bullets ripped through the kitchen, barely missing us and instead slamming into the kitchen walls. The instant we ran out of the door, we discovered where the bad smell had come from.

The mansion was on fire.

If that wasn't bad enough, the entire downstairs hallway was full of horses. I'm serious. It was like being in the frenzy of wild horses back in the blacksmith's barn, times about a hundred because the animals were terrified by the fire that shot flames and smoke out of the rooms on either side of the hallway. Loor took the lead, pulling me behind her, pushing her way through the terrified mass of horses. She actually shoved some of the big animals out of our way. Good thing she was here. I probably would have been trampled.

We made our way back to the front door, but it was engulfed in flames. No way we were getting out that way.

"Upstairs!" I shouted.

We ran up the wide, carpeted stairway to the second floor. I figured that with any luck, we could make our way to the back of the house and get out of a window before being burned or shot or trampled.

"How could this happen?" Loor shouted as we ran up the stairs.

"You're asking me like I know?" I shouted back. "I'm just as freaked as you are!"

We got to the top of the stairs and ran down the hallway, heading for a window on the far end. We were just about to throw it open, when the window shattered. Loor and I both fell to the ground as bits of glass rained down on us. Saint Dane's desperados were outside, waiting for us.

We were trapped.

Another gunshot was heard that smashed a picture hanging right next to my head. We both spun towards the stairs to see a ghastly sight. Saint Dane was standing on the top stair, backed by the burning flames from down below. He was like a demonic shadow standing there, with two six-guns drawn.

"Time is running out, children," he chuckled. "What's your next move?"

I pushed Loor into a bedroom off the hallway and slammed the door shut. This wouldn't get us out, but at least it would buy us a few more seconds to think.

"How can this be?" Loor demanded to know.

My shock was wearing off now, and my brain was beginning to function. An idea was forming. It started when we first saw those cowpokes seated around Evangeline's table. With each new disaster, my theory became more real.

"There can only be one explanation for all this," I said. I then lifted my arm, and pulled back the sleeve of my jumpsuit to see . . . I was right.

I was still wearing a silver control bracelet. Loor lifted her arm to see she was still wearing one as well.

"But we removed these," she said, totally confused.

"We thought we did," I answered. "But that's because we didn't know the truth."

"And what is the truth?"

"We're still in the jump," I said. "This is still part of the fantasy."

Crack!

A bullet tore through the door. Saint Dane had come a-knocking. I pulled Loor across the room and we huddled down behind the bed.

"Why did we not see these before?" she asked.

"Because we thought we were out of the jump," I answered. "That's how it works, if you give yourself over to the fantasy, you won't see the bracelets. But as soon as I realised we were still in the jump, they appeared."

Crack! Crack!

Two more bullets splintered the wood of the door.

"Come out, come out, wherever you are!" came Saint Dane's singsong voice from the hallway.

"So then none of this is real?" Loor asked.

"Real enough," I said. "But it's time to get out."

I lifted my arm to look at the control bracelet and the three buttons. The one to the far right was supposed to end the jump, but obviously that didn't work. The one in the middle was supposed to change the jump, but the last time I tried using that, we almost got eaten by quigs. The button to the far left was my only choice, so I hit it.

The button glowed white for a moment, and then . . .

"It's about time!"

Loor and I looked up to see Aja standing there.

"I thought you'd never figure it out!"

"Aja, what happened?" I asked.

"You never went into Zetlin's jump," she answered. "It must have been the Reality Bug. I realised it the second I inserted you, but couldn't do anything about it until you realised it for yourself and called for me."

"Are you really here?" I asked.

"No," was the answer. "It's just my image. I'm still in the Alpha Core."

Suddenly a wardrobe door blew open and flames licked out. The fire had reached the first floor. We were about to cook.

"Getting warm in there?" Saint Dane taunted from the hallway.

"Get us out of here!" I shouted to Aja.

"It's too risky," Aja answered.

"Risky?" I shouted back. "How can it get any riskier than this?"

"If I pull you out now, I may not be able to get you back in," she answered. "The Reality Bug is fighting to take over Zetlin's jump. I don't know how much longer I can keep it back, and we've still got to find Zetlin!"

"Aja," Loor said calmly. "If we do not get out of here, we will not live long enough to find anybody."

"I know," Aja said. "Pendragon, push the middle button."

"What?" I shouted. "The last time —"

"I know what happened the last time," Aja interrupted. "But while you were playing cowboy, I programmed a link."

"A link?" I asked.

Suddenly, with a crash, the door to the bedroom flew open and Saint Dane strode in.

"Time for the last roundup, buckaroos!" Saint Dane said. He raised his six-guns, ready to fire.

"Push the button, Pendragon!" Aja screamed.

I did.

Saint Dane let loose with both guns, blasting us. I heard the sharp cracks, I saw the fire come from the muzzles, but I didn't feel a thing, because a nanosecond later, everything went black.

VEELOX

I thought I was standing inside a giant colander. You know, one of those big silver bowls with all the holes in it for draining spaghetti. Everywhere I looked, I saw tiny, round dots. For a second I feared I was in some giant, fantasy kitchen, and a pile of boiling linguini was about to get dumped on me.

But that didn't make sense. Still, there were far too many of these holes to have been made by Saint Dane's six-shooter. So where was I?

I looked closer to see the dots weren't holes after all. They were little globes of water about the size of peas. There were millions, no, billions of them all frozen in space, everywhere. I lifted my hand and moved it slowly in front of my face. As I passed through the suspended drops of water, my hand got wet. Stranger still, my hand cleared a path through the drops. It was like what happens when you wipe a steamy window. Wherever I moved my hand, I cleared a trail.

"Where are we, Pendragon?" Loor was standing next to me, doing the exact same thing. She took a step forward, clearing a body-size path through the dots of water. As she moved, her green jumpsuit got wetter and wetter.

Yes, we were both still wearing our jumpsuits.

"I don't know," was my answer. I was tired of giving that answer. I looked around to get my bearings, but couldn't see much. It was like we were in a misty white cloud. The ground we stood on was paved, but I couldn't see much more than a few feet in any direction.

"What is that?" Loor said, pointing at something.

I looked to see a faint, dark form not too far from us. It wasn't moving, and didn't seem to be a threat, so I cautiously walked towards it. It was strange feeling the water cling to my jumpsuit as I walked, making it wet. As I got closer to the dark form, it began to take shape. After one more step, the mist cleared enough for me to see what it was, and I caught my breath.

It was a man wearing a green jumpsuit, just like ours. He was a normal-looking guy about my father's age. There was nothing odd about him at all, except for the fact that he was frozen in place. Seriously, the guy didn't move at all. It looked like he was in the middle of taking a step while looking backwards and beckoning with his hand when somebody hit the "pause" button on his life.

I looked to where he was gesturing, and saw two more people a few feet behind him. It was a woman holding the hand of a little girl. They seemed to be hurrying to catch up with the man, except that they were frozen too. It was like looking at a display in a wax museum. How seriously creepy can you get?

"What is wrong with them?" Loor asked.

An idea started to tickle at the back of my brain. I looked around at the billions of dots of suspended water all around us. Was it possible?

"I think it's rain," I declared. "All these drops of water. It's a rainstorm."

"How can that be?" Loor responded.

"I don't know," I said while passing my hand through the dots again. "But I think this Lifelight fantasy is somehow frozen in time."

I took a closer look at the stiff family. There was absolutely nothing wrong with them. Their eyes were clear, their skin was normal. Close-up they didn't look like waxworks; they seemed totally real. I even took a chance and touched the guy's hand.

"He's warm," I said. "This guy is stuck in time. So is the rain and the white mist. It's a storm. Everything just . . . stopped."

Loor walked a few steps past the woman and kid. She wanted to see more. So did I. I followed her and the two of us passed through more drops of water, beyond which the mist began to thin.

"Look!" Loor exclaimed.

Once we were out of the patch of fog, or mist, or whatever it was, we got a better view of our surroundings. We still couldn't see very far, but it was enough to get an idea of what this place was all about, and I have to say, it was like a surreal nightmare.

We were on a city street, but it wasn't like any city I had ever seen because the buildings were all jet black. They looked to be made from the same shiny material that covered the giant Lifelight pyramid in Rubic City.

The place was busy with people, though I guess "busy" isn't exactly the right word — they were all just as frozen as the family we had passed. There were people of different ages and races, all wearing green jumpsuits. The pavements were crowded too. Some people were in the middle of crossing the street; others rode in pedal vehicles like in Rubic City. But unlike Rubic City, this place was alive with people.

Did I say alive? It felt like we were standing inside a 3-D painting. "Alive" didn't really cover it.

We then heard a voice come from behind us. "This is incredible!"

Loor and I both jumped in surprise, then turned quickly to see Aja standing there. She was looking around with as much awe as we felt.

"So this is the fantasy of a genius," she said. "Not exactly paradise, is it?"

"Is this it?" I asked. "Is this Dr Zetlin's fantasy jump?"

Aja checked her elaborate wrist controller. "Yes, I linked you in. Now the trick is to find him."

"What happened before?" Loor asked. "Where was that other place?"

"It was the Reality Bug," Aja explained. "I'm constantly fighting it. Every time I enter a string of commands, it tries to alter them. Instead of going into Dr Zetlin's jump, Lifelight took its cues from you, Pendragon. Everything that happened was pulled out of your mind."

Loor gave me a confused look. This made no sense to her. Oddly enough, it did to me. All the things we ran into: the Old West, the stampede, Saint Dane, Gunny, everything. It all came out of my mind. It wasn't a fantasy out of the past of Veelox at all; it was a good old-fashioned Western from home.

"So, Saint Dane was not really chasing us?" Loor asked.

"Correct," Aja answered. "He was part of the fantasy."

"But now we're in Zetlin World, right?" I asked.

"Yes," Aja answered with confidence. "Sorry for the detour."

"Are you here with us, Aja?" Loor asked.

"No," Aja answered. "I'm still in the core."

Aja passed her hand through the drops of water, but her movement didn't clear a path the way ours did. This was only an image of Aja. Loor walked up to her curiously, and tried to touch her. Her hand passed right through. Loor backed away quickly. I guess touching a ghost spooked her, so to speak.

"It's okay," I assured Loor. "Everything's cool."

"Pendragon, I want to find Zetlin and leave here quickly," Loor said nervously.

"Yeah, me too. But I don't know where to start," I admitted.

"When Dr Zetlin started his jump," Aja said, "he didn't want to be bothered. Ever. The last thing he wanted was to have people from Veelox entering his jump and disturbing him."

"Which is exactly what we're doing," I offered.

"Yes, but the guy is a genius," Aja continued. "He knew there might be an emergency where he needed to be contacted."

"I think this qualifies," I said.

Aja showed us a small, blue plastic box. It was about the size and shape of a floppy disk.

"Zetlin left one of these for every senior phader, in case of emergency," Aja explained. "Entering Zetlin's jump is difficult enough. Controlling it is a whole different challenge. These are the codes to do that."

"So, what happens when you use them?" I asked.

"I don't know," was Aja's quick reply. "Let's find out."

She held out the plastic case and snapped it open, revealing a thin silver square inside. Aja took out the square and examined it.

"Two sets of codes," she announced.

"I don't suppose either is the origin code?" I asked hopefully.

"I wish," she replied. "I'll try the first."

She lifted her wrist controller and inputted a series of commands as she referred to the silver square. It must have been a complex code, because it took her several seconds to enter it. Then, with one final keystroke . . .

It began to rain.

The once suspended drops fell from the sky, soaking us. Thunder rumbled in the distance.

"Look out!" somebody yelled.

Loor grabbed me and pulled me aside as a man driving a pedal vehicle sped by.

"Careful there, folks," the guy called with a friendly wave. "The street gets busy."

Yeah, no kidding. I looked down the road to see that the painting had reanimated. People splashed through puddles, rushing to get out of the rain. The lady and little girl caught up with the man. He took the girl by the hand and they hurried on their way. The white foggy mist was now moving too. It blew down the street, rolling quickly along with the storm.

"Fascinating!" was all Aja could say.

"Let's get off the street," I suggested, and the three of us ran to the pavement and under the protection of an overhang that covered the entrance to a building.

We stood there, watching Zetlin's fantasy city come alive.

"I don't get it," I said. "Here's a genius guy who could live in any kind of paradise he could think of, and he chooses a grey, rainy city with black buildings? He may be smart, but he doesn't have such a hot imagination."

I then stepped in front of a guy who was about to enter

the building we were using for shelter.

"Excuse me," I said. "Do you know Dr Zetlin?"

The guy looked at me strangely, like I had three noses or something.

"What's the joke?" he asked.

I looked to Aja. She shrugged.

"No joke," I said. "Do you know where we can find Dr Zetlin?"

The guy shook his head in confusion. "In the Barbican," he answered. "Where else would he be?"

"Barbican," I repeated. "Okay. Where's the Barbican?"

The guy shook his head again, like I was being an idiot. He sniffed and continued on into the building without answering.

"I guess everybody around here is supposed to know where he is," Aja said.

"Yeah, everybody but us," I said. "What's a Barbican?"

"Pendragon?" Loor said softly.

She stepped out on to the pavement, staring down the street with a dumbfounded expression.

"I do not know what a Barbican is, but if I were to wager, I would say that is it," she said in awe.

Aja and I turned to see what she was pointing at. What we saw was about as incredible a sight as I could imagine.

The rain had stopped. The storm was moving through quickly and the foggy mist was blowing away. We could now see a long way down the wide street. The buildings on either side were different sizes and styles, but all were made of the same, shiny black material. As the fog lifted, more people were revealed. They were all dressed in the same dark green jumpsuit style, going about their business. It was an incredibly drab city. But what we saw at the end of the street was anything but drab.

It was another black building. Actually, it was more like a

skyscraper. I'm guessing it must have been about eighty storeys. It was way bigger than any of the other buildings on the street. But its size alone wasn't what made it stand out. The breathtaking thing about it was that this huge building was floating on its side!

Actually, it wasn't exactly floating. There was a massive, triangular brace that held it in the air. You know that big Gateway Arch thing in St Louis on Second Earth? That's what this brace looked like. Imagine that big arch with a huge, horizontal building attached to the top. That's what we were faced with. It looked like a seesaw for a giant.

The three of us stood and stared at the impressive structure. Nobody knew what to say. It was Aja who moved first. Without a word, she began walking. It was like she was being drawn towards the bizarre building. I gave Loor a quick look and we followed. We walked along the pavement in a daze. I'd guess that by the time we got to it, we must have walked a mile.

As we stood under the monstrous structure, the clouds parted. Bright sun shone through and hit the side of the floating skyscraper, making its black skin sparkle.

Loor finally broke the silence, saying, "How are we to get inside?"

"Aja?" I said. "You said there were two codes?"

"Yes," she answered.

"Try the second one."

Aja shrugged, looked at the silver square, then inputted Zetlin's second code into her wrist controller. After hitting the final key, she said, "That's it."

Nothing happened. I glanced back at the street, afraid that the second code would refreeze the fantasy. But the drab people continued to move, going wherever they were going.

I said, "Try it again —"

And that's when it happened. At first we only heard the sound. It was a loud, grinding noise that hurt my ears. It sounded like giant pieces of metal were screeching against each other because, well, that's what it was.

"It is moving!" Loor exclaimed.

We all looked up at the black building to see it was beginning to rotate. Like a monstrous Ferris wheel, the massive building slowly began to turn on its axis. I looked to the ground under the giant brace to see the outline of a huge square.

"It's the footprint!" I shouted. "The building is righting itself!"

That's exactly what was happening. The building was slowly rotating to vertical. The only trouble was, we were standing inside the giant square.

"Back off!" I shouted.

All three of us hurried back out of the danger zone. The screeching and grinding continued as one end of the building dropped nearer to the ground. It was incredible that something that big could actually move like that. But then again, this was the fantasy of a genius. I guess in Zetlin's mind, it was possible.

The whole event took about a minute. With a final rush of air that sounded like the brakes on an eighteen-wheeler, times about a thousand, the base of the building settled on to the square on the ground. The ground shook with the deep rumble of an earthquake as the base touched down. We then looked up to see an eighty-storey-tall skyscraper reaching vertically towards the sky. Its black skin sparkled with rainwater. There didn't seem to be a single window in the whole structure. But at the base, looking like a flea on a dog, was a single doorway.

"Man," I said. "This guy really makes it tough to pay a visit."

"That must be the way in," Loor said, pointing to the door. "Follow me."

"Wait," Aja said. "I should go back."

"Why?" I asked.

"It's the Reality Bug," she explained. "I have to keep putting up firewalls to keep it out of this jump. I need to be focused in the Alpha Core to do that."

"What if we need you?" I asked.

"Believe me, Pendragon, you need me in the Alpha Core a lot more than you do here. If the Reality Bug gets into the alpha grid —"

"I get it," I interrupted.

Aja looked at the ground. Something was troubling her.

"What's the matter?" I asked.

"I . . . I'm sorry, Pendragon," she said softly. "I hate that I've put you and Loor in this position."

"We're here because we're Travellers, Aja," I said. "Don't be sorry. Just keep that freakin' Reality Bug away from us, okay?"

Aja nodded. She then reached out towards me. I think she wanted me to take her hand. I looked into her eyes and actually thought I saw compassion. Did Aja really care about me? A little while ago she hated that I had ever set foot on Veelox because she feared I would steal her thunder. What a difference a few death-defying escapes can make.

"I believe," Aja said, "this is truly the way it was meant to be."

I reached out towards her, but my hand passed right through hers. After all, she was only an image of herself.

"Good luck to you both," she said sincerely. "I'll be watching."

She then disappeared in a ripple of light.

I stood there with my hand in the air, looking stupid.

"I believe she likes you," Loor said.

I quickly put my hand in my pocket. How embarrassing was that? I really didn't want Loor to think Aja and I had a "thing", because we didn't.

"Will you include that in your journal to Courtney Chetwynde?" she asked.

I couldn't believe it. Loor was teasing me. "There's nothing going on," I assured her, though I think I said it with such force that she didn't believe me.

"Very well," Loor said. "You do not need to convince me."

"Let it go, all right?" I said.

Loor looked up at the looming skyscraper. "He is in there somewhere," she said.

"Right," I added. "Let's go and find him."

The two of us then walked together towards the small door that would lead us inside the strange, fantasy world of Dr Zetlin, genius.

The creator of Lifelight.

VEELOX

We stepped into a jungle.

I'm not kidding. It was a tropical rain forest full of palm trees, dense foliage, and mosquitoes. The ground beneath us was soft, dark dirt. The temperature had to be at least ninety degrees. It was so humid, my jumpsuit was already sticking to me. I swear I even heard the sound of a distant waterfall.

"How can this be, Pendragon?" Loor asked.

I turned back and saw the black door we had just entered through. We were definitely inside the strange building called the Barbican, but it sure as heck didn't feel like we were indoors. I looked up expecting to see a ceiling, but all I saw was blackness. I half expected to see stars, but that would have been impossible. Then again, when you were inside the fantasy of a genius inventor, maybe nothing was impossible.

"This is Zetlin's world," I answered. "I think we have to be ready for anything."

A narrow path cut through the thick foliage. It was the only way to go. Loor took the lead, pushing past me and walking boldly down the path to somewhere. It reminded me of the way she took the lead down in the dark mine tunnels of

Denduron. Only this time, neither of us had any idea where we were going.

Loor walked quickly, pushing away the leafy branches that hung over the trail. I had to hang back a few feet or I would have got whacked by the branches as they swung back after she passed.

"What was that?" she asked, stopping short.

I heard it too. It sounded as if something were scurrying around in the underbrush, but it was so dense, it was impossible to see anything. Whatever was in there, I sure hoped it was just as hard for it to see us, too. We stood there for a second, listening, but the only sound we heard was the drip of moisture falling from the large, leafy plants.

"Keep going," I suggested.

Loor continued on. "What are we looking for?" she asked over her shoulder.

"I don't know, but I bet we'll know it when we see it."

A minute later the path led us to a clearing in the jungle. It was a wide open, circular space that looked as if it had been cleared for a jungle campground. All the plant life had been neatly cut away in a circle. I could see the sliced-off ends of branches all around, as if somebody had come through with a monster weed whacker. We walked to the centre of the clearing, and stopped when we both heard more rustling in the bushes. We shot each other a look. Something was definitely out there.

"Dr Zetlin?" I called out.

No answer. No more rustling, either.

"What kind of place is this, Pendragon?" Loor asked.

"There are jungles like this on Second Earth," I answered. "But Zetlin isn't from Second Earth so I have no clue what to expect."

At that exact instant, something shot out of the bushes. It was a long vine. But it was like it had been shot from a gun, because the vine flew right for us. Loor and I ducked back and the vine barely missed us. The end flew into the bushes on the far side and attached to something so that it stretched across the clearing like a rope.

Before we had the chance to react, another vine shot out the same way. Only this one flew behind us before attaching to a tree on the far side. Loor and I now stood between the two ropelike vines.

"Does this happen on Second Earth?" Loor asked.

"No, and I don't like it. C'mon," I said.

We ducked under the vine and ran for the far end of the clearing, where the path continued. As we ran, more vines shot from the bushes. They were coming fast now, shooting every which way — in front of us, over our heads, behind us. In seconds Loor and I were surrounded by a tangle of taut vines. They built up quickly in front of the trail, blocking our passage. There was only one way to describe what it looked like.

"Spider's web," I said.

As if on cue, we heard more rustling in the bushes. The sound was much louder now. Whatever was making it was coming our way. Loor and I both looked back to see movement at the far edge of the clearing. There were a bunch of places where the foliage moved, making way for whatever was coming.

I was dying to know what it was. On the other hand, I didn't *really* want to die just to know what it was. If we were about to get attacked by a giant spider, I'd just as soon be somewhere else. Loor didn't waste time thinking. She lunged for the side of the clearing and grabbed a five-foot-long branch. It looked strong enough that in the right hands, it could do some damage.

Loor had the right hands.

"Whatever it is," she announced, "if it charges, stay behind me."

I think we were both expecting to see a wild animal come out of the underbrush. Instead, what pushed its way out, slithering along the ground, looked more like a big cactus. Seriously. It was some kind of plant. It actually looked kind of pretty. It had a tubular body that was green and covered with thorns. The head was actually a violet-coloured flower. The bud was pretty big too, about the size of a beach ball. It had large petals that opened and closed, like it was breathing.

Loor and I stood and watched in wonder as more of these strange plants pushed their way into the clearing. The flower blossoms, or whatever they were, were all different colours. Bright pink, purple, deep blue, and brilliant yellow. I counted eight in all. It was like they were creeping into the clearing, taking a curious look at who their visitors were.

"They're kind of pretty," I said.

Wrong. On cue, all eight blossoms opened up and spat out vines that shot right at us! Whoa! One of the vines latched on to my arm, cutting into my jumpsuit. The thing had razor-sharp barbs on it! I quickly pulled it off, just as another wrapped around my ankle and yanked me to the ground. It then started pulling me towards it! One quick look at the plant showed me all I needed to know. Inside the blossoms were sharp, gnashing, fanglike growths. These beautiful plants were hungry, and we had wandered into their house for a bite . . . of us.

"Loor!" I shouted.

I didn't need to. Loor had already gone to work with her whupping stick. She hacked like a lumberjack at the vine that had my leg. Two quick whacks and I was free, but the plant screamed. I swear, it actually screamed in pain. I jumped to my feet to see Loor was swinging her stick like crazy, batting away more vines that were shooting out of the plants at us.

"The trail!" I shouted.

I got behind her, grabbed the back of her jumpsuit and pulled her back towards the safety of the trail. As I pulled her back, she kept swinging away at the incoming missiles like she was in hyper batting-practice mode. She nailed most of them too, knocking them off course.

I kicked at the spider's web of vines that was blocking the path. They may have been dense, but they weren't very strong because I could tear them down pretty easily. While I desperately tried to make an opening, Loor valiantly batted away the attacking vines. But there were too many of them. There was no way she could keep this up. I took a quick look back to see the toothy cactus plants were crawling closer, moving in for the kill.

"Just run!" I shouted.

Loor took one last swipe at an incoming vine, then turned with me and ran. We ducked through the opening in the web and sprinted along the narrow path. More vines zinged by our heads, trying to grab us and pull us back. As we got farther from the clearing, the vine attack tapered off. But we didn't stop running. Still, I feared we could easily be heading towards another nest of those nasty barb-shooting cactus plants.

After a few minutes of frantic chase, we both felt safe enough to take a rest. Good thing, too. My lungs were bursting out of my chest, that's how hard we were running. I think being terrified had something to do with it too. I stood there with my hands on my knees, gulping for air. Loor, on the other hand, barely looked winded. She scanned the jungle for any more signs of movement.

"There!" she announced.

"Please don't tell me it's another hungry vegetable," I gasped.

As strange as this sounds, rising up from the middle of the jungle was a spiral staircase. It led up and out of the foliage and disappeared into the dark. At first my brain couldn't compute why a spiral staircase would be in a dark jungle full of hungry predators. But then it hit me.

"We're inside a building," I said. "That must lead up to the next floor."

"Do we climb?" Loor asked.

"Do we have a choice?" I asked back.

Loor took the lead and continued along the path until it brought us to the foot of the stairs. They were made of metal, and a quick tug told us they were solid enough. The whole structure was overgrown with vines, like the ones that had been shooting at us. I touched them to see if they might suddenly spring to life and start attacking, but nothing happened. I took a step back and looked up to where the stairs led, but all I saw was black.

Loor gave me a quick look, then started to climb. I was right after her. The higher we got, the better view we had of the jungle below. The place was vast. But because it was so dense and dark, I couldn't see all the way to the far walls of the building. At least I thought we were still in a building. None of this really made sense, but then again, if it was a fantasy, was it supposed to make sense? It probably did to Dr Zetlin.

After climbing for a few minutes, we found ourselves in darkness. Looking down below we saw the jungle, and to be honest, it was making my palms sweat. We were pretty high up. I was trying to figure out how we would make our way back through the jungle to get out of here, when Loor stopped suddenly.

"Trouble," she said calmly.

"What is it?" I asked, though I wasn't sure I really wanted to know.

I looked up to see we had reached the next level. The circular staircase continued up through a large round hole in the black ceiling. Loor reached her hand up through that hole, but when she pulled it back down, I felt drops of water on my head. Huh? She showed me her hand. It was wet.

"I don't get it," I said, and climbed up past her. I put my hand up to the hole to find that it was actually a circle of water. As soon as I touched it, ripples spread out from my fingers, as if I were looking at an upside down pond. I had no idea how the liquid could be suspended like that and not gush down through the large opening. But it was and it didn't.

Loor said, "I am beginning to believe Dr Zetlin does not like visitors."

"You think?" I said sarcastically. "We gotta go through this."

"Pendragon," Loor said with a firm voice. "I cannot swim."

Oh, man, I'd forgotten. As incredible an athlete as Loor was, she was like a rock in the water. This was bad. I knew what had to happen next, and it made my stomach twist.

"We gotta keep going," I said, trying to sound confident. "I'll check it out."

I really, *really* didn't want to, but what else could I do? I could tell that Loor wanted to argue, but she knew there was no other way. So before I could chicken out, I took another step up so that my head was just below the ceiling of water. I took a couple of deep breaths to expand my lungs, then held the last breath and pushed my head up into the wet.

The water was warm. That was one good thing. I only went in up to my shoulders and did my best to get a look around. There wasn't a whole lot to see, but I think that was mostly because my vision was blurred by the water. What I wouldn't have given at that moment for an air globe from Cloral! As it was, there was nothing to see when I looked around but wet blackness.

Yet when I looked straight up, I saw light coming from above. I took a step back down and dropped out of the water. My head and shoulders were wet, but very little water spilled out from above. Unbelievable.

"It's a big pool," I said. "This is the bottom, but I can't tell how far it is to the surface."

Loor and I looked at each other. We both knew what had to happen next. Loor started yanking vines off the railing of the stairs.

"I will tie one end to your ankle," she explained.

She was a few steps ahead of me. I was still trying to get my mind around the fact that I had to swim up into the unknown. Loor was already making sure I would get back to safety. She quickly tore off a length of vine that was plenty long enough for this adventure. If I swam upward for the full length of this vine and still hadn't found the surface, there would be no way I'd have enough air in my lungs to make it back to the hole.

Loor tied one end around my ankle, then stood and faced me.

"I will hold on to your waist," she said. "Please do not lose me."

"Whoa, you're not coming!"

"It is better that we stay together and make the trip only once," she explained.

She didn't show a touch of fear, though she had to be terrified. Man, this girl was brave. I wasn't sure which was worse, taking her with me, or risking the trip by myself and having to do it twice. I decided that as long as Loor was game, we'd go together.

"Okay," I said. "But if we don't find the surface right away, we're coming right back."

Loor nodded. She tied the other end of the vine around the railing of the stairs. With a quick tug, she made sure it was secure. The rest of the vine she placed in a coil on one of the stairs. Loor then stood behind me, and wrapped her arms around my waist. I could feel the strength in those arms. I sure hoped she didn't get too scared, or she'd break me in half.

"If you start running out of breath, give me two quick squeezes," I instructed. "I'll turn us around and get right back here."

"I understand," she said.

Loor was focused, battling her fear. There was no way I was going to let anything happen to her. We stood together with my head just below the water.

"Take some deep breaths," I said. "You'll be able to hold your breath longer."

We both took three deep breaths, holding the third. With a quick nod, we both walked *up* into the water.

We had to move fast. Every second counted. It was a strange feeling. A second before, we were standing on stairs with gravity pulling us down. Now the water took over, and we were pulled the other way, up. I started doing the breast-stroke, spearing my hands up, then pulling a downward stroke with as much power as I had. Loor held tight and her weight was a huge drag. It didn't matter. All I could focus on was getting to the surface as fast as possible. There was no way of knowing how far it was. After about five strokes, I started thinking about turning back, because it was going to be a lot harder to swim down than up. I made a quick decision. Five more strokes and we'd turn around.

That's when I heard a strange sound. It was high-pitched, like an engine. Of course, it was hard to know where it was coming from because we were underwater. But there was one thing for sure: Whatever it was, it was getting louder. That meant it was getting closer.

I took a quick look straight ahead and saw lights in the distance. There were five of them at our level, underwater. They looked like torch beams, heading our way. Fast. Whatever they were, they were definitely making the whining sound.

I didn't know what to do. Were these lights a threat? Should I turn around and get us back down to the hole? Should I pull even harder and hope we would reach the surface? Should we stay where we were and defend ourselves?

I didn't have time to decide because in seconds they were on us. All five lights dipped down and passed underneath us so fast that I couldn't get a good look at what they were. They didn't hit us, but as soon as they shot beneath, I felt a hard tug that forced me to stop swimming. I knew instantly what had happened. A quick look down confirmed it.

Whatever those speeding lights were, they had severed the vine that was our lifeline to the bottom. The cut end drifted up next to me. We were floating free.

That's when Loor gave me two quick squeezes. She was running out of air.

We were trapped in a watery limbo.

VEELOX

I had to keep swimming for the surface.

We were too far away from the hole at the bottom to get back down. Besides, without the vine to guide us there was no guarantee I would even find it. No, the choice was clear. Swim up like crazy, or drown.

I kept doing the breaststroke as hard as I could. I really wished I could have kicked my legs, too, but Loor was wrapped around my lower body. My lungs were starting to ache. I think I was swimming so hard that it burned up whatever oxygen I had left.

An idea hit me: Press the button on my control bracelet and end the jump. If we didn't reach the surface in a few seconds it would be our only hope. But it was the last resort and there was no guarantee it would even work. Keep swimming.

A few agonising seconds passed and we were still underwater. I was starting to black out. We had to get air, now. Time to abort. I reached for my control bracelet, but at the exact moment before I bailed us out, something splashed down into the water only a few yards away. Whatever it was, it was pretty big and moving fast because it made a dramatic *boom* when it hit the water. But I didn't care what it was. All I knew was that if something made a splash like that, we had to be near the surface. So I didn't hit the button, and made two more desperate strokes for air.

A moment later I broke the surface, followed right behind by Loor, both gasping for air. We had made it! But there wasn't time to celebrate because we now faced another danger. Loor couldn't swim. I had to change gears fast, and take care of her. She was already starting to flail in the water. If she clocked me by accident, I'd be out cold, and we'd both be sunk. Literally.

"Relax," I commanded. "Float on your back, Loor. I've got you."

Loor rolled on to her back. She was breathing hard and her eyes were wild, but she tried to relax. I held her head above the surface and started to tread water.

"We're okay," I said, trying to sound soothing. "Let's just catch our breath and we'll get out of here."

I took the chance to look around to get my bearings. The cavernous space we were floating in was pitch black, and like the jungle below, I couldn't see the far walls of this incredible fantasy building. Again the ceiling disappeared into black. But there was something odd in the air above us. Floating midair all over this huge space were colourful, brightly lit globes. They looked to be about two feet in diameter, with each glowing a different neon colour. Orange, red, green, yellow. There must have been a hundred of them, all floating in the air above us at different levels.

"They are like colourful stars," Loor said. "What could they be?"

This was good. She was calming down.

"I have no idea," I said. "They don't look dangerous –"

Suddenly there was an eruption in the water a few feet from

us. Exploding up from below came the lights that had severed our line. But now we saw them for what they really were.

They were vehicles.

All five shot up from underwater and flew into the air. They looked to me like bright, colourful motorcycles without wheels. Each had a rider wearing a helmet. They were crouched down low like jockeys behind a conelike wind-shield. They were hauling, too. The vehicles flew out of the water and continued up towards the floating globes. These things not only travelled underwater, they could fly! All five riders charged in a pack towards a bright orange globe. They sped past it, turned sharply around it, and shot ahead towards the next one.

"They're racing!" I exclaimed. "Those globes mark the racecourse!"

The five racers flew away from us, speeding from globe to globe. They all then turned together and dived back towards the water. A second later all five hit the surface and disappeared below like a pack of hungry seagulls hunting for fish.

"How cool is that!" I exclaimed. "This is a racecourse!"

"Pendragon," Loor said calmly, "I still can't swim."

Oh, right. We had to get out of the water. I took another look around and was relieved to see another spiral staircase rising out of the water only a few yards away. A few quick strokes and I had towed Loor to the stairs. We both clung to them, happy to have solid footing again. While we sat catching our breaths, we watched as the racers erupted from the water once again, shot into the sky, and charged far off into the distance. Whoever these racers were, they were good, and they had the coolest vehicles I had ever seen.

"Are you okay?" I asked Loor.

Loor nodded and said, "We must continue up."

I gazed up the staircase to see that it disappeared into blackness.

"Man," I said. "This guy Zetlin is a piece of work."

This time I took the lead and hurried up the stairs. As we rose up, we kept watching the racers zip around the globes, plunge into the water, then fly up again and back on to the airborne course. It looked like a lot of fun.

When we arrived at the ceiling, I was relieved to see this next opening wasn't water. Instead, the staircase rose up through a large, white circle.

Loor said, "How can this be? We are no longer wet."

Sure enough, our jumpsuits and our hair were completely dry. I was beyond questioning anything that happened. If we were suddenly, magically dry, so be it. Whatever. As it turned out, it was a good thing because when I reached out to the edge of the circle to touch the white band, I was surprised to feel that it was cold.

"It's snow!" I announced.

Sure enough, I was able to dig my hand into the white edge of the circle and come back with a handful of ice crystals.

"Now what?" was all I could say.

I continued up the last few steps and arrived at a small, snow cave. It was like standing up inside an igloo. It was chilly, too. Good thing we were dry.

"I guess that's the way," I said, pointing to the opening to the cave.

Neither of us had any idea what to expect outside, but we had to brave it. So the two of us walked towards the light and out of the cave. The small cavern took a turn, and as soon as we both rounded it, we were blinded by an incredibly intense, white light. After having been in the dark of the jungle and the watery racecourse, all we could do was cover our eyes and wait until they adjusted to this new environment. It took a few seconds, but when we lowered our hands, we were met with yet another incredible sight.

It looked like Antarctica.

Not that I've ever been to Antarctica, but if I had, I'm sure it would look like this. Everything was white, which explained why we were having trouble seeing. The sky was bright white too. Again, we may have been inside a building, but this time we were enveloped in such blindingly bright light that we couldn't see walls or a ceiling.

As my eyes grew more accustomed to the light, I began to make out more detail. It seemed like we were standing on a vast field of ice. It wasn't all flat, though. There were huge mounds of craggy ice that formed hills and valleys all around us.

"This Dr Zetlin has a very strange imagination," Loor said.

Before I could agree, we heard excited shouting.

"Whooo! Yeah! Eehaaaaa!"

It sounded like a bunch of guys having an adrenalin rush. A second later five figures appeared on top of one of the icy mounds. They shot over the top, got some serious air, and then landed on the slope and slid down on what looked like snowboards. They weren't like Second Earth snowboards though. These things were round and black. They were about the size of a dustbin lid and curved up at the rim. The riders' feet were attached in the middle somehow. Man, they were good. As they sped down the slope, they did three-sixties and dodged around one another and basically looked like a stunt team. They all wore the familiar green jumpsuits, but with black helmets that covered most of their heads and faces.

Loor and I watched in awe as the five riders sped towards us. I wasn't sure if we should run, or hold our ground. I started to back away, but Loor stopped me.

"No," she said. "We cannot show fear."

Easy for her to say. But I stayed where I was.

A second later Loor and I were hit with a spray of snow as the snow riders dug in and stopped directly in front of us. It was a totally awkward moment. The five helmeted riders stood shoulder to shoulder, staring at us through dark, tinted goggles. Nobody said anything. Finally I figured it was time to cut to the chase.

"We're looking for Dr Zetlin," I said.

The five riders looked at one another and started to laugh. I didn't expect that. Then again, I'm not sure what I expected. Finally one of them got control of himself enough to step forward.

"You can't just show up and see the Z," he said.

"It's very important," I said, feeling kind of lame. "He'll want to see us."

I had no idea how to sum up quickly why we had to see Dr. Zetlin. They didn't seem like the kind of guys who would stand still for a long-winded explanation. Or care.

"Do you know where he is?" Loor asked.

Another rider walked up to her and said, "Sure, but if you want to see him, you've got to play first."

"Play?" I asked. "Play what?"

"Slickshot!" another rider shouted.

"Yeah! Slickshot!" the others chimed in.

The riders then quickly released their boots from their snow discs, tossed them aside, and started to skate across the ice. It seemed impossible because they moved like they had ice skates on, but they hadn't. They were sliding along with only their boot bottoms touching the surface. The first rider then skated back to us and stopped right in front of me.

"Here's the deal," he said. "One of you races slickshot with us. You don't have to win, just finish."

"What kind of race is it?" I asked.

The guy pointed out across the ice to the other racers who were skating along.

"It's a skating race," he explained. "There's a course over the ice marked by red arrows. We all skate the course together, first one back here wins."

"And all we have to do is finish?" I asked.

"It's not that easy," the rider explained. "There are five checkpoints. The first one has a tower with six red balls in it. One for each racer. You have to pick up a ball, then skate forward and drop it in a basket before skating to the next checkpoint. That one has six balls too. But the third checkpoint has only five balls. If you're the last one there, you're done. The next one has five balls too, but the final checkpoint has only four."

"So six start the race and only four finish," I said.

"Exactly," the guy said. "Finish the race and you can meet the Z."

"We are not here to play games," Loor said firmly.

"Too bad," the rider said with a shrug. "We are."

With that he turned and started to skate away.

"Wait!" I shouted. "I'll give it a shot. But I don't get how you guys are skating without skates."

The racer skated over to the mouth of the cave. Next to the opening was something we hadn't seen when we arrived. It was a rack full of the same black helmets like the racers wore. Next to it was a wire bin with close to forty red balls about the size of a grapefruit. I guessed those were the kind of balls that would be at the checkpoints. The guy picked up one of the helmets and skated back to us.

"Attach these to your shoes," he said while reaching into the helmet. He pulled out two wire frames that looked as if they would fit on to the sole of a shoe. Each one had two yellow pads, one for the front of the foot, one for the back. He then added, "Get used to them. We'll go set up the course."

He skated away to join the other racers.

"Maybe I should be the one to race," Loor said.

"Do you know how to skate?" I asked.

Loor looked down. She didn't like to admit defeat.

"I do," I said. "Let me try these things out."

The wires attached easily to the soles of my boots. One end clamped over my toe, the other attached over my heel. But I didn't understand how they could work like ice skates, until I put my feet down and pushed off.

"Whoa!" I shouted as I slid across the ice.

The pads must have been made of a superslick material, because I glided over the ice as easily as if I had on hockey skates. It took me all of thirty seconds to get the feel of these things and found they were even easier to control than skates. I played a couple of years of junior hockey, so I was pretty confident on the ice. With these slick pads, I found that I could turn, stop, cut, and skate backwards better than at home. My confidence was building.

But we faced a tough decision. Between the two of us, Loor was the athlete. But if she couldn't skate like me, it didn't matter how strong she was. She'd never make it to the first checkpoint.

"I think I should be the one to race," I said to Loor.

Loor nodded. She knew I was right. "Why must we play

games?" she snapped. "We are on a serious mission. It should not be decided by a childish competition."

"I know," I said. "But let's do it their way. If I finish, then we'll get to Zetlin."

"And if you don't?" she asked.

I didn't have an answer to that.

The five racers then skated right up to us and stopped in a group. "Ready?" the one who gave me the helmet asked.

"Sure," I said, trying to sound like a winner. "Any other rules I should know about?"

The racers laughed again. I hated that.

"Absolutely," the first racer said. "The main rule is: Anything goes. Finish any way you can."

I didn't like the sound of that. But this was their game; I wasn't going to start arguing the finer points of slickshot. The five racers pushed off towards the starting line. I was about to follow when Loor touched my shoulder. She didn't say anything; she simply looked into my eyes. I think she was trying to give me some of her strength and confidence. My knees went weak. In that moment I was more worried about letting her down than finding Dr Zetlin. She gave me a wink and let me go.

I pushed off while putting on my helmet and fitting the goggles over my eyes. I never wanted to win anything more in my life. For her, for me, and even for Aja. I realised that the fate of Veelox might very well be decided on this icy racecourse.

How wrong was that?

VEELOX

The five racers stood shoulder to shoulder at a tall, red post. "This is the start and finish," the first racer explained. He then pointed out the course. "The first checkpoint is dead ahead."

I looked across the flat expanse to a wall of ice that rose up in the distance. There I saw a red arrow painted on the face, pointing left.

"Just follow the arrows," the rider said. "You can't miss them. Get to the checkpoint, pick up a ball and drop it in the basket. If you miss one ball, you're out. Got it?"

"Yeah," I said.

My heart started to pump faster. This was suddenly looking like a bad idea. I had no clue as to how good these guys were. It's not like they looked like pro speed skaters or anything. Just the opposite. They were all my size. But this was their home ice. I'll bet they raced this course all the time. This was insane. But I was in it now. All I could hope was that I'd hold on long enough to stay in the race.

"On my go," the first racer said.

All six of us crouched down, ready to spring forward.

"One, two, *go!*"

What happened to three? This was a bad start. I was already a second behind and the race had barely begun. All I could do was push off and try to catch up, pumping my legs and swinging my arms for momentum. I was surprised to see that these guys didn't leave me in the dust. Or maybe I should say leave me in the frost. Not only did I keep up with them, I quickly made up the ground I had lost with the bad start. I was still last, but my confidence zoomed. Maybe I had a chance after all.

We quickly arrived at the first arrow and made the turn towards the checkpoint. I made the turn easily, crossing my feet over and trying not to lose too much speed. Up ahead I saw a rack with six of the grapefruit-size red balls. The five other racers quickly snatched one apiece while barely slowing down. I was last, but right there with them.

That is, until the fifth racer knocked the last ball off the rack. The red ball hit the ice and rolled away. I had to come to a full stop to pick it up. No way that was an accident. I guess when they said that "anything goes", they meant it. I realised there was more to worry about than just keeping pace. These guys cheated.

I snatched up the ball and took off again. A few yards ahead was a steel basket with the first five balls that the other racers had already dumped. I dropped mine off and dug in to catch up.

The other racers were skating easily. None of them looked as if they wanted the lead. That was fine with me. As long as they all were being cautious, I could keep up. This part of the course was a wide-open expanse of ice. I didn't even look for any red arrows, all I did was follow the guys in front of me.

But it got frustrating because they were all skating in one line, shoulder to shoulder. I had no hope of getting around them. I skated up behind the group, but when I put on some speed to go around, the whole group moved in front of me, blocking the way. I'd try to skate the other way, and they'd all move as one in the other direction to block me again. I was beginning to think this wasn't so much about somebody winning, as about making sure I would lose. As long as they kept me back like this, I would always be the last one to reach the rack of balls.

That would be bad news at checkpoint #3.

We quickly approached the second checkpoint. Like precision pilots the five racers smoothly moved into a single line, with me last, again. But this time I made sure to be close enough behind the fifth racer so he couldn't try anything cute with the sixth ball.

He didn't try. All six of us picked up a red ball and dumped it into the steel basket beyond the rack. This time, I was right there with them. But I was still in sixth place. Not good enough. I had to make a move.

The course then slid into a narrow canyon of ice. The walls rose up steeply on either side. There was maybe five feet between the walls where we were skating. It was so narrow, we had to skate single file. There was no way I could make up any ground.

I was in trouble. The next checkpoint only had five balls. If we stayed this way, I'd be gone. I tried to move up on the fifth racer, but it was like these guys had eyes in their butts. The whole line slid over in front of me. It was so frustrating! I was fast enough to keep up with them, but didn't have the experience to do anything else.

We were closing in on the third checkpoint. I had to make some kind of move or the race would be over. An idea came to me that was either brilliant or totally whacked. Chances were good if I tried it, I'd crash and burn. But I didn't see any other way. I looked ahead at the ice walls to either side of us. I needed a little luck, and got it. Ahead to my right I saw a spot that was a little less steep than the rest. There wasn't time to think. I had to go for it.

I made a quick move to my left and sure enough, the whole line of racers slid in that direction to block me. But then I shot to my right and skated towards the wall of ice. The slope was forgiving enough that I didn't slam into it. Instead I skated a few feet up on to the wall, forcing my chattering legs to hold firm. I then pivoted my body back left and shot for the centre. The momentum from being up on the wall gave me just enough extra speed for a slingshot between the fourth and fifth skater. It was a NASCAR move all the way, and it worked.

The fifth guy couldn't believe it. My surprise move threw off his rhythm and he nearly fell. By then we were at the checkpoint rack of balls. The fifth, and last, was mine. I scooped it up and jammed it into the basket. I was still alive.

The next section of the race was hairy. We shot out of the ice canyon and the course again moved left. I now realised we were moving in a big loop, counterclockwise, back to the starting line. The racers ahead of me broke out of formation. A second later, I saw why.

The expanse of ice before us was littered with boulder-size chunks of ice. There was no straight path through. It was an obstacle course. Blasting through at full speed would be suicide. We had to back off the speed, get more control, and dodge the boulders. For me it was a relief, because I was getting tired. I'd bet anything that these guys were in better shape than I was. My only advantage was that I had so much at stake, I couldn't lose. I was racing on adrenalin.

All five of us took a different route. It was tricky, not only because I had to get through as fast as possible, but now that

I wasn't following anybody, I had to keep an eye out for the red arrows that marked the course.

I have to admit, I was doing pretty well. I can't take all the credit though. These skate pad things were incredible. They made it so easy to shift direction, I started pouring on the speed and cutting it very close to the boulders. I saw that I was actually pulling ahead of the others. It was awesome! By the time we got to the end of the boulder field, I was out in front. The checkpoint was just past the final obstacle, and the first ball was mine. Yes! But I didn't care about winning. All that mattered was the next checkpoint. I had to get one of the next balls to make sure I'd finish. I was feeling pretty confident, though, which in my experience is the kiss of death. This time was no different.

I had just grabbed the red ball and dumped it into the steel basket, ready for the final push, when something hit me on the back of the foot. At first I didn't know what it was. But I wasn't worried . . . until I put that foot down and tried to push off. Before I knew it, I lost my balance and fell to the ice. Something had happened to my skate pad.

On the ice next to me, I saw the culprit. A red ball was lying at my feet. The first racer shot up, scooped up the ball, and dumped it into the basket.

"Sorry," he said. "It got away from me."

Yeah, right. He had thrown it at me. The ball must have knocked off my skate pad and when I put my foot down, my boot caught the ice and sent me tumbling. Sure enough, I saw the wire frame of the skate pad a few feet away. I scrambled for it, desperately pulling it back over my shoe.

I quickly looked up to see the four other skaters leaving me behind. I was done. There was no way I could catch up and pass anybody before the next checkpoint. But I didn't know what else to do. So I strapped the skate pad back on and skated after them, praying for a miracle.

The racecourse again veered left and into another canyon. This one wasn't as narrow as the first, and the walls weren't quite as steep. I pushed as hard as I could, trying to catch up, but it was useless. These guys weren't taking any more chances. They were skating hard and moving faster than they had the whole race. The sad truth hit me that up until then, they had been playing with me. They knew I wasn't a threat and barely put out any effort. But now, they had their heads down and pumped their arms powerfully. I didn't stand a chance.

That's when I got the miracle I needed.

The four remaining racers were so focused, they didn't see it coming. But I did. At first I wasn't sure what it was. It didn't make sense. But nothing about this fantasy building made any sense, so I shouldn't have been surprised. A few seconds later I saw exactly what it was and it suddenly made all sorts of sense.

High up the slope on one side of the canyon, an avalanche was starting. But it wasn't about snow and ice. It was an avalanche of red balls. There must have been forty of them, all rolling down the hill, heading for the skaters. There was only one explanation.

Loor.

I looked up to the top of the rise to see her standing there with the empty wire basket that had once held all the balls. Excellent.

I glanced down at the racers. They had no clue about what was bouncing down towards them from above. The only question now was whether Loor had timed it right. There was a chance the tumbling balls would miss them entirely.

They didn't.

The balls rained down on top of the unsuspecting racers, making them scatter. One took a header and beefed it into the canyon wall. Another spun out, lost control, and came to a dead stop. A third kept going, but had to pinwheel his arms to keep his balance. One racer dodged the balls completely and kept going. I didn't care. Fourth place was all I needed.

I flashed past the three skaters who were trying to get their balance back. They didn't know what had hit them. When I got to the checkpoint, I had my choice of three balls. I felt like taking one and dumping the other two over, just to put an exclamation point on the moment. But I figured we had already cheated enough. So I picked up one of the balls, and spiked it into the steel basket with a vengeance.

I coasted home on the last leg. By then the two other racers caught up and passed me, but I didn't care. I skated across the finish line with my hands in the air chanting, "We're number four! We're number four!"

Loor jogged up and patted me on the back. I could tell she was holding back a smile.

"Good race, Pendragon," she said.

"Good thinking, Loor," I shot back.

"You cheated!" one of the racers yelled. It was the last guy who dropped out. He skated up to the finish line looking all sorts of angry. "I call foul!"

"Excuse me," I said calmly. "I thought the first rule was: Anything goes."

"But she interfered," he protested.

"But it was okay to throw a ball at me and knock my skate pad off?" I shot back. "I don't think so."

By then the sixth skater had returned. "I want another race," he demanded.

"Tough," I said.

"There won't be another race," said the first racer firmly. It was the guy who had explained the race to us and who was the ultimate winner. "He competed in the same spirit as we did. The race was fair."

The guy walked up to me and held out his hand to shake. "Congratulations," he said. "Nicely done."

I took his hand and shook.

"Now it's your turn," I said. "We had a deal."

"Indeed," the guy said.

He pulled down his goggles and took off his helmet. He was a handsome guy, I'm guessing around sixteen years old. He had short, blond hair and an intense look in his eye. The second I saw him, I knew I had met him somewhere before, but couldn't figure out where.

"I always honour my wagers," he added.

That's when it hit me. I knew this guy. Sort of. I had seen him in a painting. A portrait. He was younger in the portrait, but there was no mistake. It was him.

"I'm Dr Zetlin," he said with a wry smile. "Welcome to my fantasy."

VEELOX

"**Y**ou can't be Zetlin," I said. "Dr Zetlin is seventy years old."

"Seventy-nine, to be exact," the kid-racer answered.

Loor and I shot each other a confused look.

"This is my fantasy," Zetlin continued. "Why would I live it as an old man?"

I asked, "So, the guy lying in the Alpha Core —"

"That would be my physical body that's seventy-nine years old," Zetlin answered. "But in here I'm a strapping sixteen. The more interesting question is, who are you two?"

After all we had been through to get here, I had to force my brain to shift gears and remember the message Aja had for him.

"We're here because Lifelight is in trouble," I said. "A virus has corrupted the processing code. We need the origin code to clean the string."

I was pretty sure that was the right message. For a second I feared it made no sense to him because Zetlin gave me a strange look. But then he turned to the other racers and said brightly, "Good race, guys! Later, all right?"

The other racers all said, "Yeah. Later! See ya, Z!" and skated off.

Zetlin then turned to us and said sternly, "Come with me."

He pulled the skate pads from his boots and stalked off. Loor and I followed right behind. It was weird. When Zetlin spoke to us, he sounded like a serious adult. But when he talked to the racers, he sounded like an excited kid. I guess his fantasy was all about reliving his youth. Whatever. All we needed was the origin code. His fantasies were his business.

"I must say, I'm impressed you two made it this far," Zetlin said. "Usually phaders don't make it past the jungle. What are your names?"

"I'm Pendragon," I answered. "This is Loor."

"Why are you hiding in this building?" Loor asked.

Uh-oh. I wasn't sure if challenging the guy was a good idea. We needed him on our side. But since the question was pure Loor, I figured I didn't have a choice.

"The Barbican is my refuge from a world I want nothing to do with," Zetlin answered. He then stopped and faced us. "And I don't like being disturbed. But you two were willing to play on my terms. You've earned the right to an audience. This way."

Who did he think he was? Some kind of king? I figured it wasn't my place to question him either, so I let it go. There were bigger problems to deal with.

Zetlin walked towards a wall of ice. I wasn't exactly sure where he was going until I saw a small black disc sticking out of the wall at waist level. Zetlin pulled on the disc and opened a door made of ice. Beyond was a small room with light blue, metallic walls. He motioned for us to enter. I figured we had come this far, we couldn't chicken out now. So Loor and I stepped inside. The room was no bigger than a lift, and that's what it turned out to be. A lift. Zetlin joined us inside, closed the door, touched a control button on the wall and we started up.

"I'm confused," I said. "I thought Lifelight had to follow the rules of reality. This Barbican thing is about as far from reality as I can imagine."

"That's because you don't have my imagination," Zetlin answered with a chuckle.

Good answer. Zetlin definitely had an exceptional mind. I suppose it followed that his fantasy could be just as exceptional.

"The people of Veelox haven't even begun to tap Lifelight's capabilities," Zetlin continued. "But they will."

"No, they won't," I countered. "Veelox is falling apart because everybody is living inside their own fantasy worlds."

If this news bothered Zetlin, he didn't show it. The lift slowed to a stop and the door opened. Zetlin stepped out first, and we followed him into a space that I can best describe as the dream home for a fifteen-year-old guy. I should know. I'm a fifteen-year-old guy and I thought the place was awesome.

The space was huge, but divided up into smaller sections so it didn't feel like an aeroplane hangar or anything. The ceiling was made of clear glass, so we could see the sky and the last of the storm clouds passing through. That meant we were now on the top floor of the Barbican.

We first walked through a wood-floored arena that reminded me of a basketball court. But this was Veelox. Their version of basketball had soccer-style nets on each of the four walls, and green balls that looked twice the size of a basketball.

Zetlin led us across the empty court, through a door, and into another space that had the Veelox version of a game I remembered playing as a kid. You know that game where you have to knock over wooden pegs set up on a table by swinging a ball on the end of a string? I think it was called Skittles.

Well, this was like Skittles, only life-size. There were five giant balls, all hanging from ropes in the centre of a round court. Instead of pegs, the idea was to knock over people. I'm serious. There was a game under way with ten kids in the centre of the big court, and another ten around the circle. The kids around the outside would grab the ball and swing it into the centre to try and hit one of the kids inside. Some of the kids inside really got clocked, too. It was like nasty dodgeball. I wasn't sure if it was fun or torture.

"Hey, guys," Zetlin called out. "Game's over. Let's play tomorrow, okay?"

Zetlin even used kid slang that sounded like Second Earth, but I guess that was because my Traveller brain interpreted it from whatever was the kid slang version of the language they spoke on Veelox.

"Yeah. Okay! See ya later, Z!" the players all shouted as they jogged off the court, heading for the lift.

"You enjoy playing child games," Loor said.

"Indeed," Zetlin answered. "It relaxes me to play simple games of skill and chance."

He led us next into what looked more like living space. It was modern, with a lot of big, comfortable couches of all colours. There were giant screens on the wall that I'd bet anything were for video games. It looked like we had just missed a big party. Plates and cups were scattered everywhere. All had half eaten leftovers of I don't know what. The only thing I knew for sure was that it wasn't gloid. There were a couple of older guys wearing green jumpsuits who were cleaning the place up.

One of them saw us and said, "We'll have the place tidy in no time, Z."

"Take your time," Zetlin responded. "I don't think we'll have anybody over again today."

Wow. He had servants cleaning up after him too. Could this place get any better?

It could.

We stepped into a modern kitchen that was full of incredible smells. A dozen chefs were scurrying around, busily cooking and frying and baking and . . . man, my stomach rumbled. I had only been eating gloid for the last few days. The idea of real food sounded pretty good right about now.

A woman chef hurried up to Zetlin with a tray of freshly baked cookies. "Can I tempt you, Z?" she asked.

Zetlin nodded for us to try the cookies. I didn't want to be rude, so I took one. Who am I kidding? They smelled great. I wanted ten. But I only took one and it was delicious. It was sweet and gooey and tasted like chocolate. Loor ate one too. I could tell by the look on her face that she liked it as much as I did. As if reading my mind, another chef appeared with two glasses that I really hoped had the Veelox version of milk. What is it about milk that tastes so good with chocolate? The liquid was creamy coloured, and I'm not sure if it was milk, but it sure tasted great.

"Thank you," I said to the chefs.

"Yes, thank you," Loor added.

Zetlin smiled and led us on. As soon as we stepped through the door into the next section, I knew this was our ultimate destination. One whole wall was made of glass, which meant we could look out on to the strange city of black buildings. The opposite wall held a computer console that looked very much like the Alpha Core in the Lifelight pyramid. This place wasn't about fun and games. This was where Dr Zetlin worked. This was where we needed to be.

"First things first," Zetlin said. He walked to the control

chair and hit a few buttons on the arm controller. The building rumbled. It felt like an earthquake.

"What is happening?" Loor asked, crouching down and ready for trouble.

"Don't worry," Zetlin answered. "I'm returning the Barbican to position number one."

The walls began to move. I realised that the massive building was turning back on to its side! We heard the grinding sound of metal wheels activating and straining under the massive load. Loor and I both looked around for something to grab on to for balance.

Zetlin laughed, "Please, don't panic. The floors rotate inside the structure. We'll remain level."

Sure enough, as the wall moved, what had been the glass ceiling became the wall. A new glass ceiling appeared which was previously the far wall. Even though we weren't actually moving, all this rotating made me dizzy. The only way I could keep from falling over was to look out at the city. The city didn't move. That proved the building was rotating around us while the floor stayed level. Amazing. A few seconds later, the building shuddered and it was over. A quick look around told me that nothing seemed to have changed.

"The building is on its side again?" I asked.

"Yes," Zetlin answered. "All the floors are perfect cubes. That's how they can rotate within the frame of the Barbican. The only thing different now is that each floor is side by side with the next. In position one, there is no need to climb between floors. Everything is on one level."

"Why do you make this building turn like it does?" Loor asked.

"To keep out the uninvited, of course," Zetlin answered.

That meant us, but I wasn't going to start apologising now. I walked over to the glass wall and gazed out at the dreary, black city.

"I don't get it," I said. "Why do you have that city out there? You could create any world you want. I'm sorry for saying this, but this whole setup is totally strange."

Zetlin joined me at the window and looked out. "This city is a reminder," he said softly.

"Of what?" I asked.

"Of life before Lifelight."

"I don't understand," I said. "Is this where you lived?"

"In a manner of speaking," Zetlin answered. "I was born and raised in Rubic City. It was a busy, thriving community, but I was never a part of it. I was too – what was the word they used? – I was too *special* to be part of the life everyone else knew."

It was strange listening to Zetlin. He looked like a sixteen-year-old kid, but his words were that of a sad old man. It was kind of creepy.

"The directors recognised my genius from the time I was an infant," he continued. "They predicted my superior intellect could change the future of Veelox." He looked at me and chuckled. "They were right."

"Then you did not live an ordinary life?" Loor asked.

"Oh, no!" Zetlin answered quickly. "I lived an extraordinary life. I was surrounded by the greatest scientific minds available. They were my teachers, but soon became my pupils. They marvelled at my theories of neural-electric compatibility. It was the theory that broke down the artificial wall between thought and reality. By the time I was eight, we created the first prototype of Lifelight. It was crude, but we were able to generate visual images driven solely by brain function. That was the moment. The breakthrough. From then on, it was simply about growth."

"But what was your life like?" I asked. "I mean, yeah, you were a genius and all, but it sounds a little . . . I don't know . . . not fun."

Zetlin didn't answer. He simply looked out of the window. It was slowly coming clear to me. Aja told me what it was like to grow up as a phader. Every minute was spent learning and being trained. There was no time for warmth or friendship. My guess was that Dr Zetlin's life had been like that, times about a thousand. This horrible, black city was the image Zetlin had of his life. His real life.

I had been wrong to think Zetlin's fantasy was about reliving his youth. It was about having the childhood he was denied. This building he called the Barbican was his second chance at being a kid.

"I had a goal," he finally said. "I worked on Lifelight for sixty years. It consumed me morning and night. But I kept going because I knew it would be my only chance to escape." He pointed out through the glass. "That city. That dark, rainy cold city is there as a reminder of what life once was, and of why I will never leave the Barbican."

I felt bad for the guy. His life was a fantasy. He had no memories of real live friends or loved ones. Everything important to him was made up in his head. Worse than that, I was going to have to tell him that it wouldn't last.

"We need your help, Dr Zetlin," I said.

Zetlin pulled himself away from the window. He was suddenly a young boy again, full of energy. He hurried to the control chair and plopped down in it.

"Right," he said. "You said something about a virus corrupting the processing code. That, I'm afraid, is impossible."

He hit a few keys on his controller and a stream of data appeared on the large monitor overhead.

"It's not impossible," I insisted. "The virus has totally infected Lifelight. It mutates people's thoughts. Instead of giving them the ideal experience, it finds what they're afraid of and hurts them. The phaders had to suspend the grid or a lot of people would —"

"They suspended the grid?" Zetlin asked in surprise.

"Yes! All over Veelox, people are in limbo waiting —"

"I know what it means," Zetlin snapped at me. He hit a few more keys and examined more data. He then stood up and announced, "I see no evidence of anything wrong."

"That's because your jump is isolated," I said. "Look, I'm on shaky ground here. I don't really know how this works."

"Then what are you doing here?" he demanded. "What kind of phader are you?"

"We're not phaders," I answered nervously. "We're here to tell you that unless we get the origin code, millions of people across Veelox are going to die."

Zetlin looked me square in the eye. "You have not convinced me," he said. "I believe this virus does not exist; therefore I will not give you the origin code. Goodbye."

Our mission was about to fail miserably. I had no idea of what to say or do to turn it around. But then we heard a familiar voice come from across the room.

"The virus is real," it said.

We all spun to see Aja. "I know it's real, because I created it. I'm a phader, and I may be responsible for the deaths of millions of people across Veelox."

VEELOX

"I know you!" Zetlin said to Aja. "You're one of the phaders from Rubic City. What is going on here? Why have these people invaded my privacy?"

Aja looked nervous. She was facing the big boss and didn't have good things to tell him.

"My name is Aja Killian," she said, her voice cracking. "I apologise, Dr Zetlin. I would never think of entering your jump if it weren't a dire emergency. I sent my friends to find you because I need to be in the Alpha Core to hold back the Reality Bug."

"Reality Bug?" Zetlin shouted angrily. He looked like his head was about to explode. For a second I thought he was going to really tee off on Aja, but he got his emotions under control and spoke calmly. "Please explain," he demanded.

Aja hesitated. I'm sure the idea of telling the most important man in the history of Veelox that his invention was on the verge of blowing a major fuse was pretty tough. Aja's rock-solid self-confidence was looking pretty shaky.

"It's okay, Aja," I said, trying to give her encouragement. "Tell him what's going on."

"Veelox is in danger," she said nervously. "Dr Zetlin, since you jumped into Lifelight, the people of Veelox have abandoned reality. They prefer to live in the fantasy of Lifelight than in their own lives."

"I don't blame them," Zetlin said.

"But you should!" Aja said with passion. "Your invention was supposed to give people a break from reality, not replace it. Our cities are abandoned. Food is disappearing. People don't communicate with real people any more, they're too busy living inside their own heads and creating characters to act in their own personal dramas. Nothing is happening. Nothing is moving forward. Nothing is real. Veelox is dead."

Zetlin dismissed this and asked, "What is this Reality Bug?"

Now came the really tough part for Aja. I hoped she wouldn't get into the whole story about Travellers and Saint Dane, because right now, it didn't matter.

"I couldn't stand to let Veelox die," she said. "So I wrote a program. The idea was to make the jumps less than perfect. The program attached to the data stream of each jumper to alter the experience slightly. I thought that if the jumps became less than perfect, people wouldn't spend so much time in them and would choose to return to their real lives."

Zetlin nodded. His jaw muscles clenched. He had just heard that somebody had sabotaged his life's work. I had to give him credit, he kept his head on straight and didn't go nuts on Aja. At least not yet.

"But this . . . *program* . . . didn't work the way you planned?" he asked calmly, though he said the word "program" with total disdain.

Aja swallowed hard and said, "No. The Reality Bug was far more powerful than I thought. It acted like a wild virus that spread through the grid. Not only did it alter the jumps, it made them hyperrealistic. The jumps became dangerous. We couldn't stop it and had to suspend the grid. Now almost everyone on Veelox is in limbo, waiting for me to purge the Reality Bug."

"And for that you need the origin code," Zetlin concluded.

Aja nodded. "There's one more thing," she said. "Since my friends entered your jump, I've been desperately programming firewalls into the alpha grid to keep the Reality Bug out of your jump. It's coming after you, sir. Every time I throw one up, the virus mutates and finds a way around my block. I don't know how much longer I can keep fooling it. Sooner or later, the Reality Bug is going to find its way into your jump, and you'll be in danger too."

Oh, great. That was a fairly crappy piece of news.

Zetlin stared at Aja's image for a moment, weighing what she had said. He then turned and sat back down in his control chair. "I won't give you the code," he said with finality.

Uh-oh.

"You must!" Loor demanded. "Holding it back is suicide. No, it is genocide."

"I told you before," he snapped. "I won't go back. If Lifelight is destroyed, so be it. Whoever survives will rebuild Veelox. I don't care one way or the other. This is my reality now. I'll deal with whatever it throws at me."

"But I can stop it from happening," Aja shouted. "I can save Lifelight."

"From what you tell me," Zetlin said, "Lifelight shouldn't be saved."

"But at what cost?" I asked. "The deaths of millions?"

"I have accepted Lifelight as my reality," Zetlin explained

calmly. "To me, Veelox doesn't exist. I will only deal with the reality of my life here. I belong here in the Barbican, with these people, in this body, with this life."

"But it's a life you don't deserve," I said.

Zetlin shot me a look. I didn't know where I was going with this, but I had to do something to get him to give up that code.

"How can you say that?" he asked defensively, jumping to his feet. "I *built* Lifelight."

"So what?" I continued. "From what I can see, it's all just maths. Being good at maths doesn't earn you a perfect life. What about the people around here? These are the only people in your life. Your only friends. Do you think they really care about you?"

"Of course they do," Zetlin answered quickly.

"Why? Because you're the Z? The guy who races with them and plays games and throws parties? Is that why they care?"

"That's exactly why," Zetlin said with confidence. "They love me."

"But they aren't real," I said. "You created them. They're puppets who do what you say. You could be a monster and they'd still love you. You took the easy way out, Zetlin. Instead of repairing your real life, you lost yourself in a fantasy. Don't you get lonely?"

Zetlin's eyes darted around the room. I was getting to him. To be honest, I think part of it was the Traveller in me at work.

"Lonely?" he said, sounding shaky. "I am surrounded by friends. We have tournaments and games. I'm the champion slickshot racer!"

"Sure you are!" I shot back. "I'll bet you're the champion at everything. It's easy when all you have to do is imagine it. I'll bet nobody ever says no to you, do they?"

This question really threw Zetlin. He didn't have to answer it.

"There's nobody to challenge you," I said softly. "Nobody to argue with. Nobody to push you and help you find new ideas. For a guy like you, that sounds like death."

Zetlin shot me a look. I had definitely hit a chord.

"You know what reality is for you?" I added. "You're lying in a tube being fed by machines. You're a living corpse. And you know the worst part? Your invention is doing the same thing to the rest of Veelox. Aja's Reality Bug may have backfired, but at least she was doing something to try and save Veelox. The whole world is on life support, barely breathing. Veelox is going to die, just like you. If that happens, your life wasn't miserable, it was tragic."

Zetlin staggered back and fell into his control chair. I had slammed him pretty hard.

Aja's image walked over to Zetlin. She stood over him and spoke reassuringly.

"Please, Dr Zetlin," she said. "You are a great man. I would love to meet you as you are, not as a memory of yourself. I want to shake your hand and say how much I admire you."

Aja put out her hand. Zetlin looked up at her. His eyes were red, as if on the verge of tears. He reached out to touch Aja, but his hand went right through hers. Aja was only an image created by Lifelight. There was no human contact.

"Come back, Dr Zetlin," she added. "Help rebuild Veelox."

Zetlin slowly turned and faced his computer array. Aja glanced over at me with a hopeful look. Had we got through to him?

"Zero," Zetlin said softly, as if he didn't have the energy to fight any more.

"Excuse me?" Aja asked.

"I said zero. That's the origin code."

"Zero?" I repeated. "That's it? Just . . . zero?"

Zetlin gave a sly smile. "The phaders are a clever bunch. I knew they would try to crack the code, and I knew they would expect it to be a complex string of commands."

Aja smiled and said, "You really are brilliant."

"Am I?" Zetlin asked.

"I'm going to purge the Reality Bug," Aja said. An instant later, her image disappeared.

"And then what happens?" Zetlin asked. "If Veelox is in such bad shape, all this will do is clear the way for its continued decline."

"That's the next problem," I said. "There has to be a way to use Lifelight without letting it control people's lives."

"If I may say so," Loor added. "If you could help Veelox find that balance, you would truly go down in history as a great man."

"Perhaps," Zetlin said, then looked at me. "Real life is so much more difficult than fantasy."

"Yeah," I answered. "But fantasy doesn't last."

Zetlin stood up and walked over to the big glass wall to look out on to his dreary city. I couldn't begin to guess what was going through his mind.

Suddenly the monitor jumped to life with an image of Aja. She was sitting in her control chair in the Alpha Core.

"We've got trouble," she said, all business.

"With the origin code?" I asked.

"No, that worked perfectly," she answered. "I went right to the processing code and cleaned the string. I totally purged the Reality Bug from Lifelight."

"Then what is the problem?" Loor asked.

"The grid went back online by itself," she explained. "I didn't do a thing. It just happened."

"So everyone on Veelox is back in their jumps?" I asked.

"Yes." Aja's voice started to crack. She sounded scared. "But something else is happening. As soon as everyone went back online, huge amounts of data began flowing from all the Lifelight pyramids to the Alpha Core."

"Data? What does that mean, Aja?" I asked, trying not to get too freaked out.

"I . . . I'm not sure."

We watched as Aja quickly inputted a series of commands and then checked her control monitor. There was tension in her eyes. Whatever was happening, it wasn't good.

"This is impossible," she said, her panic growing. "Data from all over Veelox is streaming directly towards the alpha grid."

"Alpha grid," Loor repeated. "What is this alpha grid?"

"The alpha grid is where we are," Zetlin answered, stepping up behind us.

Uh-oh.

"Killian," Zetlin said, "the firewalls you created to repel this Reality Bug, are they still in place?"

"Yes, but it's like . . . it's like the data is swarming. No, it's attacking the alpha grid and dismantling the firewalls. I can't reprogram them fast enough."

While she spoke, Aja kept making rapid-fire keystrokes on her control panel.

"Could it be the Reality Bug?" I asked.

"No!" Aja screamed back from the monitor. "I cleaned the string. It should be gone. The Reality Bug is —"

The image on the monitor began to crumble. The picture

flipped and twisted and changed until another face appeared on screen. It was the last face I wanted to see.

It was Saint Dane.

"Who is that?" demanded Zetlin.

"You don't want to know," was all I could answer.

"Hello, all you desperate little Travellers," Saint Dane chuckled. "If you're seeing this recording, it means you've tried to purge the virus from Lifelight. Congratulations for getting so close! There's just one little problem. The virus cannot be deleted. I made sure of that. In fact, trying to delete it, only multiplies its strength. Right about now, every jumper on Veelox is feeding the virus. Imagine having to battle the fears of everyone on the territory? Well, come to think of it, you won't have to imagine it at all. You're going to get the chance! I can't wait to return to Veelox and see what damage my last little surprise has wrought. Until then, sweet dreams!"

Saint Dane's image on the monitor was replaced by the sight of a zillion different numbers flashing by at lightning speed. Then every light on the control console began to glow brighter. Dr Zetlin furiously inputted commands on his control column. Whatever he was doing, it wasn't working.

"Nothing is responding," he announced.

"It's like an overload," I suggested. "There's too much data for the computers to handle."

The lights on the control console intensified, blinding us. We all covered our eyes and it was a good thing we did, because a second later, the large monitor over the control chair exploded. *Boom!* Loor grabbed Zetlin by the back of his jumpsuit and pulled him out of his chair as a wave of shattered glass hit the seat.

All three of us cowered, afraid that something else explosive might happen. Smoke filled the room, along with the smell of burning plastic. We huddled together and cautiously peered through the smoke to see an eerie sight.

The control console had gone dark. Every light was out. The monitor was nothing more than a jagged, smoking hole in the wall. We all stood, stunned, staring at the destroyed console.

But there was more.

"What is that?" Loor asked curiously, pointing down.

On the floor, covered in bits of glass from the destroyed monitor, was a black pile of goo about the size of a softball. It was as if a soft piece of tar had been spat out of the control panel when it exploded.

"Is that a piece from the console?" I asked.

"No," Zetlin answered. "I've never seen anything like it."

I took a step forward to get a closer look. But as soon as I approached it, the odd substance began to move. It was alive! I jumped back, as if it were diseased. For all I knew, it was.

"Tell me this is part of your fantasy," I said to Zetlin.

"I have no idea what it could be," Zetlin answered.

Bad answer.

The writhing black goo began to take on different shapes. A chunk grew out from the top, pushed towards the ceiling like a growing plant. It rose up a few inches, then formed what looked like a snarling mouth on the end of a black stalk! The mouth opened, revealing a set of sharp black teeth. The teeth snapped shut and the mouth sank back down into the black ooze to become part of the glob once more.

"That was . . . gross," I croaked.

The goo continued to writhe and squirm. We saw an eyeball peek out of one side, wink, then sink back into the muck. A tiny black fist then poked its way out, flexed its fingers, then pulled back into the mass. Then a sharp, spike-looking thing poked out of the side and retracted.

The three of us stood watching in awe. It was hideous and fascinating at the same time.

"It's like living clay," I said. "It's moulding itself."

As I said that, the entire black form changed into what looked like an animal. In seconds, lying before us, no more than six inches high, was a cat-looking beast with two large heads, each of which had huge fangs. The form lay on its side, writhing like a newborn. It was solid black, but as it moved, the surface subtly changed texture. For a moment it looked like fur, but it quickly changed back into black goo. It even croaked out a ratty sound.

The instant the cat image was revealed, I felt Loor stiffen beside me.

"What's the matter?" I asked her.

"It is a zhou beast," she exclaimed. "From Zadaa."

"Uh-oh," I said. "Dr Zetlin, have you ever seen something like that?"

"Never," was his emphatic reply.

"Then it came out of your head, Loor," I said. "You know what that means?"

"It means it's here," came a sober voice near us.

We all turned to see Aja's image standing there. "It broke through the firewall," she said, sounding as if she were in shock. "I couldn't hold it back."

The black cat beast then mutated. It folded in on itself, once again becoming a formless mass. But there was a difference. It was subtle, and I wasn't sure if I was seeing it at first, but once the goo started to squirm again, there was no mistake.

The thing was growing.

"The firewalls have collapsed," Aja said. "Huge amounts

of data are streaming into the alpha grid. It's feeding that thing."

The growing black clay then squirmed and grew, and took on the form of another animal. It was now the size of a small dog. The creature was still solid black, but when it turned towards us, its eyes flashed yellow and my knees went weak.

It was a quig from Denduron.

"I know what this is," I said, barely able to get the words out.

"It is a quig," Loor said.

"No," I said soberly. "It's the Reality Bug. It's taken physical form."

And then it attacked.

VEELOX

The black little beast sprang.

We scattered. The odd creature missed everybody, and when it hit the ground, its legs collapsed. It reminded me of Bambi when he didn't have the strength to stand on his own legs. But this little demon was no cute Disney deer. My guess was, it was going to get the strength to stand up pretty quickly, and when it did, we'd be in trouble. Already the black skin was transforming into the dirty-brown fur of a quig. And it was still growing. In just a few seconds it was the size of my golden retriever.

"You're done, Pendragon," Aja demanded. "Get out of the jump."

There was nothing I wanted to do more than press the bailout button on my wrist controller and kiss this fantasy goodbye, but we couldn't leave yet.

"You first, Dr Zetlin," I said. "Time to abandon ship."

Zetlin looked like he was in shock. He stared at the groggy quig, not believing what he was seeing.

"This can't be happening," he said, stunned. "The jumps don't allow it."

"They do now!" I shouted. "You've got to get out."

"You go," he said. "I'll be right after you."

I didn't believe him. I was afraid he would stay here and try to do damage control.

"Come on, Doctor, let's go!" I shouted.

"It doesn't work that way, Pendragon," Aja corrected. "When he leaves, the jump is over. You and Loor have to go first."

I looked at the mutant quig. Its body shivered as hair grew from the oozy black mass.

"Promise me you'll leave the jump, Doctor," I begged. "You can fight this thing from the Alpha Core."

"I will," he assured me. "Get going."

The quig slowly rose to its feet. It was now twice the size of my dog, Marley, and getting stronger. I looked at Loor. She had moved behind the control chair and was holding tight to the back of it. She was ready to move if the quig attacked again.

"We should go," she said to me without taking her eyes off the quig.

"With pleasure," I said, and hit the right button on my control bracelet. "We are outta here."

It didn't work.

"Why are we still here?" Loor asked.

"Aja?" I screamed.

"I don't know," Aja's image answered. "Loor, try yours!"

Loor poked the right button on her control bracelet, but nothing happened. No! I tried hitting the button on mine rapid-fire, like one of those idiots who keep hitting the lift button, thinking it will make the lift come faster. That never works, and hitting my wrist controller didn't work either.

The quig stood on shaky legs, reared back and pounced.

Loor pulled the control chair right out of the floor and heaved it at the charging beast. The black chair nailed the quig, knocking it back to the floor. It lay there, breathing hard, still growing.

"Aja!" I shouted. "Get us outta here!"

"Hang on," she called back. "I'm going back to the Alpha Core."

Her image disappeared.

"C'mon!" I shouted at the others.

Until Aja figured a way to yank us out of this jump, we had to stay alive. Hanging around with this mutating, growing monster wasn't the best way to do that. Loor grabbed Zetlin by the arm and the three of us ran across the floor and through the doorway that led to the big kitchen. When we entered, the first thing I noticed was that the chefs were gone. Can't say I blame them. They may have been fantasy creations, but they were smart enough to beat feet when there was trouble.

Loor saw the empty kitchen and had a different thought. "Weapons," she exclaimed.

She vaulted over a stainless-steel counter and ran to a table that held several nasty-looking kitchen knives. She quickly tested the weight of a few and picked two that she liked.

"If that quig gets any bigger," I said, "those knives won't do squat."

"You doubt me, Pendragon?" she asked, pretending to be insulted.

She flipped a knife into the air, spun it a few times, then plucked it in midspin with the blade ready to go. She looked like a gunslinger. Or knifeslinger. Loor had been off balance ever since she arrived on Veelox. She had to deal with technology and events that were impossible for her to understand.

But now we were in a battle. Now we were in Loor land.

The mutant quig leaped into the kitchen. It had become the size of the quig from my fantasy of Davis Gregory High. Worse, it had got stronger. It stood in the doorway and let out a grisly bellow. The mutant quig was officially ready for action.

So was Loor. She quickly threw a knife, then another while the first was still in the air. I never should have doubted her. Both knives found their mark. The first hit the quig in the shoulder, the second in the neck. It was kind of gruesome, but I didn't care. Better him than us. The beast reared up on its back legs, bellowing in agony. I thought this fight was over before it could get started.

I was wrong.

The quig reached for the knife in its neck with a paw, and brushed it away. It didn't pull the blade out, it *pushed* it out of its body, as if its flesh were made of jelly. It did the same with the knife in its shoulder. Both knives clattered to the floor. No blood. No wounds. Whatever damage the knives had done to the beast's body, it had regenerated.

We were in serious trouble.

"That cannot be," Loor said, stunned.

"Yeah, it can," I said. "That's not a quig, it's the Reality Bug."

As if to prove my point, the mutant quig growled, shuddered, and grew bigger. This thing was now getting close to the size of the quigs on Denduron.

"Outta here!" I yelled, and grabbed Dr Zetlin.

The three of us ran for the doorway that led to the video game room and charged through. This room was empty too. The cleanup crew had fled.

"Perhaps it will grow too large to follow," Zetlin said hopefully.

Crash!

The quig smashed through the doorway behind us, taking out a piece of wall as it forced its way through.

"Let's not count on that," I said, and kept running.

We made it through to the giant Skittles game. Standing in the centre of the court was Aja's image. We all ran up to her.

"What's going on?" I demanded.

"I can't stop it," she said nervously. "Data is flooding in from everywhere on Veelox. It's feeding the Reality Bug and making it stronger."

"Yeah, we see that," I said. "Can you get us out of the jump?"

"Everything is frozen," she complained. "The grid is totally overloaded and I can't take control."

"So we are trapped in here?" Loor asked.

"I'll alter the jump," Zetlin offered. He lifted his arm to reveal his control bracelet and pressed the centre button.

I winced. But nothing happened. Good news, bad news.

"We have no control," Zetlin said softly. He then looked at Aja and said, "You must try to isolate the alpha grid. Perhaps you can fool the virus by creating a duplicate program."

"Duplicate program?" I asked.

"Back up the alpha software," Zetlin explained. "Then make that back-up the default. The virus may recognise it and attack both."

"Divide and conquer," I said.

"Exactly," Zetlin added. "Can you do that?"

"I can try," Aja said, and disappeared.

"And all we have to do is stay alive," I added.

"I do not know how to fight this beast," Loor said.

"I do," I offered. "Quigs hate loud, piercing sounds. Their ears can't take it. We gotta find something to make a sharp sound, like a whistle. If this thing is just like a quig, it'll send it reeling."

"I know something!" Zetlin announced, and continued running across the court.

We followed him through the next doorway into the odd basketball court with the four nets. Zetlin ran right for a metal equipment locker. "We use whistles for the games," he announced.

I could have hugged the guy. We joined him at the locker and flipped it open. As he searched for the whistles, we heard the sound of the quig tearing through the doorway to get into the Skittles room.

"Not much time," I cautioned.

Zetlin found two whistles that looked like kazoos. He gave me one.

"We'll take turns," I said. "I'll blow until I run out of air, then you blow. The louder the better."

"What then?" Loor asked.

"We've got to get out of the Barbican," I said. "We've got a better chance of hiding from this thing out in that city than in this building."

We then heard a horrifying roar. All three of us looked to the doorway of the Skittles room to see . . .

The beast had grown. It was now way bigger than a normal quig. Its head was almost as wide as the doorway. I hoped these whistles would be loud enough to do a number on something that big.

"Please use the whistle," Loor said calmly.

I took a deep breath and blew into the kazoo thing. The sound it made was awful and perfect. It was a totally annoying, loud shriek — exactly what quigs hate. The beast lifted its head and bellowed in agony. It was working! We had power over the monster. My mind raced ahead, already calculating how we would take turns blowing our whistles to keep the quig away from us long enough to escape.

Our victory didn't last long.

I had run out of breath and Zetlin was about to take over, when the quig stopped hollering. That's because it was changing. Through the doorway we watched in horror as the quig's head began to grow and squirm and change shape. The fur disappeared and it once again became the slick, black colour it began with. Zetlin took a deep breath, but I put a hand on his shoulder.

"Don't bother," I said. "It's not a quig anymore."

The shape of the head flattened out. The black, oily skin took on a new texture that looked like scales. The eyes changed from having the round pupils of a quig, to the vertical pupils of a snake. I hate snakes. Suddenly a pink tongue flicked into the room. It had to be three feet long.

The Reality Bug had changed itself into a snake, and snakes weren't bothered by whistles.

"The lift!" Loor exclaimed.

We all ran to the door that led to the blue lift. Zetlin pulled, but it didn't open. "It's not here," he announced with dread. "The players must have taken it."

I glanced over my shoulder and immediately wished I hadn't. What I saw made my stomach dance. The snake's head was too wide to fit through the doorway, but that didn't stop it. It simply turned sideways and slipped through. I stared in awe as this giant black snake slithered on to the court. Its eyes were focused on us as the rest of its long body slid in.

"Can we get the lift here? Like soon?" I asked, trying not to sound like I was about to panic, which I was.

"It's coming," Zetlin answered.

"So is the snake," Loor said.

The mutant snake slid to the centre of the court and stopped. At least its head stopped. The rest of its snaky body kept coming.

"It is coiling," Loor announced.

As the long body slid through the door, its head rose as it formed a coil. That was bad. When snakes coil, they strike.

"How much longer?" I asked.

"Almost here," Zetlin answered.

"Almost might be too late."

The snake must have been twenty feet long, the body four feet thick. It was now in a perfect coil. Perfect for striking. It dropped its jaw and hissed, revealing a couple of nasty-looking fangs that had to be a foot long.

"Dr Zetlin?" I urged.

"It's here!" he exclaimed, and pulled the door open.

That's when the snake pulled its head back, opened its jaws, and struck.

VEELOX

We dived into the small, blue lift and I quickly pulled the door behind us. At that exact instant the snake hit with such a force that it slammed the door shut the rest of the way, knocking me into Loor and Zetlin.

"Look!" Zetlin shouted.

Imbedded in the door, having cut clean through, were two snake fangs. A second later a stream of liquid shot from each of the huge teeth.

Venom.

We all scrambled to the side of the lift to get out of the way. Zetlin's hand was splashed with the poison and he screamed in pain.

"Get us out of here!" I shouted at Loor.

She reached for the control buttons. I don't think she knew which was the right one, but it didn't matter so long as we got moving. The lift lurched and we were on our way. The fangs didn't move, though. The snake was hitching a ride. Luckily the flow of venom had stopped. It must have shot out all that it had.

"We're moving sideways," I announced. "Why aren't we going down?"

"Because the Barbican is horizontal," Zetlin winced through his pain. "All the floors are on the same level."

Oh, right. I'd forgotten.

Loor took Zetlin's hand and wiped away the venom with her sleeve. I saw that the poison had left a nasty-looking red slash on the back of his hand.

"I'm fine," Zetlin said.

"How do we get out of here?" I asked, deciding to save my sympathy until after we were safe.

"We'll take the lift across to the jungle where you first entered," Zetlin answered. "I can right the Barbican into a vertical position from there, and we can walk out of the door."

"That's fine," I said, then pointed to the fangs that were still imbedded in the door. "But as long as that thing's got its jaws in us, we won't even get out of the lift."

Suddenly, the car shuddered and stopped.

"Is that normal?" I asked.

"No," answered Zetlin. "It must be —" Before he could finish, the lift began to shake. I looked at the fangs of our hitchhiker and saw them moving. The snake had decided to take control. A second later the fangs pulled out, leaving two holes in the door.

"Now what?" I asked.

The lift began to rock. It felt like we were inside a small ship in rough seas. Zetlin looked at the control panel and announced, "We're in the weight room."

Weight room? Did Zetlin have a personal gym? He threw open a panel below the lift controls to reveal a compartment with a series of odd-looking devices like the slippery skate pads we used to race across the ice. They had the same kind of wire frames that fitted over shoes, but there was only one pad on the heel. It was a thicker pad, with a hole in the centre.

Zetlin pulled out three pairs quickly and handed them to us.

"Put these on your shoes," he commanded.

We did as we were told. The was now rocking so hard, we couldn't stand up any more. The Reality Bug was trying to pull the car off its track. He was doing a good job. The three of us were being tossed around like kids in a carnival bounce. Only it wasn't soft and fun. It hurt.

"What are these?" I managed to ask while struggling to pull the wire over my shoes.

"It's the only way to get around in the weight room," Zetlin answered.

That didn't explain anything. He then handed us each a small controller and showed us how to slip it over our middle finger like a ring. There was a button attached to the ring that rested in the palm of your hand.

"Once we're out," Zetlin instructed, "press the button. It'll activate the inertia jets."

"Inertia jets?" Loor questioned.

She never got an answer because the lift toppled and started spinning. The Reality Bug had pulled it from its track and tossed it. It felt like we were inside a washing machine as the little car rolled over and over on its side. I braced myself as best I could, waiting for an impact. But it didn't come. We just kept spinning. It seemed impossible, but the rotating lift didn't slow down.

Zetlin went for the door handle. "Follow me!" he ordered.

"Don't!" I yelled. I thought he'd kill himself for sure. But he had no fear. He pushed open the door and heaved himself out. Loor followed right after him. I figured if we were going to go down, we should do it together, so I dived for the door and launched myself out.

"Launch" was the perfect word to describe it. As soon as

I cleared the door I covered my head and curled up, ready to land hard. But I didn't. I realised after a few seconds that I wasn't going to, either. That's because I was floating. I took a cautious peek out from between my arms to see it was pitch black, with stars everywhere. I was drifting in outer space! This wasn't a weight room, it was a weight*less* room. Far off to my right, the lift car was still spinning out of control. I watched it in wonder for a second, then felt something touch me on the shoulder.

"Ahhh!" I spun around fast, expecting to see the fangs of the black snake about to close on my head. But it was Dr Zetlin. He was hanging next to me with Loor. He held her hand. They were both upside down. Or maybe I was the one upside down.

"The inertia jets shoot from your heels," he explained. "Point your body where you want to go, and touch the button in your palm. You can manouvre by adjusting the direction your heels face."

I touched the button in my palm . . . and rocketed up. Whoa! These things were powerful!

"Easy!" Zetlin ordered. "Just touch it."

I spun around and touched the button tentatively. Sure enough, I was able to control it. When I took my finger off the button, I slowed down pretty quickly. It was easy to get used to. Under other circumstances, this would be the most totally amazing, fun experience possible. It was like we were floating in outer space without space suits. But these weren't other circumstances. Somewhere out there among the stars was a giant, poisonous snake trying to kill us.

"Follow me," Zetlin announced. "I know the way to the far side."

"How?" I asked, looking around at nothing but nothing.

"I know the star formations," Zetlin answered.

I had to take his word for it. If it were up to Loor or me, we'd be floating around here forever.

That's when the snake came into view. It was far below us, floating free. At least I think it was below us. It was impossible to tell up from down.

"We're in luck," Zetlin said. "There's no way it can manoeuvre in here."

Excellent. The Reality Bug had chosen the absolute worst place to pull the lift off its track. I figured it would float helplessly in here with no way to escape. That would give us enough time to get out of the Barbican and for Aja to untangle the software. Suddenly there was hope.

And just as suddenly it came crashing down.

The snake had no way of fighting the weightlessness, so it began to change. We watched in horror as huge, human-like arms sprouted from the snake body. The hands were massive and strong. They groped around as if trying to grab on to something.

"What is it doing?" Loor asked.

A second later we had our answer. The massive hands found what they were looking for.

"The lift track," Zetlin said soberly.

The lift track was the only solid thing in this world of weightlessness. The huge hands grabbed on to the dark track and the creature had control. It moved, hand over hand, in the exact direction we needed to go.

"Hurry," Zetlin said, and took off flying, his inertia jets making a soft whooshing sound as he moved.

Loor went next. She started in the wrong direction, but shifted her legs and soon had enough control so she could follow Zetlin. I then hit my button . . . and spun in a tight circle.

Oops. I realised I had only one foot in the right position. The other was floating free. Idiot! I backed off on the button, twisted my body into the right position, made sure my heels were together, and took off. After a few seconds I had it figured out. It really was easy. Just a slight movement of my heel altered my direction and I learned how to make midcourse corrections. In no time, I was sailing along next to Loor, with Zetlin in the lead.

I glanced back and down over my shoulder to see that the Reality Bug was moving quickly along the track, hand over huge hand. But with the help of the inertia jets, we were moving faster.

Zetlin then changed direction and shot down at a steep angle. Loor and I were able to follow right behind. I looked forward and saw a small, glowing red rectangle that seemed to be hovering in space. This is where Zetlin was heading. He stopped at the door-shaped rectangle and gave it a push. It was the door out.

I looked back to see the huge black snake with the human arms gaining ground. It opened its jaws and hissed angrily.

"Hurry, please," I said to Zetlin.

Loor and I followed him and stepped through the doorway. I instantly felt the pull of gravity as we were back on solid ground. I quickly pushed the door shut behind me. It was a heavy door, much heavier than anything we had come across in this wacky building so far. It was more like a hatch than a door. When I closed it, I saw there was a heavy latch. I slammed it home. Anything we could do to slow down the Reality Bug was a good thing.

"Keep moving!" Zetlin ordered.

We were in a short, dark chamber about ten feet long. On the far end was another door that Zetlin pushed open. When we stepped through, we entered another space that I can best describe as being like the inside of a giant clock. It was a huge room full of gigantic, heavy gears. All around us and high above were massive, interlocking cogs and flywheels and I don't know what else.

"This is the centre of the Barbican," Zetlin explained as he closed the door behind us. "This machinery rotates the building. I think we're safe in here."

"How do you figure that?" I asked.

Zetlin slapped the wall next to the door we had just come through. "This wall is the structural core of the Barbican. It's five feet thick. That monster is too big to come through the doors, and there's no possibility of it crashing through this wall, I don't care how strong it gets."

"I hope you're right," I said.

He wasn't.

The proof appeared at the bottom of the door that Zetlin had just closed.

"It doesn't need to break down the wall," I said, pointing to the door.

An ink-black liquid was leaking its way into the room through the edges around the door. Like oily poison it oozed through the seams, poured on to the floor, and continued to move across it.

The Reality Bug had gone liquid.

"This way, hurry," Zetlin said, and ran off.

He didn't need to add the "hurry". We were right after him. There was no telling how long it would take the Reality Bug to ooze into the room and reform as something nasty. We had to keep moving.

"We'll take the zips," he said.

"Zips?" I asked.

We followed Zetlin through the giant machinery. I felt like an ant running through a monstrous engine, that's how big the mechanism was. He led us to a row of vehicles that I recognised from when we first arrived. They were the motorcycle-looking speeders that we saw racing underwater and in the air. Zetlin grabbed a helmet from the seat of one and jumped on.

"Whoa, we don't know how to drive these!" I complained.

"Not a problem," Zetlin answered. "A child could drive them. Watch." He grabbed the handlebars and said, "Right grip is speed, left grip is brake." He then pointed down. His right foot was resting on a pedal. "Heel back gives you nose up. Toes down, you dive. Keep your foot flat for level flight. Steering is obvious."

We then heard a gruesome scream coming from back in the machinery. It was a loud, metallic, tearing sound. The Reality Bug had reformed. Loor and I gave each other a nervous look. We then each grabbed a helmet and jumped on to a zip. We were going to have to learn how to drive these babies, fast.

"Buckle in," Zetlin said while pulling a bar around his waist. "If you're not locked in when you hit the water, you'll be thrown."

"Hit the water?" Loor asked nervously.

Zetlin then flipped a switch under the handlebars and his zip whined to life. Loor and I did the same. I could feel the hum of power coming from the zip. It felt like being on a motorcycle, like Uncle Press's. But I had never driven one myself. The closest I had come was one of those kiddie rides at the mall that you put a quarter in and it bucks around a little bit. Something told me this was going to be a little bit different. I glanced at Zetlin and he pushed his heel down. The nose cone of the zip tilted up into the air like a missile getting ready to fly.

"Let's go," he shouted, and hit the throttle. Instantly his zip launched. He shot into the air, turned sharply, and stopped, hovering over us. "C'mon!" he yelled.

I looked to Loor. Loor shrugged and followed Zetlin's lead. She pushed her heel down, the nose lifted up, and she took off. She shot past Zetlin, nearly hitting him.

Note to self: Avoid hitting things.

Zetlin turned his zip and chased after her. I had to go too, or I'd lose them. I dropped my heel and felt the front of the zip lift up. I was now pointed at the ceiling.

"Hobey-ho," I said under my breath, and twisted the throttle. The zip bucked forward and I shot into the air. The ride was incredible. It turned easily and I quickly got used to the throttle and brake. The foot pedal was a little trickier. I couldn't keep the zip level at first, and it was making me seasick. But after playing with it for a while, I was able to level out. Man, I would love to have one of these for real. Too bad it was just a fantasy vehicle.

I saw Zetlin and Loor hovering together ahead of me and quickly joined them. The three of us floated there among the giant gears, fifty feet in the air.

"Are you two all right?" Zetlin asked.

"I'm good," I said.

"I am as well," Loor said.

"Then let's keep moving."

He was about to throttle up when Loor said, "But I cannot swim."

"You won't have to," Zetlin answered.

We then heard another roar coming from deeper in the machine room. We all looked down to where we had come from, but saw nothing. The Reality Bug wasn't down there.

It was up with us.

"There it is!" Zetlin shouted.

From far back among the gears and cogs, I saw a shadow swoop up from below. I only got a glimpse of it, but what I saw I won't forget. It had the head of a bird, with a long, sharp beak. Its body looked human, with a wide, strong chest. Its legs were birdlike as well. And it had wings. Huge, black wings, like a bat.

The Reality Bug was airborne.

We all turned and pushed the zip vehicles forward. We flew in formation, with Zetlin in the lead and Loor and me together behind him. Zetlin led us on a wild ride through the incredible machinery. I guess he wanted to lose the flying Reality Bug, but Loor and I had a heck of a time trying to keep up. He flew low to the ground, under some steel beams. He then took a sharp right and led us through a narrow corridor. We had to fly single file because it wasn't wide enough for two across. We then shot out of the corridor and climbed steeply until we were near the ceiling. From up there, the round gears below us looked like curved, steel mountains.

It was amazing that we were able to keep up with him, but the zips were easy to handle. I think part of it was because these were fantasy vehicles, and in our minds we knew we had to fly them, so we did.

We were fast approaching the far wall of the machine room. There was a square opening that glowed with bright, white light.

"We're going to the glacier!" Zetlin called back.

I figured the next room in this incredible building was going to be the snowy ice field where we raced Zetlin in slickshot. That was good; we were getting closer to the jungle.

But then a shadow appeared far off to our left and in front of us. All of our crazy stunt flying was a waste. The

Reality Bug had found its own route and was racing us to the opening. We were on a collision course. We were heading straight for the opening; the bird was coming from far to our left. We had to beat it. All three of us throttled up. The freakish, giant bird sped closer. I tried to calculate who would get to the opening first. Either way, it would be close. The three of us were side by side going flat out. I squeezed the throttle, hoping it would make the zip go faster. This was totally dangerous. There was no way we could pull out going this fast. We were either going to escape, or crash right into the Reality Bug. It all depended on who got to the opening first.

A second later the three of us flashed into the white light. We had made it. The bird flew right past the opening. There was no way it could have made the sharp turn going that fast. It was going to have to circle around and hit it square on. We were going to need those few seconds to gain some ground.

We now found ourselves speeding high over the icy racecourse. Zetlin didn't try any hot, evasive manoeuvres this time. I think he simply wanted speed. That was cool by me. Speed was good. I didn't even look around to see if the Reality Bug-bird had made it into the ice world. This was all about getting across this frozen wasteland as fast as possible. It was a flat-out race.

After a minute Zetlin motioned that he was going down. He dipped his nose and shot for what looked like a sheer wall of ice. We had reached the far side of the ice room. But I didn't see any openings. We had to trust that Zetlin knew where he was going. I didn't think he wanted to splat against the ice like a bug on a windscreen.

On the snow below, I saw a winged shadow. The bug was behind us and moving up fast.

"There!" Loor shouted.

I saw it too. There was an opening cut into the ice. It was our doorway to the next room.

"We've got to go underwater!" Zetlin shouted back to us. "I doubt the bird can follow us."

What made him think that? From what I'd seen, the Reality Bug could do anything it wanted. Still, maybe the extra few seconds it took to transform into something else would give us the edge we needed.

But Loor couldn't swim.

"Loor?" I shouted.

"Do not worry," she said. "I will make it."

She was going to have to be incredibly brave. I knew she would be. Zetlin shot into the ice tunnel with us right behind. We sped through the short tunnel, blasted out the far side and entered pitch black. There was nothing to see but the series of colourful globes hanging in the air that marked the racecourse.

"Crouch down low before you hit the water," Zetlin ordered. "Don't slow down. Keep breathing." He then dropped the nose of his zip and shot for the water.

We followed him blindly. Man, I was scared. For Loor, and for me, too. I didn't know what to expect when we hit the water. Was it going to be so jarring that I'd get ripped off the zip? Should I really keep breathing? Should I wet my pants? I crouched down low inside the clear nose cone and gritted my teeth. The water came up fast. Zetlin hit with a splash. Two seconds later Loor and I hit too.

It was a jolt, but nothing I couldn't handle. The pointed nose cone must have absorbed most of the shock. Better still,

I could breathe. The helmet must have had something to do with that.

I glanced to Loor to see she was charging along right next to me. She was incredible.

It was easy to see Zetlin because the moment we hit the water, our headlights came on. The water rippled over the top of my nose cone, making the whole vehicle shiver. Turning was only slightly tougher than in the air. That must have had something to do with the water resistance. Still, we were moving fast.

I heard a huge splash in the water behind us. There was only one thing that could have made that sound. The Reality Bug was now wet. I wondered if the bird creature also went underwater, or had the bug mutated itself into something sharklike. I had to shake that image out of my head.

Our trip underwater didn't last long. Up ahead I saw the vague outline of another square opening. Zetlin aimed his zip towards it and we steered for Zetlin. Seconds later we blasted through the opening . . .

And out into the air high over the jungle. I glanced back at the opening to see it was a square of water. Nothing poured out, just like the strange round opening Loor and I had gone through when we first arrived. It was impossible, yet there it was. I noticed that my clothes weren't even wet. Unbelievable.

Zetlin gunned his zip and beat it for the jungle floor. I didn't want to run into any more of those vine-shooting plants, but it was better to get lost in the jungle than to be flying wide open for the Reality Bug to see us.

Zetlin flew his zip right for the deck. He levelled out a few feet above the jungle floor, speeding along a path. Loor was right behind him and I was right behind Loor. We were moving fast. I kept my eye on her back, looking for any movement that would warn me when the next turn was coming. We were on the home stretch. Soon we'd be at the entrance to the Barbican and home free.

After a few minutes of jungle jumping, Zetlin slowed down as he approached the far wall of the building. We had been racing for a while now, and my heart was thumping like crazy. Zetlin stopped his zip, jumped off, and ran up to a control panel that was built into the wall. He opened up the cover and started hitting buttons.

"Why don't we fly the zips out of here?" I asked.

"They don't work outside the Barbican," Zetlin answered. "We've got to go to position two so we can walk out."

He hit a few more buttons, and the building started to shake. I heard the far-off sound of screeching metal and could imagine the massive gears starting to turn. I could only hope they'd turn fast enough so we could get down and out of here before the bug found us. The building rumbled and started to move.

"It won't be long," Zetlin assured us.

We heard a tortured squealing sound, as if metal were being torn apart. A second later the building stopped moving.

"What happened?" Loor asked.

Zetlin went right back to the controls. He furiously hit a few keys, but nothing changed.

"I don't understand," he announced nervously. "All the indicators say we should be moving."

"When we were back in the machine room," I said, "there was a horrible sound. Could the Reality Bug have messed with the machinery?"

We then heard a piercing shriek come from deep within the jungle. We all looked up.

"I don't know," Zetlin said. "But the Barbican isn't moving. If it doesn't go vertical, we can't get out."

VEELOX

Another shrill squeal echoed through the jungle.

It was so loud that it felt like needles to the brain. A flock of colourful birds took flight not far behind us. We then heard the sound of crashing, crunching trees. Whatever the Reality Bug had changed into, it was big.

And it was coming.

"This can't be the only way out of here!" I complained.

"There is one other way," Zetlin said. "It is an emergency corridor, but I have never used it."

"I think now would be a good time to give it a shot," I said quickly.

More crashing trees. Closer this time. I could hear the tearing and crunching of plants as the Reality Bug moved through the jungle, looking for us. Hunting for us.

"Where is this exit?" Loor asked.

"Back in the machine room," was Zetlin's answer.

"Machine room?" I shouted. "Why didn't we use it when we were there?"

"Because I didn't know the Reality Bug was capable of sabotaging the Barbican," was Zetlin's logical answer.

"Okay, no problem," I said, trying to keep calm. "We gotta get back there."

That's when we saw it. Crashing through the tropical trees only yards away came a terrifying sight. The Reality Bug had transformed itself into, well, into some kind of green bug. It had multiple, tarantula-style legs, a long scaly body, and a massive head with pincers that snapped in front of its red, fleshy mouth. And it had grown. This beast now towered over us like we were in some kind of Japanese monster movie.

When it appeared through the trees it stopped, reared its head and let out another one of those painful shrieks.

"We are in the wrong place," Loor announced, and gunned her zip. She shot into the air, making sure to keep out of reach of the monster bug.

But she didn't get far. No sooner had she taken off than the bug turned its head towards her and shot out a clear, ropelike cord from its mouth.

"Loor!" I shouted, but it was too late. The thread caught the back of her zip in midflight and held her there like a kite at the end of a string. Loor gunned the throttle, trying to shake it, but the filament held firm. I saw that it was reeling Loor in like a fish on the line. The pincers around its mouth snapped in anticipation. The spider had caught its prey and was ready to feed.

"I'm gonna bail her out," I shouted, and was about to fly up and get her off her zip and on to mine. But Zetlin was quicker. He shot off the ground and throttled up to full speed. I thought he was going way too fast to stop right next to Loor, but that wasn't his plan. He aimed his zip halfway between the struggling Loor and the giant bug, blasting into the taut filament, snapping it in half. Totally smart move. Loor sped forward as if propelled from a slingshot.

"Yes!" I shouted, and instantly wished I hadn't. I was now alone, with the Reality Bug looming over me. Oops. I might as well have shouted: "Here I am! Come and get me!" It was time to go. I turned hard, to my left to stay as far away from the beast as possible, and throttled up. Out of the corner of my eye I saw it turn towards me and shoot out another cord. I quickly pushed my toe down, making the zip dive. The cord shot right over my shoulder, barely missing me. By the time the big bug reloaded, I was gone. A quick look over my shoulder showed me that it was scrambling back the way it had come, following the wide trail it had already cut through the jungle.

The race was back on.

I retreated in the direction of the water portal and soon caught up with Loor and Zetlin.

"Nice move," I shouted at Zetlin.

"I am very good," he answered.

He *was* good. Not modest, but good.

"Follow me back to the machine room," he announced, and throttled up. Loor and I gunned our zips and settled in behind him. I was confident we would make it. The Reality Bug was getting bigger and that meant it was slower. If we kept the pedal to the metal, we'd beat it to the machine room and get out of there with no problem.

Or so I thought.

The big liquid square that was the portal to the water room appeared in the distance. The three of us were flying towards it at full speed. In a few seconds we'd hit the water and be on our way. Zetlin turned back to us and shouted, "You two okay?"

We both nodded.

"Don't slow down. We can beat this thing," he added with confidence.

Because Zetlin was turned back towards us, he didn't see that something had appeared ahead. We were on a direct course for the big square of water, moving as fast as ever. But in that quick moment, I saw that there was something covering the opening. It took an instant for my brain to compute, but I realised what was stretched across the square.

It was a web. The Reality Bug must have spun a web after it came through, and it was about to catch a couple of speedy flies.

"Look out!" I screamed.

Too late. Loor and I turned hard and pulled out, but Zetlin didn't have a chance. He barely had time to look forward when he slammed right into the web. I had a fleeting hope that it would snap like the cord Zetlin severed before, but it didn't. This wasn't just one cord, it was an interlocking web.

Loor and I circled back quickly to see that Zetlin was stuck in the sticky cords. His zip had crashed to the ground, leaving him tangled and helpless like, well, like a fly caught in a spider's web. I wasn't even sure if he was conscious. Or alive.

Loor pulled her zip right up to Zetlin and hovered next to him.

"Are you all right?" she asked.

Zetlin nodded. Whew. He was shaken, but alive and awake. He was also trapped in a spider's web. I looked down to the jungle below to see the giant bug in the distance, scurrying towards us. Its eight legs were thrashing hard to speed it along to see if anything tasty was caught in its trap. We had to get Zetlin out of there fast. But how?

Loor had the answer. She reached into her jumpsuit and pulled out a vicious-looking kitchen knife. I didn't know she had kept one, but I was glad she had.

"Help me, Pendragon," she ordered. "Go below him."

I eased my zip down and underneath Zetlin. Loor went to work cutting away the web. I grabbed hold of Zetlin's legs, ready for him to drop down on to my zip. While Loor sliced away, I sneaked a look back down. The Reality Bug was getting closer. If it decided to change into a bird, it could fly right up and have us. But it didn't. The giant bug just kept charging through the jungle.

A few seconds later Zetlin fell loose from the web and Loor eased him on to the zip in front of me.

"Are you with us?" I asked him.

"Yes," he said, but sounded loopy. We didn't have time to rescue his zip, so Zetlin leaned forward into the nose cone of my zip, giving me a clear view forward.

"I suggest you hurry," Zetlin said.

I looked up to Loor and asked, "Is the web clear?"

"Clear enough," she answered.

The two of us then pulled away from the web, made a wide circle back, and gunned the vehicles towards the hole she had cut. Loor was first and sailed through with room to spare. I was right behind her and shot through the tendrils and into the water.

Speed was everything now. Loor and I drove our zips side by side, squeezing the throttles, coaxing every last bit of power out of the strange but cool fantasy machines. Loor made the first move to surface. Zetlin and I were right behind. We both launched up and out of the water, headeding for the icy opening that would lead us to the slickshot course.

Minutes later we blasted through the ice tunnel and shot out over the bright, frozen glacier. We kept pushing the zips forward, not even taking a second to turn and see if the Reality Bug was on our butts.

Zetlin never looked up from inside his position in the nose

of my zip. Just as well. Both Loor and I knew where we had to go, and a short few minutes later we were sailing over the giant gears of the machine room.

"There's the trouble," I said while pointing down.

Sure enough, two massive metal bars had been jammed between a set of gear wheels. When the Barbican started to move, it jammed up the works. Not only was the Reality Bug vicious, it was smart.

I motioned to Loor for us to land, and the two of us guided our zips down to the floor.

"Dr Zetlin," I said. "We're in the machine room. How do we get out of here?"

Zetlin pulled himself up from the nose of the zip. He looked groggy.

"Are you hurt?" Loor asked.

"Just rattled," Zetlin answered. He looked around, scanning the vast machine room. "There!" he announced. He pointed to a round, vertical tube not far from us that stretched from the floor to the ceiling. It was made of the same light blue aluminium as the inside of the lift.

"That's the dead centre of the Barbican," he said. "And our way out."

"We should leave these vehicles and travel on foot," Loor said. "We do not want the monster knowing where we are."

Excellent idea.

"Let's go," I said and the three of us hurried across the floor of the machine room, heading for this blue cylinder. We kept looking back, expecting the Reality Bug to appear. But it didn't. I was beginning to think it had run out of tricks and was trapped back in that jungle. Good. I hoped the vine-shooting cactus plants were gnawing away on it.

It only took us a few minutes to get to the cylinder. It was about four feet wide and shot straight up. Zetlin directed us to a square hatch that had a wheel built into it.

"This leads down into the arch that braces the Barbican," he explained while spinning the wheel. "We can climb all the way to the ground inside the arch."

He pulled open the hatch and entered first. Loor went next and I followed last. It was dark inside the round tube, especially after I closed the hatch and spun the wheel that locked it. Our eyes adjusted in a few seconds and I saw a metal ladder that ran the length of the tube. Zetlin got on the ladder and climbed down. Loor and I followed quickly. The ladder went down several feet to a platform.

"This platform is the very top of the arch," Zetlin explained. "There are metal stairs on either end that will take us down."

Yikes. I thought back to seeing this arch from outside. It was huge, which meant it was a long way down. I was beginning to realise why this wasn't Zetlin's first choice of escape route.

Loor was thinking the same thing. "If the Reality Bug follows us in here . . ."

She didn't have to finish the sentence. We knew we'd be trapped.

"I know," Zetlin said. "But it's the only way down."

I didn't want to waste any more time, so I started walking towards the end of the platform. I must have gone about thirty yards when I came upon a set of metal stairs with metal handrails. The stairs curved down and away into the dark. Gulp.

"Be careful," Zetlin said. "It's a long way down."

I didn't need that reminder. I turned around and went down the stairs backwards, with a death grip on the handrails to either side. Loor followed me and Zetlin was last. It was tough at first because the stairs weren't very steep. It was like walking on my hands and feet. I thought back to the shape of the arch to remember it curved at the top. I figured that the farther down we got, the steeper it would get and that is exactly what happened. Soon I was climbing nearly straight down, as if on a ladder. I moved as fast as it felt safe to go. Speed was good, but if I tripped . . . *splat*. I didn't know what scared me more: falling into this dark hole, or having the Reality Bug attack from above. Either way, it was good motivation to keep moving.

None of us spoke on the way down. There wasn't a whole lot to talk about. But I knew we were all thinking the same thing. Keep moving, get down and out of here before the bug finds us.

Suddenly the entire structure shook. It was so fast and hard, it nearly pulled me off the stairs. We all stopped, clutching the handrails for safety.

"What was that?" I called out.

"I don't know," answered Zetlin. "Keep going, but use caution."

I started down again. Another minute went by and the structure shook again. We all held tight and didn't move.

"It's gotta be the bug," I said. "Maybe it's trying to break through one of the walls."

We started moving again, but now with the fear that at any moment we could get thrown off the stairs by these mysterious jolts. It happened three more times, and each time we held tight. Then, finally, after what seemed like a lifetime, we made it to the ground. Nobody stopped to celebrate. We were now at the base of one side of the arch, in the widest part of the structure.

"There is the way out," Loor said, pointing to a door not far from us. We all ran to it and Loor pulled it open.

It was pouring rain outside, but I didn't care. We were out! We hurried away from the arch, trying to get as much distance between us and the Reality Bug as possible. We must have run at least half a mile down the wide street before we felt safe enough to stop. The three of us found refuge in the entryway of one of the black buildings.

As we stood there, catching our breath, I looked back at the incredible structure that was the Barbican. What an impossible, amazing, breathtaking building. It hung in the air, on its side, offering no clue as to the wonders inside. It seemed both spectacular, and sad.

I glanced to Dr Zetlin and saw he wasn't looking at the building. He was actually looking down the rainy street of his dreary fantasy city. It was a place that was here to remind him of a life he had fled. Now it was his refuge.

"Dr Zetlin?" I said softly.

"I swore I would never return," he said, his voice cracking.

I looked out at the city to try and see it through his eyes. Rain bounced off the grey streets. It was a pretty depressing place. It struck me that there were no people. From the time the Reality Bug started to wreak havoc, I hadn't seen a single soul. I didn't know if everybody had fled, or the fantasy had somehow altered and wiped out everybody but the real people. Us. I guess it didn't matter. We didn't belong here. None of us did.

"This isn't reality either," Loor reminded him.

"It is to me," he said.

We then heard a sound that at first I thought was thunder. It was a deep, violent booming sound that came from the direction of the Barbican. We looked at the building, but there was nothing unusual to see. We heard two more loud booms.

"Whatever it is," Loor said, "it is what made the arch shake when we were climbing down."

But what was it?

The answer came quickly. We heard another huge booming sound. Zetlin gasped.

Something was attacking the Barbican . . . from inside. Chunks of the building were tearing away and crashing to the ground below. I think we all knew what it was, but didn't want to believe it.

"It wasn't trying to break down a wall," I gasped. "It was trying to break out."

Then a huge black shape erupted from the far end of the building. It was the end that held the jungle. We watched in awe as a massive fist pushed its way up and out of the building. The sound of wrenching metal and breaking glass cut through the pounding rain. The fist pulled back into the building and another shape pushed up. It looked like a monster was being hatched from the horizontal structure. The black mass pushed up and out of the hole, tearing it wider, sending chunks of wrecked building to the street. The mass writhed and twisted, and then opened its eyes.

It was the head of the beast and it was a creature from hell. It looked like an animal, but no animal I had ever seen. The shape was like a boar's head, with a snout and long, curling teeth. The eyes were snake eyes with vertical slits. The beast had gigantic horns that curled up and around like a ram. The whole head was covered with black, oily fur.

The beast forced its head up through the hole and opened its mouth to bellow as it struggled to push out of the building. The gaping mouth was bloodred and full of multiple rows of yellow teeth.

We watched, mesmerised, as the beast punched out another hole. Its fist blasted out, making the escape hole even bigger. It then punched its other fist through so both arms were free. Now it could lift its colossal chest out of the structure. Its chest and arms were almost human, with massive muscles. The thing was still growing as we watched. It was now too big to fit inside the end of the building. We could hear the sound of wrenching metal as the beast's weight pushed down on the one end. If it grew any bigger, the building would collapse.

The beast howled again and smashed its fist down on top of the building. It blasted open another huge hole and water came flooding out. It had broken open the room that held the underwater racecourse. Tons of water spewed from the building like a waterfall and crashed on to the street. There was so much water that, in just a few seconds, the surge made it all the way to us, and we stood knee-deep in a river. But we didn't move. We were already soaking wet from the rain. A foot more of water wasn't going to make things any worse.

The beast pushed against the top of the building and lifted one leg out, then the other. We saw that the bottom half of the monster was furry, with hooves for feet. It heaved itself out of the hole and stood on top of the horizontal building. Last out was the creature's tail. It was long and bone white, like a rat's tail. The monster stood on its two hoofed feet, with its tail wrapped around one leg, and howled. It was a horrible, angry sound that made my blood freeze. We were staring at the physical being of the Reality Bug. All the fears of the people of Veelox had fed this thing, made it real, and let it grow.

The three of us were absolutely powerless against it.

The monster then climbed off the building and slid down one side of the arch. Now it was on the ground. The question was, would it start looking for us? It stood tall, looked around, and sniffed the air. I saw its piggy snout moving as it searched for smells. I really hoped we were downwind. Any second I expected the beast to catch our scent and start coming.

But it didn't. It gave one last look around, then fell to its knees.

"What is it doing?" Loor asked.

The beast balled up its monster hand into a fist, raised it into the air, brought it down hard, and punched the ground. The force was so strong it shook the street as if it had been slammed with an earthquake. The monster did it again. Its muscles rippled with strength as it punched the ground again. And again. And again. He kept punching at the same area, eventually blasting a crater in the cement.

The look on Zetlin's face told me he didn't have any better idea than we did about why the beast was punching the street.

"What's happening?" came a frightened voice from behind us.

The three of us jumped in surprise, and turned to see . . .

Aja. She walked past us with her eyes fixed on the beast.

"What's happening?" I asked back. "You tell us! We've been running from that thing since we saw you. Are you gonna get us out of here or what?"

Aja didn't answer me. She just kept staring at the Reality Bug.

As the beast pummelled the ground, its head changed. It went from the strange, piglike creature, to the head of a bird with a long, curved beak. The beak opened to reveal huge, pointed teeth. Its body then changed to something like a reptile. Its head then changed again. It became a gruesome, fleshless skull with dead eyes and fanged teeth.

"It's feeding on the fear of the whole territory," Aja gasped.

"Aja," Loor asked calmly. "Do you know why it is punching the ground?"

Aja turned to us. Her face was totally blank. "I think it's trying to escape," she said.

"It already escaped," I said. "Look at that building. It's destroyed."

Aja shook her head. It was creepy to see her like this. Aja was brilliant and she showed it in her eyes. But those normally sharp eyes now looked vacant, as if her mind wouldn't accept what was happening.

"No," she said. "It's trying to escape from the fantasy."

Zetlin shot her a look. "What do you mean?" he demanded.

"The Alpha Core," she continued as if in a trance. "It's being torn apart. Every time it pounds the ground, I can feel it in the core."

"That's impossible," Zetlin said. "The Alpha Core is reality."

"That's what I'm trying to tell you," Aja said with finality. "The Reality Bug has got more powerful than Lifelight itself. It's trying to escape from this fantasy . . . and break into reality."

VEELOX

Was it possible? Could the Reality Bug rip a seam in Zetlin's fantasy and escape into the real world? If this monster got into the pyramid through the Alpha Core, it would tear the place apart. The people in the pyramid would be doomed, not to mention the rest of Veelox. Could that really happen?

Of course it could. Why would I doubt it? None of the rules of reality applied to anything I'd seen on Veelox, what made me think they would start to kick in now? No way. If this thing got loose, it would lay waste all of Veelox.

And Saint Dane would have his first territory.

"Why is this happening?" Loor asked with a firm voice. She sounded a lot more in control than I was feeling.

I had no idea how to answer that question, until I saw that she was holding up her wrist controller. The square button to the far right was glowing white. I quickly lifted up my wrist to see the button on my controller was glowing as well. A glance to Zetlin showed that his was glowing too.

"Aja?" I yelled. "What does this mean?"

I held up my wrist controller for her to see, but she kept staring at the monster beast as it crashed its fist into the street over and over. This nightmare was her creation. I think she was in shock. I jumped in front of her, getting right in her face.

"Aja!" I screamed, and held my controller up to her face. "Why is it doing this?"

Aja slowly focused on the controller. She looked at it strangely for a second, as if not knowing what it was. Then I saw her eyes focus. An idea was forming. Aja was coming back. "Just before the Alpha Core began to shake," she said slowly, "the alpha grid opened up."

"What does that mean?" Loor demanded.

"I think the Reality Bug is focusing all of its strength to fight its way out," Aja said. "That might give us control of the jump, at least for a little while."

I quickly spun to the others. "We're getting out, now! Loor! Hit the button."

Loor didn't question. She immediately hit the glowing button . . . and disappeared.

"Yes!" I ran to Dr Zetlin, who was staring vacantly at the monster. "Dr Zetlin, I'm getting out of the jump. You've got to follow me."

Zetlin didn't take his eyes from the monster. I grabbed the guy by the shoulders and forced him to look at me.

"Listen!" I screamed. "We've got to end this jump. Maybe that'll stop the Reality Bug."

"And if it doesn't?" he asked slowly.

"We've got a better chance of you fighting it from the Alpha Core than running away from it in here. My faith is in you, and Aja. You gotta end this."

Zetlin glanced back at the beast. I saw something change in his eyes. He became focused and alert. He looked back to me and nodded.

"Go," he said. "I'll be right behind you."

This time I believed him. I looked to Aja's image. "I'll see you in the Alpha Core, all right?"

"Hurry," she said, and disappeared.

"I'm gone!" I said to Zetlin, and hit the right button.

The world went black.

I had enough sense not to move right away. The last time I did that, I slammed my head on the inside of the jump tube. But was I back? Had I finally returned to reality?

My answer came quickly. Light crept into my jump tube as the silver disc slipped sideways into the wall. The table slid out of the tube, and all I saw was Loor. She stood over me, looking like an angel that had been sent to my rescue.

"Are we back?" I asked. "For real this time?"

"I believe so," Loor answered.

I hopped off the table and ran out of the cubicle, heading for the Alpha Core. Seated in the control chair was Aja. When she saw me, she jumped out of her chair and threw her arms around me in a huge hug. I half expected her to fly right through me like a ghostly image. But she didn't. She was solid. It was her. The real deal. We were back.

"I never thought you'd get out of there," she said.

I hadn't expected this big welcome, but I wasn't complaining. "What's happening?" I asked.

Aja pulled away from me and sat back in the control chair. I was happy to see she was focused again.

"As soon as Dr Zetlin left his jump, everything stopped," she explained while pointing to the monitor, which was black. "The pounding stopped too. I think when he ended his jump, the Reality Bug ended with it."

Loor had joined us. "Could it be that easy?" she asked.

Aja hit a few buttons on her console. A data stream appeared on the monitor. She scanned it, then announced, "I think so. Lifelight is back to normal." She turned to me and giggled. "It's over."

"So where is Zetlin?" I asked.

Aja leaped out of her chair and ran into the jump cubicle. The centre disc was still closed. Aja hit a few buttons above it, but then hesitated. I could guess what was going through her mind, because I was thinking the same thing. Opening up this jump tube felt like we were unsealing a tomb. Zetlin hadn't been out of there in years. It was exciting and creepy at the same time.

"It's okay," I said, trying to be reassuring. "It's time for him to come out."

Aja nodded, then hit the last button. The silver disc slid back from the centre tube, and with a soft hum, the table emerged. The three of us stood together, nervously waiting to get our first view of Dr Zetlin. The *real* Dr Zetlin.

Lying on the jump table was an elderly man with closed eyes. He wore the familiar green jumpsuit and had his hands folded in front of him. His skin was pasty white for lack of sun. His head was bald, and he had a scraggly beard. That made sense. He hadn't shaved in three years. There was a definite Rip Van Winkle vibe going on. He even had his round glasses on. I wasn't sure why he needed those in the jump tube, but who am I to judge? It was incredible to think this was the same guy we had just been racing through a fantasy with . . . when he was sixteen years old. The only proof was the red slash mark on the back of his hand, where he had been splashed with venom. This was Dr Zetlin all right. In the flesh.

For a second I feared he was dead. He sure looked dead. But then he slowly opened his eyes and squinted from the light. After all, his eyes had been closed for a long time.

"My head hurts," he whispered.

I guess he was still hurting from his collision with the web. He began to sit up, so the three of us quickly helped him. The guy felt frail. No big surprise. He was seventy-nine years old and hadn't had any exercise in a while.

"I'm as weak as a kitten," he announced.

We got him up straight, and he took a deep breath. He felt his beard as if it were an alien attachment. He took off his glasses and rubbed his eyes. He then took his first look at all of us. I now recognised the guy we knew from inside the fantasy. He may have been in an old body, but his eyes were the same. He looked at each of us in turn, then asked, "What is the status?"

Aja took a step forward and reported, "We think that when you ended the jump, it destroyed the Reality Bug. There's no sign of it anywhere. And may I add, it's an honour to meet you in person, Dr Zetlin."

Zetlin looked Aja up and down, then said, "Yeah, whatever."

He slid off the table on to wobbly legs. We all rushed to keep him from toppling over, but he pushed us away.

"I'm a little rusty," he said gruffly. "Not feeble."

We backed off.

Zetlin took a couple of unsteady steps, then stopped, and stood up straight. "I'd forgotten what it was like to be in this body," he explained. With every step he took, he got more sure of himself. He made his way out of the jump cubicle and headed for the Alpha Core. By the time he made it to the control chair, he was looking pretty steady. Suddenly, seventy-nine didn't seem so old any more.

Zetlin dropped himself into the chair as if he owned it.

Actually, he did. He glanced up at the data on the monitor, looking for something. I'm glad it made sense to him, because to me it was nothing but a jumble of numbers and symbols.

"Killian!" he barked.

Aja ran up to him and stood at attention. "Yes, Doctor?" she said professionally. She was now working for the master.

"You've examined the entire alpha grid, and the main grid?" Zetlin asked.

"Yes," she said. "Lifelight is back online. The jumps are performing normally. I don't see any sign of the Reality Bug. Anywhere."

Slam!

The entire room rocked. It was such a strong, sudden impact, I lost my balance. Loor had to catch me and hold me up.

Slam!

The room was jolted again. I heard something crash to the floor in the jump cubicle. What I saw through the door was impossible, yet there it was. A hole had been blasted into the ceiling beyond. Debris covered the floor. But it wasn't the damage that rocked me. It was what I saw peering down from the hole above.

It was the hollow socket of a giant skeleton head. The bug wasn't dead. It had just broken through to reality.

None of us could move. We were frozen in shock. The head moved away and a second later a massive, black fist slammed into the hole again, smashing it open wider.

I looked back to the control console where the monitor was suddenly going haywire. Numbers flashed by incredibly fast. Aja and Zetlin were furiously hitting buttons, trying to get control.

"Where did it come from?" Aja screamed.

"It must have fled to another part of the grid when my

jump ended," Zetlin said quickly. "But it found its way back."

Oh, yeah, it found its way back, all right.

The pounding continued. The ceiling was collapsing and the hole was growing wider. The monster now started grabbing at the damaged area, ripping up pieces to make its entryway into our world bigger.

Loor glanced around the room, searching for a weapon. But it was futile. There was no weapon any of us could use to stop this thing.

Another crash. I looked into the cubicle to see its fist had broken all the way through. It wasn't going to take this beast very long to tear apart the entire pyramid.

"Look," Aja said, pointing to the data on the monitor. "It's drawing data from all over Veelox. That's how it got so powerful. It's still feeding on the fears of all the jumpers."

"Then stop feeding it!" I shouted.

Aja and Zetlin shot me a look like I was crazy.

"It's feeding itself, Pendragon," Aja answered impatiently. "We don't have a whole lot of say in the matter."

I heard a guttural growl and turned towards the cubicle. What I saw made me forget to breathe. The giant skull had pushed its way down through the hole and was peering at us. Being so close, I could smell its decay. We all watched in stunned fear as flesh began to grow on the skeletal head. Eyes grew from the sockets and oily skin spread out over the face to form features. In seconds, the beast had become a hideous baboon-looking head with white, pupil-less eyes. The monster grunted, and pulled back up into the ceiling. It was about to start its final assault.

If we were going to do something, it had to be now.

"There's gotta be a way!" I argued. "Can't you cut off the power supply?"

"Didn't you hear me? It's coming from every jumper on Veelox," Aja answered.

"So what!" I shouted back. "Shut it down! Shut it all down. If people aren't jumping, the Reality Bug can't feed on their fears!"

"I told you, we can't do that!" Aja shot back. "It's too dangerous!"

"More dangerous than this?" Loor asked calmly.

Boom!

A foot crashed through the ceiling. It was birdlike, with huge sabre claws.

"That's why we suspended the grid before," Aja argued. "We can't shut Lifelight down."

"But if we don't stop it, it's going to destroy the pyramid and turn on the rest of Veelox," I yelled. "If it's getting strength from the jumpers, we've got to cut it off!"

"The grid cannot be shut down, Pendragon!" Aja shouted back.

Crash!

The huge bird leg was now kicking at the doorway into the Alpha Core, smashing it wider, opening the portal between fantasy and reality.

"Dr Zetlin," I screamed. "It's a machine! There's gotta be a way to shut it down."

Zetlin didn't answer. He didn't even look at me. He was hiding something.

"Dr Zetlin!" I screamed. "Can we shut this down?"

The beast kept kicking at the doorway, cracking it open. Chunks of material flew across the room. Zetlin was hit by a flying particle. It jolted him and made him look up at the horror that was fighting to get at us. To get at Veelox.

"My whole life has been about Lifelight," he said in a daze.

"If I shut it down, my life will have been worthless."

"That means it *can* be shut down?" Aja asked with surprise.

"Dr Zetlin," Loor said calmly, "your life has not been worthless, and it is not yet over. But unless you do all you can to stop this horror, it *will* be over and you will forever be known as the man who let Veelox die."

Zetlin winced. Loor's words had got through to him. But he continued to stare at the beast that was nearly on us.

"Doctor," I said, trying to will him to listen to reason. "If you can do something, you have to do it now."

Zetlin gave me a quick look, then spun back to the control console. He had made a decision. He was shutting down Lifelight.

"What can I do?" Aja asked.

"Nothing," Zetlin said with sadness as he made some rapid-fire entries on the console.

"Will this cut off the data feeding the Reality Bug?" I asked.

"Theoretically," Zetlin shrugged. "But I truly don't know. I've never encountered this situation before."

Yeah, no kidding.

The Reality Bug began mutating again. The giant birdlike leg began to twist and mould until the foot transformed into a repulsive insect head. Most of the head was made up of a round mouth that was ringed with multiple rows of gnashing, pointed teeth. The leg itself grew into a snakelike body.

In this form, the hole from Lifelight was now big enough for the Reality Bug to slither into Veelox.

"Hurry!" I shouted at Zetlin.

Zetlin was calm. He reached around his neck and pulled out a red plastic card on a chain, like the green one Aja had used to suspend the grid.

The Reality Bug dropped farther into the jump chamber.

Its snaky body made wet, squishing sounds as it hit the floor.

Aja, Loor, and I huddled together near the control console as the nasty-looking creature slithered into the Alpha Core, its teeth making a revolting sucking sound as it sought its prey. Us.

Zetlin stayed focused. He jammed the red card into the slot and made quick keystrokes on the control pad.

"Do you need verification?" Aja asked, without taking her eyes off the bug that was slipping closer.

"No," he said sadly. "I have control."

He then reached up to a clear plastic cover that protected a red toggle switch. He flipped the cover up to reveal the switch, and glanced back at the Reality Bug.

The bug opened its round, evil mouth, ready to descend on us.

Zetlin closed his eyes . . . and threw the switch.

The Reality Bug froze. In that single second, it went from a living entity to an immobile statue. It was like a freeze-frame in a movie.

Every light on the control console went dark. It was as simple as that. Lifelight had been turned off.

The four of us stared in wonder at the frozen Reality Bug, waiting for the next move. It stayed in that same, rock-solid position for a moment, then its skin began to change. The entire surface of the beast became a vast series of numbers. It was as if we were looking at the raw data that had been gathered to create the monster. The shape of the creature remained, but every bit of detail was replaced by numbers. Billions of green, glowing computer numbers.

The numbers then began to count down. Each set of digits sped on a freefall to zero. As each numeral reached zero, it disappeared, taking a small chunk of the monster with it. It was like the beast was decaying, bit by bit, number by number. The Reality Bug was being deleted before our eyes. The whole process took no more than thirty seconds. But when it was done, there was nothing left. The only sign that it had ever been there was the gaping hole left in the ceiling of the jump cubicle.

The Reality Bug had been starved to death.

And Lifelight was dead.

VEELOX

The next few days were spent in a blur of activity. Because Lifelight had been shut down, thousands of jumpers had no choice but to leave the pyramid and return to their lives in Rubic City. It was a strange thing to see.

People wandered out of the pyramid, hiding their eyes from the bright sun. Most seemed dazed, as if they weren't sure what they should be doing or where they should go. I saw a few people arguing with phaders, demanding to be put back into their jumps. But the phaders could only shrug helplessly. Lifelight was dead. Whether the people of Veelox liked it or not, they had to deal with real life once again.

While the jumpers had to come to grips with the reality of reality, there were big doings among the people who ran Lifelight. Bottom line was, Lifelight had been shut down and the directors wanted to know why. Most of what happened over the next few days I couldn't take part in, because, well, I didn't belong. But there was a major inquiry and poor Aja was at the centre of it. Luckily for her, she had a pretty good ally . . . Dr Zetlin. Together the two of them faced the directors to answer the tough questions about why Lifelight was no more.

There was nothing Loor or I could do to help, so we went to stay with Evangeline and wait for news. But rather than sit in the quiet old mansion, wondering what was going on at the pyramid, Loor and I took a pedal vehicle and toured Rubic City to watch it come back to life.

It was pretty cool.

The streets were now full of people. Stores reopened for business. Once-grimy windows were washed sparkling clean. People even began to change out of their green jumpsuits to wear normal clothes again.

As we rode through the streets we listened in on people's conversations. Of course the number one topic was Lifelight. People wanted to know what went wrong. But as the hours passed, we began hearing other conversations. People spoke about normal things like wanting to repaint their houses, or when they might expect fresh vegetables at the market, or about how much they had missed seeing each other. I could only imagine that the same things were happening all over Veelox.

It was all good. The territory wouldn't be reborn overnight, but it was definitely on its way. As happy as I was for the people of Veelox, this news had much bigger meaning for Loor and me. It meant that Saint Dane had been turned back once again. He thought he was in a no-lose situation. He wasn't.

I have to admit, I was feeling pretty good about myself. Yeah, it was great and important to beat Saint Dane. That's the main thing. But after having been embarrassed on First Earth, I felt that on Veelox I was able to pull the Travellers together and get the best from all of us. Aja was certain she had beaten Saint Dane before I even showed up, and make no mistake, she played a huge part in our victory. Maybe the most important part. But without the help of Loor and myself, it would have been a disaster.

As Loor and I pedalled around the reawakening city, I was actually beginning to accept the idea that maybe I *was* the lead Traveller. I still had no idea why I was chosen for the job, or who did the choosing, but my confidence was starting to grow. I went so far as to think that if I could continue to lead the Travellers the way I did on Veelox, then the ultimate victory over Saint Dane was possible.

I had come a very long way from that night when Uncle Press first brought me to the flume.

Aja didn't return to her house for a couple of days. Evangeline was a wonderful host. She fed us gloid (we avoided the blue like the plague), and made up comfortable rooms for us. It was the first time I had spent with Loor when we weren't in the middle of some crisis.

I didn't hate it.

She told me about her life growing up as a warrior-in-training, and I told her about Stony Brook. Okay, my life wasn't exactly as exciting as hers, but she listened and pretended to be interested. It was a great time. Loor and I had been through some hairy adventures, but we were now connecting on a whole new level. I think they call it "normal". I always had a ton of respect for her. Now I felt as if I had found a friend.

I could have gone on like this forever, but it wasn't meant to be. For on the afternoon of the third day, while the two of us pedalled through a new neighbourhood, Loor made an announcement.

"There is nothing more for me to do here, Pendragon," she said. "I need to return to Zadaa."

This hit me out of left field and my thoughts were jumbled. "But, I thought . . . I was hoping . . ."

"What were you hoping?" Loor asked.

I took a breath to get my head together, then said, "I don't see why we should split up. Saint Dane is going to show up again, I guarantee it. It would be better if we were together to deal with whatever he throws at us. Right?"

Loor gave this some thought, then answered, "You are right. We do not know where Saint Dane will surface. But I do know there is trouble on Zadaa. I want to be there and ready."

"Okay, I get that," I said. "But Saint Dane went to a territory called Eelong and Gunny followed him. I think we should go to Eelong."

"I agree," Loor said. "But we do not know for certain where Saint Dane plans to strike next. Yes, he went to Eelong, but Zadaa is on the verge of a civil war. How are we to know which he plans to attack first?"

I couldn't argue with that.

"Go to Eelong," she continued. "I will return to Zadaa. When events come clear, we can always find each other."

I racked my brain trying to come up with reasons for us to stay together, but couldn't undo her logic. What I had to admit to myself was that the real reason I wanted us together was because I didn't want to be alone. Uncle Press was gone, Spader had issues, and Gunny was on Eelong. Even Aja had her hands full here on Veelox. The truth was that if Loor went back to Zadaa, I would be on my own. That scared me.

"Maybe I should go to Zadaa with you," I offered.

"Then what of Eelong?" Loor asked. "Gunny has not returned. I believe you should find him."

Gunny was only supposed to be on Eelong a short time. The plan was for him to get a quick look around and then return to Veelox. He didn't. I got so caught up in Lifelight that I couldn't go looking for him. Loor was right. What had to happen now was obvious. Saint Dane went to Eelong. Gunny followed him. Gunny didn't come back.

I had to go to Eelong.

Without another word of argument, I turned the pedal vehicle and headed for the flume. It was a little trickier dropping into the manhole this time because the street was no longer deserted. We had to wait until nobody was watching, then quickly lift the metal lid and drop into the derelict subway below. A few minutes later the two of us stood at the mouth of the flume. This day had not turned out the way I had expected.

"Say goodbye to Aja for me," Loor said. "And Evangeline."

I nodded. I didn't want to say goodbye to anybody. Especially Loor.

"Thank you for coming to Veelox," I said.

"Gratitude is unnecessary," she declared. "I am a Traveller."

"But I threw you into a pretty nasty situation without a whole lot of warning and . . . you are an amazing person, Loor."

I wanted to hug her, but she wasn't the sentimental type. So I was surprised when she reached forward and touched my cheek. It was a tender gesture. Something I had never thought she was capable of.

"I feel the same about you, Pendragon," she said sincerely. "I am glad you are our leader . . . and my friend."

I felt a swell of pride and emotion. I hate to admit this, but my eyes started to tear up. There was no way I was going to let her see that, so I willed myself to get a grip. She backed away and stepped into the flume.

"*Zadaa!*" she called into the dark tunnel. The flume came alive with light and sound. The far off musical notes were on their way to grab her and take her home. I had to fight the urge to jump in after her. That wouldn't have been cool.

"Find me," was all I said.

"I will," Loor answered.

The grey stone walls melted into crystal as the light grew so bright I had to squint. The last image I saw of Loor was her silhouette. A moment later she was gone.

And I was alone.

I didn't leave for Eelong right away. I needed to know how the Lifelight investigation went. Our mission on Veelox wouldn't be over until all the loose ends were tied up. So rather than jump into the flume, I went back to Evangeline's house.

When I arrived, I was surprised to find Aja sitting at the kitchen table with Evangeline, eating gloid.

"Where's Loor?" was the first thing she asked.

"She went back to Zadaa," I answered. "She asked me to say goodbye to both of you."

Aja nodded and continued eating. She looked tired as she sat there enjoying her gloid, not saying a word. I was dying to know what had happened, but I didn't jump all over her. I knew she would tell me when she was ready.

Evangeline said, "I'll leave you two to talk," and left the room. Uh-oh. I had the feeling that Aja had news, and it wasn't necessarily good.

"There's a public meeting tomorrow," Aja finally said. "The directors are going to announce the findings of their investigation to all of Veelox."

"What did you tell them?" I asked.

"Basically, I lied," Aja admitted. "I said there was a software problem that corrupted the jump data and threatened the safety of the jumpers."

"That wasn't a lie," I said.

Aja sniffed. "No, but it wasn't exactly the whole truth."

"They believed you?" I asked.

"They had to. I had Dr Zetlin on my side. The directors may be powerful, but they don't mess with the Z."

"So he backed up your story?"

"Every word," Aja quickly answered. "He didn't say anything about the Reality Bug and took full responsibility for shutting down Lifelight."

"And they bought it?" I asked.

"Remember, Pendragon, we were the only ones who saw the Reality Bug, but there were thousands of people all over Veelox whose jumps had gone sour. People were scared. They knew there was trouble."

"What about the damage to the Alpha Core? How did you explain that?"

"We played dumb. To be honest, neither of us could come up with a logical explanation so we told them we didn't know how it happened. They had to believe us because there was no way we could have done the damage ourselves."

"You've been gone three days," I said. "Were they questioning you the whole time?"

"No. Most of the time we spent troubleshooting the grid, checking every possible bit of data to make sure nothing else was corrupted," she answered. "Of course, I was also looking for any sign of the Reality Bug."

"And?"

"It's gone," she said with confidence. "Totally."

"So you're a hero," I said with a smile. "The people of Veelox see you as the coolheaded phader who averted disaster."

"Maybe," she said. She then put her spoon down and sat back in her chair. She didn't take her eyes off me. "What do *you* see me as?"

This was a loaded question. I knew how important this was to her.

"I see you as the TravelLer who beat Saint Dane and saved her territory," I answered with authority.

Aja smiled. "With a little help," she said coyly.

"None of us can do it on our own," I reminded her.

Aja nodded. "Did we really do it, Pendragon?" she asked tentatively. "Did we save the territory from Saint Dane?"

"You gotta take a look around Rubic City," I said. "The place is coming alive. You've given them a second chance."

The look on Aja's face said it all. She felt as if her entire life had been about preparing for this challenge. It may not have played out exactly as she'd imagined, but the result was the same. She had succeeded. The look on her face was one of pure relief, and satisfaction.

"So what is the public meeting about?" I asked.

"I think they want to explain to the people what happened," she answered. "People all over Veelox will be watching. Who knows? Maybe they're going to give me a medal."

The big meeting was held early the next morning.

It was all very exciting. Thousands upon thousands of people streamed into the pyramid to gather on the central floor. After getting used to Rubic City as a ghost town, it was amazing to see so many people flowing through the streets, all heading for one place.

I went with Aja and Evangeline. With the huge crowd flooding into the pyramid, it felt like we were going to the Super Bowl. As we walked along the glass corridor of the core, it was eerie to see all of the control stations dark. Not a single monitor or indicator light was lit. We entered the main chamber of the pyramid. It was even more breathtaking now because it was loaded with people. Not only was the main floor packed, but there were people standing on every level above us, looking down at the floor. Everyone was orderly, but there was electricity in the air.

As in the core, all the Lifelight indicator lights were out. The thousands of lights that had marked the jump cubicles were all dark. Seeing this made me believe that Lifelight was truly dead.

Aja led us through the crowd to the centre of the pyramid floor, where there was a round stage. It was raised just enough so that everyone could see it. On the stage were fifteen chairs. Aja didn't need to explain. This was where the directors would sit.

"We can go down the front," Aja explained. "I'm sort of part of this."

"This is so exciting!" Evangeline exclaimed.

No sooner did we arrive at the platform, than the general buzzing of voices stopped. The show was about to begin. A section of crowd parted for a line of people who were walking to the stage. These people wore yellow jumpsuits and walked in single file. I looked at Aja. She nodded. These were the directors. They were all adults, some with grey hair. They climbed a few steps to the platform and marched in front of the seats.

I saw that the last person in line was Dr Zetlin. I had to do a double-take because his beard was gone and he didn't look as ghostly white as when he first came out of his jump. He looked almost human, and definitely more like the young guy we raced through the Barbican with . . . plus about sixty years. He glanced down, saw us standing in front, and winked.

All fifteen people sat down, except for one woman who walked to the front of the stage. She looked to be the oldest person of the group, except for Dr Zetlin, that is. She had short, sandy-coloured hair and sharp eyes. The woman surveyed the crowd, making sure to look up to the heights of the pyramid. It was like she was trying to make eye contact with each and every person there. The crowd of thousands went eerily quiet.

"That's Dr Kree Sever," Aja whispered, "the prime director."

"Is she, like, the boss?" I asked.

"Yes," Aja answered. "You're staying in her house."

Right. I knew that name sounded familiar. This was the woman who was nice enough to let Aja and Evangeline live in her mansion. Now that she was out of Lifelight, I wondered if Aja and Evangeline would have to find a new place to live.

"Welcome to all those who have come here today," Dr Sever began in a strong voice. "And to those who are watching from distant parts of Veelox."

Her voice was amplified throughout the pyramid. I guessed she had a microphone, which is also how they heard her at remote locations.

"After three days of exhaustive research," she continued, "we, the directors of Lifelight, have come before you in order to explain recent events, and to present the decision we have made regarding the future."

The woman sounded kind of like a politician running for office, rather than a scientist. I think she liked being in front of a crowd.

"We are honoured," she continued, "to have with us a man whom we all know, but few have had the privilege to see in person, until today. I'm speaking about none other than the creator of Lifelight himself, the esteemed Dr Zetlin."

The pyramid broke out in wild applause. It was deafening. Zetlin didn't move. In fact, he looked embarrassed. After five minutes of this standing O, Dr Sever quietened the crowd and continued, "What better person to explain the confusing events of the last few days, than the one man who knows more about Lifelight than any other? It is my great pleasure to present to you the legendary Dr Zetlin."

The crowd erupted again. I was betting this kind of applause was happening all over Veelox. Dr Zetlin slowly rose to his feet, nodded to Dr Sever, and walked to the front of the stage. He raised his hands to quieten the crowd. Nobody wanted to stop. It took another five minutes before the place finally quietened down.

"My friends," Dr Zetlin began, "I stand before you today a humbled man. Never, in my wildest imagination, could I have foreseen the events that happened here and across Veelox."

I looked around to see that every eye was focused on Dr Zetlin. He was a legend. No, he was a superstar. For these people to see him in person must have been pretty awesome.

"I'm not speaking of the problems that were encountered with Lifelight that prompted me to shut it down," he continued. "I am speaking of the state my beloved Veelox has fallen into because of my invention. For that, I am ashamed."

A slight nervous murmur went through the crowd. I don't think they were expecting to hear bad news.

"I designed Lifelight to be a celebration of life, not a substitute," he continued. "Living an ideal existence is difficult to resist. I know. I am just as guilty as any of you. My intent was to stay inside the perfect world of my choosing, never to be bothered with the challenges of reality again. But it is a fool's paradise. We have become a society of individuals whose only concern is our own comfort, pleasure, and amusement. By embracing Lifelight, we have turned our backs on our cities, on our neighbours, and worst of all, on our loved ones."

There were thousands of people in the pyramid, but they

were as silent as a painting. It was kind of creepy.

"I believe the problems we encountered a few days ago may very well prove to be our salvation," Zetlin said. "Corrupt data had infected the grid, disrupting many of the jumps."

Corrupt data? That was a nice way of describing Aja's Reality Bug.

"Thanks to the quick and fearless actions taken by Aja Killian, the senior phader in Rubic City, the problem was contained."

Dr Zetlin pointed to Aja. The crowd applauded. Aja stepped forward and raised her hand in acknowledgment. When the applause died down, Zetlin continued, "But in order to purge the grid of this corrupt data, I made the difficult decision to shut down Lifelight entirely. We were doubly successful. The grid was cleared, and Veelox was given a second chance."

Dr Zetlin was doing an excellent job. He was not only explaining to the people of Veelox why Lifelight had been shut down, he was telling them why it was a good thing.

"It is my wish that until we can learn how best to utilise Lifelight for the good of all of Veelox, that we not even consider bringing it back online."

Another concerned murmur went through the crowd. That last statement surprised them.

"And I pledge to work with the directors, and with all of you, to find a balance that will bring as much joy from living in the reality of Veelox, as we found in the fantasy of Lifelight. Thank you."

The people all applauded, but not with the same enthusiasm as when Zetlin was first introduced. I don't think they liked the idea of not being able to jump back into Lifelight. But I figured they didn't have a choice. They were going to have to learn how to deal with reality again, whether they liked it or not.

Dr Zetlin sat down at his place and gave us another look, and a nod. I smiled at him. It must have been tough to stand in front of the entire population of Veelox and announce that his life's work was flawed. But I truly believed that with his help, the people of Veelox would one day figure out how to get the best from Lifelight, without giving up their real lives.

Dr Sever then stood and addressed the crowd, saying, "We have much to thank Dr Zetlin for. His genius and vision not only created the wonder that is Lifelight, but he rescued Veelox from a potentially disastrous incident by making the hard decision to shut down the grid. Moreover, he and his colleague, Aja Killian, have worked tirelessly to ensure that the problem that nearly destroyed Lifelight is no more."

That was followed by a round of applause.

Sever continued, "We respect Dr Zetlin's considered opinions as to the future of Veelox and of Lifelight. We, the directors agree that we must work to find the proper use of Lifelight in our ever changing society. However . . ."

However? She let the word hang. I had the feeling that something was coming, and it wasn't going to be good.

"We disagree with Dr Zetlin in how to go about that. We feel that the only possible way to best understand how to utilise Lifelight is to explore those options . . . while it is fully operational."

Uh-oh. An excited buzz went through the crowd. Zetlin jumped to his feet in anger.

"No!" he shouted. "That defeats the purpose! If people go back into their jumps, we'll be right back where we were!"

"With all due respect, Doctor, we don't think so," Sever said with a superior attitude. "Lessons have been learned. It is the decision of the directors to bring Lifelight back into operation immediately."

Sever waved her hand. It was a signal. Suddenly the Lifelight pyramid sprang back to life. People looked around in wonder as the operational lights came back on. It was like Christmas had come to Veelox as the pyramid was once again alive with the multiple lights of Lifelight. Once the people realised what was happening, they cheered. They actually cheered. It was like their team had just pulled out a surprise victory in sudden death.

"What is happening?" Evangeline asked, confused.

"Did you know about this?" I screamed at Aja to be heard over the crowd.

"No!" she answered. "When they wanted us to troubleshoot the grid, I didn't think they wanted to go back online!"

People started pushing to get off the floor. The once orderly crowd had been charged with energy. None of them wanted to be left out. They were all hurrying to get back to a jump cubicle and reenter their fantasies.

"We've gotta stop them!" I pleaded.

Aja jumped up on to the stage and ran to Dr Zetlin.

"Do something!" she begged.

Zetlin said, "If we can get to the Alpha Core before the jumps begin, I can take control."

Aja grabbed him by the hand and pulled him off the stage.

"Hurry!" Evangeline shouted.

We left her by the stage and the three of us pushed our way through the surging crowd, back to the Alpha Core.

"What are you going to do?" I asked Zetlin as we fought our way through.

"They know the origin code now, so they have control," he panted. "I can override the phaders, but only if they haven't got the grid back online yet. Once that happens, I won't be able to control anything from the Alpha Core. We'll be at the mercy of whatever the directors want."

"Stop those people!" Dr Sever ordered from the stage, pointing at us.

A group of phaders started after us, but they were having just as much trouble getting through the massive crowd as we were. I looked up into the pyramid and saw jump cubicle doors opening up all over. Some people pushed others out of the way to get in first. Young people took advantage of the weak and pulled them out of the cubicles to take it for themselves. It was a musical chairs, nightmare riot. Nobody wanted to be left out. They didn't care what Zetlin had said. They didn't care about the future of Veelox. They were addicted to their own fantasies and would do anything to get back in.

We had to take control and shut down Lifelight, for good.

We finally made it back into the core. Down the long corridor of glass I saw phaders taking their places in the control chairs, preparing to begin the jumps. But there was still time. The control stations were still dark.

Aja ran to the door leading to the Alpha Core and inserted her green card. The door didn't open. She tried it again; it stayed closed.

"Your card has been disallowed," came a voice from behind us. It was Dr Sever. She walked up to us with several strong-arm-looking phaders.

"Your actions over the last few days are still suspect, Aja," Sever said. "Until we complete a full investigation, we can't allow you access to Lifelight."

"Dr Sever," Zetlin said calmly, "please, give it some time. You hold the future of Veelox in your hands. Won't you please wait?"

"I'm sorry Dr Zetlin," she said with a smile. "I'm afraid it's too late. Every pyramid on Veelox is moments away from going back online."

As if on cue, the core came to life. The millions of indicator lights flashed once again as images appeared on the thousands of monitors. The jumpers were back in their fantasies. Dr Zetlin closed his eyes and dropped his head in defeat.

I was stunned. Moments before, I felt sure we had pulled Veelox back from the brink of collapse. But now the territory was in as much danger as the moment I first arrived. No, it was worse. Aja's Reality Bug had failed. Veelox had reached a critical turning point, and was pushed the wrong way.

There was no other way to say it:

Saint Dane had won.

"This is all thanks to you, Dr Zetlin," Sever said. "You got rid of that nasty little bug quite nicely. Now we can return to normal."

Bug? Did she say bug? Nobody knew about the bug except . . .

Dr Sever then leaned down to me and whispered in my ear. There was a subtle change in her voice. To everyone else she still sounded like Dr Kree Sever, prime director of Lifelight. But the cold tone of her voice said something very different to me.

"How does it feel, Pendragon?" she said with an iciness that made me shiver. "The first territory of Halla is mine."

● SECOND EARTH ●

Bobby's image disappeared abruptly.

Mark and Courtney were left staring at nothing. They had left the Sherwood house and returned to the privacy of Courtney's father's basement workshop to watch the journal.

"That's it?" Courtney asked, upset. "He stopped recording his journal right there? That's not fair!"

Before Mark could offer an opinion, another image flickered to life. The recording wasn't yet complete. Courtney and Mark watched in wonder as the 3-D projection formed in front of them.

"There's more!" Mark exclaimed.

But the image that appeared before them wasn't Bobby's. It was Aja Killian's.

"Hello to you, Mark Dimond and Courtney Chetwynde," Aja began. "My name is Aja Killian, the Traveller from Veelox. Pendragon has told me all about you two, and that he trusts you both very much. This is why I am completing his journal for him."

Aja took off her small yellow glasses and rubbed her eyes. She looked tired.

"Pendragon is gone," she continued. "He left Veelox shortly after Lifelight was brought back online. His destination was the territory of Eelong to search for the Traveller named Gunny. I feel as if my duty is to stay here to do all I can to keep Veelox from falling further into decay. I have the help of Dr Zetlin, but I'm afraid we are fighting a losing battle. The directors have all returned to Lifelight. Most of the phaders and vedders have also left on their own jumps. There aren't enough people left in reality to monitor the jumps, let alone care for their real lives. The pull of fantasy was just too strong. Saint Dane has won. Veelox is near dead."

Aja was holding back tears.

"Pendragon asked me to finish his journal so you would know the state of Veelox, and to send it on to you. It is the least I can do. I feel as if I have failed the territory, failed the Travellers, and failed Pendragon. My only hope is that we can stop Saint Dane on the other territories, so that the only casualty of this evil war will be Veelox. My home."

She swallowed hard and then said, "In my heart, I know this is not the way it was meant to be. This is the end of Bobby Pendragon's Journal Number Fifteen. Goodbye."

Aja's image disappeared. The journal, and Bobby's adventure on Veelox, was now complete. Mark picked up the small silver projector and stared at it, as if hoping there were one last bit of news that would leap from it to give this story a happy ending.

There wasn't.

"So what does this mean?" Courtney asked nervously. "Saint Dane always said that as soon as the first domino fell, the others would fall easily."

"I-I really don't know," Mark said sombrely.

Courtney jumped to her feet and paced. "I hate this!" she

exclaimed. "I feel totally helpless. All this stuff is going on and all we can do is sit around and hear about it like a couple of nimrods."

This made Mark smile. "I thought you only wanted to worry about school and soccer and normal life?" he asked.

Courtney stopped and looked straight at Mark. "The hell with soccer," she declared. "I thought we were supposed to be acolytes?"

"Now you're talking!" declared Mark.

Early the next morning the two were back sitting on the couch in the apartment of Tom Dorney. Together they watched all three of Bobby's journals from Veelox. Afterwards they described to Dorney what happened at the Sherwood house with the quigs and the stunning appearance of a flume.

"If that doesn't say we're ready to be acolytes," Courtney concluded, "then tell us what will."

Dorney scratched his chin. He then hoisted himself up out of his easy chair, grumbled, and shuffled into the kitchen.

"Does this mean he's pulling our chain again?" Courtney asked.

Mark shrugged. "Give him a chance."

Dorney shuffled back into the living room with a glass of water. He didn't offer any to Mark or Courtney. The guy wasn't exactly a great host. He sat back down in his chair, spilling some water on his lap.

Courtney rolled her eyes, but neither said anything. The ball was still in Dorney's court.

"You're going to get messages," he said calmly. "Sometimes from Travellers, other times from acolytes on other territories."

Mark and Courtney sat up straight. Things had just got very interesting.

Courtney asked, "What kind of –"

"Let me speak," Dorney snapped.

Courtney shut up.

"They'll come to you through the ring," Dorney continued. "Like the message I sent to you. They may tell you that a Traveller will be arriving and that you need to provide Second Earth clothing. That's usually the case. But Pendragon may need something specific."

"Like when you had to take care of Press's motorcycle," Mark jumped in. He couldn't resist. He was getting excited.

"Yes," Dorney answered, then took a sip of water.

"What about the quigs?" Courtney asked.

"Protect yourself," Dorney answered. "There's no magic wand you can wave to make them go away. They aren't always around, but you have to be prepared when they are. I'll tell you one thing, they're afraid of the flumes. Don't ask me why. When a flume activates, you won't see any quigs around."

"Can we contact other acolytes?" Mark asked.

"Look at your ring," Dorney ordered.

Mark held up his hand so he and Courtney could see the heavy ring with the dark grey stone surrounded by the odd, carved symbols.

"Each of those symbols represents a territory," Dorney explained. "There are ten in all."

"Ten territories," Mark repeated softly, as if he had just been given the secret of the ages.

"If you know the name of an acolyte," Dorney continued, "take the ring off and call out that name. The symbol from their territory will activate the ring and you can send a message."

"So if I took off the ring and said: 'Evangeline', the symbol for Veelox would open up the ring and I could send a note to her?"

"That's right."

"Is that how we should get in touch with you?" Mark asked.

"You could," Dorney answered. "Or you could pick up the telephone."

"Oh. Right," Mark said, feeling dumb.

"Can we contact Bobby through the ring?" Courtney asked.

"No," was Dorney's quick answer. "Only the acolytes. Travellers don't need to be bothered with our problems."

"Is there anything else?" Mark asked.

Dorney took some time to think about that answer. He looked out of the window, his mind seeming to fly a million miles away. Courtney and Mark looked at each other. They weren't sure if Dorney had tuned them out, or was having deep thoughts.

"You are the acolytes from Second Earth now," Dorney finally said. "With Press gone, I'm no longer needed. It may be an easy job compared to what the Travellers do, but I think you'll agree it's an important one."

"We do. Absolutely. Yessir," they assured him.

Dorney looked back out of the window with a frown on his face.

"Is there something you're not telling us?" Courtney asked.

Dorney sighed and said, "It's just a feeling."

"What?" demanded Courtney.

"I don't know," Dorney said anxiously. "I didn't like what I heard about Veelox."

"Yeah, no kidding," Courtney said.

Dorney looked at them. For the first time since they'd met him, Mark and Courtney actually felt as if he were softening up a bit.

"What I mean to say is," Dorney continued, "be careful. Saint Dane has finally had a victory, and there's no telling what's next. From this point on, I can't guarantee that the old rules still apply."

◆　　◆　　◆

Mark and Courtney took the train back to Stony Brook with that ominous warning still on their minds. Neither said much. They both had to get their minds around the fact that they now were officially acolytes. The only question was, what next?

"I want to go to the flume," Mark announced.

"Why?" Courtney asked.

"We'll bring some of our clothes to leave there."

"But nobody told us they needed clothes," Courtney countered.

"I know. Just thinking ahead."

The two fell silent for a moment, then Courtney said, "That's just an excuse to go there, isn't it?"

Mark was ready to argue, but decided not to. He nodded. "I guess I just want to see it again. To prove it's real."

"I hear you," Courtney said. "I do too."

When they got off the train in Connecticut, they both went home and gathered up a bunch of clothes they thought a Traveller from some distant territory might need to blend in on Second Earth. Courtney picked out a bunch of simple, functional things like jeans, T-shirts, a sweater, socks, hiking boots, and underwear. She debated about bringing one of her bras, but figured that was overkill.

Mark gathered up a bunch of clothes that were totally out of style. It wasn't like he had a choice. That's all Mark had. He found sweatshirts with logos that meant nothing, no-name jeans, and generic trainers. Style was not something Mark concerned himself with. He hoped the Travellers wouldn't either.

Mark brought one other thing from his house that he hoped he wouldn't need. He borrowed the sharp poker from his parents' fireplace toolset. It was woefully inadequate to deal with an attacking quig-dog, but it was all he could find.

Mark and Courtney met in front of the gates to the Sherwood

house, each with a loaded backpack. They didn't say a word to each other as they walked around the side of the property to the tree that would give them access to the yard. Once over the wall, Mark held the fireplace poker, ready to defend them against a rampaging quig. Courtney saw that Mark's hand was shaking like jelly, so she gently took the poker from him. If either of them had a chance of fighting off a charging quig, it would be Courtney.

But they didn't run into any of the yellow-eyed beasts. They made it through the house, down to the basement, and into the root cellar that held the flume. No problem. They emptied their backpacks and neatly folded the clothes in a pile. Courtney looked at some of the geek clothes Mark had brought, and chuckled.

"Oh, yeah, Bobby's gonna blend right in wearing a bright yellow hooded sweatshirt with a red logo that says, *Cool Dude!*"

"Give me a break," Mark said defensively. "It's my favourite sweatshirt."

Courtney shook her head in disbelief. When they were finished, they both gazed into the dark tunnel to the territories. They stood together silently, each with their own thoughts as to what the future might hold.

"I'm scared and excited at the same time," Mark finally said.

"Really," Courtney added. "I want to be part of this, but it's scary not knowing what to expect."

"Can you imagine being a Traveller?" Mark asked while stepping into the mouth of the tunnel.

"Well, no," Courtney answered, "to be honest."

"Well, I've thought about it a lot!" Mark declared. "It would be awesome, stepping into a flume and announcing the next amazing place you'd like to go."

"It's pretty unbelievable," Courtney agreed.

"Look at this thing!" Mark said, scanning the flume. "It's kinda like having a jet fighter."

"It is?" Courtney asked with a chuckle.

"Yeah. You know what it's capable of, but have no idea what to do to make it go."

"It's not all that hard," Courtney said, "if you're a Traveller."

Mark smiled, turned to face the dark tunnel, and shouted out: *"Eelong!"*

He looked back to Courtney and said, "Could you imagine if –"

"Mark!" Courtney shouted.

Mark saw the terrified look on Courtney's face. She was looking deeper into the flume. What was back there? Mark spun quickly to see the impossible.

The flume was coming to life!

Mark jumped out of the tunnel and ran to Courtney. The two backed away towards the far wall of the root cellar, hugging each other in fear.

"D-Did I do that?" Mark asked.

"Or is somebody coming?" Courtney added.

The light appeared from the depths of the tunnel. The musical notes were faint at first but quickly grew louder. The rocky walls began to crackle and groan. Mark and Courtney could only stare in awe.

"I-I don't really want to go to Eelong," Mark cried. Courtney held him tighter, ready to hold him back if she felt him getting pulled into the flume.

The grey walls melted into glorious crystal as the bright light and sound arrived at the mouth. Mark and Courtney had to squint. They didn't dare put their hands in front of their eyes, though. They were too busy hanging on to each other.

They soon realised they weren't about to be pulled into the tunnel. Something else was heading their way. Through the bright light they saw a tall, dark silhouette walk out of the flume. Oddly, unlike everything they had ever heard about how the flumes worked, once the passenger arrived, the sparkling light didn't go away. The jangle of music stayed too. Whatever was happening now, it was out of the ordinary. Mark and Courtney opened their eyes. What they saw made them want to close them again, because standing in the mouth of the flume was Saint Dane.

He had arrived on Second Earth.

The two had never seen him before, but there was no mistaking the tall demon with the long grey hair, piercing blue eyes, and dark clothes. The light behind him continued to burn and the walls remained crystal. This had never happened before, at least not that Mark or Courtney knew.

"And so it begins," Saint Dane cackled. "The walls are beginning to crack. The power that once was, will no longer be. It is a whole new game, with new rules."

Saint Dane roared out a laugh. With a sudden burst of light from deep inside the flume, his hair caught fire! His long grey mane exploded in dancing flames, burning right down to his skull. Mark and Courtney watched in horror as the flames reflected in his demonic eyes. Saint Dane laughed the whole while, as if he were enjoying it.

Mark and Courtney didn't move. If Courtney had had her wits about her, she would have felt that Mark was trembling.

The fire burned away all of Saint Dane's hair, leaving him bald, with angry red streaks that looked like inflamed veins running from the back of his head to his forehead. His eyes had changed too. The steely blue colour had gone nearly white. He fixed those intense eyes on the two new acolytes and smiled. He then tossed a dirty, cloth bag at their feet.

"A present for Pendragon," Saint Dane hissed. "Be sure he gets it, won't you?" Saint Dane took a step back into the light of the flume. "What was meant to be, is no longer," he announced.

Saint Dane then began to transform. His body turned liquid and he leaned over to put his hands on the ground. At the same time his body mutated into that of a huge, jungle cat. It was the size of a lion, but speckled with black spots. The big cat then snarled at Mark and Courtney, and leaped into the flume. An instant later the light swept him up and disappeared into the depths. The music faded away, the crystal walls turned back to stone, and the light shrank to a pin spot.

But it didn't disappear entirely.

Before Mark and Courtney could get their heads back together, the light began to grow again. The music became louder and the walls went crystal again.

"My brain is exploding," Mark uttered.

A second later the bright light flashed at the mouth of the tunnel and deposited another passenger.

"Bobby!" Mark and Courtney shouted, and ran to him. They threw their arms around him in fear and relief. The tunnel then returned to its normal, quiet state.

But Bobby wasn't there to give them comfort. "What happened?" he demanded.

Mark and Courtney pulled away. Both of them were supercharged with adrenalin. "It was Saint Dane!" Courtney shouted. "His hair burned! It was horrible!"

"He said the rules have ch-changed, Bobby," Mark stuttered. "What did he m-mean?"

Bobby took a step back from the others. Mark and Courtney felt him tense up.

"What did you do?" Bobby demanded. It sounded like he was scolding them.

"Do?" Courtney said. "We didn't do anything!"

Both Mark and Courtney focused on Bobby. He was wearing rags. His feet were bare, his hair was a mess and he had a coating of dirt all over his body. He didn't smell so hot either.

"What happened to you?" Mark asked.

"It doesn't matter!" Bobby shouted back. He was just as charged up as they were. "Did you activate the flume?"

Mark and Courtney looked at each other. It took a while for them to register what Bobby was asking. Finally Mark said, "Uh, I g-guess so. I said 'Eelong' —"

"No!" Bobby shouted in frustration.

"What's the matter?" Courtney asked. "We're not Travellers. We can't control the flume."

"Things have changed," Bobby shouted out. "Saint Dane's power is growing. He's got his first territory. It's all about changing the nature of things."

"So . . . that means we can use the flumes?" Courtney asked.

"Don't!" Bobby demanded. "It'll just make things worse."

Mark then remembered something. He ran back to the door of the root cellar and picked up the bag Saint Dane had thrown at them.

"He said this was for you," Mark said, handing the bag to Bobby.

Bobby took it like it was the last thing in the world he wanted. He turned the rotten bag upside down, and something fell on to the floor.

Courtney screamed. Mark took a step back, not believing his eyes. Bobby stood firm, staring at the floor, his jaw muscles clenching.

Lying at his feet was a human hand. It was large and dark skinned. As gruesome as this was, there was something else about it that made it nearly unbearable to look at. On its finger, was a Traveller ring.

"Gunny," Bobby whispered in agony.

The three stood there, unable to move. Finally Bobby took a brave breath, picked up the hand and jammed it into the bag.

"Bobby, what's happening?" Courtney asked.

"You'll know when I send my journal," he said. He then turned back and ran into the mouth of the flume, clutching the bag with Gunny's hand. "*Eelong!*" he called out. The flume sprang back to life. The light and music started on their way back for him.

Mark was nearly in tears.

"Is Gunny all right?" he asked.

"He's alive," Bobby said. "But I don't know for how long."

"Tell us what to do!" Courtney pleaded.

"Nothing," Bobby answered. "Wait for my journal. And whatever you do, do *not* activate the flume. That's exactly what Saint Dane wants, and it is not the way things were meant to be."

With a final flash of light and jumble of notes, Bobby was swept up and into the flume, leaving his two friends alone.

Mark Dimond was ready for an adventure.

He was about to get one.

To Be Continued

The adventure continues in

PENDRAGON ⊕

BLACK WATER

⊙ **PROLOGUE** ⊙

Acolytes

That's what this was all about.

It was also about saving humanity from being crushed by a villainous demon named Saint Dane, but that was a little much for Mark Dimond and Courtney Chetwynde to tackle right off the bat. They figured becoming acolytes was the best way to ease into the whole universe-saving thing. The two friends sat together on a musty old couch in a small New York City apartment. They were there to learn the mysterious ways of the acolytes. Not exactly dramatic surroundings, considering they were hearing words that would change their lives forever.

"You are the acolytes from Second Earth now," said Tom Dorney, whose apartment it was. "With Press gone, I'm no longer needed. It may be an easy job compared to what the Travellers do, but I think you'll agree it's an important one."

"We do. Absolutely. Yessir," Mark and Courtney assured him.

Dorney turned to look out of his window and frowned. He was an old guy with short-cropped grey hair and excellent posture. He was once a soldier. Old habits die hard.

"Is there something you're not telling us?" Courtney asked.

Dorney sighed and said, "It's just a feeling."

"What?" she demanded.

"I don't know," Dorney said, troubled. "I didn't like what I heard about Veelox."

"Yeah, no kidding," Courtney said.

"What I mean to say is, be careful. Saint Dane has finally had a victory, and there's no telling what's next. From this point on, I can't guarantee that the old rules still apply."

This was chilling news for Mark and Courtney on their first official day as acolytes. Dorney's ominous warning was very much on their minds as they left his apartment and took the train back to Stony Brook, Connecticut. Just before the train pulled into Stony Brook Station, Mark announced, "I want to go to the flume."

"Why?" Courtney asked.

"We'll bring some of our clothes to leave there."

"But nobody told us they needed clothes," Courtney countered.

"I know. Just thinking ahead."

"That's just an excuse to go there, isn't it?" Courtney asked.

Mark didn't argue. "I guess I just want to see it again. To prove it's real."

"I hear you," Courtney said. "I do too."

When they got off the train, they both went home and gathered up a bunch of clothes they thought a Traveller from some distant territory might need on a visit to Second Earth. That's what acolytes did. They supported the Travellers on their mission to protect Halla. Courtney picked out a bunch of simple, functional things like jeans, T-shirts, a sweater, socks, hiking boots, and underwear. She debated about bringing one of her bras, but figured that was overkill. Mark gathered up a bunch of clothes that were totally out of style. It wasn't like he had a choice. That's all he had. He found sweat-shirts with logos that meant nothing, no-name jeans, and generic trainers. Style was not something Mark concerned himself with. He hoped the Travellers felt the same way.

Mark brought one extra item, but hoped he wouldn't need it. It was the sharp poker from his parents' fireplace. It was a woefully inad-equate weapon to deal with an attacking quig-dog, but it was all he could find.

Shortly after, Mark and Courtney met at the iron gates in front of the empty Sherwood house. They silently walked around to the side and climbed the tree to get over the high stone wall that surrounded the spooky, abandoned estate. Once over, Mark held the fireplace poker out in front of him, ready to ward off a rampaging quig. Mark's hand was shaking like warm jelly, so Courtney gently took the weapon from him. If either of them had a chance of fighting off a charging quig, it would be Courtney.

Luckily they didn't run into any of the yellow-eyed beasts. They made it through the big empty mansion, down into the basement, and into the root cellar that held the newly created flume. No problem. They emptied their backpacks and neatly folded the clothes in a pile. Courtney looked at some of the geek clothes Mark brought, and chuckled.

"Oh yeah, Bobby's gonna blend right in wearing a bright yellow sweatshirt with a red logo that says, *Cool Dude!*"

"Give me a break," Mark said defensively. "It's my favourite sweat-shirt."

Courtney shook her head in disbelief. When they were finished, they both gazed into the dark tunnel to the territories. The flume. They stood together, each with his/her own thoughts as to what the future might hold.

"I'm scared and excited at the same time," Mark said.

"Really," Courtney added. "I want to be part of this, but it's scary not knowing what to expect."

"Can you imagine being a Traveller?" Mark asked while stepping into the mouth of the tunnel.

"Well, no," Courtney answered, "to be honest."

"Well, I've thought about it a lot!" Mark declared. "It would be awesome, stepping into a flume and announcing the next amazing place you'd like to go."

"It's pretty unbelievable," Courtney agreed.

"Look at this thing!" Mark said, scanning the flume. "It's kinda like having a jet fighter."

"It is?" Courtney asked with a chuckle.

"Yeah. You know what it's capable of, but have no idea what to do to make it go."

"It's not all that hard," Courtney said. "If you're a Traveller."

Mark smiled, turned to face the dark tunnel, and shouted out: "*Eelong!*"

He looked back to Courtney and said, "Could you imagine it –"

"Mark!" Courtney shouted.

Mark saw the terrified look on Courtney's face. She was looking past him, deeper into the flume. Mark spun quickly and saw something he thought was impossible.

The flume was coming to life.

Mark jumped out of the tunnel and ran to Courtney. The two backed away toward the far wall of the root cellar, hugging each other in fear.

"D-Did I do that?" Mark asked.

"Or is somebody coming?" Courtney added.

The light appeared from the depths of the tunnel. The musical notes were faint at first but quickly grew louder. The rocky walls began to crackle and groan. They had seen all this before, but only when the flume was activated by a Traveller. Never, ever had a flume been activated by a non-Traveller – until now.

"I – I don't really want to go to Eelong," Mark cried. Courtney held him tighter, ready to hold him back if he got pulled in by the power of the flume.

The grey walls of the tunnel melted into glorious crystal as the bright light and sound arrived at the mouth. Mark and Courtney didn't dare put their hands in front of their eyes because they were too busy hanging on to each other. But neither felt the tug of the flume, because someone was heading their way. Through the bright light they saw a tall, dark silhouette appear and step out of the tunnel. Oddly, the sparkling light didn't go away. The jangle of music stayed too. This had never happened before, at least not that Mark or Courtney knew. But none of that mattered as much as the man who now stood facing them.

It was Saint Dane. He had arrived on Second Earth. The two had never seen him before, but there was no mistaking the tall demon with the long grey hair, piercing blue eyes, and dark clothes.

"And so it begins," Saint Dane cackled. "The walls are beginning to crack. The power that once was, will no longer be. It is a whole new game, with new rules."

Saint Dane roared out a laugh. With a sudden burst of light from deep inside the flume, his hair caught fire! His long grey mane exploded in flames, burning right down to his skull. Mark and Courtney watched in horror as the flames reflected in his demonic eyes. Saint Dane laughed the whole time, as if enjoying it.

Mark and Courtney didn't move, except to tremble.

The fire burned away all of Saint Dane's hair, leaving him completely bald, with angry red streaks that looked like inflamed veins running from the back of his head to his forehead. His eyes had changed too. The steely blue colour had gone nearly white. He fixed those intense eyes on the two new acolytes and smiled. He tossed a dirty, cloth bag at their feet.

"A present for Pendragon," Saint Dane hissed. "Be sure he gets it, won't you?" Saint Dane took a step back into the light of the flume. "What was meant to be, is no longer," he announced. With that, he began to transform. His body turned liquid as he leaned over to put his hands on the ground. At the same time his body mutated into that of a huge, jungle cat. It was the size of a lion. His coat was brown, but speckled with black spots. The big cat snarled at Mark and Courtney, and leaped into the flume. An instant later the light swept him up and disappeared into the depths. The music faded, the crystal walls returned to stone, and the light shrank to a pin spot.

But it didn't disappear entirely.

Before Mark and Courtney could get their heads back together, the light began to grow again. The music became louder and the grey rock walls transformed back into crystal.

"My brain is exploding," Mark uttered.

A second later the bright light flashed at the mouth of the tunnel to deposit another passenger before returning to its normal, dormant state.

"Bobby!" Mark and Courtney shouted. They ran to him and threw their arms around him in fear and relief.

"What happened?" Bobby demanded, all business.

Mark and Courtney were both supercharged with adrenalin. "It was Saint Dane!" Courtney shouted. "His hair burned! It was horrible!"

"He said the rules have ch-changed, Bobby," Mark stuttered. "What did he m-mean?"

Bobby took a step back from them. Mark and Courtney sensed his tension.

"What did you do?" Bobby demanded. It sounded like he was scolding them.

"Do?" Courtney said. "We didn't do anything!"

Mark and Courtney focused on Bobby. He was wearing rags. His feet were bare, his hair was a mess, and he had a coating of dirt all over his body. He didn't smell so hot either.

"What happened to you?" Mark asked.

"It doesn't matter," Bobby shot back. He was just as charged up as they were. "Did you activate the flume?"

Mark and Courtney looked to each other. Mark said, "Uh, I g-guess so. I said 'Eelong' –"

"No!" Bobby said in anguish.

"What's the matter?" Courtney asked. "We're not Travellers. We can't control the flume."

"Things have changed," Bobby shouted. "Saint Dane's power is growing. He's got his first territory. It's all about changing the nature of things."

"So . . . that means we can use the flumes?" Courtney asked.

"Don't!" Bobby demanded. "It'll just make things worse."

Mark remembered something. He ran back to the door of the root cellar and picked up the bag Saint Dane had thrown at them. "He said this was for you," Mark said, handing the bag to Bobby.

Bobby took it like it was the last thing in the world he wanted. He turned the rotten bag upside down, and something fell on to the floor. Courtney screamed. Mark took a step back in shock. Bobby stood firm, staring at the floor, his jaw muscles clenching. Lying at his feet was a human hand. It was large and dark skinned. As gruesome as this was, there was something else about it that made it nearly unbearable to look at. On one finger, was a Traveller ring.

"Gunny," Bobby whispered. It was the severed hand of the Traveller from First Earth, Vincent "Gunny" VanDyke. Bobby took a brave breath, picked up the hand, and jammed it into the bag.

"Bobby, what's happening?" Courtney asked.

"You'll know when I send my journal," he said. He turned back and ran into the mouth of the flume, clutching the bag with Gunny's hand in it. *"Eelong!"* he called out. The flume sprang back to life.

"Is Gunny all right?" Mark asked, nearly in tears.

"He's alive," Bobby said. "But I don't know for how long."

"Tell us what to do!" Courtney pleaded.

"Nothing," Bobby answered. "Wait for my journal. And whatever you do, do *not* activate the flume. That's exactly what Saint Dane wants. It's not the way things were meant to be."

With a final flash of light and jumble of notes, Bobby was swept into the flume, leaving his two friends alone to begin their careers as acolytes.

It wasn't a very good beginning.

☉ SECOND EARTH ☉

Four months had passed since that incredible, frightening episode in the basement of the Sherwood house.

Mark Dimond and Courtney Chetwynde had done exactly what Bobby told them to do. Nothing. They stayed away from the flume and waited for the arrival of another journal. They waited. And waited. And waited some more. Mark found himself staring at his ring, willing it to activate. He so desperately wanted a sign that being an acolyte meant more than sitting around like a load, pretending all was normal. A few times he called Tom Dorney to see if he had got any messages from other acolytes. Dorney's answer was always the same: "Nope." No detail. No chitchat. Just "Nope". Dorney was a man of few words. To Mark, he was a man of *one* word. "Nope."

Mark went to the safe-deposit box at the National Bank of Stony Brook, where Bobby's journals were securely kept. He sat by himself for an entire day, reading them all, reliving the incredible journey that his best friend had been on for the last year and a half. So much had changed since that winter night when Bobby left Stony Brook with his uncle Press to discover that he was a Traveller, and that his destiny was to protect the territories of Halla.

The same night Bobby left, his family disappeared. Any record that they had ever existed disappeared right along with them. More importantly, the curtain was pulled back on the incredible truth that the universe didn't function the way everyone thought. Bobby's journals explained how every time, every place, every person and every thing that had ever existed, still did exist. It was called Halla. Halla was made up of ten territories that were connected by tunnels called flumes that only the Travellers could use. But the most frightening truth contained in the journals was that an evil Traveller named Saint Dane was doing his best to destroy Halla. Saint Dane would travel to a territory that was about to reach a critical point in its history, and do all that he could to push events the wrong way and send the territory into chaos. It was up to Bobby and the other Travellers to stop him. They had been pretty successful, too. Denduron, Cloral, First Earth – all victories over Saint Dane and his evil plots.

But then came Veelox.

Veelox was a territory doomed to crumble because people chose to live in Lifelight, the wonderful, virtual-reality world created by a supercomputer, instead of in real life. It marked Saint Dane's first victory over Bobby and the Travellers. Mark worried that the toppling of Veelox meant Saint Dane had even more power than before. He worried that the rules had changed and that the demon would now be more difficult to defeat. He worried that the battle would soon come to Second Earth. He worried that this was the beginning of the end for Halla. Mark worried a lot. He was good at it.

And on top of it all, Mark and Courtney were now acolytes. Up to this point their job had been to read Bobby's journals and keep them safe. Basically they had been librarians. Now they were in it. Being acolytes meant they would support any Travellers who came to Second Earth and help them blend in with the local culture. They were psyched and ready for the challenge. Finally, they had the chance to take an active role in helping Bobby.

But in spite of all these exciting and scary developments, it turned out that there was nothing for them to do. Mark felt like an anxious racehorse stuck in a gate that wouldn't open. He'd walk through the halls of Davis Gregory High, where he was a sophomore, look at the other kids, and think, *Do they know the danger we're all in? Do they have any clue that I'm one of the few people in Halla who is trying to protect them?* The answer was, of course, no. To the other kids at school, Mark Dimond was nothing more than a nervous brainiac who ate too many carrots and didn't wash his unkempt, greasy black hair often enough. Guys like Mark were like wallpaper . . . always hanging around but totally invisible.

Things weren't going much better for Courtney. Life had changed drastically for her since entering high school. Courtney had always been the girl who had it all going on. She was pretty, with waist-length brown hair and deep grey eyes. She had lots of friends and, most notably, kicked butt in every sport she played. Courtney was a legend. It didn't matter what sport either: soccer, volleyball, softball, track . . . She even wanted to play football, but the rules wouldn't allow it. But since coming to Davis Gregory High, things had changed. Courtney wasn't the best any more. Maybe it was because the other girls had caught up. Maybe it was because she never had to try very hard, and it was paying off for those who did. Or maybe it was because she had lost something intangible. The spark. The magic. Whatever. The result was that Courtney looked bad. In soccer she was demoted from varsity to JV and then quitted the team. That was big. Courtney never quitted anything. Ever. But she quitted soccer. She sought refuge in volleyball, her favourite sport. But things weren't any better. Courtney didn't even make the team. She got cut. Cut! Courtney had never been cut. It was humiliating. At first the other kids were happy to see the queen dethroned, but after a while they started feeling bad for her. Courtney didn't want pity. That was the worst.

If there was one word you could use to describe Courtney

Chetwynde, it was "confident". But that confidence was taking a severe beating, and she was starting to question herself. It affected the rest of her life too. Her grades took a nosedive; she stopped hanging with her best friends, and she fought with her parents. She hated their constant, worried looks that silently asked, "What's wrong with you?" The frustrating truth was, she didn't know. It was eating her up.

But Courtney wasn't totally self-absorbed. She knew her troubles were puny compared to the bigger dangers lurking about. Bobby Pendragon, the guy she'd had a crush on since she was four years old, was flying around the universe battling an evil demon who wanted nothing less than the destruction of everything. Courtney realised that on a scale of one to ten where ten was the worst, getting cut from volleyball was around negative forty. Knowing this, Courtney felt guilty when she worried about her own little problems. But she couldn't help it, which made her feel worse. She couldn't control events in Halla; she could only deal with her own life . . . and she wasn't dealing so well.

Mark and Courtney were an odd couple. Under normal circumstances they would never have been on each others' radar. Shy nerds didn't hang with awesome jock girls. It was one of the realities of high school. But these two were joined by their friendship with Bobby. They knew Saint Dane had to be stopped and were prepared to do whatever it took to help their friend. But after months of being acolytes, they hadn't done a single thing that had anything to do with life outside of boring old Stony Brook, Connecticut.

It was making them absolutely, totally crazy.

The only thing that kept Mark from going off the deep end was the Sci-Clops science club at school. The summer before, Mark had designed and built a battling robot for the state science fair. He won first prize and got an invitation to join the prestigious club. Mark wasn't used to being rewarded for doing something that was usually considered geek territory, so he welcomed the chance. Mark found that Sci-Clops was full of brilliant students who shared his curiosity about the world around them. A Sci-Clops meeting was a mini-vacation from the relent-less social pressure of high school. It also helped get his mind off the imminent destruction of the universe.

Four months to the day after they saw Bobby and Saint Dane at the flume, Mark anxiously watched the clock tick towards the end of the school day. Mr Pike, the teacher who led Sci-Clops, promised that a special guest would be speaking that day, and Mark was dying to know who it might be. When the bell rang, he gathered his books and walked quickly towards the science wing. He hurried across the student centre, entered the science wing, and was halfway up the back stairwell when his day began to unravel.

The adventure continues in

PENDRAGON ⊕

THE MERCHANT OF DEATH

Bobby Pendragon is a seemingly normal fourteen-year-old-boy. He has a family, a home, a best friend and a possible new girlfriend. But then something happens that changes his life forever . . .

Pulled away from the comfort of his family and surburban home, Bobby is launched into the middle of an immense inter-dimensional conflict. It's a journey of danger and discovery for Bobby, and his success or failure will do nothing less than determine the fate of the world.